PRAISE FOR BURSTS OF FIRE

(Publishers Lunch *Buzz Books* 2019 selection)

"An emotional story of familial love, tension, and mistrust among three sisters and three brothers . . . Readers who relish adventure mingled with a message will be engrossed in the plights of the two sets of siblings."

—*Publishers Weekly*

"Forest depicts strong female characters, with varying motivations and personalities adding plenty of action in daring raids, battles with war machines, and magical time walking, though equal attention is given to exploring relationships between the sisters and their allies. This exciting new series will have fantasy fans eagerly awaiting the next installment."

—*Library Journal*

"The first book in the Addicted to Heaven series promises an exciting political fantasy with realistic representation of mental illness and addiction and is sure to entertain fans of epic adventures."

—*Booklist*

SUSAN FOREST

FLIGHTS OF MARIGOLD

ADDICTED TO HEAVEN

BOOKS BY SUSAN FOREST

Addicted to Heaven series
Bursts of Fire
Flights of Marigold
Scents of Slavery (forthcoming)

Immunity to Strange Tales
(short story collection from Five Rivers Publishing)

BOOKS EDITED BY SUSAN FOREST AND LUCAS K. LAW

Laksa Anthology Series: Speculative Fiction
Strangers Among Us: Tales of the Underdogs and Outcasts
The Sum of Us: Tales of the Bonded and Bound
Shades Within Us: Tales of Migrations and Fractured Borders
Seasons Between Us: Tales of Identities and Memories (forthcoming)

Flights of Marigold

Addicted to Heaven
Book Two

Susan Forest

LMG
LAKSA
MEDIA GROUPS

LAKSA MEDIA GROUPS INC.
www.laksamedia.com

Flights of Marigold
Addicted to Heaven (Book Two)

Copyright © 2020 by Susan Forest All rights reserved
This book is a work of fiction. Characters, names, organizations, places and incidents are either a product of the author's imagination or are used fictitiously, and are not to be construed as real. Any resemblance to actual situations, events, locales, organizations, or persons, living or dead, is entirely coincidental.

Laksa Media Groups supports copyright. Copyright fuels creativity, encourages diverse voices, promotes free speech, and creates a vibrant culture. Thank you for buying an authorized edition of this book and for complying with copyright laws by not reproducing, scanning, or distributing any part of it in any form without permission. You are supporting writers and allowing Laksa Media Groups to continue to publish books for every reader.

Library and Archives Canada Cataloguing in Publication

Title: Flights of marigold / Susan Forest.
Names: Forest, Susan, 1953- author.
Series: Forest, Susan, 1953- Addicted to Heaven.
Description: Series statement: Addicted to Heaven saga
Identifiers: Canadiana (print) 20190196335 | Canadiana (ebook) 20190196351 | ISBN 9781988140216
   (hardcover) | ISBN 9781988140223 (softcover) | ISBN 9781988140230 (EPUB) | ISBN 9781988140247
   (PDF) | ISBN 9781988140254 (Kindle)
Subjects: LCSH: Large type books.
Classification: LCC PS8561.O6785 F55 2020 | DDC C813/.54,Äîdc23

LAKSA MEDIA GROUPS INC.
Calgary, Alberta, Canada
www.laksamedia.com
info@laksamedia.com

Cover by Samantha M. Beiko
Interior Design by Jared Shapiro
Map by Holly Totten
Edited by Lucas K. Law and Leigh Teetzel

FIRST EDITION

To Dale

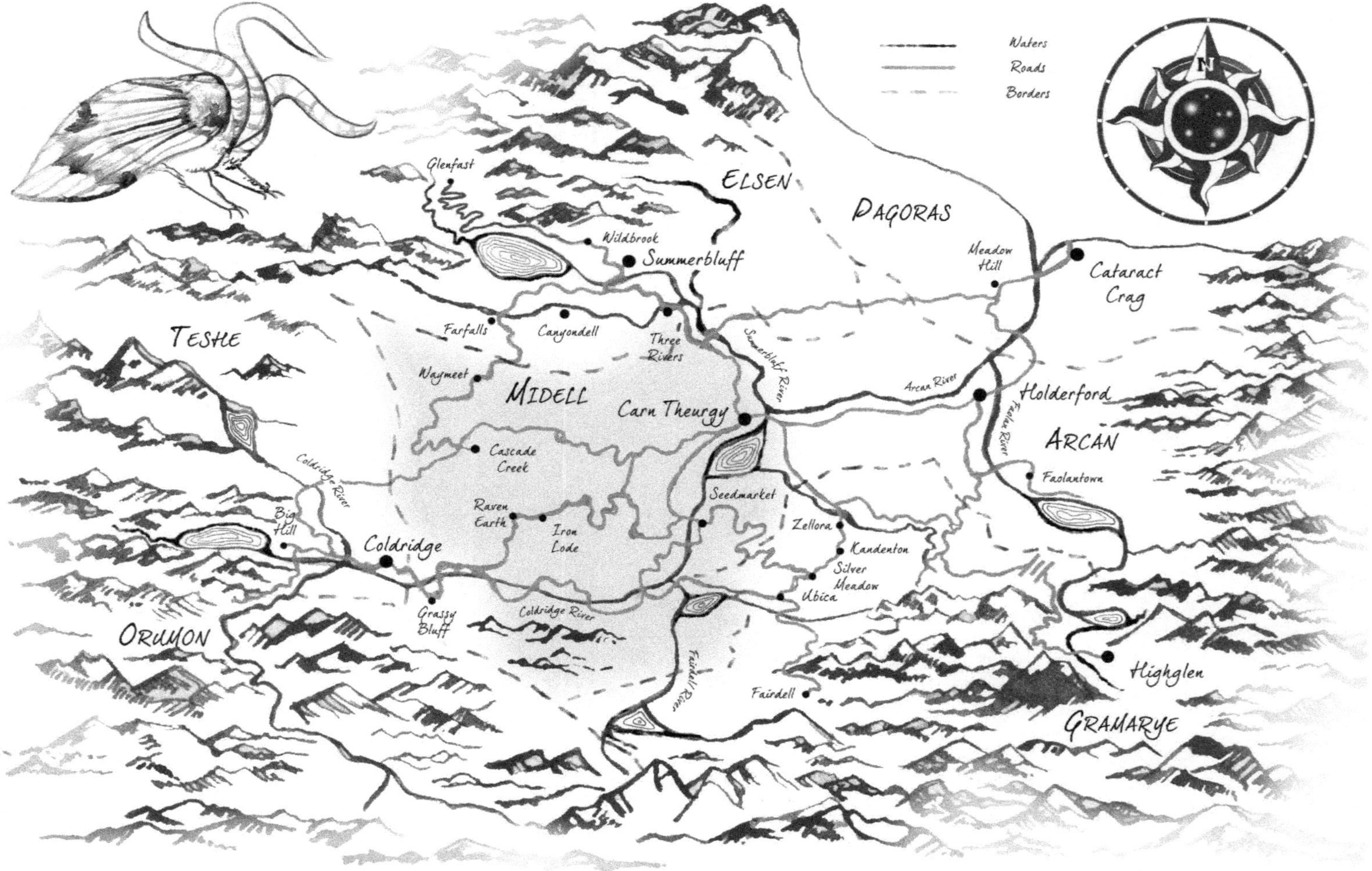

Waters
Roads
Borders
N
Glenfast
ELSEN
DAGORAS
Wildbrook
Summerbluff
Meadow Hill
Cataract Crag
TESHE
Farfalls
Canyondell
Three Rivers
Summerbluff River
Arcan River
Holderford
Waymeet
MIDELL
Carn Theurgy
Faolan River
ARCAN
Cascade Creek
Coldridge River
Faolantown
Seedmarket
Raven Earth
Iron Lode
Zellora
Big Hill
Coldridge
Kandenton
Silver Meadow
Ubica
Grassy Bluff
Coldridge River
ORUMON
Fairdell River
Highglen
Fairdell
GRAMARYE

CAST OF CHARACTERS

COUNTRY OF GRAMARYE
Capital: Highglen
Prayer Stone: Chrysocolla (destroyed)

Inaccessible except by a narrow road up a steep headwall in the southwest of Shangril, Gramarye is largely a high, mountainous country known for the quality of its yak wool. King Dwyn Gramaret was deposed during the unification of Shangril, when High King Artem gifted the country to his youngest daughter, Hada, to be ruled by a regent until she came of age. The regent chosen was Raef Gramaret, his son, who declared fealty to the Delarcan Royal Family.

Royalty
  King Dwyn Gramaret: Deposed. Now lives in hiding as the King-in-Exile.
  Queen Hada Delarcan: Nineteen-year-old sister of High King Huwen, Artem's son; named Queen of Gramarye by her father, Artem, at the age of nine.
  Regent Raef Gramaret: Son of King Dwyn Gramaret; pledged allegiance to High King Artem during the unification of Shangril, and was appointed Regent until Princess Hada came of age.

Magiels
  Yolen Barcley: Deceased. Father of Gweddien Barcley.

Gweddien Barcley: The last remaining male magiel who can trace his lineage to the One God. Prisoner and some-time refugee.

Court and Servants

Lord Vael: Wealthy land owner and Raef's sycophant.
Lord Andred: Wealthy land owner, possibly a political supporter of Queen Hada.
Lord Lydon: Wealthy land owner, possibly a political supporter of Regent Raef.
Lord Bron: Wealthy land owner, possibly a political supporter of Queen Hada.
Lord Oliver: Wealthy land owner, possibly a political supporter of Queen Hada.
Tuien: Hada's maid

Merchants and Guildsmen

The Verlin Family: Wool Merchants.
   Sieur Verlin: Patriarch, Master Draper to the court and aristocracy.
   Sieura Verlin: Sieur Verlin's mother, who manages his household.
   Yon Verlin: Sieur Verlin's eldest son and Master Merchant.
   Xoran Verlin: Sieur Verlin's youngest son and Apprentice Dyer.
   Tyg Verlin: Sieur Verlin's youngest daughter.
   Rennika Falconer (Rennikala Falkyn): Magiel of Orumon and one of three remaining female magiels who can trace their lineage to the One God, hiding her identity by posing as Sieur Verlin's adopted daughter; Journeyman Dyer.
   Wynn: Sieur Verlin's stableman.
The Naid Family: Weavers.
   Ide Naid: Rennika's friend.
Sieur Miach: Journeyman tanner sympathetic to the uprisers.
Sieur Charl: A Master Dyer.
Sieur Gurd: A Master Potter.

Peasants
- Xadria: Madam, and owner of the Three Corners Alehouse.
- Vellefair: An older reprobate, well-connected with the thieves' network.
- Belden: A young thug.
- Sieur Yaquob: Free trader who re-sells appropriated wares of persecuted magiels
- Raoul: Sieur Yaquob's son and pickpocket.
- Colin: Deceased. Former servant of King Dwyn, who cared for Rennika when she first came to Gramarye; Yak herder.

COUNTRY OF ARCAN
Capital: Holderford
Prayer Stone: Ruby

Abutting Shangril's mountains in the east, and bordered by Pagoras, Theurgy, and Gramarye, Arcan is a country of rolling farmland ruled by High King Huwen Delarcan, whose father, Artem, died uniting the seven realms of Shangril. The peace is an uneasy one, however, and Huwen has his hands full fulfilling his father's vision of empire.

Royalty
- High King Artem Delarcan: Deceased.
- High King Huwen Delarcan: Ruler of the seven kingdoms of Shangril.
- Queen Ychelle Delarcan: Huwen's wife.
- Princess Shalire Delarcan: Huwen and Ychelle's infant daughter.

Court and Servants
- Sieur Igua: Huwen's chancellor and chief adviser.
- Sieur Daxtonet: Royal tutor.

COUNTRY OF ELSEN
Capital: Summerbluff
Prayer Stone: Azurite (destroyed)

Situated in the north-east of Shangril, Elsen is a mountainous country of minor political importance known for iron mining and forestry. Its sparse population and many uninhabited glens make the country a good place for uprisers to hide.

Royalty
King Quinlan Brille: High King Huwen's uncle.
Lady Saffen Brille: Deceased. High King Huwen's cousin.
Anwen: Saffen's maid and Huwen's one-time mistress.

Uprisers
Fearghus: King-in-Exile Dwyn Gramaret's general in northern Shangril.
Colm: Fearghus's second in command.
Nia: An upriser healing woman.
Tonore Warrick: An upriser soldier and Meg's former lover.
Vonte: Deceased. Tonore's lover.
Peate: A young upriser.

COUNTRY OF TESHE
Capital: Coldridge
Prayer Stone: Amethyst (destroyed)

A small country in the west of Shangril producing fur and softwood; a political backwater until the unification of Shangril, when its strategic importance as the gateway to Orumon made its capital, Coldridge, a contested city. In the past ten years, Coldridge, occupied by High King Delarcan's forces, has been under intermittent attack by uprisers, primarily because it was the location of High King Huwen's Marigolds.

COUNTRY OF PAGORAS
Capital: Cataract Crag
Prayer Stone: Emerald (destroyed)

Located in the north-east of Shangril, Pagoras is a flat land perched on a dramatic, almost unscalable cliff that falls away to mysterious lands inhabited by strange people. Because of massive elevators, constructed only in the last thirty years, limited trade goods with the country of Aadi have made Pagoras wealthy. Ruled by Jace Delarcan, who is more interested in trade than politics (and wealthy enough to ignore his older brother's more repressive laws), magiels seek refuge in Pagoras where they are less likely to be persecuted.

Royalty
King Jace Delarcan: High King Huwen's younger brother, third in line to the throne of Shangril.

Peasants
Kirst: Woman displaced by war living in a shantytown outside of Cataract Crag.
Nola: Kirst's daughter.
Toothy: Part-magiel healer, working in a brewery to improve the beer with magic.
Hane: Man displaced by war living in a shanty in Cataract Crag.

COUNTRY OF ORUMON
Capital: Archwood
Prayer Stone: Amber (presumed destroyed)

Occupying a long valley surrounded by mountains in Shangril's south west, Orumon is the source of most of Shangril's precious gems and metals, as well as stone. Its isolation allowed it to have some warning when the King of Arcan embarked on his mission to unify Shangril under a single High King, and withstood his attacks for almost a year and a half before capitulating. Orumon's magiel, Talanda, cursed the country on her death bed to make it uninhabitable until the contested Amber Prayer Stone was reinstated.

Royalty
- King Ean Olivin: Deceased.
- Queen Elana Olivin: Deceased.
- Princess Faris Olivin: Deceased.

Magiels
- Talanda Falkyn: Deceased. Mother of Meghra, Janatelle, and Rennikala Falkyn.
- Meghra Falkyn (Meg Falconer): One of three remaining female magiels who can trace her lineage to the One God; now an upriser.
- Janatelle Falkyn (Janat Falconer): One of three remaining female magiels who can trace her lineage to the One God; now an upriser.
- Rennikala Falkyn (Rennika Falconer): One of three remaining female magiels who can trace her lineage to the One God; now concealing her identity and living in Gramarye.

Servants:
- Nanna: Deceased. Meghra, Janatelle, and Rennikala's nurse.

Uprisers:
- Sulwyn Cordal: Deceased. Journeyman merchant, now an upriser. Janatelle Falkyn's lover
- Colm Cordal: Sulwyn's cousin, now an upriser.

COUNTRY OF MIDELL
Capital: Theurgy
Prayer Stone: Citrine (destroyed)

A rich country of rolling hills, orchards, and mixed farming, Midell borders all six of the other countries in Shangril. King Eamon Delarcan uses the magic of the Prayer Stone of the Ruby, which he has stolen, to wall his country off from his neighbours.

Royalty
- King Eamon Delarcan: Second in line to the throne of Shangril. Eamon controls the Prayer Stone of the Ruby, the most powerful prayer stone of the original seven.

Magiels

<u>Dannle Lock</u>: Eight years old. First child born of the Marigolds, raised from infancy to wield magic in service to Eamon.

COUNTRY OF AADI
Capital: unknown
Prayer Stone: None

Little or nothing is known of the lands beyond the borders of Shangril, except the elevation is lower and the climate warmer. In the past thirty years, limited trade has commenced, bringing silks and spices to Shangril. In recent years, Shangril has imported steam technology from Aadi.

Others

<u>Orville Haye:</u> A foreigner who first introduced steam technology to King-in-Exile, Dwyn Gramaret.

PROLOGUE

Sleeping woods cast a silhouette of branches over the night sky. Early spring rain had shriveled the last of winter's snow into pale mounds crouching under trees and in sheltered places, and the path leading into the village had turned into a churn of frozen mud.

The fugitive tapped on a rough wooden door.

No candlelight seeped from behind the loose flaps of waxed linen in the hut's windows. The thatched roof, so familiar, was now heavy with lichen.

No greeting, no sound. The home he remembered from his youth had decayed gracelessly into ruin. Ranuat, Goddess of Murderers and Thieves, had turned her back on him and his family.

What to do?

He looked around the small open space before the house. The well's pulley was missing and stones along one edge of its protective wall were tumbled and moss-covered, but the woodshed, door askew, was half full and an ax had been left against the chopping block. His father's home and workshop might have been left to deteriorate, but it could not have been abandoned for long.

Where was Mother?

Father, he'd learned from a stranger who'd heard from an acquaintance, had died in the civil war. His sisters would, by now, be married and gone. He'd left them behind—what, twenty? Twenty-five years ago?—on a bright summer morning, riding the sturdy mare, off to make his way in the grand city of Archwood. No longer his father's apprentice but full journeyman, he'd been hired to work and study with a master jeweler in the capital city of Orumon.

Grand city. He shook his head.

He tried the latch to the house. The door drifted open.

"Hello?" He took a tentative step inside. Food had been cooked here recently.

He closed the door and made his way through the clutter, hands extended before him in the murk. "Hello?"

A scrape.

He turned.

Someone launched toward him, but reflexively he swiveled and caught her. "Mother?"

Beneath his hands, his assailant's arms stiffened, and her head snapped up to peer at him in the dark. "Odryn?"

Relief and joy engulfed him, and laughter bubbled up from his depths. "Mother!" He pulled her sparrow bones to him in a jubilant hug, and she burst into answering laughter and tears. He pushed her back. "How are you? I came as soon as . . ." His words faded. His arrival was too late to be of any good to anyone. He was no kind of a son.

She blinked rapidly, then, and pulled herself into him, head against his chest. "Your Uncle Bertran," she said in her thin, high voice. "He's gone."

Dead. Yes. Two days ago, a few villages to the south, a vagabond had told him. The grief of that loss had sent him on this foolish pilgrimage home. Haunted him as he traveled.

Uncle Bertran had sold the remains of Father's wares—jewels, gold, tools—one by one, to keep Mother fed when her love of dice had robbed her of everything. In the years of quiet drudgery of the High King's war, Bertran—the vagabond said—was the man to go to with anything of value to be sold, no questions asked. But Bertran could not outdistance Mother's debts, and the lenders to whom he'd succumbed made an example of him. A permanent example.

Odryn's mother sagged in his arms, and he found her a chair.

She looked at him where he sat beside her, holding her hands. "You're alive," she marveled. "You're here."

"I am." He smiled, though Ranuat twisted his heart. It was folly to come here, to be seen near his childhood home. He'd been hiding these seven years since the fall of Archwood, knowing despite all hope that the High King's men would never cease their pursuit of him.

"Everything's gone." Her face, bewildered, searched his for answers. "We have no money."

"I know."

"Your uncle tried to help, but—"

"I know."

"—since your father died—"

"Hush." He held her hands. "What do you need?"

The desperation in her eyes was pitiful. "Can you stay here? Work? Repair your father's studio?"

No. To work as a jeweler again . . . that was his dream. But it would only call attention, bring the High King's soldiers. "I think Father's tools and gold have all been sold," he said as gently as he could.

"But you could get more," she cried, life returning to her countenance. "Your work was always so fine, Odryn. Why, you were the personal jeweler to King Ean of Orumon—"

"King Ean is dead, Mother. Archwood—all of Orumon—is under a curse."

"But you saw the Amber." Her eyes glittered with fanatical vision, as though she had only to reach out to touch a life of golden ladies in silk robes and gilt ballrooms, eating sweet delicacies, dancing to the trill of flute and harp. A life he'd lived in some small way at King Ean's court.

Would that he hadn't.

"The Amber Prayer Stone . . ." His mother gazed into the darkness, distracted by . . . whatever wishes or memories sustained her now.

The Amber Prayer Stone. Gift from the one God to his worldling mistress, jewel second in magical power only to High King Huwen's Ruby. The reason the High King had put Archwood under siege, and the reason the city had endured a grueling year and a half of encirclement before the amulet's protective magic finally faltered with the death of King Ean and his magiel.

"The Amber is magic. It can still save us," she muttered.

"With no king and no magiel to wield it? No, Mother." Besides, surely she'd heard the story. Everyone knew all the prayer stones, but the Ruby had been crushed. A display of High King Huwen's power: the last of the rival prayer stones, gone; the people's hope of communing with the Gods, gone; their hope of obtaining a death token to take them to Heaven when they died, gone.

Odryn had not personally seen the axman smash the Amber. The ceremony had taken place after the capture of Archwood; after the capitulation of the refugees; after the curse had fallen on the city. Odryn had been on the run by then.

But he knew the story of the Amber's destruction was, in fact, a lie.

Because Odryn had crafted an amber jewel—an exact copy of the Prayer Stone—in secret, at High King Huwen's command. Because when Archwood fell, the Amber was not found.

King Huwen and his armies had marched home in triumph—fleeing Orumon's curse—but they did so empty-handed. King Huwen had needed a substitute for his deception. Odryn the Jeweler had seen the original. He knew what it looked like.

His mother slumped, eyes glazed, fully in the grip of memory and fantasy.

Odryn's fingers drifted to his tunic, felt the hard outline of the smooth marigold-colored stone that hung from a golden chain around his neck. He'd held it, protected it, for so long, afraid to divulge his secret.

But Mother was destitute. He could protect the gem no longer.

Now.

How could he sell this jewel without ending up on High King Huwen's gallows?

CHAPTER 1

A wisp of incoherence in the corner of Meg's eye interrupted her pacing. A ghost, drawn to this place. There would be death tonight in the hamlet of Glenfast. Had been death.

She calmed, listening, her fingers creeping to the death token in her collar.

Yes. There. Footsteps, running up the stairs. A fist pounded on her door, but before Meg could respond, it slammed open. "Meg, quick! Casualties," Nia panted, her fair, sleep-tousled tangles a wild dishevelment.

The blur, like fog, swirled and dissipated. Nia was a force of energy, of life.

"Colm's raiding party. He's back." Nia remained half in the corridor, too agitated to enter.

That meant Meg's sister, Janat, would be back, too. Meg shoved on her boots.

But—Colm. Stroke of good fortune, or bad? Colm would've ridden at a measured pace and arrived midafternoon with some ostentation, had the mission fared well. An unannounced midnight arrival with wounded—how badly had the raid gone?

Meg thrust the thought aside. Colm was *here*. Her opportunity. Finally. She snatched a cloak from the peg by the door, more to cover her nightclothes than to shield herself from the night. Despite Glenfast's altitude, the air had not fully lost the heat of the summer day.

"They've ridden from Wildbrook." Inverted shadows cast by Nia's candle mocked her scarred face as she hastened to the landing. "Some are injured."

"From Wildbrook? In one day?" Meg pulled the attic door closed and followed Nia. "Are the women readying the house of healing?" Janat, the raiding party's healer—like Meg, a magiel—would be tending the wounded. She hoped. *Oh, Kyaju, let Janat be caring for them.*

"Yes. We're trying to arrange billets for those too injured to return to the barracks." Nia hurried down the narrow stairs. "I've sent women to stoke the fires and boil the water. I'm going to look after the broth and bread."

Meg had to speak to Colm before he left again. Now she wouldn't have to wrack her brain for some excuse to be given permission to go to the upriser camp outside Coldridge to see Dwyn Gramaret, king-in-exile, a fortnight-long journey skirting contested territory. Colm could deliver the plan in her stead when he reported in. And, if Colm had failed in Wildbrook, all the more reason the upriser king and his short-sighted tacticians should listen to her.

Meg and Nia descended past the glazier's rooms where sounds of rattling pots and the glimmer of candlelight filtered in from the kitchen. The glazier's wife was no doubt appropriating the morning's simmering oats for the returning men. They hurried through the main floor workrooms to the dirt lane. Nia turned downhill to alert others to bring food, while Meg hastened toward the cobbled square, now bright with the flicker of torchlight and ringing with the stamp of hoofs.

Glenfast had once been the last retreat of the kings of Elsen, walled against attacks by warring neighbors. But in the past five hundred years of the Gods' Peace, the fortifications had been taken apart, its stones used for houses and cobbles, as the holding prospered into a goat herders' village. That peace ended when Meg was seventeen.

Now, the square before the country house, once the center of the hamlet, thronged with soldiers, horses, carts, and villagers routed from their beds. Thronged, too, with smudges. Ghosts, invisible to worldlings, barely discernible to magiels. The silent visitors were impotent, but—what?—curious? Drawn to death.

Meg shook off the presence of the spirits. Janat would be here. Somewhere. Meg's stomach tightened. Gods, she prayed that giving Janat work—important work, in battle—was the balm her sister needed.

She pushed worry aside and made her way through the crowded square. *Kyaju, what kind of fiasco had occurred at Wildbrook?*

Before the great hall doors, a handful of horses stomped nervously—farm horses unused to cobbles beneath their feet. Exhausted foot soldiers stood in small groups looking for some sign of instruction or sank, uncaring, to the ground. Townspeople disheveled with sleep bustled through the chaos.

Meg spotted a familiar form. Tonore.

A companion who'd traveled with Meg and her sisters years ago when they were highborn refugees from the earliest upheavals of the war and persecuted for their political value. He'd been her partner in war tactics at the king-in-exile's table in the upriser camps, and a one-time lover she'd flirted with across a feast table in a crowd of celebratory rebels, beneath an arch of stars.

Now, he slumped against his sack of meagre supplies—clothing, weapons, personal effects. His hair hung in greasy strings over his grubby face and clothing, the scar from his missing ear visible in the dim light. Smears of dried blood caked his beard on one side—his blood or someone else's, Meg couldn't tell. He'd begun to go bald in the past few years, though he was no older than Janat. This, and his hollow eyes, made him seem ancient. But then . . . this war had aged them all.

He bent over an unmoving form at his side, listening, quivering with denied tears. Vonte. The man's lips moved, and Tonore stilled at the words. Premonition crept into Meg's stomach as she watched. She'd seen this before. Lived it too many times. Death.

Tonore nodded, a brief, unconscious assent. He tugged with trembling fingers at the strings on his lover's filthy chemise, opening it at the neck to expose the band of cloth fastened there, and Meg knew. Wisps of indistinctness drew closer. Ghosts.

Tonore fumbled with the band of cloth, releasing a disc a little larger than a coin, flat and pale in the inconsistent light of the torches. Vonte's entreating eyes lifted to Tonore's, and Tonore smoothed his lover's hair back, his touch lingering on his face. He leaned in and kissed the man, delaying, denying what must come. Then, with a tautness of resolve, he placed the death token on Vonte's tongue. He bowed his head, silently shaking.

Meg watched, unable to turn away. The soldier's eyes closed, his features softening, body relaxing onto the cobbles beneath him.

Tonore's face pinched, and he shuddered in grief. The spirits melted into the miasma of their brethren.

Meg crouched beside Tonore and placed a hand on his shoulder.

Tonore covered her hand with his, hard and fierce, and turned to bury his head in her embrace, shudders wracking his body.

"I'm sorry," she murmured. Sorry for Tonore, even Vonte . . . but for herself, her own losses, too? Perhaps. Vonte was fortunate to have a death token, gift of the Gods. Fortunate to have had Tonore, a good man. Fortunate to have someone help him place his death token on his tongue. Now, he would not be condemned to wander the earth, a ghost among too many ghosts, restless and unrooted for eternity, but would ascend to one of the Heavens. The lowest sphere of Ranuat, Goddess of Murderers and Thieves? Or higher, perhaps to the realm of Kyaju the Devout? Or, even as far as the Heaven of the One God? There was no way to know.

Tonore pulled from her a little, composing himself. He ran a sleeve across his nose.

"Do you need anything? A Serenity?" she asked.

He shook his head, lips pressed together against speech. "I'll stay here a bit."

She nodded. In their years together, he'd never taken any palliative but willow tea. Even the time he took an arrow to his chest during the Farfalls raid, less than a season after he'd come to her bed the first time. That had been a bad one.

Someone pushed past her and she leaned into Tonore's side, trying to stay out of the way. "Where's Janat?" she asked as gently as she could.

The softness vanished from Tonore's face. "Don't know." His voice became harsh. "But Colm should be here by now. Pulling up the rear, most like. His notion of a leader's place." He twisted to face her. "Listen. Meg. You have to talk to him."

"I will."

"Now." He took her hand, punctuating his insistence. "I heard he's leaving at once to report to King Dwyn. You must get Colm to convince the king to come to Glenfast and settle these infernal disputes. Fearghus orders one thing, Colm undermines him, men are killed. It can't go on."

"Once the wounded are seen to."

"It'll take time to transport the wounded to the house of healing. You have a moment, Meg. Colm doesn't listen to me. Or Fearghus."

"They don't listen to me, either," she said.

"You're King Dwyn's magiel. Colm has to take your messages to him."

She turned to the cacophony around them. "There are so many hurt."

"Your healing women are trained," he insisted. "They can sort the bruised and crippled from the critical." And the dying.

"I need to find Janat."

His face darkened. "Help the people you can help, Meg."

She shot him a sharp look.

"Meg." His grip tightened. "Save a handful of men tonight? Or save a hundred men, or a thousand, by averting more disasters like this?"

He was right. She gripped his hand hard, hugging him with her other arm, and he responded as fiercely. "I'll go."

She rose, but he put a detaining hand on her arm. "We haven't eaten since yesterday. Colm's whipped us beyond all reason."

"The village is doing its best. I don't think Fearghus knew you were coming tonight. I was only called a few minutes ago."

"Colm didn't send a runner?"

Meg didn't know. She squeezed his shoulder. "I'll see what I can find."

A shift, a murmur, rippled through the throng. Meg looked to the main road.

Colm had entered the square, the last of his struggle of uprisers to arrive. He was a small man but made of sinew and muscle, and he had quick, assured movements that spoke of impatience with fools. His worn leather armor was the color of mud in the thin torchlight. His face, usually clean-shaven in the foreign fashion for spying on royals, straggled now with a week's growth of dirty beard. He guided his horse with his one good hand through the throng and dismounted near the doors to the great hall.

"Take care," Meg said to Tonore. She pushed forward past a cart laden with sacks.

Colm glared at Fearghus, under the torchlight, emerging from the great hall at a fast hobble, shoving an arm into the sleeve of his vest. Colm pointed to the cart. "*That* was the price of five good men's lives." He didn't bother to lower his voice.

So. A botch.

Fearghus buttoned his vest, scowling, the lines on his aging face sharp in the inconsistent light. "Tend to your men's needs. We'll talk tomorrow." He jostled past his officer.

"Four carts." Colm caught his elbow. "Oats and barley. Two dozen bags of last fall's apples. We couldn't get near enough to take the gold. Not enough money or food to get us through to the fall harvest."

Four cartloads? That was all the raiders had been able to take from Wildbrook? Not a single prayer had been answered, then. Meg had lived in Wildbrook for the better part of a year. It was a rich holding. *Had* been a rich holding.

Fearghus snatched his elbow away. "We'll talk tomorrow."

"Do you know what they have? The High King's royal army? *Muskets. Foreign muskets.*"

Fearghus glowered, but his hesitation told Meg he hadn't known. He turned on his heel and called to the tavernkeeper across the press.

"We cannot stand against muskets!" Colm called to his retreating commander. "Even with fear-blocking philters—*which* were lacking because our magiel swills her own spells—"

Oh, no.

Fearghus whirled. "You're saying I could have predicted *muskets*?"

Colm shoved his way through the knot of followers hanging on the exchange, to confront his commander. "I'm saying you should've listened when I told you forty swords and twenty horses could not breach Wildbrook's walls."

Fearghus snarled, then swiveled back to shout orders.

Colm threw up his hands in disgust and strode in Meg's direction.

"Colm Cordal," Meg cried. "A word!"

"You have work, Magiel Falconer." He pushed past her. "The house of healing will be full tonight."

"When do you leave? I must speak with you before you go." She would go to the house of healing without delay. But first she must secure an appointment. He had put her off too many times.

He halted and pierced her with his eyes. "And I would have a word with you." He changed direction and shouldered his way to the back of a cart. Reaching in with two hands, he hauled someone by the armpits from the straw bedding.

Janat.

Gods, had she been—

He deposited Janat on her feet. She giggled, clutching at the side of the wagon. A hodgepodge of ragged skirts escaped the cinch of a down-valley bodice beneath shreds of a too-large traditional robe over her bare legs. The grime ground into her knotted hair was of a greasier sort than the blood and mud of the soldiers—older and clammier. It abraded into her elbows and feet. She slithered to the ground, a heap of stick legs and arms, the magiel shimmer of her skin blurring her in the dark.

Meg's stomach squirmed in relief and disgust. Her sister's high forehead and pretty dimples were a sad imitation of their mother's elegant loveliness. Meg wanted to crush her into a hug, hold her, and keep her safe.

But Tonore. The men. She couldn't lose this moment. "Sieur, a meeting—"

"This magiel," he growled in Meg's face, "is worse than useless. Her spells did not work—what spells our men *got*—because she tasted most of them herself."

Gods, Janat taking her own spells was exactly what Meg'd been trying to prevent by pleading with Colm to let her sister go to war where there was useful work for her to do. A sense of mission to displace Janat's unaccountable drive to deaden herself. "I must consult with you—"

"This is not the time, Magiel."

She bit back her anger. "Please."

He blew out a breath in annoyance. "Tomorrow night. Not before," he warned.

She closed her eyes in thanks to Kyaju.

"And not before every one of my men is tended to." He scanned the chaos, his attention already flown. Her face flared with heat. He implied—Kyaju, she would never abandon her charges.

Janat wobbled where she sat, then leaned over and vomited.

Oh, Gods. Oh, Kyaju, what more could she do for her sister?

"Ah!" Colm flinched from the stink, whipping his cloak back. "You govern her," he clipped, "or I will imprison her for the duration of this war, I swear."

"Colm, Sieur, she's not—"

"Or hang her as a traitor."

CHAPTER 2

Meg gathered up Janat and took her to the house of healing where she found a girl to sit by her as she slept off whatever potion she'd consumed. Then Meg descended into the frantic disarray that was the main area of the house. Nia had a list for her.

But she'd barely examined the first patient, a soldier with a musket ball in his abdomen, bleeding from an unknown source—spleen? Liver?—when she was called back to Janat's room. The young girl stood outside the door, gripping the knob as Janat shrieked and thumped beyond.

"Let me out!"

Nia, bolting up the stairs, shot Meg a look of warning.

Janat's antics could not be brought to Colm's attention. "I'll talk to her." Meg nodded a dismissal to the girl and took the knob.

Nia put a hand on Meg's arm. "We need you, Meg. That boy will die," she said in a low voice. "Others, too."

Meg had calmed Janat before, but sometimes it took hours. She'd also made things worse, agitating rather than soothing her.

The door thumped. "Let me out!"

Meg tightened her grip on the knob.

Nia must have read the doubt on her face. "Have you no soporific?"

Of course, she did. "I can't fuel her dependence." That would worsen everything.

Nia leaned close. "You must."

Nia was right. There were too many soldiers.

She gave Nia a faint nod and reached into an interior fold of her robe where she'd sewn hidden patches with small openings, in the magiel way. She withdrew a potion. Together, they entered the room.

Meg worked. When her eyes blurred and her shoulders ached, she prayed for strength and took a breath of the wakefulness spell that gave soldiers alertness in battle. She worked on through the night and late into the next day.

The sun was westering over the green hills when Meg, having finally visited the shrine to Kyaju, mounted the marble steps to the village's great hall. Colm's suite spanned the tip of the south wing's second floor, at the end of an echoing corridor lined with statues of onyx and alabaster. A boy had been posted at the once-gilt door, for the soldiers were far too exhausted from their long march and weeks of summer campaign to do more than minimal duty.

"Sieur Cordal is not to be disturbed, Magiel." The page looked at her with a mixture of defiance and fear.

It was the shimmer of her skin. A blur of time vibrations that had once been a mark of beauty and divinity, commanding reverence. But with the war and the High King's decree, worldlings had begun to hunt magiels, forcing them into ghettos and prisons. Magiels had to become adept at hiding their faces in hoods, or arranging meetings for the dark of night, in alleys or back rooms.

But there were times when worldlings' fear of her was useful. Meg's plain, strong features gave her an air of authority. She regarded the boy with a frosty gaze. "Inform Sieur Cordal that Magiel Falconer is here to see him. As he commanded last night."

It was hard to tell if the boy's pallor increased, but his eyes flinched at this information. For a moment, he looked as though he would argue, but then he bobbed his head and disappeared through the peeling double door.

Meg tapped her fingers against her thigh and restrained herself from pacing. She would not revert to crawling the walls in the confines of her room, agonizing over gossip of mishandled strategies and continued oppression by the king of Arcan who'd set himself up as High King of Shangril. Not without at least presenting her plan. Gods, she missed sitting by the king-in-exile's side in his military tent, pouring over maps and listening to reports from messengers from across the seven kingdoms of Shangril. She missed speaking to men at council, discussing the logistics inherent in her suggestions.

She even missed their challenges to her logic, debates that sharpened battle plans.

The door opened. "Sieur Cordal will see you," the boy said.

Relief. A familiar eagerness pumped through her.

The reception room for what had once been the guest quarters was not unlike similar chambers in Castle Archwood where Meg had grown up. Late afternoon sunshine streamed through a narrow window, and the warmth of high summer with it, throwing into shadow all but the corner of a table, a chair, and a strip of carpet.

Colm, rumpled and still unshaven, entered the anteroom from the suite's bedroom. In this softer light of day, he looked gaunter than Meg remembered, more like his cousin. Sulwyn, whom Meg and Janat had both loved, each in her own way. Sulwyn, who'd divided them, and in death, brought them together again.

"Your visit is most inconvenient." Colm stood in the gloom with his hands clasped behind his back, angled to deflect her attention from the infirmity of his left arm, an old battle souvenir. He wore only a shirt and Aadian breeches, his feet bare, and he did not offer her a seat.

"Sieur." *Colm.* She should've addressed him by his first name, the name she'd used so easily when they campaigned together in the early days of the war. Over the years, he'd risen in rank and she, apparently, had fallen. Their relationship—never close—had become more distant. Formal. "Thank you for agreeing to meet with me. I—"

"I did not agree to meet with you. I gave you all the information you required last night. Your sister is a morally corrupt woman. I will not have her associating with my men. Not to administer spells, not to heal, not in any other capacity. I will not banish her." He paused as if to emphasize this statement.

He expected gratitude. Subservience.

"Not out of generosity," he continued when Meg said nothing, "but because she can't be trusted. Should royal forces capture her, they would extract far too much information about us. Control her, Meg."

"It's not because of my sister I've come to see you."

"I *will* have her tried and hanged," he said. "Don't think I won't."

"So you said last night. That's not why I am here."

He took a breath and looked down, as if exhibiting unwarranted self-control. Deep bags circled his eyes. "What could you possibly speak with me about, that you have not already communicated to Commander Fearghus?"

"I couldn't be certain anything I said to Fearghus would reach your ears. He has no high opinion of my ideas." She took a chance. "Or yours, it would appear."

This seemed to surprise and soften him. "Fearghus is an old man with no imagination who only follows direct orders or repeats worn strategies."

"You, at least, once listened to me."

He ran the finger of his good hand along the edge of the table and allowed his rigid stance to ease. "Dwyn should have put the uprisers of Elsen under my command."

This was it. His mind was on tactics. "High King Huwen is ignoring *Highglen*."

Colm waved a hand in dismissal. "Highglen is in Gramarye. We are to secure a toehold in Elsen. Summerbluff, or failing that, Canyondell."

"But we're not! We're doing no more in Elsen than raiding a few noble holdings, trying to survive until winter. Once the king of Elsen's had enough complaints, he'll comb the mountains to find us and root us out." She came forward to the table and put both hands flat on it, looking up at him. "Harassing local lords and villages only makes people afraid of us. Drives them to bury their heads, to defend a High King who promises to keep the roads safe for free traders."

"Meg—"

"*Highglen* is ruled by a regent with no authority to act." She *had* to convince him. "All summer our forces have been squeezing Coldridge. *Now,* Colm. While our men have Huwen pinned down. He can't use his Ruby Prayer Stone as long as his brother refuses him. *Now* is when we need to take Highglen."

Colm straightened in bitter satisfaction. "I listened to you when you asked me to bring your sister on this raid instead of you. You said she'd come through if she was just given a chance. I put my name on the line for you, Magiel. Do you know how much that cost me?"

She knew he was playing on her emotions. She couldn't let him distract her. "Highglen is isolated and vulnerable. There's a solid upriser contingent in the city. Their people would rise up. All they lack is a leader."

He bit. "On what authority do you come by such a statement?"

"A sympathetic free trader from Highglen."

Colm eyed her, listening.

"Princess Hada has gone there," Meg pushed. "She's claimed her inheritance, Castle Highglen. She and her brother's regent are divided, wrestling over the country's governance. Colm, she's *nineteen*."

"So simple?" Colm said condescendingly.

"It *is*! Don't ignore me." Before he could argue, she went on. "We can get there, infiltrate, take the city before Huwen mounts his cannons on wagons!"

"You don't understand, do you?" he responded. "Maybe. Eventually. When King Dwyn realizes Commander Fearghus has hung himself with his idiocy and nepotism, perhaps the men will come to fight behind my banner. But until then—"

"Sieur! You must—"

"Do you never quit, Sieura?"

Behind him, the door opened, and a woman peered into the room. "Oh! Colm, you—"

"I bid you good day," Colm said, striding toward the woman in the doorway.

Meg drew in a sudden breath. Fearghus's wife. The woman, comely for her age, gray-peppered hair still full and now disarrayed fetchingly about her face, wore only a sleeping robe.

The woman startled in recognition when she saw Meg. A flicker of disgust dried on her face. "Colm." She gave him a pointed look and disappeared back into the bedroom.

He paused in the doorway. "Your concern is irrelevant, Magiel," he said. "This war is bigger than any individual. You—all of us—need to do our jobs."

Meg left Colm's rooms, mind racing, a cascade of questions slowing her steps. *Tonore's talk of internal disputes, Colm undermining Fearghus. Fearghus denying Colm the swords and horses he needed to secure the band's rations. To what end? With what ramifications?*

At the kitchen of the house of healing, she dipped a cup of water from the bucket, intending to take it to the girl spinning wool at Janat's side as her sister slept. Or raved. *Fearghus's wife in*

Colm's chambers—private chamber. How long had he been cuckolding his commanding officer? Gods, she needed a moment to pray. To understand.

She checked with Nia. The convalescents were stable. Janat had woken, and Nia had given her a mild worldling tea to ease her vomiting, as Meg had instructed. Janat had rested then, weeping, and slept again. A number of the wounded had been discharged, and more were doing well enough to sit up, some even helping with small chores at supper. Nia told Meg to rest.

Rest.

That would not happen. Meg's anger only mounted as she drew inevitable conclusions. Before she relieved Janat's minder, she needed to go to Fearghus's home.

Fearghus's steward directed her to the granary. The commander was seated at a rickety table in the candlelight, fingers stained with ink, as a clerk inventoried sacks of oats. Deep fissures lined his leathery face and his fingers had thickened with years, but he was hale and his eyes were bright beads in his face: sharp. He glowered at her arrival, then returned to the tiny figures in neat columns on a sheet of rough parchment before him.

"Fifteen sacks with only a touch of rot," his clerk called out.

Fearghus bent over his record and scratched with a quill. "What do you want?"

"Do the lives of your men and the souls of the people of the seven kingdoms of Shangril," Meg clipped, "rest on the whims of your jealousy?"

The commander's fingers stilled. A breathlessness descended on the circle of candlelight within the granary and the clerk's head whipped around, hands motionless on the pile of grain sacks.

Fearghus lifted his head and, catching the clerk's eye, nodded toward the door. The clerk hurried out, and the stir of air from the closing granary door flickered the candle.

Fearghus set his quill in the ink well and straightened on his stool, his lined face coloring subtly. He tightened his jaw, as if to prevent his eyes from softening. His voice was low. "He flaunts her?"

Regret at her harsh words constricted Meg's throat, dried her denunciations.

"What has Colm told you?"

"That you refused him the equipment—"

Fearghus waved his hand in dismissal. "He blames me. Of course, he does. For holding back a few blades to defend Glenfast in his absence. He blames his men, too, did he tell you that? He blames your sister, though in that case I agree." Fearghus leaned back against the wall and folded his hands over his spare stomach. "He blames everyone for his failures but himself. It's no wonder men don't rally to his call." He eyed her. "Now he impugns my wife?"

Meg shook her head, unable to meet his gaze. "I . . . saw her. In his chamber."

The silence in the shed admitted the distant sounds of wind and men and dogs. A shine sprang into Fearghus's eyes. "I do not govern the uprisers of Elsen on the basis of revenge against my generals," he said huskily.

No? Then— "Sieur, I beg you. If you have no politics with upriser factions, petition King Dwyn to send men to take Highglen."

"This, again?" He glared at her. "I said, 'no,' and I mean, 'no.' We defend Glenfast and our remaining forces are directed at Coldridge. There are no men to waste on a third fortress." He let out a short breath. "Meg, I like you. But you're a woman. A healer, not a tactician. You have no place at the councils of men. Battle strategies are not your concern."

"It *is* my concern! It is my life and my sisters' lives, and my peoples' lives and souls—"

"It is your concern to heal, make potions to strengthen our soldiers, and pray for victory."

"You focus on one hill, one village, and lose sight of the central goal. I see things—"

He stood. "Your predictions, *Magiel*, have no validity."

"I'm not talking about seeing the future. I'm talking war plans. We must procure the Ruby Prayer Stone for the good of the people. To do that, the uprisers need a place of strength from which to speak on equal footing with the royals. A fortress. A citadel. A defensible castle from which to expand our influence."

"And you think I don't know that? Right now, I need cabbages to prevent scurvy." The commander leaned on his table. "I need generals—and magiels—who recognize their place and do as they are commanded."

She breathed fury at him. The idiot. The arrogant, stupid idiot.

"But—Sieura Falconer—neither of us is about to get what we desire. Go home and care for your charges."

CHAPTER 3

Powerless! Meg was powerless.

The crunch of her boots reverberated off cobbles and walls as she crossed the dark square before the great hall.

Powerless to convince Colm or Fearghus. But they were only field commanders. Dwyn Gramaret, King-in-Exile, held the highest authority over the uprisers. He'd listened to Meg in the past.

Her steps slowed as she reached the edge of the square, and she stopped, a hand on a corner of the baker's shop. A spitting rain had begun to fall, and a pair of dogs growled over a dead rat. She surveyed the wide cobbled space. She saw no smudge of ghostly presence, but spirits were there. This sphere had become more and more crowded since the civil war—since the High King had smashed all but one of the prayer stones. Meg prayed to Kyaju for the thousandth time, and to Ranuat, and to all the Many Gods, to show her some way to come to them in Heaven, that she might return to her people with the death tokens they needed.

King Dwyn could send men to Highglen. But he was in the west, directing an increasingly futile war against the High King's forces in Coldridge. A long journey with autumn only weeks away. Neither Colm nor Fearghus would give her leave to go there to petition the king.

But she'd been left with no choice. She must.

She returned to the house of healing. Those patients, who remained, slept on pallets in the house's many small rooms. Only a few healers were needed to watch over them.

Meg could afford to leave these men in the hands of her assistants. She would plan and prepare, then steal away, alone. If the people of the seven kingdoms ever were to regain their spiritual link with the

Gods, the uprisers must convince the High King to stop warring on his own people. They must entice him—or force him—to share the Ruby Prayer Stone.

To do that, the uprisers needed a base of power from which to negotiate. Glenfast was an inconsequential hamlet at the end of a box canyon that could be taken the moment the king of Elsen thought it worth his time to seize. Coldridge, in the west, might never be taken from imperial forces wielding cannons. They *needed* Highglen.

But . . . Janat.

Meg crept through the warren of hushed rooms. The heavy smell of sweat and vomit and blood had lessened with the windows open to invigorating rain. She mounted the ladder to her sister's attic chamber, fumbling in the dim light filtering from the open doorway to kneel beside Janat's pallet.

The bed was empty.

The tiny space was a flurry of wadded sheets and scattered straw, Janat's usual disarray. But she was not here. *Piss*.

The young girl assigned to report on Janat's movements rose from the floor where she'd fallen asleep. "Mistress Falconer?"

"Your charge is gone."

The girl took in a sharp breath, fully awake, her eyes a gleam in the dark. "Sieura Falconer! I'm sorry! I—"

Meg softened. "When did she leave?" she asked in a gentler tone, sitting back on her heels and groping on the shelf for a candle.

"She was asleep when Nia brought dumplings for supper, and for a good time later. After sunset, Sieura."

Meg struck flint on steel. A spark fell onto the tinder and puffed into flame. She lit the candle before the tinder died, and held it up. She recognized Janat's thin cloak on the rumpled bedclothes. On the floor beside the pallet, her sister's buckled shoes. She couldn't have gone far.

Piss, piss, piss. Meg needed Janat to sober up and see the precariousness of her position. She needed Janat to take her place as magiel for the Glenfast uprisers and stay clearheaded for at least the next few weeks, if not into the winter. Meg was uncertain whether she'd be able to go to Coldridge and return before snow blocked the roads in the mountain passes. "Have you any idea where she's gone?"

"No, Sieura." The child's small face was stricken in the candlelight.

"Hush. Don't worry." Meg checked the chamber pot. Empty. "It's not your fault. Stay here. If she returns, come find me or Nia."

The girl nodded, and Meg covered her hand reassuringly.

Where to look? She climbed down the attic ladder, through the upper level to the main floor, and found Nia with the local midwife and apothecary in a small room off the house's entry. They sat at a table in the relative brilliance of three tallow candles. A scatter of vials, small cloth sacks, and clay pots littered the table before them. Inventorying their stock of worldling spells. Nia looked up as Meg entered the storage room, closing the door behind her. "Nia—"

Nia shook her head, mouthing numbers. "Twenty-four," she said, and the apothecary's wife, seated at a tiny table, wrote the number on a scrap of linen.

High summer would be gone in a blink. Everyone was taking inventory. Winter would be particularly long and hard this year, with such low stockpiles. Meg dipped a finger in a potion, checking for strength and vitality. It was good. She could feel ingredients that were too old or too fresh to bring their fullest potency to the spell, and a slight imbalance in measures, but it would work. Good worldling magic was often enough without magiel intervention.

"I sent a boy for you," the midwife said, pausing in the midst of groping through a sack.

Not good. If the men were recovering well, the house of healing should have no need of her before morning, and then, only to confirm decisions correctly made. "I'm here now. What is it?"

"The Heartspeed," Nia said. "I could have sworn the storeroom had fifteen vials this morning."

This sounded right. Meg did a mental calculation. She'd made thirty over the last few weeks—Heartspeed was beyond a worldling's skill to make—and except for the ten she'd sent with Colm on this last raid, none should be used until men went out to war again. She had suggested Fearghus take a quarter dose each morning since the excitement yesterday, just to keep his heart steady. Colm had asked for two vials for a runner he'd sent to King Dwyn. Another might have been used—Meg was so tired, she couldn't remember. But if Nia said there were fifteen, then there must have been fifteen. "How many do we have?"

Nia held up a handful of vials. "Six. Did Colm or Fearghus send men out on some new raid and ask you for them?"

"No." The men were not up to another raid so soon. Double piss. Meg did not have time to hunt for missing inventory or puzzle out how and why the bickering commanding officers undermined one another in bids to prove each other wrong. She had to—

Janat.

"By all that's Holy."

Nia gave her a sharp look. "What?"

"Have you seen my sister?" Her voice thickened with fury and dread.

Dawning comprehension and repulsion crept onto Nia's face. "She's not asleep upstairs?"

"No. I checked."

The three women exchanged worried glances, and the midwife let the sack on her lap collapse to the floor.

Meg thrust her candle into a globed lantern.

"We'll help you look." The apothecary's wife put her quill down and pulled her shawl from the back of her chair.

Nia leaned close, her voice low. "Let her go."

Meg gave Nia a sharp look.

The other women slipped from the room, and they were alone.

"Meg, you've done everything for her. Everything a person can."

Meg opened her mouth to . . . what? What could she say?

"We need you. Not just as a healer. We need your battles with Fearghus. You might think he doesn't listen, but after you've spoken to him, we get supplies. But you're so distracted by Janat—"

"I can't leave her."

"What can you do to help her that you haven't already done?"

Meg bit her lip, her head shaking slowly in powerlessness. "I . . . have to look for her. Nia, I'm sorry. She's my sister."

Nia tilted her head.

Meg turned to the door, covering her head against the rain. "I'd rather she be found before Colm hears of her disappearance. Or hears of the loss of the Heartspeeds."

⁂

The village of Glenfast was not large, but it contained nooks enough to hide a woman, especially if she did not want to be found. Meg went first to the attic room she shared with her sister. Janat was not there, and the glazier had not seen her.

The public house was quiet and dark, but the tavernkeeper told

Meg sleepily she might check the stable. Meg had found Janat there more than once.

The homes of her sister's few acquaintances were inky and silent.

Which left Meg combing the streets, peering into corners and crevices, scattering rats. She prayed. The rain was soft, but it had stolen the heat of the village's structures, and a light breeze poked chill fingers through her woolen cloak.

She was in Little Lane, near Cliffside, when she heard a man shout, followed by a shrill scream. She darted to the end of the snaking alley.

Mist and rain softened the tableau before her into shades of gray on gray. A man, arms outstretched, stood with his back to her reaching over the city wall, which was not as high as his head at this point. The wall's masonry was decayed, a broad pile of slabs balanced on the edge of a deep protective cleft in the mountain, above a rushing river. On top of the wide crumbling wall, Janat, her blurred face puffy with tears and bruises, her eyes wild with fear, leapt back from his fingers. Her feet bled and her bodice was torn to rags, exposing her shoulders and one breast.

"Bitch!" The man was too cowardly or too clumsy to climb the wall, too infuriated or too far into his cups to use persuasion. He swiped ineptly at her ankle. "You get over— Bitch!"

Janat hopped, managing to stomp his wrist into the stone slab. "I don't know when you—are! When I . . ." A pebble broke from under her other foot, tumbling into the precipice.

"Janat!" Meg's cry over the noise of the river startled them. For an instant, Janat and the man were caught, motionless, in the pearly light of the pattering rain. Meg had no idea what had infuriated the man or why Janat was afraid, but whatever the argument—a senseless drunken quarrel with a forgotten cause, no doubt—the top of this wall was no place for a shoving match.

Behind her, someone banged a shutter closed against the disturbance.

"Meg?" the man choked. One of the tinker's gaggle of unmarried sons. He'd been recruited by uprisers on promise of a quick war, maybe six or seven years ago. Hardened, now. Bitter. But at Meg's interruption, he turned and ran along the wall, possibly searching for a stair.

"Janat," Meg repeated, trying to soften her voice, to coax, to draw her sister's attention.

Janat half crouched, her eyes bright and muscles stiff, watching the soldier.

"Janat. Come down." Meg could never tell how Janat would respond. Lethargic and uncooperative, or silly and obstructive. Tonight, though, there was a wildness in her posture, a recklessness in her movements, a fretfulness in her hands. As if she'd taken Heartspeed.

Janat darted a glance at her, then back to the soldier. He'd found a stair to climb onto the wall, and now came at a drunken run along the wide barrier. Twice, flagstones dislodged beneath his feet and tumbled, silent under the drum of rain, into the gush of water far below. "I paid you! Strumpet!"

"Janat!" Meg's pulse leapt as the soldier, murder on his face, neared. She dashed to the wall. "Janat," she screamed.

A demented grin lit her sister's face as the man pounced. Janat dodged toward the street, but her bare foot dislodged a rock from the crumbling rim, and she slipped on the wet rampart, tumbling to her hands and knees.

Meg sprang up and snatched Janat's arm, imploring the Gods for strength. Flinging spell words at the wall, she searched for a time in its construction when the stones beneath the soldier's feet had not yet been plucked from their beds.

For an instant—all Meg could manage over distance and without potions—the lip was not there. Surprise and terror streaked his face as the wall beneath him disappeared. His arms windmilled, back arcing. His shriek broke off, and Meg stared into Janat's wild eyes as both strained to hear above the roar of the river and the patter of the rain.

A glimpse, in her mind. The man Meg had killed. Eight years ago. Wenid.

Janat tugged against Meg's iron grip, but Meg thrust herself back into the street, pulling Janat with her. They landed in a heap in the mud.

"Shut up down there!" A man's voice over the banging of shutters. "People are trying to sleep."

Janat tore herself loose from Meg. Slipping, she managed to gain her feet.

"Janat!" Meg's plea was sharp, her voice lowered.

"Why should I?" Janat whirled on her.

Would she run? Or gouge at Meg's face and arms? "Janat." She tried to calm the thump in her chest, keep her voice low and calm as she climbed to her feet. "Please. Stop. Come home."

"Home?" Janat stared incredulously. "What home?" She paced, furious, fingering the collar at her neck. "You killed a man. There on the wall, just now. He didn't have time to put his death token on his tongue."

A pang shot through Meg, a sharp remorse. The man. Soldier. Tinker's son. Condemned to wander this sphere forever. A ghost. She should have done something else to stop him, something . . .

Wenid's face as he lay on the floor, contorted by the poison she'd given him. The blood, where she'd sliced him.

"And you used magic," her sister said. "You'll be useless in a couple of candlemarks and I can do as I like. Fly like a flower—" She danced and laughed.

"Janat." Meg shoved the flashes of nightmares back. Kyaju, the soldier had been about to rape her sister. "Come back to the room with me." Away from the ire of watchers. "Let me talk to you."

"Lecture." But the girl didn't run. She paced, sweating. Angry, but calmer. "You don't want me. You sent me away. I embarrass you. I mess up. I'm a failure, a freak, a Marigold—"

"You're not!"

"Liar!" She spun black eyes on her.

"How can you say—"

"You feed me. You nurse me. You lie for me." Janat's eyes blazed and tears gleamed on her rain-wet cheeks. "You pick me up and put me on my feet so I can do your little chores." She laughed, as at a new thought. "You make potions for me, and don't know it. Now you've killed for me." She rushed forward and grabbed Meg by the shoulders, face feral. "And I break every promise I make." She laughed a high, chilling laugh, and again, her fingers found their way to her collar. To her death token.

"Janat—" But Janat was right. The man, the tinker's son. What was his name? Meg had killed him, cursed him, as she'd done to Wenid. Sent his spirit from his body with no death token to bring him to Heaven.

Her sister shucked her away and tried to scrabble up the wall.

Meg sprang to her feet and wrapped herself around her sister's body, pinioning her to the stone. She cradled her for a moment as

Janat wriggled, emitting a guttural snarl. Then her body went limp. She turned, flinging angular arms around Meg's neck, and wept bitterly into her shoulder, shivering under Meg's embrace.

An image of Janat, a toddler, filled Meg's thoughts. *Castle Archwood. Aureoled in sunlight shining through the nursery windows. Her first necklace of real gold.*

"Shh, shh," Meg soothed. *Janat, humming tunelessly, telling Nanna in a childish lisp she was a princess dancing at a royal ball.*

"I . . . can't . . ."

"Hush." Meg stroked Janat's arms, her hair. *Twirling. Falling down, dizzy.* Meg pushed the memories back.

"I can't. I can't stop, Meg."

"You can. You will." Meg had to be here for her sister. Now.

Janat lifted her head, and her beautiful face twisted with grief. "I want to. You don't know how much I—"

"I know."

"You *don't* know. You can't know." Janat slumped against the wall, letting herself slide down into the mud, and Meg slid down with her. "And Meg, when I haven't felt it for a while, when I haven't floated . . . I can't think of anything else. I can't . . . all I can think of is, where is the poppy milk, where is the berserker mushroom, when are you looking the other way, when are you making more Heartspeed—"

"You're right," Meg interrupted. "I don't know how you feel. But . . . if you want to stop—"

"And I *don't* want to stop. Meg, I don't." She struggled for a moment, as if she would try again to climb the wall.

"I'll help you. I'll beseech the Gods for you."

Janat turned in Meg's enfolding arms, irritation creasing her brow. "You say that but you don't mean it."

"I do."

"No, you don't. Your work is too big. You are the great magiel to the king of the uprisers. You're fighting to restore the people of *seven realms* to their Gods. Seven realms, Meg."

Meg suppressed a growl in her throat. *Gods.* Janat, for all her stupidity and blindness could cut through the complexities of her world and pin Meg to a rock. By all that was Holy, Meg had spent her life preparing to be the spiritual leader of her people. For almost ten years, since she was seventeen, she'd battled the High King's armies, battled superstition and prejudice, and now battled infighting amongst the uprisers. And, always, her goal slipped from her fingers. Even now, she was so close—so close—to finding a toehold, a sanctuary in which the uprisers could rebuild. A garrison. To reclaim the peoples' access to Heaven.

"Let me go, Meg."

Meg blinked the rain from her lashes and peered at her sister's shivering form.

"Let me go." As Nia had said.

"To climb that wall? Put your death token on your tongue?"

"To free myself."

Meg wrapped her sister closer and pulled her head to her shoulder.

"To free you, Meg. To do what needs to be done. It will be my act of patriotism."

Janat had read her thoughts. That it might be possible for them to remain with the uprisers. For Meg to continue her work. To pause, care for Janat for a bit until she was better, all the while pursuing her claim with Fearghus, smoothing things over with Colm, and petitioning King Dwyn. Scrabbling for supplies, money, men.

But tonight, Meg had killed a man. An upriser soldier.

She'd killed before; she was a soldier, too, for all Colm and Fearghus might deny it, and she knew the philters she brewed were used to destroy men. But . . . hand-to-hand, that was different. And she'd killed an upriser. There would be questions. No doubt witnesses had seen Janat and the tinker's son earlier.

I'll hang her as a traitor. Don't think I won't. Colm's words.

Meg could confess her own role, defend Janat, and plead self-defense. But Colm had made up his mind. Janat had not a single shred of goodwill left.

She leaned her cheek onto Janat's sopping hair, let her head move slowly from side to side. "No."

"Meg—"

Meg pulled away enough to look again into her sister's face. Folded her sister's fingers in her own palm. She shook her head. "No. I won't let you go."

Janat bit her lip, but distress found its way again into her eyes.

"I've been breaking promises, too."

Janat's brows dipped in a momentary frown.

"I've promised to help you, and . . . you're right. I lecture. I get angry. I neglect you. I sent you away." She took a deep breath. "No more."

Janat's frown of confusion deepened.

"We'll leave Glenfast." Meg hadn't really thought of going until the words were said. But . . . yes. There it was.

"Leave—"

It was the only choice. It was true, and deep within, Meg knew it. Janat shook her head slowly.

The pressure of battle tactics. The violence of the raids. The temptations of drunkard soldiers. How could such a life be good for Janat? The revolution had been Meg's ambition, never Janat's. "Tonight." Tonight, everything would change. Their lives would change.

Meg would never give Janat potions again.

Janat blinked and her shivers turned to shaking. "And go . . . where?"

Meg didn't know. And yet, she did. One country had stayed out of most conflicts and had not demonized magiels.

"The edge of the world," she said.

Pagoras.

CHAPTER 4

Huwen's daughter, in all her chubby, pink-cheeked perfection, opened her mouth, seeking. Ychelle lifted her breast, brushing the babe with her nipple and the little one latched on with the expertise of seven weeks' practice. The little one settled, eyes closed, jaw working, as afternoon sun streamed through the open balcony doors. The sun brought with it a cooling breeze, and his wife looked up at Huwen in languid contentment. She lifted a lazy hand, and he took her fingers in his own to kiss them.

A child. Their own. It was difficult to believe.

Huwen hadn't believed it. When Ychelle told him the little one would be born in the summer, when the midwife confirmed it, even when he felt the wondrous quickening in his wife's hard belly. Ychelle had brought two others to term, stillborn. Three more had not lived even that long.

Now, *Shalire*. Huwen had to smile, just at the thought of her. Seven weeks.

A daughter. So, not the heir he needed. But yet, she *lived*. She breathed, she cried, she slept, she puked, all unconscious of her own miracle.

The tap on the door was barely audible. Huwen was of a mind to ignore it, but Ychelle pulled a silk scarf over her shoulder, covering her naked loveliness and her baby. His queen, young and comely, was not what most would call beautiful. But she was lovely to Huwen.

"Come," she called.

The girl who entered dipped a curtsey, averting her eyes. "Your Majesty," she said to Huwen. "Chancellor Igua would meet with you in your war room."

Igua. An old crow with a harsh, rasping message. "Tell him I'll meet with him tomorrow."

Ychelle lifted her hand in his, touched his cheek. "Love," she said. "He's been waiting for you since morning."

"He can wait." Huwen meant his words to be soft for his wife, but it was difficult to keep his irritation in check.

"We'll be fine," she reassured him. "You won't be gone more than a few candlemarks. Shalire will be sleeping when you return, and we can have dinner."

He sighed. "Very well. Have Cook send our meal here, so we can eat privately."

Humor danced in his wife's eyes.

He smiled at her flirtation, kissed her, and strode from the room. *Let's get this over with.*

When Huwen arrived in the war room, Igua, two generals, and an aide were studying maps spread out on a large table. The uppermost map, Huwen could see even at a distance, was a plan of Coldridge and its environs. Of course. Uprisings there were a constant thorn. Huwen had practically memorized every line on the parchment. But nothing had changed in Coldridge for almost eight years, except to worsen. Huwen did not need his few moments with his daughter interrupted for some minor point of strategy on the far side of Shangril.

The tacticians straightened, heads bobbing in quick salute.

"What is it, Igua?" Huwen stopped well short of the table. He would not be drawn in.

"Your Majesty." Igua was not one to mince words, a trait at once irritating and useful. "Rebels have taken Coldridge."

This was unexpected. Huwen's face must have betrayed shock, as a moment of smugness flickered in Igua's eyes.

God, How?

Igua pointed to the map, drawing the attention of the general and the aides, though the chancellor spoke to Huwen. "It was sudden," he reported. "In the middle of the night, five days ago." He raised a brow pointedly. "Six days ago. An act they would not have dared in the spring when Your Majesty directed the royal troops."

Huwen noted this chastisement but did not acknowledge it. Yes, he'd left the fortress to return to Holderford to be with his wife in her confinement. Yes, he's remained here for the past two months as his daughter proved she was not on the verge of dying in her cradle. Huwen was not about to apologize to anyone for that. He gave a short nod for Igua to continue.

"The city had been surrounded by rebels for two weeks before the attack."

Huwen hadn't known this. Or maybe he had. Or maybe Igua and the generals had handled it themselves, following Huwen's instruction.

"Uprisers appeared *within* the castle walls. We were aware of ancient tunnels connecting the keep with a cave system in the hills, from conflicts before the God's Peace, but they were guarded. We suspect spies or bribes. We're ferreting that out, now."

God. Huwen drifted toward the balcony door, the sunshine, and the breeze. A page, unbidden—unless Igua had given him a signal—brought him a goblet of wine.

Huwen was weary of this never-ending war. "Magic?"

"We don't think so. The rebels have no magiels of significant power, and most of the half-breeds are imprisoned, ghettoized, or otherwise no threat."

Or executed. His chancellor had omitted that. "You've taken steps to retake it." He sipped his wine. A groom brushed a lovely mare in the bailey beyond the balcony's stone railing. There was peace, he reassured himself. In some parts of the world.

"We are," his chancellor confirmed. Of course, Igua was taking care of it. That was what he did.

But today, there was a hesitation in Igua's voice that made Huwen turn.

"We defended the castle and city with cannons. They are in rebel hands, now."

Huwen frowned at Igua, working through this statement. Nonsense, surely? But, no, his chancellor's demeanor was grave. The rebels controlled their cannons? That would add a complication to retaking the fortress.

"There's more."

More? No. What more could there be?

"They've freed the Marigold prisoners."

Huwen blinked. This would be laughable. Was laughable. But no one was laughing. "Freed them."

"Yes."

"From the prison."

"Yes."

"Into our waiting troops."

The aide lowered his head and the generals looked uncomfortable.

"We recaptured many of the escapees," Igua said. "We are hunting down more."

Huwen stared at him. Unarmed prisoners—women and children—had escaped into royal hands but slipped through. It was not possible. Was his army made up of idiots? "Tell me this is a joke."

"It was night. Raining. There was a flood of them scattering in every direction. The prisoners were armed, and the rebels provided covering fire from the cannons," one general—Huwen didn't even remember his name—said. "We were taken by surprise." His words sank in the silence. Weak excuses.

Heat began to rise in Huwen's chest. "Two years ago, you lost Gweddien."

Igua licked his lips.

Gweddien. The last remaining full-blooded magiel. Male, able to father strong children. "I've heard no recent report saying you've found him."

"We are searching, Your Majesty. He has great skill in disguise, and there are those who would shield him. He has not sought shelter in places we expected him to go."

"Then look where you do not expect him to go." Obvious.

Igua lowered his head in a truncated bow of subservience.

Huwen turned on his heel, fury barely contained. Ychelle waited. And Shalire.

"Your Majesty."

Exercising restraint, Huwen turned.

"You must return to Coldridge," Igua said in a low voice. "Your generals need your leadership."

His leadership. Huwen would've accused Igua of mocking him, but he knew his chancellor was speaking in earnest. Huwen felt like anything but a king, anything but a leader. Everything he touched soured.

Still. He could not deny the soundness of Igua's judgment. That he put the good of the realm ahead of his own welfare, at the risk of offending his lord. Above Huwen's selfish and cowardly motives. He acquiesced with a sigh.

Igua gave the faintest nod of acknowledgment.

"But Gweddien must be recovered." At all costs. Huwen hated giving the order. He hated calling for his childhood friend to be boxed, coerced.

"The order has already been given."

There it was.

Huwen had no choice. The war must come to an end. It must. The strife was crippling him, crippling Shangril. Crippling his ability to finally unify the seven realms, to bring prosperity.

Crippling his ability to recover the Ruby.

Fearghus and Colm might disagree on many things, but Meg was under no illusion about how to unite them. Both would give orders for her and her sister to be hunted down: Janat to face charges, and Meg to come to heel, that she might churn out the potions a worldling could not concoct. No, she and Janat must leave in secret, stay off the roads, travel swiftly, and melt into some unexpected backwater.

None of which was possible. Glenfast was a small hilltop redoubt, walled, with one gate. It was deep in Elsen's borderlands with nothing but wilds and orums surrounding it on three sides, accessed by a single road that wound down through cliffy, dense forests. To plunge into the woods would be to flounder in the dark, leave a trail any dog could track, and risk breaking their legs—or necks—on a sudden rain-slick precipice. Yet to remain on the road meant trying to outpace pursuers on horseback. And the few hamlets along the road were huddles of extended families where concealment would be futile.

Still, Meg was not without alternatives.

She could not trust Janat, mercurial and agitated with Heartspeed, to follow an instruction or even to stay put, so she towed her to the house of healing. She tried to keep her sister silent as she shoved charms into hidden pockets—Confusions, Disguises, Memory Losses, even two Serenities—and took her to the glazier's home to pack clothing and coin, and to steal food. She pushed the cache of supplies over the city wall where it tumbled into a tangle of low bushes far enough from the gate to be masked by the wall's curve, to be recovered later.

The rain had steadied to a soaking drizzle before they drew near the city gate. A sentry hovered in the doorway of the gate house, bow lowered but strung and nocked, as the sleepy gateman pulled his oiled hood up and brought a lantern to investigate their approach. Meg had known better than to hope the late candlemark would catch them drowsing. Still, a part of her had hoped.

"Meg and Janat Falconer." She lifted her own pig-fat-smeared hood in the flickering light to reveal her identity, the one she'd taken since fleeing her name at the outbreak of civil war. "Requesting permission to pass." Janat fidgeted at her side but, thankfully, stayed quiet.

The man—the baker's grandfather—drew his craggy face into a map of suspicion. "It's almost two chimes, by my reckon."

"Collecting juniper berries by the waning solstice stars." Meg knew the movements of the constellations despite the cloud cover, as did the gateman. What the gateman didn't know was that juniper berries were more effective when collected in the dark of an autumn equinox. But his ignorance worked to Meg's advantage. "We need them for..."

The night wavered and disappeared.

Piss! The spell she'd cast on the brittle stone wall had disrupted the linearity of her experience of time. Payment for the use of magic. Ripples of time tossed her—forward? Back?— to live some other portion of her life—

She stood in a castle bailey in the predawn light of early spring. Janat's arm, heavy, draped over her shoulder, her head lolling. Janat wore a rumpled gown of Aadian fashion, and Meg was dressed in the livery of a servant. Smoke and the distant sounds of battle filled the air, and a crowd of townspeople milled or sat, exhausted, in the gravel. Barring their way was the castle's back gate.

Coldridge. Eight and a half years ago. She'd come to prevent the High King from using the Ruby Prayer Stone to pray to the Gods for victory in war.

By assassinating his magiel. Wenid.

It had been a useless attempt to restore a world vanished with the lunatic king's attack on his neighbors; an attack ending five hundred years of peace. She'd struggled for the return of the aristocracy's usurped lands; the return of her people's Gods and way of life. The assassination had been the final act of Meg's transformation from coddled princess to soldier. She'd been fighting this futile war ever since.

Well, no more. Now she'd fight for Janat.

A handful of King Huwen's cavalry spurred past her. She shifted Janat's weight on her shoulder, to hide in a shadowed corner of the compound. She knew by dint of eight years of memory, the castle's main gates would open in a moment. The High King's reinforcements were leaving to finish off the last of the uprisers who dared to wage war against their betters. The battle, which had begun with such promise, had reversed suddenly at its height: despite Meg's murder of the king's magic wielder, someone had used the Ruby Prayer Stone. A magiel and royal had touched the Ruby—the sole Prayer Stone to survive the lunatic king's purge—and gone to Heaven to pray for victory in battle.

The Gods had intervened on behalf of the royals.

The bailey flickered. Meg had vacated her existence at that point in time, and . . .

Plunged into some other part of her life.

Meg was . . . she looked around, tried to take in—she was in Mama's apartment. It was the night Mama had called her to her rooms to perform magic so Mama might see a future invisible to her, through Meg's eyes.

It'd been so long . . . so long since she'd seen Mama.

Meg sat up in the bed, taking everything in. The fire on the hearth glowing in the shadows of deep night. The canopy overhead. The softness of downy quilts.

Mama, sitting beside her, took Meg's hand. Mama's shimmering face was filled with worry. "Meghra?"

Tears pushed up from Meg's chest into her throat.

"When are you?" Mama asked.

"Years from now, Mama." She forced the words past the cramping in her windpipe.

Mama's eyes softened. "You're alive. You survived. Then, I will be right to send you away from me."

Meg nodded, unable to speak. Gods, she'd been only seventeen. And Mama . . . so soft. So plump. "Do it as soon as you can, Mama. Don't wait."

"Janatelle? And Rennikala? Your sisters, are they—"

"Rennika—Rennikala—Mama, we changed our names. She's fine, I think. I haven't seen her for . . ." Years. Should she say this to Mama? Who would die only months from this moment? Who would never see her three daughters again? "I haven't seen Rennika for a while, but she's fine and healthy—"

"And Janatelle?" Mama had caught Meg's avoidance. "Meg, you must care for them. You are the oldest . . ."

And then, Meg leapt from one part of her life to another. A future? No, another past. She recognized *a fire flickering under a night sky spattered with a river of stars*. Bright-lit faces, Fearghus and Colm and King Dwyn. This was . . . four or five years ago, when they were still hiding in the woods south of Fairdell.

Tonore, pouring from a wine skin into her chipped mug, a silly grin on his face in the firelight.

"We're going to rise again," Colm asserted. "Huwen better watch his ass, because we're going to be stronger than ever."

A general assent, bordering on a cheer. Meg felt light-headed, as if her body had consumed more wine already than was good for her. She looked around and saw Janat there. Yes, sitting on the grass, leaning back against some young man's knees—what was his name? Meg had forgotten. Janat's head was tilted up to kiss him as he bent over her.

"Forty recruits joined us just this month," Fearghus bellowed, ever the accountant, even when drunk. Meg shook her head. There'd never been forty recruits in a single month.

"It'll be a new rebellion," Dwyn said quietly. Ardently.

"To a new rebellion," someone cried, and someone else struck up a lute.

The dark road. Meg blinked. She was walking down the hill, Janat at her side.

"The uprisers argue constantly and treat us like slaves," Janat prattled, "and *then*, they seem to think we should be grateful—"

Rain pattered on Meg's oiled hood as she stumbled behind Janat. She turned. Trees screened the gate, but the walls and towers of Glenfast rose behind them, lost in a blacker sky.

"Are you back?" Janat asked.

"For now." Meg blinked, focusing on the path ahead. Back, yes. Here. Now. She was wearing her backpack under her cloak. Janat must have led her other self, the one that had inhabited her body while she was away, to the cached supplies once they were through the gate. "When was I? How did we get out of Glenfast?"

"I saw you were gone, so I told the gatekeeper what juniper berries are used for. I'm not completely useless. He let us through. Don't worry, you didn't have to do anything. You looked pretty stupid. I got us out."

That was what worried Meg. How much had her sister given away about their plans? Meg could have kicked herself for telling Janat she intended to take her to Pagoras. At least, she hadn't said *where* in Pagoras.

"You were from, I don't know, maybe a couple of years ago," Janat prattled on. "You didn't have a clue what was going on, but you wanted to take charge. Like you always do."

Meg tripped over a stone. The fatigue of using magic was catching up with her. Still, they must put as many miles as they could between themselves and the uprisers who would follow. "Do you have any Heartspeed?"

Janat moved away from her, wary. "I don't know."

"You took nine from the supply room."

"It wasn't nine!"

Meg gave a weary sigh.

"You haven't changed. Picking apart everything, every detail, all the numbers. I just talked to you when you were, like about, twenty or something. You always had to be the boss then, and you still do. You want to carry the spells because you don't trust me. You always treated me like I was a baby and you still treat me like I'm stupid."

Meg could barely keep her eyes open. She stopped where the road bent, and swayed a little, trying to focus on her sister. "I need some, Janat, or I'm going to fall asleep right here."

Janat stopped and glared at her. "You—"

"I promised to help you. I promised to get you away from Glenfast. Somewhere safe." She wouldn't repeat the name, *Pagoras*, though Janat was clever and that was probably the one word she would remember. "I can't do that if they catch us. Please, Janat. I need some Heartspeed if we're going to get away."

A sly smile spread over Janat's face. Of course. Her sister's silly obstinacy was only an artifact of the potion. "I might have one."

Meg let her lids fall closed in frustration. "You didn't imbibe eight of them," she said. "You'd be dead. I need three."

"You don't need three!"

A wave of dizziness came over her and she fell into Janat's side, clutching her sister's arm to stay upright. She held out her hand. "Three," she whispered.

Janat nudged her upright. "I hate you." She rummaged in some purse or magiel pocket beneath her cloak and produced three vials and shoved them into Meg's hand.

Meg pulled the cork from one, swallowing its chalky contents.

Janat was right. One Heartspeed was more than enough to keep her awake and walking at a brisk pace well into tomorrow afternoon. She shoved the other two into her purse. By then, they might both need another.

CHAPTER 5

Janat stopped at the top of the hill and shaded her eyes, squinting into the early morning sun. A sound, like distant, continuous thunder drifted on the wind. Gods, she was tired. The road might be an engineering marvel, raised above flat fertile farmland and straight as an arrow, but it was endless, disappearing into a faint mist on the horizon. She could melt into the road, right here, but Meg would only poke her again.

They'd left the mountains and powder-dry cart tracks of Elsen days ago, and to their relief they'd only been closely scrutinized—by what Janat assumed to be upriser sympathizers—twice since then. The second time had been touch-and-go. Five men had sprung an ambush along the road with some of their number spread out, hanging back beyond any air currents that could carry a whiff of Confusion. But a local who'd needed a healing potion for her crippled mother vouched convincingly for them, and their disguises held.

Near Wildbrook, the countryside became rolling and settled. Roads proliferated and they were able to travel by back ways; Fearghus's men could not patrol every route, especially so close to the royal garrison, on high alert since the raid. Just as well, as Meg was becoming very parsimonious in doling out wards, or spells of forgetting. They'd completely run out of aging and skin-steadying creams for disguises.

And Janat's vials of Heartspeed were long gone, and with them her stamina.

Meg poked her, and she trudged on, aching for another Heartspeed to make the miles disappear beneath her feet.

As the day wore on, fields laced with irrigation and drainage ditches became more frequent. Many were heavy with rice, barley, vegetables, fruit, and grapes. Free traders, singly or in trains—none accompanied by more than a few outriders—increased in number, as did side roads leading to distant villages and towns.

It was late afternoon when, on the horizon, Janat made out a vast shantytown huddled against the walls of a sprawling city. The constant thunder of falling water had grown as they approached, and above the horizon, a plume of mist caught the sun's waning rays. Meg hadn't said where they were going, but this had to be their destination. The edge of the world, Cataract Crag. Somewhere along the King's Road, they must've entered the country of Pagoras.

A candlemark after nightfall, the road brought them through the smelly, lantern-lit warren of shacks to the city gates.

Closed.

Janat staggered to a halt and sank to the cobbles.

"Janat."

She couldn't go a step further. There, just below the road, a handful of people sat around a fire, drinking ale and singing rowdy songs. These were shimmering people—half-magiels at least—and they looked friendly enough. The aroma of food made her stomach cry with hunger.

She felt, more than heard, her sister's exasperated sigh. "Don't think it," Meg said tiredly. "We're not staying here."

Janat closed her eyes. Their packs were thin, and the gates were shut. They weren't getting into the city. Not before morning.

She hadn't dozed, she didn't think—at least not for more than a few seconds—but a young girl of maybe nine years old was talking to Meg. "You could stay with my mam," she said in the clipped accent of the north, pointing into the spark-lit dark.

And then Meg was tugging Janat again, hauling her to her feet, and they were stumbling among the shanties. Many were dark, hushed with snores or muted conversation. At one or two places, faces looked up at their passing, then turned back to a meal or fire. In the distance, someone played a stringed instrument and voices joined in a soft, lilting lament.

The little girl stopped, and Meg set down a bucket of water she'd acquired from somewhere. Janat was too tired to ask where.

A woman, maybe Janat's age, was sitting cross-legged on a rug applying pig fat to a pair of boots in the inconstant light of a few burning coals. "Nola." She frowned at the child. There was a disheveledness, a detached quality to her expression Janat recognized. Coveted.

"Mam—"

The little girl was unhealthy-thin, but her mam was starvation-thin, with sores on her face and arms.

"No one claims the ground," the woman said irritably, guessing their intent. Her sharp consonants were not as sharp as those Janat had heard when they'd traveled north before. "There's no room in the shanty, no food, 'n no fuel." Food. It smelled spicy and strange, and made Janat ache.

"See how her skin dances, Mam," the child, Nola, whispered. "I bet she can make your charms stronger."

The woman peered at Meg for the first time. "You from Coldridge?"

"No."

Odd question. Janat's eyes drifted closed. *Please, let us stay. Please.*

"I have a chetram I haven't spent," Meg said. "We could pay you. We'll leave tomorrow."

"A chetram?" The woman snorted. "A *gultram* buys nothing in Pagoras. Try five."

But there was a moment's silence, and Janat opened her eyes to see Meg placing coins in the woman's hand.

"Nola. Find a bowl. Get some soup."

Yes! Janat sank to her knees, letting the pack slip from her back. The fire was small but threw a comforting heat.

"You can share the hearth." The woman spoke slowly to make her words clear. "But there's still no room in the shanty."

Janat observed Meg. Her sister couldn't see their host's languor. Her quiet euphoria.

Meg sat by the fire. "We have oiled cloaks against the rain. What can we call you?"

"Kirst."

From an iron pot beside the fire, Nola ladled two steaming bowls of thin soup augmented with wild rice and purple turnips and marigold flowers, and even some bits of bamboo snails. Janat bolted the foreign food as quickly as she could without burning her tongue.

"Sleep on your pack with a knife handy," Kirst advised distantly, scratching at her arm.

This was a given. They'd slept thus every night since leaving Glenfast. They'd camped, avoiding villages, not only because of those who—presumably—followed them, but because a worldling, spotting them as magiels, might call for a king's man to harass them. For sport, or to make them move on.

"We heard magiels are safe in Pagoras." Meg blew on a spoonful of soup.

"High King's law is the High King's law," the woman said, letting the boot she was greasing ease into her lap. The night was full dark, and the River of Stars arced overhead, a splash of brilliance in the blackness. "Magiels. Worship of the Many Gods. Fighting for the uprisers. They're all still forbidden. But," she said carelessly, "Pagoras's a rich country, 'n High King Huwen turns a blind eye. Needs King Jace's harvests to feed his armies. Needs King Jace's money from trade with Aadi."

"And King Jace doesn't mind magiels?" Meg gave the woman a sharp look. Ah. She was beginning to notice.

"Rich people can have anything. Magiels in Cataract Crag make spells no one can get anymore in all of Shangril." Kirst smiled, as at a secret pleasure. "Though most here are only part magiel. Barely make more than a worldling spell." She rubbed her arm, its muscles string-thin and peered at Meg. "You full magiel?"

Meg snorted a gentle laugh. "No such thing. Not anymore."

The woman eyed her as if deciding whether to believe her or not, then shrugged, disinterested.

Janat finished the soup and gave her bowl to Nola, encouraging the sharp-eyed little thing with a smile. She looked about the small campsite for whatever else the family might have to offer.

"You asked if we were from Coldridge." Meg attacked her soup. "Why?"

The little girl reached into some dark cache and added a chunk of peat to the coals. Janat took up the hem of her under robe, a shade less muddy than the rest of her clothes, and ripped off a strip. Meg shot her an exasperated look. Janat didn't care.

"Lot of magiels coming from Coldridge the past few days." Kirst set her boots aside and leaned back on her elbows on her rug. "Uprisers finally took the city."

"What?" Meg stared at the woman.

Nola took the boots from her mam, pushing them under the edge of the shanty. Janat folded her bit of cloth, tucking and weaving.

"They say." Kirst scratched absently at a sore. "Freed the prisoners. Before Huwen's troops surrounded it."

Prison. The word, unexpected, plunged Janat into icy memory, and her fingers stilled. Lightless stone dungeon. Chilled. Crowded. Filled with magiel women.

Marigolds.

"Bribed their way through some tunnels. What I was told." A faint smile touched Kirst's lips. "Bet Huwen was riled."

"Uprisers took Coldridge?" Meg confirmed. "Against Huwen's cannons?"

Janat shivered. *Prison.* Soldiers with blinding torches and echoing boots, lining Marigolds against one wall. Pulling certain ones forward. Those with the most inconstant skin. The most magic.

Kirst pushed her lips into an indifferent pout. "S'what they say." She let her head sway back and forth, as if she was too tired to shake it in negation, or as if she enjoyed the sensation of moving her head. "Few days of freedom, then the army puts 'em under siege. To starve. To die of wounds and cursed water." She let her gaze slip sidelong to Meg. "Some of the High King's men are here, rounding up the dodgers. In case, you know. In case, you care."

Janat couldn't keep the images back. Each time, one woman was selected, taken from the cell. Not seen again.

Kirst spoke to the arch of stars, to the constellation of Ranuat, the seven murderers surrounding the one bright merchant, low in the north. "High King stole our right to pray to our own Gods," she whispered. "Our right to have magiels to bring us death tokens. No wonder people hate him."

Janat's skin shimmered less than most, a blessing from a mother so powerful she could bear her child to appear however she willed. Janat was passed over by the prison guards for weeks. Then—

She shook herself and knotted the strip of cloth in her fingers.

Gweddien. Dread and anticipation crawled through Janat, sending a chill down her back. Could he be here? A freed prisoner?

Janat pushed away the thought and showed Nola the doll she'd made from the strip of cloth. The girl smiled shyly. Janat held it out, and the child took it.

"Uprisers have raided the castle at Coldridge all summer," Meg whispered. "No, since . . ."

Janat tugged her pack open, pulled out clothing, and laid it down to insulate the cold ground. She turned her back to the fire and covered herself with her cloak, shoving the images aside. *Shut up, Meg.*

"Coldridge . . ." Meg's voice grew thoughtful. "Must have fallen weeks ago."

Janat squeezed her eyes closed. *Shut up, Meg. Shut up.*

2

Kirst's words buzzed in Meg's head like flies about an open wound, catching her unawares as she towed Janat up Cataract Crag's crowded streets, or waited for an apprentice to summon his master, or studied an empty rice bowl.

Uprisers had taken Coldridge. They had a defensible base of operations, then. Good. And if—*if*—they could hold Glenfast too, it was the beginning of a network. Bases in two countries, Teshe and Elsen. Yes. After eight years, something solid. Better than mere harrying insurrections to irritate royal forces, immediately crushed. Progress.

Gods, Meg wished she was there.

But, why should she? Her contributions weren't valued. Holding two strongholds didn't mean the uprisers weren't still divided by faction. No, she was better off here, in the rich lands of Pagoras, where magiels were appreciated. Where she could care for Janat. Not the life Mama had envisioned for her—magiel to the Amber Prayer Stone of Orumon, transcending to Heaven to pray for death tokens for the people of an entire nation—but it was, apparently, what the Gods desired of her.

She shifted the massive bundle of laundry on her hip and shuffled in a throng of other laundresses through the city's west gate toward the river. Janat, similarly burdened, walked the dusty path just ahead of her.

Meg couldn't complain. The work was honest, they had a room to themselves in the city, and the weather was fine. Though the cooling seasonal rains would soon fall in the mountains of Glenfast, late summer in Cataract Crag was hot. Hot and muggy.

Slabs of water-smoothed limestone sloping gently into the river made a perfect place for the city's women to scrub and beat and lay out their laundry on sunny days. The muted roar and fine, misty spray of the cataracts downstream was a constant reminder of the power of the great falls. Here at the edge of the escarpment, the wide, sluggish Arcan River, braided into a delta of innumerable swampy islands. Final drainage of all seven countries of Shangril, it spread across the flat lands, then fell away into awe-inspiring falls.

Meg had taken Janat to the overlook to hear the deafening boom and view the elaborate pulley system that raised goods from the valley of Aadi and lowered them from Shangril. Foreign trade made Pagoras the richest of Shangril's seven nations. They said the first stranger from Aadi had only braved the cliffs from the basin thirty years ago; machines for trade had been operating far less than that. People never took the perilous journey from Shangril to the lowlands, except for the engineers who maintained the machines, or the odd artist or adventurer. The people of Aadi were said to be too strange, their language too incomprehensible.

Meg had met an Aadian, Orville Haye. He, certainly, had oddly small eyes and his body was corpulent, and he had perplexing ideas. His exotic steam technology and black powder cannons would have won the first battle of Coldridge for the uprisers, had the Gods not intervened for High King Huwen. Cannons. Orville's cannons had changed everything.

But Meg was done with that now. She'd found work for herself and Janat cleaning rooms at an inn in the affluent east side of the city overlooking the vast sweep of Aadi, where the great houses and wealthy markets of King Jace's courtiers welcomed magiels. When she asked, the innkeeper told her magiel spells of healing, cooking, and pleasure were appreciated by the bankers and money-lenders and investors of Cataract Crag.

Meg had found a garret above a warehouse for them to live in. She gave their surname as Hawkins and their story as refugees from Big Hill, a village burnt to the ground in the first wave of war. By adopting the local accent and saying little—not uncommon among those scarred by strife—and giving modestly of her work and talent, she hoped to weave a kinship of allies here. She not only wanted a network to back them, particularly if Colm's uprisers or the High King's soldiers came sniffing, but to give Janat a feeling of support.

They unrolled their bundles among the washerwomen at the water's edge, finding a place between the magiel everyone called Toothy, and Nola's mother, Kirst.

"Tastes of suds." Kirst sat on a log, wrinkling her nose at the cup in her hands as Nola lathered soaproot in a tub of clothing. The doll Janat had made her was protectively close by, on the ground by the child's basin. Meg could have berated Janat for tearing her only under robe—Janat never thought ahead—but the doll seemed to be the only toy the child had.

Well. Meg found a ceramic basin, left by the river for this purpose, and filled it with water.

"Need a sip of the demon that nipped you," Toothy smirked, assembling a set of wooden shafts to construct a drying rack.

Meg saw Janat's gaze snap to Kirst, but her sister said nothing.

"Tried that," Kirst said ruefully. She shaded her eyes with one hand. "The powder you gave me helped." Toothy had been a village healer somewhere in Arcan before the war. Now she improved beer in one of the better taverns and complained about inns that claimed to have magiel cooks when they didn't.

Nola watched her mother warily as Meg set down her basin, heavy with water, and Janat gave her a chunk of soaproot.

"So?" Toothy adjusted her rack to balance on the uneven ground. "Must have been a revel. Did the bard at the tavern bring news?"

"'Course."

"Come on, then. Tell."

"Princess Hada Delarcan." Kirst sipped from her cup again and grimaced. "The High King's sister. Gone to the city of Highglen in Gramarye to claim her kingdom."

Meg had heard this news, but Toothy's brows shot up.

Kirst grinned at the attention. "Took four wagons of dresses and furniture, twenty personal servants, a hundred household guards."

Meg caught Janat's glance, washing sheets in the basin beside hers. Her sister put her head down and scrubbed the inn's bedding.

But Meg had heard this rumor, too. Gramarye wasn't Hada's kingdom, though it'd be ill-advised to say so here. High King Huwen's father had stolen the kingdoms of Shangril from their rightful owners before his death and bequeathed them to his children. The king of Gramarye, after the Delarcans invaded the country, *should* have been Dwyn Gramaret.

Toothy plunged her husband's smallclothes into her basin. "Hada's not of age to take rule from the regent, is she? What will Huwen say?"

Kirst gave a sly grin. "That young wolf? Uprisers under siege in the west and a disobedient younger brother defying him in Theurgy? Hada is way down his list. And," she leaned on one arm and whispered, "his first born is a *daughter*." She snickered. "He'll have to do better than that, next time."

A daughter. That . . . was interesting. Two previous still births. No heir.

Janat took her sheets to the river to rinse. Meg continued scrubbing, an excuse to listen. Gods, Princess Hada was *nineteen*. Meg had first seen her when the Delarcans had come on a state visit to Archwood. Meg had been maybe six or seven, and never been out of Archwood palace. Hada had been a spoiled baby, then, squalling if she dropped a biscuit. If this girl intended to take over actual *rule* from Gramarye's regent, the transition and chaos, compounded by her inexperience, made *now* the ideal time for uprisers to attack Highglen. It was all Meg could do to keep from screaming in frustration.

"But do you know who the regent is? In Gramarye?" Toothy pressed, grinning at her as though she held back a secret.

Kirst sipped from her mug. "I don't keep track."

"Raef Gramaret," Toothy said.

Meg had a vague memory of him. A crippled child. Dwyn, his father, had disowned him. The boy—man, now—had become Huwen's creature.

Kirst frowned incomprehension. "The uprisers' king-in-exile? You're joking."

"Not Dwyn Gramaret. *Raef* Gramaret. His son," Toothy said. "He was captured and swore allegiance to the Delarcans when they took Highglen and executed his mother. It was only his father, Dwyn the Coward, who escaped and tried to raise an army."

Meg had heard the story. Dwyn's advisers had smuggled the king away from the war-torn country for the good of his people, promising to rescue his family. It hadn't happened.

"Why would Hada care who is regent?" Kirst said. "She's a Delarcan. She'll take what she wants."

"Hada won't take governance of Gramarye from Raef Gramaret." Toothy squeezed the water from her husband's underthings. "The people of Gramarye love him. He's one of them. And he has the High King's blessing."

"And Raef has no contact with his father?" Kirst asked.

No.

"Dwyn Gramaret renounced him," Toothy said. "Or so they say. But some want Raef as King of Gramarye because they think it's the door to taking their country back from the Delarcans."

Dwyn might have been labeled a coward, but over the years he'd come to see his son as a traitor.

Janat returned with her basin of rinsed laundry and, after setting it on the ground, began squeezing out the excess water, saying nothing, watching her.

Right. Meg's sheets were as clean as they were going to get. She took her basin to the river. Dumping the soapy water, she spread a sheet in the river and shifted it to let the gentle flow rinse away the soap. The watercourse here was not loud, but she was too far from the women to distinguish their words.

Did Dwyn know Hada had gone to Highglen? Colm wouldn't have told him. Gods, to be stuck here and to overhear such fragmentary and tantalizing details. To be so helpless.

But the uprisers had taken Coldridge in the west. Between consolidating his conquest and holding Glenfast, would Dwyn have enough men to take Highglen, even if he knew the opportunity existed? Not likely. The cities could not be more geographically separated. Moreover, would Dwyn have the will to take Gramarye from his disowned son?

It would take so little to capture Gramarye. If they acted now.

Meg squeezed the water from the sheet and returned it to the basin. There might be uprisers in Cataract Crag, but Meg hadn't tried to make contact. There was no one she trusted, no one she could send to Dwyn with the message. Gods, she wished she could go to the king-in-exile to plead her case.

Janat was doing well.

Meg hadn't left her side since leaving Glenfast, but after her sister's first few days of agitation and tears, she'd quieted. She'd regained her appetite, though she was still restless at night with dreams. But that would pass.

Still, no. Meg couldn't leave her. She'd promised. So, that was that.

Meg returned the last sheet to the basin and hauled it back up the sloping rock slabs. Toothy had meandered down the river to talk to some of the other women, and Kirst and her daughter were gone. Janat had spread her sheets over some bushes in the sun where the breeze could dry them. She held out her hands, offering to help Meg spread hers as well.

Janat looked healthy enough. Her appearance had never been as hard to focus on as Meg's or Mama's, and her red-brown hair was thick and glossy. A few days' binge on Heartspeed had not affected her weight any more than war and starvation had done. Her muscles were strong. Physically, Janat would be able to make the journey with Meg to Coldridge to petition King Dwyn.

But Janat didn't smile. Perhaps that was normal for her. Now. Meg couldn't remember her sister smiling—really smiling—for . . . she couldn't remember how long.

"Janat."

"Hmm?" Janat lifted her head from their work.

"What do you dream about? At night?"

Her sister cocked a curious brow at the question but shrugged and was silent as they laid the last of the sheets over a bush. "Nothing," she said finally.

"But you move and jerk. You cry out."

Janat put her basin by the path.

"Janat?"

"I don't know. I don't . . ." Again, the diminutive shrug and shake of the head. "I don't remember."

"But . . ."

"Leave it, Meg. I don't remember."

CHAPTER 6

A spitting rain misted the air the next morning as Meg and Janat left their boarding. The warehouse district was located on the north side of Cataract Crag, near the carters' sheds lining the cliff-side platforms where great pulleys worked from sunup to sundown loading and unloading trade goods. But it was some distance from the nearest farmers' market where Meg and Janat ate a watchful breakfast on their way to the inn. Each day, Meg took her rice bowl from a different vendor, expecting at any moment for some upriser to pull her—or Janat—into a lane or onto a cart to be brought back to Glenfast.

"Sieura Hawkins!"

Meg startled. Janat laid a hand on her arm.

The little girl—Nola—darted toward them through the crowd of merchants, dogs, and carts, her small face pinched, intense. "Come quick. You must help my mam."

Meg's steps spurted forward, her years as a healer responding without question. "What's wrong?"

"She's bad. Maybe to die." The little girl increased her pace, weaving among the early risers of the mercantile district. She carried the doll Janat had made.

Janat lagged, her expression wary. Odd, that. Meg knew she didn't like the work at the inn, but . . .

Her own steps slowed. "What makes you think I can help?"

The girl turned, alarm changing her intensity to desperation. "You're full magiel."

Meg let Janat catch up. "Not everyone with blurring skin is full magiel." They couldn't be late at the inn. There were plenty of unskilled workers in the shantytown looking for employment; the wealth of Pagoras drew a glut of destitute workers. The innkeeper could take his pick. The only reason he'd hired Meg and Janat was to get two maids for the price of one. Meg needed to develop a quiet reputation. Being inconsistent would do them no good.

A touch of anguish crumpled the child's face and she bit her lip, swallowing despair. People and carts and goats pushed past them.

"I'm sure there are many healers in the city. My sister and I only know a few country spells for cuts and bruises."

Disappointment and defeat welled up in Nola's eyes and she shook her head emphatically.

Janat tugged the child to the side of the street, out of the way of the crowds. "You have no money for a healer."

Nola shook her head fiercely, mouth clamped closed.

Janat turned. "You go ahead, Meg," she said softly. "Tell Innkeeper Ebanis I'll be along in a bit."

No. Janat was doing well, but Meg wasn't going to let her go off somewhere alone, not so soon.

Janat read something in her face. She bent and murmured into Meg's ear, "Kirst gave us food and a fire when we first came." She lifted her eyes to watch Meg's face.

Calling too much attention to themselves with heroic acts of healing would make them conspicuous. Colm's men would find them. Or any in the royal faction still interested in rounding up magiels with high ancestry for their disgusting Marigold scheme.

"We're early. We have time," Janat pointed out. "Sieur Ebanis never rises before mid-morning. He won't mind if we're a bit late."

"*Sieura* Ebanis does." More to the point. Still, Janat was right. As long as the beds were changed and the chamber pots cleaned before incoming guests arrived, the innkeeper's wife was not a rigid taskmaster.

Meg gave a brief nod and Janat smiled gratefully, taking the girl's hand. "Show me."

⁂

The hovel Nola took them to was not Kirst's shanty beyond the city gates, but a blind alley on the south side of the city near the shambles and tanneries. A hodgepodge of sheds and tents filled the reeking lanes between slaughterhouses and brothels, and Nola wound her way among them, finally opening a rug-like flap that served as a doorway to a wooden lean-to propped against a dice house.

Meg followed Janat in from the sharpening rain. It took a moment for her eyes to adjust to the dim seep of light within. Two forms sprawled on blankets on the uneven hard pack. A smudge of ghosts hovered in the corners.

This was not going to be a simple healing. The potions Meg carried in her hidden pocket would likely not be of use. And if this healing took magiel magic, they would not be able to work later. This had been a bad idea.

"She didn't come home last night." Nola whispered, staring at the unmoving bodies. "I looked for her. All night. Toothy said, check the shambles."

Janat sank to the nearer woman's side. "It's Kirst." She turned and held out a hand to Nola. "She's alive."

Nola burst into tears and folded into Janat, her doll crushed between them. Meg gestured Janat back and examined the woman. It was hard to tell in the dim light, but other than her slow breathing and unresponsiveness, all Meg could see were the sores on the woman's skin, many now crusted with what looked like yellow mud. She pointed to it.

"What is it?" Janat asked.

The lean-to jiggled a little, and a shaft of lesser darkness fell into the confined space as the rug-door was flung onto the shanty's roof. Someone squatted in the opening, silhouetted against the pattering gray day. "Boneblood. They also call it Itch. Who are you?"

Meg glanced at Janat who kept her eyes pinned on the newcomer as Nola shrank into her. "Friends," Meg said carefully. "We know a little healing."

The figure, a man in shape-cloaking rags, slumped into the hovel and leaned against the dice-house wall, his knees steepled over Kirst's sprawled legs, seemingly oblivious to the stream of rain trickling between the wall and the roof planks, and onto his shoulders. "Can't do anything. They might not be dead now, but they're as good as."

Nola shot him a look of hatred.

Meg gave a short, sharp frown. "Who are you?"

The man chuckled. "Hane." He spread his hands and looked up at the structure. "Owner of this fine establishment." He pulled a bit of hard bread out of a satchel and proceeded to bite into it. "Welcome."

"We can help," Janat said in a low voice to Meg. She had set Nola back and was inspecting Kirst's head, neck, chest, and stomach. She placed a hand on Kirst's forehead, probing. "There's a poison." She picked off a bit of the yellow salve crusted on Kirst's arm and the sore beneath it bled. "It's deep. But we can drive it out together."

Meg bit her lip.

"Bring your potions," Hane invited. "You can try. Won't work. Not for long."

Nola trembled, staring at her mother, face streaming.

Meg wedged herself between the girl's mother and the wall. She didn't want Janat to do the healing and become lost in the muddying of her time stream, but her sister had already begun. "What's Boneblood?" she asked Hane, placing a hand on Kirst's belly, another on her arm. The poison came from the crusted salve and was continuing to seep into her body through the sores.

"Don't know where it come from," Hane said, watching their work with detached interest as he ate. "Maybe Aadi. Only been around maybe three, four years, that I know."

Meg scraped the dried unguent from the lesions.

The other occupant, a woman lying face down, made no move or indication she even knew they were there. Ghosts hovered near her.

"See, to start, you gotta dig yourself a little hole in the skin," Hane offered, apropos of nothing.

Meg checked beneath Kirst's clothes. There were sores on all parts of her body, but the ointment appeared only to have been smeared on the wounds of her arms and face.

"But after a bit, your skin makes more holes, so you can put the Boneblood there, too."

"Gods, why?" Meg placed her hands on Kirst's heart and belly, searching for a time when her blood and tissues were healthy, to bring them forward in time to replace the corrupted flesh.

"You never do ganja? Never do Dream Incense? It's *better*. Like flying into the sweetest flower . . ." He put the last of the bread in his mouth and brushed his lips with his sleeve. "One small hole. No one knows. You're fine."

"She's not fine!" Nola cried.

Meg dug deep, back in time, finding Janat's presence hunting there as well. The woman's flesh had not been free of one taint or another for a long time.

Hane gave Nola a long, steady look, but she met his gaze with smoldering anger. "Well." He nodded at the woman behind Janat, now rolled toward the shed's canvas wall. "It isn't a good idea to spread it on lots of sores. Or get your friend to spread it on you when you're sunk too deep to raise your own fingers."

Kirst's eyes fluttered and she took in a sharp breath.

Meg gave Janat a slight nod. Both drew back, and Nola pushed between them, wrapping her arms around her mother.

"Nola, Honey," Kirst murmured, struggling beneath her daughter's weight to sit up. Then she rolled on her side and vomited.

Meg shifted toward the door. They'd done what they could, and she needed to get Janat some place safe before they both left their bodies to inhabit some other snippet of their lives.

"There!" Nola spun fiercely in her mother's arms to face Hane. "I knew they could do it! You're wrong!"

"This time." He rested his forearms on his knees and nodded at Kirst, eerily calm. "Doing all right?"

Kirst pulled herself to a sitting position away from the foul-smelling puddle and wiped her mouth on her sleeve, smiling as she stroked her daughter's hair. "Good. You?"

"Can't complain." He reached out a foot and kicked the other woman. "Think Ra's gone, though."

The ashen skin. The limpness. The indefinable essence, no longer there. Even the ghosts had departed. A sick surprise flitted through Meg. She turned the woman over.

Ra had no death token collar at her throat. Meg shot a glance at Kirst.

Kirst regarded the woman patiently. "Ra never had a death token. Don't know why."

"Guess she thought she'd never die," Hane said, with that same unnatural tranquility.

Nola shoved herself against her mother, hugging her hard and holding her doll, glaring at Hane.

Meg rose and touched Janat's hand. It was time to go.

Janat raised herself to a crouch beneath the low ceiling and spoke to Kirst. "We can see you safely home before we go."

Kirst smiled over Nola's head as she stroked her daughter's hair. "I think I'll rest here a little longer."

Nola lifted her head. "No, Mam. Let's go." She turned her back on the corpse against the wall. "Let's go!"

"Shh." Kirst smiled, scratching at a sore on her elbow. "In a bit, Nola. In a bit."

※

Janat's fingers crept to the death token sewn into the collar she wore. She couldn't get the image of Kirst and her daughter out of her head. That child. Soon, she'd face life without a mother, grow up alone. Janat had felt the depth of illness in Kirst's flesh. Hane was right. She and Meg had not truly healed her.

"Janat." Meg grasped her elbow to keep them from being separated by the morning market crowds. They steered around a cart-and-four laden with casks of beer. "I've been trying to—"

A round room of high-arched stone with windows of glass on every side. Janat wore a fashionable dress, of Aadian design with a narrow bodice and full skirt. Janat shook her head. Time ripples. But—Gods, no, not here, in the middle of the street. She and Meg needed to return to their room—

Gweddien, also dressed in the Aadian fashion, sweating, avoiding her gaze. Wenid, staring at her in predatory disbelief. "You are Talanda Falkyn's daughter?"

And the time stream flickered. Gods, she could have wept in relief. She didn't want to ever go back to that moment.

Dark—no, the dim light of candles at night. Three men laughing around a dinner table, plates empty, beer mugs full.

"Watch." The men peered at something on the table. And Meg was there, but young, her skin untouched by sun or suffering. Janat let herself relax into the tingle of a faint inebriation . . . she remembered these meals, back in the early days, before the uprisers had formed an army. The planning, the rousing arguments, the conviction of righteousness.

She leaned into Sulwyn, her lover, her . . .

She closed her eyes. Sulwyn was dead, now.

A soft huffing sound, and they all took in a breath. The toy. The little steam engine.

"That's amazing. How does it work?" Sulwyn asked.

Janat opened her eyes. Yes. Orville Haye was at the table. The chubby Aadian inventor pointed to the glass vessel of boiling water and the narrow spout. It powered a small wheel, like a water wheel spinning in a gush of steam, turning a gaily painted set of sails. "Steam has power," *Orville was explaining.* "More power than you can imagine. Where I come from, trains of wagons carrying hundreds of people are pulled by engines like this, but a thousand times bigger."

Someone stifled a laugh. In the years since this moment, Janat had seen Orville's machines of war. Of destruction.

But this *moment, a little drunk and leaning on Sulwyn's arm . . . would only last an instant. She closed her eyes and held her lover close.*

CHAPTER 7

Janat woke with a gasp. The thing, the—

She oriented herself. Sloping attic roof, dormer window, shuttered and curtained. Pitcher and basin on the table, chamber pot below. A flutter and cluck—she'd woken the chicken she and Meg had bought. Across the rush-covered floor, Meg was still asleep on her straw pallet.

Meg must have brought her home and put her to bed.

But the thing, the dream. It had been here, just within reach. The . . . She had no name for it. Horror. Thing. And then, as usual, the ground had opened, and she'd plunged through the blackness. A nightmare that left her heart pounding and her skin slick with sweat.

She pulled herself up to sit against the wall and tucked her blanket around her. A slit of late afternoon sunlight filtered between the curtains. She and Meg had missed an entire day of work. They'd be in trouble.

The dead woman in the shanty. The ghosts.

Janat shucked her blanket and, donning her clothes and boots, pulled her cloak from its peg and eased herself through the door. Gods, she was going to spend a few minutes without Meg glued to her side. Her heart rose, thumping in her chest at the thought. She held her breath to creep down the ladder to the warehouse owner's apartment. Just for a moment.

The daughter lifted her head from her spinning wheel, and the wife looked up from skinning a rabbit. "Janat," the wife said.

Janat bobbed her head in acknowledgment.

"You and your sister slept all day."

"Yes, Sieura."

"Are you ill?"

She shrugged. "A bit of tainted meat, I think."

"Oh." The woman nodded vaguely.

"I thought I'd get some air. Can I fill the water bucket at the well?"

"Yes. Certainly."

Taking the bucket from under the sideboard, Janat made her way down the stairs and into the street.

The afternoon light was failing, and the street was full of dockworkers, shopkeepers and free traders, dogs, mules, and a flock of sheep. The air was scented with the earlier rain; though the cobbles were drying, puddles still filled the gutters, splashing up beneath cartwheels.

Janat sat on a stone wall. She watched as half-magiels and worldlings mingled, contented and purposeful. Gods, she hadn't felt so free, in . . . She shook her head. A long time.

Meg. Meg had given up her dream, her life's work—Mama's last wish—that Janat might have this freedom. It'd been Meg's destiny, from the time she was born, to continue Mama's work, bring people death tokens from Heaven. Meg had foregone her calling, foregone everything, to give Janat the strength she needed to put her troubles behind her. To find work, a home, a life.

The fact that Mama's plan failed, that High King Huwen broke the siege at Archwood and smashed all the prayer stones but his Ruby, did not lessen the generosity of Meg's sacrifice. Janat would never be able to repay her.

The image of the dead woman in the shanty flashed in Janat's thoughts.

Janat pushed herself into the flow of people, crush of workers heading home or to the tavern. The water bucket dangled at her side. *Gods, that could have been her. But for Meg. So close. So close.*

She was still fatigued from her use of magic that morning, though she'd let Meg do most of the work. Meg wanted to do it all, of course, but Janat needed to start being useful. She had a lot to make up for.

Her flights into other parts of her life seemed to be over, at least for now. Her time shifts had been unremarkable. Hiding in a hayloft with Meg, giggling over the look on the farmer's face when Meg told him she could heal his syphilis. Curled up next to a campfire amongst people celebrating . . . something, a tankard in her hand. She hadn't sipped from it, even though the body she inhabited—in her future, she thought—would have to deal with any hangover.

Laughing with Meg as they tied up Tonore with ropes when his team was winning at Prisoners' War.

Janat smiled. They'd had no money, no jewels, or castles, but there had been good times.

She came to the plaza. By the central well, a gaggle of magiel women, some of whom she recognized, gossiped as they waited their turn at the crank. Janat leaned her rump against the wall surrounding the well shaft, content just to *be*.

"Hey, Janat," one of them greeted her.

She nodded in acknowledgment.

"Meg not with you?"

She shrugged a little. "She's a bit sick. Something she ate."

Another turned her head from the group. "Were you in Coldridge?"

This was out of the blue. Her stomach flipped. The escaped prisoners.

Two or three of the group joined her. "Have you heard?" one asked.

"Gweddien's here," another one said. Rahd, that was her name.

They all stared at her. She knew she blanched. *Marigolds*.

"Tell Meg," the first one said. "Was she in Coldridge prison too?"

"Tell any magiel woman you see to watch out for him."

Janat blinked at the circle of faces. *The weeks in that dungeon. Each night, one woman taken.*

To Gweddien.

Rahd put an arm around her. "Sorry," she whispered.

"He's here?" Janat managed.

Two others drew closer. "Rahd saw him."

Janat looked into Rahd's face. "You're sure?"

Rahd nodded.

"All magiels come to Pagoras," someone whispered.

"Where?" Janat asked. "Where did you see him?"

"The Duke and Emerald," Rahd said. "Looking for a room."

The Duke and Emerald turned out to be a low-ceiled basement tavern, well out of the center of Cataract Crag on its south side, though not as close to the shambles as the alley to which Nola had brought Janat and Meg that morning. From a small table near the door, Janat could see everyone in the room and keep an eye on those who came and went. The rain had started up again.

She had no money. Meg paid for everything. Janat understood. She couldn't be trusted with money. But she had a purse with a few oddments in it, and she held it, visible on the tabletop. She'd manage the problem of payment later.

The young server brought her rice with beans and vegetables and a bit of frog meat. She took a glass of ale. With food, it would have no effect, and ale was almost water, in any case. Anyway, it was all right. She'd had no liquor of any kind since . . . Glenfast.

She savored the first sip. It tasted like home.

Not like Orumon, not like her childhood, no. But comforting. Familiar. Calming, after the difficult day. Before what promised to be . . . well, she didn't know.

Her meal was done, her plate taken, and she'd carefully nursed two goblets of ale before she saw him.

That face, burned into her memory. Tall, thick dark hair, blurred with time shifts. Regular features, long creases on either side of a wide mouth that made him look as though he smiled, even when he was serious. Lean, but not starved. A face she hated. "Gweddien."

Fear in his gray eyes flicked to recognition when he registered her, and then to distasteful memory, then to something softer, something she couldn't quite hate. He hesitated as if he considered approaching her. Then his gaze twitched to an interior doorway. Stairs to the rooms, likely. Seeing her had interrupted something.

She opened her hands to show she was unarmed and gestured to the second chair at her table.

He came over, then, and leaned close enough to speak softly and be heard above the chatter and laughter in the confined space. "Janat." He smelled of whiskey.

"Join me."

His brows compressed in a quick frown of surprise, but he took the offered seat. "Are you following me?"

It was her turn to be surprised. Yet, she had traced him here. So, in a way, perhaps, she was. "No."

He took the seat and signaled the wench.

"I have no money. You can pay for my meal."

He eyed her.

"You owe me much more than that."

He shrugged in agreement. His eyes had the soft, unfocused look she knew too well. "I see you got out of Coldridge. When?"

"Back then," she said. "During the battle. Meg saved me."

"Meg." Wonder focused him into the moment. "She was there?"

"She killed King Huwen's magiel, Wenid." Janat wondered what potion he'd found—beyond the whiskey—to ease his evening, and if he had more for her.

"Good." A viciousness in his tone betrayed a hatred she shared. "I knew Wenid was gone, but of course, no one told the prisoners why. Just that he was dead."

The wench brought two beers.

"She's been saving me ever since." Janat quaffed the beer, and it was deep and rich and satisfying. "Not that it's done much good."

He nodded, thoughtful.

"You? You were freed with the other Marigolds this summer?"

He stroked the side of his goblet. "No. I convinced a guard to spirit me out. And surprisingly, he didn't betray me. He was actually a magiel sympathizer."

"When?"

"Two years ago." He lifted his head. "I had the advantage of being held neither in a dungeon, nor under strict guard caring for a child, like the other Marigolds."

So. Not in the dungeon. No, not Gweddien. She sneered.

His eyes hooded, wandering over her features. "You're right. Things got better once Wenid was gone. I was given good food." He held up his mug. "Wine. I wasn't forced to impregnate a new woman every night." He leaned forward on the table and spoke fiercely, pinning her with his eyes. "But I was still a prisoner, Janat. It was still a breeding scheme."

"And you had to cooperate."

"Yes, damn it."

"A serial rapist."

His eyes became daggers. "You make it sound like I wanted to be there. *Gods, Janat!*" he exploded under his breath. "You know what Wenid did to me. I was his puppet and victim, just like the women. Just like all the Marigolds."

Marigolds. At least High King Huwen had the grace to be ashamed of his own bestiality. He hid the scheme under an innocuous name.

Gweddien drank his beer and looked away.

Still. She couldn't help herself. "With Wenid gone, no one could compel you."

He looked at her sharply. "What do you care? I never touched you."

Shock punched her chest. "What?"

He snatched up her hand and gripped it, hard. "Not *that* way."

"You—you—" She yanked back, heart thumping wildly in its cage, but his hand crushed hers into the table like an iron band.

"What I did to you was worse." His eyes bored into hers, coals. "You think I don't regret that? Every day? Every minute?"

She breathed hard through her nose, trying to get control of the wild thoughts and memories shoving themselves into her brain.

He gave her hand a small shake. "Do you hear me?" he said, still in that low, intense voice. "I regret that. Get it into your brain. I would take it back, if I could."

"Rape would have been better," she whispered bitterly. Part of her reared, panicking at the thought, but another part knew it to be true.

His grip lessened, the pain—almost unnoticed—easing, but he did not let go. "If I ever get the chance, Janat, I will make things right." He held up his other hand. "Don't ask me how."

"But you let him—Wenid. *Led* him—to do it to *me*!" The enormity of Gweddien's betrayal hovered over her, blotting out the world, and she held it back only with desperate will. "Did you think that by throwing me to Wenid, he would let you go?" It was ludicrous.

Gweddien pressed his lips together, his eyes shining, but a hint of a smile, regretful triumph touched his mouth. "Given the circumstances," he said, "you would have acted differently?"

She breathed hard. He'd caught her.

"You know." Gweddien bit his lip, still drilling her with his eyes. "You know."

She knew. There was no escape from Wenid's glim. She licked her lips and glanced at the others in the tavern. No one seemed to have noticed their suppressed argument, or at least, no one cared. Patrons talked and laughed and drank, just as before.

His grip softened to a plea, a desperation.

Gods, she'd pushed away the thought of glim, unsuccessfully, every day, every candlemark, every minute, since that night. The Heartspeed, the Serenity, the whiskey, the poppy . . . helped, but only briefly. "Do you . . ."

He caught her meaning and released her hand, almost violently, and sat back in his chair. "Wenid's dead."

"But—" Wenid couldn't be the only magiel to know of the existence of glim. He'd found it. Somewhere. It wasn't his invention.

"If I had glim, do you think I'd be here?" Gweddien snarled. "I'd be in a corner somewhere, far from this earth. Or dead."

She blinked, breathed, took a sip of her beer. Her rage had subsided. Somehow, his apology—not an apology, maybe—his *pain*, that was her pain, had taken the force from her anger.

He shook his head and drank his beer. "Other people can stop." He shrugged and looked at his tankard. "I can't." He signaled the wench. "Something is inherently wrong with me."

Janat had long known this same thing about herself.

"Huwen had my likeness drawn," Gweddien said, out of nowhere.

She peered at him. Very well. New topic. The last one had run its course. Become too painful. "Why?" She sat back in her chair, asking out of ritual more than interest.

He smirked. "To hold over me as a deterrent from escaping."

"How?" This conversation made little sense, but she no longer cared.

"At the time, I laughed." He fingered his tankard. "But a month ago a soldier from Arcan had it."

She squinted at him. "The original?" Impossible. "A copy?"

He finished his beer. "If it was a copy, there was not a hair's difference from the artist's rendering. But what kind of uncanny magic could make such a copy? And, if Huwen can make exact copies, how many are there?"

She shook her head, mystified. "So?" And then— "Huwen went to that effort, even before you fled?"

"I am surpassingly valuable to him. The most powerful magiel in all of Shangril. Present company excepted, of course." He tilted his head to her, and his mouth twitched in a charming smile. "We should make our own baby."

She rolled her eyes. "No." He was handsome, but two broken people were not candidates for parenthood. Even she could see that.

His gaze flicked to the door as if weighing his options, then he leaned fractionally closer. "I still have a couple of hours. Let's have fun."

She emptied her mug. "That is such a bad idea in so many ways." She grinned.

He grinned back. "It's my money we're drinking." Gweddien caught the wench's eye and held up two fingers. "And whiskey," he said, and the girl nodded. He leaned in to Janat. "Inability to stay sober can be a real problem."

She laughed.

He watched the serving girl. "You and Meg still fighting the good fight?"

This was the last thing Janat wanted to talk about. "What else?"

The girl brought their beer and two small glasses of Teshian whiskey. The best.

"No . . . rumors of the Amber?" He tossed back the liquor and nodded to the girl.

Janat gave him a pained look. "Really?" She considered sipping her whiskey, enjoying its burn down her throat and the slight heat spreading through her with each taste. But, no. She copied him, swallowing the whole thing, choking back its fire and squeezing her eyes closed. Gods, it was good. It'd been so long. She blew out, short and sharp, and glowed in pleasure at the relaxation creeping through her.

He lifted a shoulder. "That prayer stone was important to you at one time."

"Important to Meg," she corrected.

"And your mother."

She glared at him. He had no right to bring up Mama. "The Amber was smashed. End of story." And all her mother's hopes and dreams, and the uprisers' hopes and dreams, and Meg's hopes and dreams, even her own . . . everything had been lost in that one sledgehammer blow.

That was it. She had to go home. Gweddien had no glim. Meg would be furious with her. She'd better go to bed and suffer through Meg's sharp tongue and sympathy. And guilt. She rose.

But the wench arrived with more whiskey and Gweddien put a hand on her wrist. His skin shimmered beautifully in the candlelight, and his eyes were soft and warm.

The whiskey was paid for. She sank back into her chair. "One more. That's all."

CHAPTER 8

The Duke and Emerald. Piss.

Meg elbowed her way through rain-drenched streets lit only by lantern light seeping from taverns and brothels and dice houses. She'd left lanes signed with names behind in the market district, and the people she met on the street gave her conflicting directions.

A tavern. Rahd sent Janat to a *tavern*. By Ranuat, Meg had just got her sister clean. And, for some bizarre reason, Rahd sent her to Gweddien. Gweddien, a ghost from the past. And . . . why, under all the Heavens, was Janat even interested in finding him? Whatever lay between them, Meg was sure it was unsavory.

Meg shouldn't have slept, shouldn't have done that healing magic on Kirst. It was only good fortune someone by the well remembered seeing Janat talk to Rahd and had known where Rahd lived.

At least Janat's absence hadn't turned out to be an abduction. Meg thanked Kyaju for that. Still, Meg kept an eye open for suspicious figures. She and Janat had changed their names, but two magiel sisters, one ill with her own spells, could be tracked, even among the liberal districts of Cataract Crag. Their whereabouts could be known to uprisers Meg had never seen.

Piss.

If they missed work tomorrow, their jobs would be gone. Meg would have to be convincing to prevent that.

A crest gleamed in the rain outside a set of narrow steps leading to a doorway half-sunk below street level. Duke and Emerald? Yes. Stepping carefully to keep from twisting an ankle, she descended the stair and opened the door into a dim, noisy pub and threw her hood back.

The tables were crowded, and a dozen patrons crammed into corners or against a wooden serving bar. Most seemed animated with drink. A few in one corner sang, and some scattered through the room had joined them in an attempt to drown out all conversation. No sign of Janat. Or of Gweddien—whether Meg would recognize him again after all these years, she wasn't sure.

She cast about, uncertain. Where to look?

She eased back into the street, contemplating her search. Cataract Crag was far too big to inspect one street at a time, as she'd done in Glenfast. She settled into a shadowed doorway where she could watch the tavern entrance, her hood pulled up against the rain. Maybe she'd missed Janat returning to their rooms by way of a different route. That would've been easy enough to do. Yet Meg couldn't simply give up and go back to the warehouse. Wait. Worry. Pace.

A few patrons left, in ones and twos.

It was late—past midnight. The once-bustling streets had emptied.

A familiar figure emerged from the tavern. Gweddien? Yes, even after all this time, even cloaked against the weather, some part of her was sure of it.

He left the tavern, scanning the deserted street, wary. For an instant she thought he looked her way, but no. He walked, a trifle unsteadily, past her hiding place and around a corner.

Should she follow him? Might he lead her to Janat?

Maybe, but unlikely. Meg left her cranny and returned to the tavern. There were fewer patrons now, some undoubtedly having gone to their rooms, and the rowdiness had diminished. But Janat was not there.

Piss.

Meg dashed out the door to the street, rounding the corner Gweddien—if it was him—had taken.

The lane was empty.

She splashed down the dark way, scanning each intersection, panting.

And then. There. Just disappearing around the next bend, a figure. She followed.

A man—magiel, by the time shifts dancing on his skin—leaned against the door to a cart shed, standing guard in the thin rain. Gweddien had gone inside, but Meg had no idea if Janat was in there as well. Meg had, with some difficulty, followed Gweddien to a second tavern where he'd met this man who'd brought him here. There was no way Meg would get past this magiel. Not without using magic.

But perhaps the cart shed was not fully secure. She withdrew into the shadows and made her way back down the lane, circling the buildings, looking for some access to the back of the shed.

She found a narrow passageway, barely wider than her shoulders, between two buildings, that ended in a glistening stair. She climbed and was rewarded by finding two crooked doors off their hinges leading to a hatch with a pulley overhead. A hayloft, built over by shops and warehouses. She wormed her way inside as silently as she could through rustling hay, cast in shadow by a dim flicker of candlelight from below. She crawled toward the edge of the loft, hoping her movements sounded no more sinister than the scurry of a rat. The space was warm enough and dry but for a drip-drip-drip from a few places in the roof. It smelled richly of horse manure.

She peered down. Slumbering cart ponies occupied three stalls, and wagons of different sizes, but of a similar pattern, were lined up before a closed double door.

A man stood on the far side of the center cart facing Gweddien, whose back was turned to her. A candle rested on the cart's tail board. Janat was not there.

Kyaju, despite years that had done him no favor, she recognized Gweddien's contact. She'd seen him as a child, in Archwood. Odryn, King Ean's jeweler.

"You can't!" Gweddien's voice sounded low and savage, even in his own ears. He could not believe what he was hearing.

The jeweler stood before him, short, thin, and dirty, his hair ragged and his robe threadbare, and he shook his head. "It's finished," Odryn said. "I don't have it."

"You don't know what I've done." By Ranuat, Goddess of Murderers and Thieves, Gweddien had left Coldridge for Orumon the *hour* he'd been freed, hunting for any rumor of the Amber. The stories, the twists, the near disasters. But he found a thread, a rumor. Tenuous, teasing. He'd followed it, backtracked false tales, despaired and persisted across the entirety of Shangril. "What I've been through—"

"I could say the same." Odryn's words were a harsh whisper, matching Gweddien's for suppressed intensity. "I got it out of Orumon, by the Gods. That country is cursed."

"Who did you sell it to?" Gweddien swayed over the worldling, itching to throttle the man.

"I wouldn't tell you that!"

"To the High King? To a royal?" Gweddien's fists balled. "Someone who would have it destroyed?"

"No." But the jeweler's heat was gone.

Had he sold it to someone who *might* sell it to Huwen? Gods, no—Gweddien gripped the side of the cart with both hands, forcing himself to find something to do with them other than to strangle the jeweler. Ranuat, why had he not brought a spell with him? Of compulsion? Such spells were difficult to make and uncertain in result, but possible.

"I'm sorry," the man whipped. "But you have no claim on it. I had to get rid of it, don't you see? I needed the money. I don't need every magiel and thief and king's man and swindler in Shangril hounding me for it."

"Just tell me," Gweddien wheedled, "who. And I'll leave you alone."

The man took his candle and backed toward the door. "You leave me alone," he threatened.

Gweddien watched him go, took a step to follow. No.

Putting both hands back on the side of the cart, he rattled it, roaring his frustration.

※

In the shadows of the hayloft, Meg held her breath.

The *Amber*?

The voices in the room ceased and a door banged shut. Only the patter of the rain could be heard, and a low growl as Gweddien shook the side of one of the carts.

Huwen's father, the old High King, had died at the siege of Archwood, the day it fell. Huwen's first act as the new High King was to have the city searched for the Amber Prayer Stone. He found it and smashed it. The army that had followed him into the city had even been assembled to witness the stone's destruction before they fled the curse Mama had laid on the city.

But Meg had spoken to Mama in fleeting moments of her past, and Mama had tried to tell her something—that there was still hope.

No. *There was no Amber.*

Yet, rumors lingered that the Amber still existed. That only a fake had been smashed that day in Archwood.

Meg had convinced herself over the years that those who said so were only wishful. A fairy tale, a story uprisers told to stoke their passion.

Gods, could it be possible?

Meg stared at Gweddien gripping the cart below.

The Amber. The last remaining link to the Many Gods, that High King Huwen would—*must*—destroy.

The Amber had the power to deliver the seven nations of Shangril to the uprisers.

Her mother's prayer stone. Meg's inheritance.

6

At sunrise, Meg arrived at the Hawk and Hound, the inn where she and Janat worked. She hadn't slept.

After leaving Gweddien's rendezvous, she'd returned to the neighborhood of the Duke and Emerald, to search street by street. She found Janat, soaked and freezing, half-conscious in an alley. Her sister had sobered enough by then to follow her to the room they'd rented, and Meg had spent the remainder of the night by Janat's side, stroking her sister's hair. Thinking.

But Meg did not dare miss two days' work in a row, and Janat was safe enough in their room and out of the rain. Meg let her sleep. With summer waning, the Hawk and Hound wouldn't be full, and by the time Meg changed the sheets on all the beds, she'd make it back to Janat's room before she woke.

The inn's common room was empty. Most of the tables had been cleared, though flagons and goblets stood on a few, and there were cloths with spills to change. She hung her cloak on a peg in the kitchen, rolled up her sleeves, and began cleaning. She'd finished the dishes and was finding linens for the beds when Sieura Ebanis found her.

"There you are." The innkeeper's wife leaned on the door frame and held a robe closed over her night clothes, frowning querulously at Meg.

"I apologize, Sieura," Meg said. "My sister and I ate cursed meat and were ill yesterday."

"I had to do all the cooking and all the cleaning and all the serving," her mistress said. "I was run off my ass. And I'm not young like you."

Meg lowered her head, holding the sheets over her arm. "We should have sent a runner."

"Fat lot that would do," the innkeeper's wife said. "Where's Janat?"

"Still cursed."

"There's plenty of rogues in the shantytown as would like the coin I give you."

"Yes, Sieura." She kept her eyes down.

"Your sister stole two pears when she was here last."

"Oh?" Meg set the sheets on a table and fished in her purse. "I have a gultram."

"Three," the wife said.

Meg poured the coins into her hand. She had four and gave three to her mistress.

"And my husband pays two of you to work. If she doesn't come, it's only half pay."

"I'll do the work for both," Meg said, trying to keep her voice from sounding argumentative.

"You owe at least that much for missing yesterday."

Meg bobbed her head and picked up the sheets. Having work through winter was more important than missed pay for one day.

The innkeeper's wife sighed, her voice softening. "Meg," she said gently. "You shelter her. You shouldn't."

Meg let herself look into the woman's face.

Sieura Ebanis put a hand on her arm. "Let her drown, if that's what she's about."

Meg drew back. "Do you know the story of the ogre that was a paragon during the day?"

"Surely."

"If you drive a sword through the heart of the ogre, you drive it through the heart of the paragon."

Sieura Ebanis dropped her hand in helpless regret. "Go on, then," she said. "The free trader in the blue room said he was leaving at dawn. You can start there."

Meg bobbed her head again and took the linens to the blue room, stripping the sheets from the bed. The innkeeper's wife seemed to have forgiven her. She followed Meg into the room and fluffed the feather mattress on its rope support and helped Meg make the bed, chatting on about stories relayed by the clientele. Meg smiled at her tales, encouraging her to tell more, and the morning passed. At this rate, Meg wondered if she might be freed up to check on Janat after the noon meal. She would feel better once she knew her sister had recovered from the night's misadventures.

They were cleaning the third room when the Sieura Ebanis asked, "Why don't you do that, Meg?"

"Hmm?" She lifted her head. "Do what?"

"You weren't always a maid," the woman said obliquely.

Alarm brought Meg's full attention to bear. "What . . . makes you say that? I'm just a village healer."

A corner of Sieura Ebanis's mouth quirked. "Plenty of rich folk were forced out when Huwen's father took their lands. I can tell."

Meg knew what confession the woman wanted, but she said nothing.

"You speak proper when you forget to sham. I daresay you read."

Meg tucked the upper sheet under the foot of the mattress. She could think of no response.

"And your lineage." She nodded at Meg, meaning her skin. "I'm betting you can do magic better than most."

She dropped the quilt onto the bed. Best to keep quiet.

"I know folk from wealthy families," the innkeeper's wife said, tugging the corners of the quilt. "I could introduce you."

"I'm fine," Meg said noncommittally, stuffing a pillow into its case.

"But a rich man's mistress—" The woman smiled meaningfully. "—could lie abed as much as she liked and eat the best foods." The woman put the last pillow on the bed. "And you'd remember me, from time to time?"

Meg straightened, trying to school the horror from her face. "Of course," she whispered. "But I'm fine, here." *To come to this? From daughter of the Magiel of the Amber Prayer Stone to . . .*

"Well, you think about it," her mistress said.

... to a drab?

"Of course, if you don't want to do what's best for you . . ." The woman picked up the sheets but stopped at the door. "King Jace's Master of Treasury," she said. "In the castle. Do think about it."

"Think about what?" Janat stood in the doorway, bedraggled.

"You're late," Sieura Ebanis said, brushing past her. "If you can't be here on time tomorrow, don't come."

"I'm sorry, Sieura. It won't happen again." Janat dipped a perfunctory curtsey as Sieura disappeared.

Meg took up her dust rag. She could hug Janat. And she could strangle her. "I'm glad you're here." The words meant both.

Janat chose her second meaning. "You're not my prison guard."

A pang pierced Meg's chest, and her words emerged harsher than she intended. "I don't want to lose this job."

Janat checked the pitcher and basin. "Neither do I."

There was a gash in Janat's sleeve. Just below her shoulder, stained with blood. "Janat, you're hurt."

"Don't." Janat pulled away from her and took the last set of sheets down the hall.

Meg followed, bringing the broom. "It looks like a knife wound."

Janat pulled the quilt and dirty sheets from the bed.

Meg reined in her irritation, unfurling a clean sheet. "You tell me over and over I wouldn't understand. Can't understand. You never give me the chance to try."

Janat caught the far edge of the sheet as Meg flipped it out, but she said nothing.

"I can't understand if you won't tell me what's wrong."

"Just a drinking wound," Janat clipped. "I don't know how I got it."

Meg blinked.

Janat tucked her side of the sheet under the mattress, working in silence.

Lecture. That was what Janat had accused her of. Meg straightened her side of the bed. She knew she sounded reproving, but what was she to do? She'd done everything she could think of.

Janat flipped the quilt back onto the bed.

Meg smoothed the quilt. "Listen, Janat. Let's not fight."

Janat stuffed a pillow into its case. "What did Sieura Ebanis want you to think about?"

This topic wasn't much better. "Pandering me as King Jace's Master of Treasury's mistress."

Janat jerked, holding the pillow. "She could do that?"

"As a favor," Meg said, dusting the table. "In return for whatever I could do for her later."

Janat found a pillowcase. "You'd get a house. Or at least a set of rooms."

"Maybe." Meg ran her cloth along the window casement.

"We'd have clothes." Janat stuffed the pillow. "We wouldn't have to work. It would be like being back in Archwood."

"I'm not doing it, Janat." She polished the mirror.

"If you don't, I bet she finds an excuse to let us go." Janat sank onto a chair.

"I'm not doing it."

Janat closed her lips in a straight line, and Meg knew she'd heard the finality in her voice. "Then let's go to Highglen. When we're fired."

Meg pivoted. "Highglen?"

Janat gave a one-shouldered shrug. "Why not?"

Was Janat mad? "Because people here don't hunt down magiels."

Janat frowned in annoyance. "What if I want to go? You can't stop me."

Meg stared. "Why do you suddenly want to go to Highglen? You never wanted to go there before."

"Rennika is in Highglen." The tone made Janat's words sound like an excuse.

Their sister. A full magiel, but one—the only one, as far as Meg knew—whose skin did not shimmer with time shifts. "You haven't spoken two words about Rennika for a year. Why do you suddenly want to travel to another country to see her?"

Janat threw her head back and sighed. "Gweddien's in Cataract Crag. I met him last night. He's going there, all right?"

There was something between her sister and Gweddien, but Meg could swear it was not love. Her sister's sudden—

Gweddien's decision to go.

Last night, he'd learned—who had the Amber. He must have.

Meg flipped through the events. The jeweler had said he sold the Amber—*if* it was the Amber, she couldn't get ahead of herself—but wouldn't tell Gweddien to whom, or where that person was taking it.

Gweddien had been furious. Determined. Rash. But now, suddenly, he was going to Highglen.

After Meg left the stable, Gweddien had to have found the jeweler again. Made him talk.

Meg pulled the chamber pot from beneath the table.

Janat must have seen Gweddien since then. This morning.

Janat had no interest in the Amber. But Gweddien was a full-blooded magiel, descended from the House of the Chrysocolla. Did Janat see him as . . . a mate? An ally, protector?

An avenue to rid herself of . . . Meg. Her nagging.

"Well?" Janat challenged.

"No."

"Meg!" Janat jumped to her feet.

"We're safe *here*, Janat. We have a place *here*. We're building friendships *here*." Sooner or later, they had to stay in one place. A place where Janat had a chance to recover her health.

"You are so—so—"

Meg had done Janat enough damage by chasing her own dream. That hogwash between Gweddien and the jeweler last night? Nothing but words. Meg had seen no prayer stone, and neither had Gweddien. Pursuing such a fantasy would only distract Meg from caring for Janat.

The Amber did not exist, and Meg had no reason to chase it.

CHAPTER 9

The free traders who came to the Hawk and Hound's common room for a late midday meal did not want the trout stew Cook had made for the earlier patrons, and they were willing to pay. They shook the rain from their cloaks and pulled up cushioned chairs before the fire, and Sieura Ebanis called Meg from the laundry to serve while she helped Cook with the tricky preparation of the chic Pagoran-Aadian cuisine. Meg didn't mind. Janat was in a grumpy mood, and laundry was hot, heavy work when done indoors.

She covered her rumpled clothes with a clean apron and brought the men, the only patrons just now, a list of the inn's wines.

"The Meadow Hill Black Pine?" the money lender suggested. "Something light?"

The silk trader studied the list. He was costumed as Meg had seen frequently at the inn and in the wealthier districts, in the colorful, closely fitted Aadian fashion. "I think we should try the Blackbird." He tapped the list and gave his companion an impish look.

The money lender lifted a brow and smiled. "The Blackbird," he ordered.

Meg dipped a curtsey and withdrew.

"Blackbird?" The innkeeper's wife, rolling dough, twitched an irritated frown. "It's an Aadian wine. They will expect to be served properly. Do you know the protocol?"

Meg cast back to her childhood. Banquets she'd attended had limited mead—not that she'd been old enough for more than a single glass—poured from silver or golden decanters. Each person seated at the king's table had his own page, and at the lower tables, one page poured for two diners. As far as she could remember, they almost never had anything from as far away as Aadi. "Pour from the left?"

Sieura Ebanis pushed back a lock of her hair with a forearm. "In Aadi, there's a ritual. Show the label, ease the cork and allow the patron to smell it, pour a taste and if he accepts it, half-fill each glass, beginning with the guest. Use glass chalices, and leave the bottle, but offer to refill frequently."

Meg nodded her understanding and found the wine in the cellar. She hurried back to the customers.

"The princess isn't going to rule," the money lender was saying, leaning in to the other, placating.

She laid the glasses and showed the label. The money lender waved his assent.

"Youth didn't stop Huwen from ruling," the silk trader countered.

"More's the pity. Too bad his brother died, the older one."

"Huwen had an older brother?"

"Bastard. Never would've ruled, but he would've made a better king." The money lender shrugged. "Murdered."

The trader rolled his eyes. "Depravity and corruption."

"No." The other shook his head. "Robbers. Years ago, somewhere up Elsen way. I forget the details."

The silk trader waved his hand. "But this Delarcan girl, trying to make a point to her brother. Familial politics is death to trade."

They discussed the politics of Highglen. Meg blinked. Of course. By these men's reckoning, they were alone, their conversation private. She was a servant, and therefore, not present.

Meg twisted the cork from the bottle and set it before the money lender.

"She's not stupid, whatever you may have been told." The man absently sniffed the cork and gestured for Meg to pour. "She won't impose rule. Locals see her as a foreigner."

Meg poured a taste of wine into the goblet.

"You give the child too much credit," the silk trader argued. "Youngest Delarcan. A woman. Taking her brother's distraction in Coldridge as an excuse to hie herself off to seize a crown. I don't like it."

"There's no cause for concern." The money lender held the glass up to the light, sniffed, and rolled the liquid in his mouth. He lifted a brow in appreciative surprise.

"I told you. Aadi is the country for wine," the silk trader said. "Far better climate."

The money lender gave Meg a brief nod, swallowing the remainder of his sample. "There will be no disruption to trade in yak wool or furs. Even if the princess does prove to be a silly creature, she has advisers. And, worst case, a brother who will rein her in."

Meg poured for his companion, and he, likewise, appreciated the vintage. "Very well, then. Tell me about this Raef Gramaret. What kind of a regent is he? I'm told he's very young and that he has dubious connections. A cripple?"

Meg poured again for the money lender, then withdrew, but waited by the kitchen door, eyes cast to the floor. The men's voices were low and almost muted beneath the snap of the fire. "Assuage your fears," the banker soothed. "The lad's father disinherited him when he cast his lot with the Delarcans. The boy's forward thinking and entrepreneurial. Transformed the country's wool trade. Gramarye is producing more and better woolen thread than ever in its history."

Gweddien was going to Highglen. The Amber—*maybe*—was going there; to Hada, a secondary heir to the throne of Gramarye.

Magiel, Prayer Stone, royal. Gweddien, Amber, Hada. The three, once joined, would rise to the Heavens where Gweddien could commune with the Gods. Where he could deliver the people's prayers for prosperity, health—victory in war—and death tokens. Or where he could pray for whatever whim took his fancy. Whatever caprice Hada Delarcan convinced him to pray for.

Gods. The Amber was *Meg's* birthright. And Gweddien planned to usurp it.

※

Meg could not credit what she was hearing.

"Janat? Gone." Sieura Ebanis's scorn said she'd expected nothing less. "My husband tried to find her to scrub dishes when them free traders come."

Gods. At least two candlemarks gone. Where, this time?

Sieura Ebanis put a hand on Meg's arm before Meg was even aware she'd turned toward the door. "Let her go, Meg."

But, how could she?

"Listen. There're potatoes to peel and water to haul and still a stack of midday dishes unwashed. There's good work for you here."

Meg was at the door, pulling her cloak from its peg.

"If you go now—"

The door banged closed behind her, but Meg already knew how the sieura's plea would end.

※

By midafternoon the next day, Meg could stumble no further. She found a scrubby willow overhanging a rock wall along the road and wormed her way under it. Despite her worry, she fell into an exhausted sleep.

She'd spent the remainder of yesterday and into the small hours in the all-too-familiar routine. Hunting for Janat. Nothing.

But a small certainty underlying every thought, every inquiry, every futile search, grew until Meg had no choice but to listen. Janat had left Cataract Crag.

Meg had returned to her attic chamber. She brewed potions to cache in the pockets of her robe. Some, she made as a worldling did, with no manipulation of time to make the ingredients more powerful. She also made others. Stronger, magical spells. Well, she'd have to trust whatever version of herself inhabited her body over the next few hours to shepherd her along as best it could. Then she filled a travel sack with her few possessions, and blankets, money, food—she prayed to Ranuat for forgiveness—pilfered from the warehouse owner.

In the dark before dawn, she slipped from Cataract Crag and took the King's Road south.

To Highglen.

※

Meg put her head down and marched at a dogged pace. Janat had most of a day's head start, and the only thing Meg could depend on was her sister's unpredictability. Janat might, in fact, be drunk somewhere in the warrens of Cataract Crag, promising herself she'd leave for Highglen anytime. Or she might've left precipitously without supplies. She might've plunged onto some cross-country route south among winding roads to farmers' cottages. But her sister was also capable of a rational, direct, and swift travel. Perhaps absurd, but Meg gambled on the King's Road.

Her intuition was correct. At dusk, a day's journey south of Holderford, she spied a lone figure ahead of her on the road. She called out her sister's name. The figure turned and stopped.

Yes. Janat's form. Her stance. Meg's steps quickened until she broke into a run, a bubble of joy welling up in her chest. She engulfed her sister in an enormous embrace, heart pounding in relief.

Janat only shook her head with a rueful half-smile. "I should have known."

Meg held her at arms' length, looking her sister all over. She was fine, unharmed, eyes clear and calm. Meg took in a huge breath and pressed her smile closed, a million words blocking her tongue. Then she, too, merely shook her head and threw an arm around her sister's shoulder.

They knocked about down the road, and Meg gave Janat a butt in the shoulder. Janat thrust her back, and they both dissolved into peals of laughter.

If it was to be Highglen, so be it.

South of Holderford, the road to Highglen was no more than a back country track, dotted at long intervals with unmarked hamlets. Villagers along this road considered themselves part of the country of Arcan, and most believed magiels to be demon worshippers and uprisers were common bandits. Life might be worse under High King Huwen, but there was nothing the villagers could do about it, and fear of war and robbers made them welcome the protection of royal soldiers. Having a limited number of Heartspeeds and Confusions and Disguises, Meg suggested they give wide berth to villages whenever they could.

The risk of discovery—by magiel haters, or by uprisers looking to return them to Glenfast—lessened when they left the Faolan River valley, following a steep track, narrow and deeply trodden, into the high, treed foothills skirting the southern mountains. But the risk of getting lost increased the further they went, as animal tracks and paths to woodsman's huts crisscrossed the main trail, eventually becoming indistinguishable from the track they followed. The weather deteriorated as they climbed to cooler altitudes where autumn approached. Ghosts haunted dells and shadowed places.

Yet, Meg found the journey surprisingly restful. They built simple shelters at night and kept each other warm under the same blanket by the cook fire. They woke to brisk sunrises and drank from crystal rills; they prayed under breathtaking vistas of stars. The countryside reminded Meg of their days on the road with Dwyn's armies, the early days, the days of hope and big talk, before reality set in. Before they understood that the revolution must begin again, rise from small pockets of new recruits.

"Remember the time we came to Fairdell and that caravan was there?" Janat mused. They were following a winding track, now all but nonexistent, through boreal forest along an undulating ridge.

"The performers?" The image made Meg smile. "Remember the juggler?"

"Who told jokes?" Janat laughed. The trail crested the ridge and began to descend.

Meg saw the boy's big eyes and earnest fear. Afraid Dwyn wouldn't let him join the upriser army. Meg shook her head, holding her skirts up on the sliding gravel.

Janat giggled. "That was when I was making those little figurines of the Goddesses."

"Drawing portraits." Meg stepped over a log. "You were good at that, Janat. I think you should have kept it up."

Janat turned to her in surprise. "After seeing the Mysteries?" She shook her head and turned back to the descent. "No, Meg, I *had* to be an actor."

Meg's laughter broke off as the path emerged from the forest, and they looked out over a steep-sided valley that plunged to a rushing mountain river.

"The Zellora River?" Janat asked.

It had to be. "Look." Meg pointed out a line in the trees on the far side of the valley that was too straight to be natural.

"The King's Road," Janat said. "You were right."

The road to Highglen. Meg guessed they were only a few candlemarks' easy walk from the road. If nothing went awry, they could make Highglen in the south by nightfall.

CHAPTER 10

Fortune smiled on Gweddien in Meadowhill. He met up with a band of itinerants heading south: a knife grinder, a tooth puller, and a bard.

Travel was not only safer with companions, but more pleasant as they shared drink and stories and songs. When their way took them into Arcan, territory hostile to magiels, Gweddien remaining hidden in the woods, and his companions brought him food and requests for spells to earn coin: a cough suppressant in one hamlet, a pair of curses in a second, an easement for childbirth in a third.

The bard left them when they turned from the Faolantown Road to cross the hills to Gramarye, but two artisan traders—magiels both, and quietly nervous—joined them on the King's Road from Zellora. Despite the weather turning wet, they made reasonable time. As they journeyed, Gweddien heard no rumor of Yaquob, the free trader he followed, so he could only hope the jeweler had told the truth, that the man's destination was Highglen. But the spell Gweddien had used to compel the jeweler's confession had not failed him yet.

And . . . Highglen. Interesting destination. Princess Hada had gone there to claim her inheritance; something that might prove advantageous.

The magiel artisans, as luck would have it, though, were being followed. Their story, something about a miller's daughter, came out in the late afternoon of the tenth day when, from a resting place atop a bluff, they looked back down the way they'd come and saw a company of Arcanian soldiers. Following them. With dogs.

Piss. Gweddien had been caught before, twice; though thank the Gods, he'd managed to escape before being taken back to Coldridge prison. Both times, like this, it had happened toward the end of a long journey when his stockpile of potions was depleted.

The tooth puller and the knife grinder disassociated themselves from Gweddien and the other two magiels, and the three magic wielders were forced to hasten toward Gramarye with all speed. But the King's Road was climbing steadily, and Gweddien estimated they must have crossed into the country of Gramarye some time ago.

Gweddien, at least, carried a few spells, but no Disguises. He had used up all his Confusions; he had a Memory Loss, but it was not in powdered form for wide dispersal. The artisans—a brewer and a tinker—carried even less.

By late afternoon Gweddien was more sober than he could remember being, and his head ached from the climb and his want of beer. At least they'd left the heat of the valley behind. He was glad for the cool weather of low cloud cover and brisk wind.

They rounded a turn in the path. And found—a gate?

Though he'd spent a good deal of his youth in Holderford, Gweddien was born in Gramarye, and he'd never seen such thing barring a road. Any road he'd traveled in all of Shangril, for that matter. By the smell of the lumber, it was newly built. Carpentry tools were visible, and the sound of hammering rang from the forest.

The gate stood open but was guarded. Archers appeared on the wall's battlement when they approached, and a group of young men-at-arms stepped onto the road and called for them to halt.

"Friends!" The brewer cried out, his short locks tossing about his head in the breeze. He held up his hands to show he was unarmed. Gweddien and the tinker did the same.

"Magiels," the leader of the men-at-arms growled. "Not welcome in Gramarye. Turn around."

Ranuat. Arcanian soldiers were on their heels. But . . . the gate. Open. Could Gweddien turn it to his advantage? If only he was on the other side of it. Imprisonment in Gramarye—anywhere—was preferable to returning to Huwen's prison.

The brewer blanched. "Sir, I am a master beer maker and my brews are incomparable in their perfection. I beg you—"

"We are awaiting a contingent of Arcanian soldiers, come to escort a party of breeding magiels to prison in Coldridge," the leader of the Gramaryan guards interrupted. "You're welcome to join them."

Marigolds. Gweddien had no desire to return to Coldridge.

The wind was rising. Hoofbeats. Unhurried, but approaching from down mountain. Huwen's soldiers.

The men-at-arms were watching the bend in the road expectantly. Gods, what did Gweddien have that could help? As unobtrusively as he could, he slipped a hand into a concealed pocket in his swirling robe, feeling the shapes of the vials. A Memory Loss, an Attraction, an Anti-Nausea. Nothing he could use for an attack.

The Attraction, though . . . It couldn't hurt. He slid it into his sleeve.

Then, Gweddien raised his hands to show he meant no harm. Slowly, he crouched to adjust his bootlace. As the horsemen drew to a halt drawing the guards' attention, he uncorked the vial and drank its contents. He raised his hood.

When he rose, the commander of the Arcanian forces, a lieutenant by his insignia, had dismounted. The captain of the Gramaryan guards emerged from a building visible through the gate's opening and came to discuss with him the transfer of the prisoners. Their words were muted by the rustle of the wind until the captain nodded in the direction of Gweddien and his companions. "Might as well take these, too," he said over the tempest. "We don't admit vagabond magiels. Pickpurses and thieves."

Gweddien averted his face. Gods, he hoped the Arcanian lieutenant hadn't seen the drawing identifying him.

"Those two." The shout came from the direction of the mounted men.

The Arcanian lieutenant broke off his conversation with the captain of the guards.

Gweddien stole a glance at the scene. A man—the Arcanian's second in command, as near as Gweddien could guess—had dismounted and was striding forward, his eyes never leaving the artisans. "They raped the governor of Zellora's daughter," he was saying. "We've been looking for them."

༆

The afternoon was waning behind leaden rain clouds and rising wind when Meg stopped, listening. A distant rumble. Ahead, on the King's Road. Hoof beats? Cries?

She and Janat shoved themselves into the woods which ascended steeply here. Panting and catching their cloaks on rose bushes and evergreen branches, they climbed a low cliff and flattened themselves to look down on the road.

Two figures ran past, cloaks flying in the gale, their inconstant complexions announcing them magiels. Neither was Gweddien.

An instant later, a handful of mounted soldiers followed, shouting for the fugitives to stop. All disappeared around a bend in the track. Cries intermingling with thumps and shouts announced the horsemen's success. Meg held her breath. Shortly, the soldiers—wearing High King Huwen's colors—brought their captives back up the road and again out of sight.

***

The magiel artisans had sprung into the center of the riders, wafting something caustic into the air, startling men and horses. They dashed down the road and were around the bend before the soldiers, crying out and swiping at their eyes, managed to get their panicked mounts under control. But the delay was short lived, and a half-dozen cavalry peeled from their companions and spurred after the magiels fleeing back down the road.

The Arcanian lieutenant's gaze snapped to Gweddien. His eyes sharpened in sudden recognition.

He'd seen the sketch. Must have.

"Him," the lieutenant shouted, pointing. "Take him! Now!"

Gweddien wheeled and dashed through the gate. A handful of Gramaryan guards seized him. Gweddien clapped a hand on the back of the neck of one of his captors. "I'm valuable," he hissed into the man's face, capturing his attention. "Tell Princess Hada."

The Arcanian lieutenant and his remaining soldiers plunged to a halt in a semicircle just inside the gate, stopped by the guards' drawn swords and the nocked arrows of those atop the wall.

Yes. The charm Gweddien swallowed must have taken effect.

The captain of the Gramaryan guards pushed into the open space between the adversaries. "What's going on?" he demanded.

"This man is High King Huwen's most wanted fugitive," the Arcanian lieutenant spluttered. "Turn him over, immediately."

The Gramaryan captain turned to Gweddien. Gweddien locked eyes on him. "Ask the Arcanian why I am so valuable." His voice was sharp with significance. *Please, charm. Do your work. Persuade.*

The captain's expression flickered in doubt.

Gweddien pitched his voice low, for the captain's ears only. "This man is not your master. The princess is." And a captain outranked a lieutenant.

The captain studied him for a long moment, then turned belligerently to the Arcanian.

"This is outrageous," the lieutenant cried. "Does Gramarye turn treason against its High King?"

The captain lifted a hand and the archers' nocked arrows tightened on their bows. "I have no evidence this magiel is wanted," he said slowly.

So. The Gramaryan captain had not seen Gweddien's sketch. Perhaps the uncanny copies had not made it as far south as Gramarye.

The lieutenant purpled, but the archers stretched their strings.

"If, as you say," the captain went on, "this magiel is to be turned over to the High King, I will certainly do so."

The lieutenant breathed harshly through his nose, glaring at the man in the rising gale.

"But I will do so on orders from my own commanders."

The captain signaled, and the men holding Gweddien grasped his elbows roughly and marched him through the cluster of gawking magiel prisoners to the barracks.

"In the interim, you may take the magiel prisoners we have assembled, as agreed."

The guards pushed Gweddien into the building, and he heard no more.

He would have to use this potion more often.

Meg and Janat waited for a long time, straining to listen, but heard nothing above the rising tempest. Then the soldiers, augmented to double their number, reappeared, marching at a steadier pace with at least a half-dozen captives, hands bound behind them. Magiels. Marching downhill. North, away from Highglen.

Meg and Janat waited a long time but heard no more.

"Meg." Janat's whisper was barely audible beside her. "We've got to be in Gramarye by now. Aren't we?"

Meg thought so. The road had risen steeply into the mountains.

"Those soldiers. They're Huwen's, from Arcan."

Arcanian soldiers. Taking magiels away from Gramarye. To prison? To execution? To slavery?

Rain began to fall.

They sought shelter beneath the ground-sweeping branches of a great spruce tree, ate, and rested—it was too cold to actually sleep—until the rain stopped and the clouds became pearly-bright with the light of the River of Diamonds. Wet and shivering, they shook themselves from their blankets and made their way down the steep bracken beside the low cliff, and to the road. There was no sound here, but for the constant mutter of the river and the rattle of the wind in the trees. They saw no movement but the sprinkle of reflected starlight on wet underbrush swaying in the breeze. And the occasional ghost.

Meg led the way, watchfully, up the road.

They'd walked only a few minutes when something, a sound, gave Meg pause. She stilled, pulse racing, and Janat halted beside her.

A footstep on gravel, far ahead.

Meg peered forward, muscles tight. There was a blot, a sense of darkness more complete than the vertical stripe of trunk and lace of branch.

"Hear something?" A man's voice, barely audible.

Silence. Whoever was ahead listened. Meg listened, too, but heard nothing over the rush of blood in her ears and the river below the road.

The wind sighed.

Another voice. "Just the horses." That was what Meg thought he might have said.

So, the road was guarded?

She exchanged a look of puzzlement with Janat.

After a long moment, one of the men asked the other some question Meg couldn't make out, and the other responded. Daring to breathe only a little, Meg nodded for Janat to ease back along the road. When she was out of earshot around a bend, Meg followed, step by careful step.

They returned to the place where they had hidden.

"What's going on?" Janat asked.

"I don't know."

"Why would they block the road?"

Meg shook her head.

"You think Gweddien made it to Highglen?"

"I don't know."

"So?" Janat whispered. "What do we do?"

Meg looked around the forest. Gods, to have abandoned all her good intentions, to have left a city that was safe, where they were making a home, only to find themselves blocked—made her want to scream. "No point in staying here."

Janat pulled up her collar against the chill of night.

"Do you want to go to Zellora?" Meg asked.

Her sister's dark form gave a small response Meg took to be a shrug.

Go back to Cataract Crag? It was discouraging to backtrack. Though perhaps it was best.

"Can we get around them?" Janat asked. "Rennika's still in Highglen. As far as we know."

Meg quirked a frown at Janat. She wanted to keep trying. Huh.

Meg peered into the forest, climbing steeply above them. "We might be able to circle around."

"I don't want to stumble blindly in the dark. There could be cliffs."

Meg peered up the slope through the trees. "It's not that dark." It was true. The wispy clouds had drifted away, and the river of the Gods' stars was full and bright. Rocks and tree boles stood out in shades of gray.

"I guess we could try. For a bit." Janat squared herself to the slope and waited for Meg to lead.

Meg took them a good distance back from the road, climbing a high rounded ridge where the trees opened out and they had a view of the land. Though the road was no longer visible, the river valley was, and Meg could see where it snaked up, climbing a steep headwall into a gently sloping upland valley surrounded by lofty peaks.

Maybe.

Picking her way through the hilly forest, she led Janat on a wandering course roughly parallel to the road for what felt like a long way, gradually easing back toward the sound of the river. Eventually—much later than Meg would have liked—they saw the road once more through the trees.

Again, they watched and waited, resting a while to snack on a bit of cheese and bread, but neither saw nor heard evidence of movement.

They descended to the road, and again, moved as stealthily as they could, watching and listening, until the constellation of Ranuat set behind the mountains.

✸

Early morning sun shone in a cold, blue sky when Meg led Janat down a crunch of shale toward Highglen's back gate. They'd come within sight of the closed and guarded main gate before sunup, and again plunged into the woods to climb well up and around the city. This second detour had been steeper and more difficult than the first, and Meg wondered if all their struggles in the woods would bring them anywhere at all. But as the sun rose, they came out onto a high ridge and found themselves well behind the city.

For a moment, Meg was alarmed when they caught sight of the cluster of palaces and shops and warehouses crammed behind wide stone walls. A plume of black smoke rose from a massive building in the center of the city, on the eastern bank of the river. But after a minute, she saw that the smoke, even from here faintly acrid, came from four tall chimneys. So, not a mishap. But she wondered what these hearths burned to make so much black fume, and why. An odd, rhythmic sound like many horses stomping on some hard surface oscillated dully on the wind.

But her curiosity was immaterial. The gates on this side of Highglen stood wide.

CHAPTER 11

Highglen's Yak Herders' Gate was little used and unguarded, but Meg and Janat kept their hoods up as they passed into the city. Meg saw no time-flickering faces on the bustling streets within. They walked purposefully, heads down, sidling into back streets away from the grand houses of the aristocrats. The city was more prosperous than Meg remembered from her visit years ago when their sister Rennika, still a child, had sheltered here against soldiers hunting heirs to the great magiel houses.

On the bridge over the Gramarye River, the strange, rhythmic din drew Meg and Janat to the railing to stare at the building with the high chimneys. The structure was enormous, a featureless brick rectangle the size of three great halls, end-to-end, punctuated with rows of identical glass-paned windows. What on earth was it for?

Janat touched Meg's elbow and they pushed on, winding their way downhill toward narrower, fouler quarters crowding muddy lanes. Here, a glimpse of time-flickering skin wasn't as closely guarded, and despite the drizzly weather, half-magiels chatted on doorsteps or shopped in the markets.

Meg inquired after Rennika, dredging her memory for any information about her sister that could help, but their sister seemed not to exist. Meg asked about Colin, the yak herder Rennika had lived with years ago, but laborers and thieves and drabs knew little about the herdsmen of Gramarye's backcountry. As she queried, Meg kept an eye open for uprisers. She had no desire to be recognized, if Fearghus's inquiries had reached this far south.

Finally, well into the afternoon, as she and Janat were sitting in a tavern considering where to stay for the night, a pub keeper pulled up a chair at their table. "Are you weavers?" she asked in the round-voweled accent of the south. "There's work for weavers in Highglen."

"No," Meg said. "We're here to find a relative." For the twentieth time, she described Rennika. "Twenty-one. Blonde." And, to all appearances— "Worldling."

"She might be the journeyman dyer," the woman said. "The draper's apprentice."

"She said something once, didn't she, Meg?" Janat asked. "About a young wool trader she liked. An apprentice, almost a journeyman? What was his name?"

The name popped into Meg's head. "Yon."

"Yon Verlin." The pub keeper nodded. "Largest wool and fabric sellers in Highglen." The woman nodded uphill. "Big house on Highmarket Common."

※

A fortuitous overcast and lightly falling rain provided an excuse to cover their heads as the afternoon light waned, and Meg and Janat ventured back toward the more prosperous neighborhoods of Highglen.

Highmarket Common was anything but common. The large plaza, filled with the scent of roasting yak meat, the bleats of lambs, and racing boys and dogs, stood above the rest of Highglen, just below the queen's castle. Under the shadow of a shrine to the One God, well-dressed servants bargained with prosperous tradespeople as gossiping grandmothers fingered early fall produce at large free traders' tents and artisans' stalls. The common was bounded by walled great houses that harkened back to the dignified architecture of the Great Peace, each accommodating an elegant shop on its main floor spilling light onto the wet cobbles from many-paned windows: a jeweler, a gold smith, a silk importer, a spice merchant, a furrier— and, the draper.

Meg and Janat talked quietly together on a stone bench near the draper's shop, tucking their packs under their feet. Meg strained her eyes and ears, alert for any soldier who might happen along, and for some sign Rennika was anywhere nearby.

The rain was letting up near dark, when Janat abruptly poked her and pointed.

A cart had pulled up before the draper's shop, and a woman in a plain but well-cut cloak descended from the rear seat, bringing a package with her. She spoke to the driver.

Rennika.

Fair-haired, where Meg's mane was dark, and worldling-skinned where Meg and Janat shimmered. But there the differences ended. Rennika shared their mother's wide forehead, diminutive size, and long-lashed brown eyes. Their sister had grown into a slender, good-looking woman. Not as pretty as Janat with her flash of dimples—neither Rennika nor Meg were—but strong and confident. A pang touched Meg's chest. Gods, when had her little sister grown up?

Janat hurried between the shoppers to catch Rennika's attention.

Rennika straightened, staring, then engulfed Janat in a hug.

Meg breathed.

There was a brief animated conversation, muted by the sounds of the busy plaza, then both looked to her. Rennika darted across the flow of patrons to grasp Meg's outstretched hands. "Meg!" And she wrapped her arms about her as Janat rejoined them. "When did you get here? How did you find me?" she cried, pushing herself back to peer under Meg's hood.

"This morning," Janat said.

"You're known for your dyeing, apparently," Meg supplied, tightening her nostrils at the rank smell of dyes that still clung to her sister. "Even in the lower town."

"Where are you staying?" She cast a quick glance at the shoppers, her voice low, but went on before Meg could answer. "Have you heard about Princess Hada?"

Meg shook her head to prompt her sister's words.

"She came up from Arcan this summer and she's been repressing magiels, even more than Raef Gramaret did," Rennika said. "I'm surprised you got into the city. I heard she even had a gate built on the road where she says Gramarye ends."

"We managed to avoid the gate," Meg said, matching her tone. "We came across country, around the back."

"We have no place to stay," Janat whispered. "We hoped we could stay with you."

Rennika startled. "Oh—" She looked from Janat to Meg.

Meg let the silence speak.

"I . . . have a room above the draper's family, but . . ." Rennika shook her head ". . . magiels aren't generally allowed in the upper city. I don't know if Sieur Verlin would let you in."

"He doesn't know you're a magiel." Of course. How stupid of her. Rennika's skin had no trace of shimmer, a gift from their farseeing and powerful mother. Rennika looked anything but a magiel.

Rennika's eyes widened with shock. "Sieur Verlin can never know. None of them."

"What have you told him?" Janat asked.

Rennika let her gaze flick around the common, but the crowds were thinning as night came on. The windows of a few of the shops had darkened, and the driver of Rennika's cart had taken the horse and wagon into the draper's yard to unload.

Rennika tugged Janat's arm and the three squeezed onto the stone bench. "The same story I used when I first came here. That I was orphaned in the fighting, and Colin was my uncle."

Colin. The yak herder was once King Dwyn's master of horse. He'd concealed Rennika at the outbreak of the war. "Where's Colin now?"

"He died. Five years ago."

Meg's breath caught. Her sister had done well in the interim. Very well. "So," Meg said slowly, "there'd be no one to contradict you if . . ." Her mind flickered through ideas. "If you told this draper that before he died, your father had remarried a woman with two capricious-skinned children. That we *are* your sisters."

Rennika studied her, hesitant. "No," she conceded.

Meg lifted a shoulder. "For a few days?"

Rennika's eyes narrowed and Meg had to remind herself Rennika was not a child. Highglen was a long way from the rest of Shangril. Too far to come for only a few days.

Meg pushed her lips together in cajolery. "Or longer."

Rennika's lids fluttered as if she reevaluated possibilities. "Of course," she said, but without conviction.

"Listen. I know this puts you in a difficult spot," Meg conceded.

"What are you doing here?" Rennika asked.

To be fair, her sister needed to know. "We've left the uprisers."

"What?"

Janat took in a deep breath. "We need to find some place, Rennika. Please. Some way to . . ." She gestured at their sister. "Make a life. Away from politics. That's all."

Rennika bit her lip.

"Please."

Her sister looked over at the draper's shop fronting its prosperous quadrangle. Its lower windows were now dark, but from those on the floor above, where the family lived, light seeped through thick curtains. "I'll do what I can."

Janat was impressed with Rennika's rooms. She had the entire attic to herself, and her bed was raised from the floor, with a down mattress on a rope net. Unlike the common sleeping rooms Janat was used to in Glenfast, Rennika's apartment was more like the palaces of aristocrats, divided into separate sleeping spaces for individuals or couples. The attic of the ornate old house had clearly been intended as a space for at least three or four servants, but the draper had built his business from nothing, and even now he had no house servants. His family ran his home and his business. Rennika was the only apprentice he'd taken on, beyond his two sons-in-law.

Janat lowered her pack to the floor in a small spare room.

"I'll see what I can do to find you something to use for a pallet." Rennika affixed one of her candles in a sconce. Her fingers were dark with splashes of blue and purple and red. "I never use this room."

It was wonderful to have shelter and warmth against the night chill. And a room to herself!

Rennika showed Meg a second, equally disused room, then disappeared, returning in a few minutes with a small cauldron of thick red rice and lentil soup, and yak sausage. She set the food on a table in the apartment's main room near a small brazier, along with two more candles. Her gaze lingered on Janat's thin bag and ragged clothes, then darted away in embarrassment. But she bit her lip and nodded to Janat's cloak. "I have a few things . . . that might be warmer than what you're wearing." She shrugged with one shoulder. "A few things I don't need. I can take them in to fit."

Janat luxuriated in a cushioned armchair by the brazier. "Really?" Janat knew she was sticks and bones, and winter in the mountains would feel all the colder unless they had a place to live. "Rennika, that would be wonderful."

Meg took the straight-backed seat. "I know we're imposing, Rennika. You don't have to clothe us, too."

"I have a second cloak." Rennika found a stool somewhere and served the soup into three small bowls. "Janat can start with that. I'm sure one of the girls, or maybe my friend Ide, has something they don't need."

"Thank you." Meg's gaze ran lightly across the room's interior, its cushions and tapestries and carpets. She nodded to Rennika's deep mauve robe as she took her bowl. "Is this your work?"

Rennika blushed a little. "Most of it, yes."

Meg shook her head in admiration. "It's delicate craftsmanship. And the hues . . . really quite amazing."

Janat had to agree.

"Thank you." Rennika gave Janat a bowl.

"And thank you for persuading Sieur Verlin to let us stay." Meg dipped her spoon in the chunky broth. "You don't know how much this means."

"Two days was all he would give," Rennika said apologetically, serving the sausage. "His wife is dead, but his mother runs the house, and she's nervous." She didn't have to say, *about magiels*.

"We'll stay out of the way," Janat said. The food was delicious.

"It isn't that." Rennika, who'd missed eating with the family, poured tea, adding a dollop of butter to each mug giving the brew a rich flavor. "Since Hada came, soldiers in the lower town have taken to entering magiels' homes and shops and tossing their furniture about and smashing it."

Janat looked at Meg. They'd heard tales of such acts in Arcan.

"You can't be seen in the common, or anywhere above the river," Rennika said. "Use the servant stair if you have to leave the attic. I'll try to bring you most of what you need."

"Are there uprisers here, then? Or a thieves' network?" Janat asked. "Someone who could help us?"

"I don't know." True to her word, Rennika had left the rebellion behind. Moved on with her life.

Meg put her hand on Rennika's. "We'll find our way, Rennika. We always have."

Rennika took a deep breath but said nothing.

Meg gave her attention over to her meal. "This is a beautiful house. Is there a library?"

The change in topic was a reprieve, of sorts. But what were they going to do?

Rennika nodded. "Quite a good one. Sieur Verlin has a copy of Eric Stewart's definitive poem cycle. I could ask him if you could look at one of the volumes."

Meg gave her a surprised smile. "Political *satire*?"

Rennika gave her a one-shouldered shrug. "Sieur Verlin's an educated man."

"Tell us about him." Janat bit into the hot sausage, solid and fatty and delicious. "About you and this house. Sieur Verlin's a textile merchant?"

"Well, we buy fleece and spun wool from yak herders, thread from the factory, and woven fabric from local weavers." Rennika cradled her tea. "Yon is Sieur Verlin's eldest son and a master trader. Sieur Verlin is a master draper to the castle and most of the courtiers, and he's allowed me to apprentice with him."

"Yon." Janat remembered. "You mentioned him when we were in Coldridge."

Rennika gave a small smile, then. "He's . . . good. Very fair. A good trading master."

Janat returned her smile and set her empty bowl on the table. "Do you love him?" she teased. At twenty-one, Rennika was more than old enough to be wed.

Rennika blushed. "Oh, no! He's . . . above my station."

Meg lowered her mug, staring. "You were born in a palace."

Rennika shot Meg a withering glance, and there was a biting silence.

"You're a Falkyn, Rennika," Meg said quietly.

Falkyn. The name they'd been born to.

"No matter how you hide it. Magiel to the Amber Prayer Stone of Orumon. And, ignore the rebellion or not, you can't stay out of politics."

Rennika darkened. "I can. I have. And I will."

Janat reached out and covered Rennika's hand with her own.

Meg shook her head slowly. But she bit her tongue and turned the topic to other things.

CHAPTER 12

Coals nestled beneath the row of blackened cauldrons, shedding a warm glow in Rennika's workshop. The wind, a capricious mutter and rattle, slapped cold raindrops onto the waxed-linen windows. The dull rain smelled of autumn, though the equinox was still three weeks away. The dyeing enclosure—hers, now—overlooked Highglen from a promontory a candlemark's ride from the city's east gate. Here, fresh water could be drawn from the creek, fabrics could dry in the breeze, and the stink of mordants could blow far away, over the mountains to the aeries of the orums.

Rennika lifted a loop of rope from the second vat and drew the skein of linen yarn onto a pan, pressing the wet tangle with a wooden paddle to squeeze some of the solution from it.

Rennika carried the pan, crimson drips unheeded on her apron, to the door to inspect her work. A festival had been announced for the equinox, a day of prayer and celebration of the One God. Singers and jugglers and puppet troupes were to play in all the town commons and there would be free bread and ale. Orders for new robes and gowns were already coming in, and Verlin expected more.

The day's overcast did not provide the most favorable light for judging color. She flicked the yarn this way and that with stained fingers. The color was uneven, varying between fuchsia and magenta, with touches of deeper red. The variation was beautiful, though Sieur Verlin was not likely to approve, despite the fact that linen was notoriously difficult to pigment. "Xoran," she called.

The boy, Verlin's second son, taller this year and growing out of his clumsiness, dropped his long paddle in the vat and came to the door.

She pointed to the inconsistencies in the yarn. "How would you make each strand take true?"

Her apprentice examined the sample in the gray light. "Agitate and separate strands. Add a cup of vinegar to the mordant."

"Master!"

She lifted her head.

Wynn, the stableman, half obscured by the steady rainfall, held the halters of a pair of draft horses just inside the double gates of the compound. Ah. The collier had arrived to deliver charcoal. She gave the hank to her apprentice and, drying her hands, reached for her oiled cloak. "Exactly. Do as you said and leave it another day." He'd done well—she should consider assigning him a test piece for his journeymanship.

She followed the team and cart to the charcoal shed where the collier was backing his wagon up to the bin. The man—Jack, she remembered—nodded to her as he slipped from the seat. "Journeyman."

"Journeyman," she responded.

The collier, tall and spare, found a spade. He was a strong man, for all he had a narrow frame. His hair was fair almost to white, and his face never browned but every time she saw him it was either pale or burnt with sun. She swore that the fine, silt-like powder of the charcoal he worked must be ground into every pore of his body, and just now it streamed down his face in gray rivulets. He and the stableman began shoveling charcoal. "Where's Master Quennell?"

"Arrested. Exiled." Rennika's jaw tightened at the reminder. Quennell had been a hard taskmaster, but fair, and she had respected him. But his complexion had been too inconstant for Hada Delarcan's taste.

Jack tilted his head as he shoveled. "Fortunate for you, then. I never liked him. Magiel. You've assumed his office?"

"Yes." She'd passed no examination, nor been admitted to any dyer's guild. Quennell had only assigned her masterpiece this spring, a suite of matched wool, silk, linen, and leather pieces in five complementary colors, solid and two prints, suitable for a nobleman's ensemble, adopting the style now fashionable from Aadi. He'd been in the course of examining her work when he disappeared. It took Sieur Verlin a week to track down what had happened, but by then the exile had been implemented. Verlin had complained bitterly that the dye master's skills were irreplaceable, and a special dispensation should've been made to keep the man in Highglen, but nothing could be done.

"Pissing magiels," Jack said. "Glad the Delarcan is doing something about them. That two-tongued regent never did." He spat.

"Yes. Well, I believe Sieur Verlin owes you something for the charcoal?"

"Twelve gultra." The men were making short work of the shoveling. "Price is going up, next delivery."

She tilted her head in query.

"Heavy call for charcoal in Arcan." He shoveled. "Not enough to go around."

Well. What could be done? "I believe Sieur Verlin left a payment at the office. I'll see you there when you're done?"

The man nodded and kept shoveling.

But the payment was not at the office. For the past two years, Rennika had been taking on all aspects of managing the workshop's finances, inventory, and schedules alongside Quennell, but today there was no purse set aside in the lock box for charcoal. The few chetra there would not cover the bill and were needed for other expenses. "I'm sorry," she said, as Jack stood by the door, hands and clothing black with soot, fastening his cloak. "Sieur Verlin does not appear to have left the payment. I can ride to Highglen and be back by midafternoon."

Jack shifted on his feet. "It'll take me all day to get the team back to Kandenton. I have another delivery in Zellora tomorrow."

Verlin was usually good about payments. "I apologize. Would you accept a promissory note until you return? I will talk to Sieur Verlin."

Jack looked vexed but loathe to speak his mind. "Tell him I charge a fee for late payment."

That was only fair. She nodded, wrote and signed the note, making a copy for Sieur Verlin. Jack put his mark on both. A gust of rain chilled the room as the collier took his leave.

Rennika sank into the armchair before the desk, turning it to warm herself by the fire and study her masterpiece displayed on the far wall, arranged there for Quennell's inspection. She'd envisioned the materials she'd dyed fashioned into garments combining the traditional layered robes of Gramarye with fitted vests and sleeves such as the wealthier free traders from Pagoras wore, copying clothing imported from Aadi. The vibrant, exotic colors appeared hauntingly rich, muted in the faint light of the waxed linen windows.

Her work deserved a master's designation. Not only was her craft almost flawless—the imperfections that blazoned out at her were visible to no one but herself and Master Quennell—but her piece was ambitious and creative, pushing the colors to exceptional vibrancy. Quennell had used his limited magic ability—he was only part magiel—to search the ages of the ingredients he worked with, honing them to stronger intensities or muting them to pastel softness to create the effect he wanted. No worldling dyer would have understood how he achieved this, though all stood in awe of his precision of hue. But Rennika understood. And she could use the same magical techniques. As long as she didn't show off, no one needed to know of her heritage.

A blast of wind rattled the building.

She rose. Enough daydreaming. She should finish inspecting the saturation of the other linen hanks. But, as long as she was in the office, she might as well calculate the materials requirements for the new set of matched dining chair seats the glazier's wife had ordered yesterday. She found her bundle of fabric samples and spread them on the table.

The door opened and Sieur Verlin entered with a patter of rain. He stamped his boots and removed his outer cloak. "Sieura," he greeted her. "Xoran told me you were here."

"Sieur." She dipped a truncated curtsey.

He pushed her samples aside and half-sat on the end of the table. "Rennika, I've been thinking, and I have a proposal for your sisters."

She leaned her hip against the other end of the table, mirroring him.

"Your sisters are magiels. Your one sister is quite talented, am I right?"

"Both are part magiel." This was the story they'd agreed upon.

"But they can both work magiel magic?"

"Yes."

"You know it's hard for me to have them stay in the house. Makes my mother nervous."

Rennika lifted a shoulder and sighed. "Sieur, no one is happier to see them than me, after all this time, but had I known they were coming, I would have counseled them against it."

"I might be willing to let them share your attic."

She could not suppress the surprise that lifted her brow. She'd always found Sieur Verlin to be a tolerant master, generous to the poor, and willing—in private—to commiserate with the plight of the magiels. But she'd also known him to be a conservative man, sensitive to prevailing attitudes, and practical. He was not the sort to risk himself unnecessarily. "Sieur?"

He clasped his fingers around his knee, leaning back on his perch. "Like it or not—and you know I'm not one to have political opinions—magiels have provided commodities that are becoming scarce. Commodities some of my clients are fond of."

She tilted her head. Sieur Verlin was hired by the wealthiest of Highglen's courtiers. But he offered fabrics and colors, measured men and women for garments, and rooms for draperies. His business did not depend on magic the way, say, a physician's might.

"If your sisters would be willing to create Dream Incenses, I could get them a good price, even after a small commission."

She straightened.

"You may not be aware, but until recently, such incenses were a popular entertainment at a number of the lords' and ladies' soirees. If I could be instrumental in supplying such small gifts, my clients' gratitude would not be bad for my business. I'm not the only draper in Highglen."

She thought he outcompeted his rivals through sheer efficiency. No house servants, and Rennika his only journeyman, and he treated her as a member of the family. Yon sold good Highglen wool to middlemen all over Shangril and purchased cotton, silk, and linen in the lower lands to bring here for spinning, dyeing, and sale to Highglen's elite. Verlin's daughters spun and wove, his portly mother did his writing and numbers, and his youngest son, Xoran, was Rennika's apprentice. His only other workers were two stable men and an occasional contract laborer. Now, she saw there was more—perhaps considerably more—to his business acumen.

"For the sake of appearances within the family, your sisters should provide some small service," he said. "Cooking or cleaning. I would not want this arrangement generally known among my children. Or by Sieura Verlin."

A place to stay and a source of work. Exactly what Meg and Janat sought. Rennika's stomach fluttered. She could provide them with a home. To have her sisters back . . . "For how long?"

"As long as they can escape arrest, provided that each of us profits by the arrangement. If the soldiers come sniffing, I'd have to disavow harboring them."

"Of course."

He gave a small nod. "Can they make such magics?"

And Rennika's position with the disapproving Sieura Verlin, who hated yak herders' nieces like Rennika, would not be hurt if her sisters cleaned and cooked. "Both of them would be quite able."

"And would they agree?"

She took in a deep breath. "I will present them with your most generous offer, Sieur."

The cell in which Gweddien had been shoved appeared to once have been a large stone-walled cold cellar beneath Castle Highglen. He was manacled to a stout beam embedded in one wall. The room had been divided with thick posts of down valley timber into several small chambers, most of which, as near as he could tell, held magiels. They spoke rarely, as conversation resulted in whippings, but in the deep night he overheard their whispers, queried them about the lay of the country. The cells had no doors, but chained as he was, the lack of door was immaterial. Unlike the part magiels, he had the skill to shift the tumblers within the locks of his fetters, and escape. But that, currently, was not his plan.

He was cold. They'd taken his magiel robes, of course, to search for pockets and potions they knew could be hidden within. A steady rain had been falling since his arrest, and water trickled from the stairwell to puddle on the hard earth floor. Just now the little pools provided drink for three rats. He didn't mind. Watching them in the dim gloom of the overcast day was a small diversion from waiting, and they hadn't tried to bite him. He knew by the headache and first few spasms of his limbs that soon the vomiting would start, and he would have no thought for anything but the retching of his body and torment of mind for want of potions.

A step sounded on the stair, and the rats scrambled into the shadows. The guard arrived with his meal.

Gweddien sat up and his chain rattled. "Thank you."

The guard grunted and set the bowl before him. Rice.

"Did you deliver my message?" He tried to keep the eagerness from his voice, though the nausea already creeping into his gut chafed at the delay.

The guard shrugged an affirmation. "For what good it will do. I don't talk to royalty."

"But you told your captain?" Keep the tone light, charming. Confident.

He shrugged again, meaning he had.

"And you gave my name?" This had been a gamble, as likely to get him sent back to Coldridge as not. But just now with his stomach roiling, even the thought of Coldridge failed to deter him.

The guard shrugged a third time, another assent. "If you're wrong, if the princess doesn't think you're worth her being bothered, I'll bring you a whipping." The tone of his voice suggested that *said whipping* would not be of the same caliber as the others.

Should he have had the message go to Raef Gramaret instead? Which governor, the princess or the regent, was hungrier for power? He mentally chided himself. Hada. It had to be Hada. Gods, he prayed the message had gone beyond the captain. "She'll be glad you told her," he said with a little grin. "I swear."

Raef Gramaret, furious, swept into the ballroom of Highglen Castle's Great Hall—the best he could, encumbered by his lame leg and cane—Lord Vael at his heels. The long, ornate chamber was bright-lit through tall glass-paned doors admitting late afternoon rays, as the sun dipped below the clouds to skim the mountain tops. He faltered for a moment, scanning the echoing chamber. Hada was not here.

There. The west terrace. He strode to the door, moderating his pace as he crossed the flags to the cushioned benches where three ladies sat. A woman reading poetry broke off at his arrival, and the ladies looked up from their embroidery. The late summer sun was still warm here, overlooking the city and the sweep of Gramarye's lower realms to the distant plains of Arcan, but the air was tinged with frost. Snow was coming.

Raef came to a stop and, as much as it galled him to do so, gave the princess a curt bow.

"Lord Regent," Hada said mildly, lowering her sewing. She was a pretty thing, slender with thick fair hair and dewy eyes like her brothers', but better favored. Doubtless, her physical attributes fetched her as many gifts as her rank.

But not from him. He eyed her young man-at-arms. "Your Highness, some disturbing news has only this hour come to me, and it is incumbent on me to address it with you."

Hada flicked her hand and the poet, bowing, withdrew. "Please. Sit." She gestured to a bench angled toward hers, and the lady-in-waiting there shifted her position to make space.

Now to come to it. Raef perched on the edge of the bench, holding his cane at arm's length. "I am told trade goods from Pagoras and Arcan are being taxed at your infernal gate."

Hada rested her hands on the sewing in her lap. "Yes."

"That it is manned by your household guards."

"Yes."

The simplicity of this woman was astounding. A thousand rebukes sprang to his mind, but he kept his question short for the benefit of her simple nature. "Why?"

"Free traders and guildsmen benefit from our roads. They should pay some of the cost of upkeep."

He blinked at the stupidity. "The gate . . . has no fence. Anyone can walk around it."

"Carts cannot. And the fence is being built. Begin with a first step."

He was speechless with competing objections. "Sieura—" He chose the term intentionally. "With all respect, governance of Gramarye is not your concern."

The woman did not appear to notice his insult but waved her hand and resumed her embroidery. "A matter of formality," she said. "You are regent only until the coronation."

Again, astonishing. Her grasp of politics was so simple as to be laughable. To argue she was a woman and not heir, that her position was symbolic, that she had no background, training, or understanding of governance, that High King Huwen was monarch of Shangril and his appointment of Raef as ruler had not—and would not be—annulled, that the support of wealthy and powerful lords was critical in any rule—he shook his head. It was pointless. She would not—could not—understand. He took a breath. "Your Highness, Gramarye's wealth is founded on our trade in wool and textiles." He doubted she knew even this much about her own realm.

She glanced up from her sewing with a brief smile. "Yes."

"Trade. Carts. Horses."

Again, she acknowledged him with a small smile.

"Sieura, the road from Highglen to Arcan and Pagoras must be *widened*. Not *blocked*."

A frown flicked across her brow. "The gate is sufficiently wide."

How could he explain in terms simple enough? "Sieura, I am importing four power looms from Arcan."

She lowered her sewing. "Sieur, please stop addressing me by a wrongful title. It reflects badly on your comprehension of rank."

One of her women covered a smile with her hand. Heat slammed Raef's heart and boiled into his ears.

Hada gestured toward him, the same wave she'd used to dismiss her entertainer. "You may go."

Vael drew in a sharp breath.

Raef was on his feet. "The gate must be dismantled."

Hada lifted her head, a small "o" of surprise on her lips. "Sieur. No." She wiggled her fingers a second time. "You may go."

Speechless, he stared at her. "You—" He spluttered, his mind blanking to a million insults.

"You are a Gramaret, Sieur, and son of a rebel outlaw. You administer this province only until the details of governance can be transferred." No humor or doubt in her stare. "Now. Please go."

The man-at-arms shifted forward.

God! The impertinence—

He whirled and hobbled from the terrace.

CHAPTER 13

Something about Sieura Verlin disturbed Janat.

Janat had been left in the draper's compound to perform sham chores for Sieur Verlin's mother while Rennika worked in the leather shop and Meg rode out on one of the mountain ponies to harvest incense ingredients, if any could be found after last night's fresh snow. Sieura Verlin, a stout woman with coiffed, iron-gray hair and fingers stained with ink from her accounting, appeared to mask distaste behind an impassive visage, and failed. Janat was not surprised. Rennika had said Sieura Verlin was uncomfortable with their arrangement.

No, it was something else about the matron that disturbed Janat. But, as the feeling seemed mutual, Janat was given her tasks and the matron retired to her office, leaving the youngest girl, Tyg, to show Janat where to find supplies.

Left on her own, or with Tyg, Janat didn't mind cleaning up or beating rugs or preparing food for midday. What became awkward, in her ill-defined position of servant-guest, was sitting with the family to eat.

And someone was bound to offer her ale. She'd promised Meg she'd take only apple juice, which could pass for cider, but . . .

She was more than aware of the door to the cellar where barrels of ale and beer, and bottles of wine and whiskey, stood next to the root vegetables and crocks of preserves.

No. A slip and an embarrassment, that's how *that* would end. Janat would find herself overhearing people whisper about how to manage her. No. She was determined. Not again.

She was loitering by the kitchen door, trying to work up courage to enter the dining room, when Tyg emerged from the cold cellar with butter and honey. "Come eat."

Janat bit her lip. "Where's Rennika?"

"Oh, Rennika usually doesn't take a noon meal," Tyg said. "Then she comes, midafternoon, looking for a snack."

"Oh." Janat didn't know the family's etiquette but was not above taking a chance. She brought the cheese she'd sliced to the dining room where Sieura Verlin and the family were gathering, and bobbed a curtsey. "Sieura, Tyg tells me Rennika will eat in the warehouse today. Might I bring her a bowl?"

Sieura Verlin, blinking at the curtsey, seemed relieved. "Certainly. Yes. Do that."

Janat wasted no time filling two small bowls with dumplings, lentils, and nuts, and making herself scarce across the quadrangle at the leather warehouse.

Rennika, arms spotted with stains to the elbows, was bent over a massive wooden table beneath two chandeliers, using a chunk of dyed, hardened grease to trace the outlines of a fabric pattern onto an enormous tanned yak hide. Her fair hair was caught up in a kerchief, leaving her oval face unadorned. She really was quite lovely, in a quiet way. She lifted her head and smiled at Janat's tray. "Oh. Lunch."

Janat cleared a few oddments from a small table near the hearth—a book, a slate scribbled with numbers, chalks, chamois—and arranged the cups and bowls there. She poured tea, and its rich, earthy fragrance curled into the light that filtered with surprising brilliance through the waxed linen windows. "Marigold tea with cinnamon and cloves. Delicious and healthy," Janat said, seating herself. "And lucky, or so they say."

Rennika finished a mark and set her grease crayon aside, studying her work.

Janat nodded at the leather. "For the glazier's dining chairs?"

Rennika brightened. "Yes. The seats will be horsehair-and-fleece-stuffed leather. The backs will be filled with wool fabric. Cheaper, without looking cheap."

Janat quirked a grin. "Clever. And you'll dye the leather?"

"Yes." Rennika washed her hands at a basin. "The leather and the fabric are to match, which is the tricky part."

A cheer erupted from the main house, and Rennika turned at the sound.

"And cutting the leather falls to you?" Janat asked, pouring the tea.

Rennika pulled her attention back to Janat. "In this case, yes," she said, dragging a stool to the table. "I need to match the grain and ensure I dye enough hides to—"

The door burst open, and Tyg burst in. "Rennika! Rennika, come quick!"

They both jumped to their feet.

"Lord Raef is coming to the house!" Tyg cried, rushing to take her hands. "Papa's won the contract to supervise all the dyeing from the new textile factory, and we're entertaining Lord Raef! The *regent of Gramarye!*"

"Oh!" Rennika cried, hugging her back. "When?"

"In two weeks! And Princess Hada's *very own* Holder of Histories will seal the agreement, before he goes back to Holderford!" Tyg hopped on both feet. "All the trade masters are to be invited, and Papa's going to have the butcher slaughter a pig!"

Janat wiped her fingers from the dumplings and set her napkin on the table. A celebration. Drinking. But she wouldn't be in attendance. She'd have to stay well out of sight.

Rennika smiled stiffly at Tyg. "That's wonderful."

"You have to come, right now. And you have to have Ide sew up your masterpiece into the best gown, ever!"

Rennika blushed. "I don't think—"

"You'll be the most important one there!" Tyg tugged at Rennika's hand. "Come! Papa's telling everyone all about it."

Rennika blew out an unsteady breath. "I'll be right there. You go."

Tyg ran out into the sunshine.

Rennika slumped back onto her stool, her face pale.

Janat leaned forward. "Rennika. This is . . . phenomenal."

Rennika blinked and focused on her. Her head made a slight nod, yet she didn't speak.

What? "You don't seem . . . excited."

Rennika took a deep breath. "There were rumors this could happen."

"What worries you?"

"Master Quennell is gone." She looked up. "Princess Hada's men did a sweep of Highglen when he was in the market, and they sent all the magiels they found there to Arcan."

"So? That makes you master, then," Janat reasoned. "You said you finished your masterpiece."

"But my examination wasn't complete. I haven't been admitted to the guild. There are no women in the Dyers' Guild."

Janat squeezed her hand. "You don't think—what, that Sieur Verlin will take on a new master for this contract?"

Rennika lifted a shoulder.

"You're better than all of them."

Rennika cast her a small smile. "You don't know that." But her face told Janat her words had hit their mark. Rennika rose and wandered back to her work, fingering the leather. "I'm not saying I'll have to go back to my journeymanship," she said quietly. "Just . . . it's hard to say how this will affect . . . well, the whole family."

Janat joined her at the table.

"And there are so many free weavers here. When Lord Raef's weaving factory opens, they'll all be out of work, like the spinners were when his thread factory started."

Janat didn't know what that meant. She'd never been in a city where the mechanical wheeze of a steam engine thrummed beneath everything, every conversation, every patter of rain, every measure of music.

A tiny frown creased Rennika's brow. "I'm borrowing trouble," she said with a cautious smile. "This is good news."

But the contract was not the boon it appeared.

"Let's go congratulate Verlin."

Meg woke, rigid and sweating on her pallet in the dark.

She pressed her eyes closed and opened them again, reassuring herself of where she was. Dreams of blood . . . battle. Wenid's death. They still ambushed her, even now. Asleep or awake.

The soldier who'd attacked Janat, pinwheeling from the wall.

Such visions sprang upon her less frequently than they used to, and less forcefully, but they still came. She forced herself to breathe slowly and listen to the sounds of the house, the distant throb of the steam engine. Let her heartbeat calm.

Animated chatter wafted up through the floor from the Verlins' living quarters. The initial excitement of the contract announcement two days ago had died down, but barely. Perhaps it was dinnertime or early evening.

Meg must have slept away most of the day. She cast back to the flashes of other parts of her life she'd lived as a consequence of performing this morning's magic, but nothing stood out; no informative hints from her future. She had the vague impression she was destined to live an unremarkable life, or a short one. Or one in which she would guard her use of magic with great care.

Meg rolled from her pallet and wrapped herself in a robe and a blanket from her bed against the chill of the alpine night. She eased open the door to Rennika's sitting room, thinking of food. She'd prepared a mild Serenity spell for Janat this morning, a little different from the one she usually made. Janat didn't shake and start at every sound anymore, but Meg wanted to monitor her, even so.

Rennika sat in the light of three candles next to the brazier, a book in her lap and ink and paper on a small table beside her. She turned at Meg's entrance and nodded to a bowl of yogurt and cranberries, with sausage sliced on top. "I thought you might be hungry."

Meg pulled up the cushioned armchair. "Thank you." The meat was cold but still delicious. "Where's Janat?"

"In bed, asleep." Rennika rested her quill in the ink pot. "She was helping with laundry today. She was tired."

Meg nodded. "Did you give Sieur Verlin the Dream Incense I made?"

Rennika poured her tea, adding a spoonful of butter. "Yes. He left you a purse." She nodded to a shelf over her worktable.

Meg set aside her bowl and fetched the pouch from among a scatter of slates and rags and dishes. She returned to the circle of candlelight to pour the coins onto her palm. Two gultra and twenty chetra, as promised. She would lock this in the puzzle box she'd purchased in Cataract Crag.

"Sieur Verlin is honest," Rennika said, watching her return the coins to the purse.

"Oh, I have no doubt of that." Meg tucked the purse away and took up her bowl again. Then without eating, she leaned back in the chair and let the moment of peace settle within her. "You're fortunate, Rennika."

Rennika looked up from her book.

"Sieur Verlin. His family . . ." She let her finger run lightly over the nubby tapestry of the chair's arm. "They're good to you."

"Yes. They are."

"And you've been good, to shelter Janat and me." Meg hesitated before continuing. Janat might be asleep, but still, she lowered her voice. "Rennika, you should know." How to say it?

Rennika tilted her head.

"Janat is . . ." She didn't want to be unkind. But— "She doesn't make good decisions. Not even . . . when things are going well."

Wariness replaced the tranquility in Rennika's eyes.

"She's a thief."

Rennika lowered her quill into her ink well. "We all had to learn how to survive during the war."

"No. Something happened." Meg tried to find a way forward in words. "I don't know what. I've tried to ask her, but she puts me off. She . . . she's a drunkard. A spell-eater."

"What?"

Meg let out a long breath. This was difficult. "I know she thinks I don't listen to her. She thinks I . . ." She shrugged. "I don't know how to get through to her. I try to show her I care. Do things for her. But she thinks I should just give up on her. I really . . ." Meg's body betrayed her, threatening to close her throat. "I don't know what to do anymore."

Rennika let the book fall closed on her lap.

Meg shook herself. "Anyway. You should know. You can't let her have money. She shouldn't drink anything stronger than ale or cider. And she shouldn't do magic."

Rennika scrutinized her, a look of disbelief on her face. "She looks fine." Her eyes flicked. "She looks so much better than she did before I left the two of you."

Those days. Meg stared into her bowl. After the battle at Coldridge the uprisers had been driven back, forming pockets struggling to surprise the king's armies, attacking and withdrawing. They used spells and potions to cover infiltrating raids, to spook horses and confuse the enemy. They used spells to give their own fighters endurance and drive away fear. They traveled constantly on low rations and little sleep. They'd all been shadows, deadened. If Janat had been more so, no one noticed. "She's doing all right. Now. I've been watching out for her a bit more." But Gods, it was a lot of work. Trying—so hard—not to be constantly beside her. Trying to keep distance. Being *normal*. All the time.

"Meg, are you all right?"

"By Kyaju, Rennika," she whispered, her chest tightening. "She's my sister. And I . . . I've hurt her, and ignored her, and . . ."

"It's not your fault."

"No?" Meg put her uneaten food on the table and rummaged for a handkerchief, something, to press against her nose. "She's a different person from what she was when you were with us."

"It's not your fault."

"Then, why?" Meg blew her nose. "We *all* lost Mama. We *all* lost our home. We *all* had to survive on the road. What made things different for Janat?"

Rennika looked small and pale in the candlelight. "I don't know. You had your anger to keep you going. I had a home, here, with Colin. I didn't see all the things you saw."

Anger. To keep her going. Yes, perhaps that was part of it. Janat didn't rage against what had happened to them. She just wanted to turn back the clock. Return to the way things had been.

"Maybe Janat was born different," Rennika guessed. "More sensitive to spells."

"She and I—we had a falling out." Meg hadn't told anyone this.

"When?"

"Way back. Before the battle at Coldridge." The images of that night stabbed Meg's vision. "She and Sulwyn were lovers."

"Sulwyn? Really?"

Meg reflected. "I'd traveled a lot with him that winter—with the uprisers. When we came back, Janat thought he and I . . ." Meg shrugged. "But Sulwyn and I had never so much as looked at each other that way. At least, I hadn't. I was pretty young. Idealistic. I was only there for the cause."

"Janat was younger."

"She ran off." In her mind, Meg saw Janat's stricken face. "I didn't see her again—none of us did—until the battle at Coldridge. I think, I don't know, something happened to her in Coldridge."

Rennika placed her hand on Meg's. "At Sulwyn's funeral, when we cremated him, she was . . . it was like she was in deep grief. Catatonic, almost. I thought it was because of Sulwyn's death."

Grief. Yes, that was the word. "That's what I thought. But . . . I don't know. Something else. I don't know."

"A lot of things were done to magiels in those days," Rennika said. "In the chaos. A woman, alone. An aristocrat turned refugee. It wasn't possible to *not* be damaged. What did she tell you?"

"That's just it. Nothing." There had to be some explanation.

Rennika's hand on hers tightened. "Whatever it was, Meg. It wasn't your fault."

But Sulwyn . . . had confessed love for Meg. A love she didn't want.

"Meg? Listen."

Meg blew her nose. Gods, Rennika—*Rennika*, of all people—was trying to comfort her. Rennika the princess, the child. Rennika, the little one kept safe in the hinterland, who never faced the worst of the wars. "I've become cynical, I guess."

"Janat seems genuinely happy."

"Thank you. For listening." Meg covered Rennika's hand with her own. "For seeing the good." She was wide awake, though the house had quieted now.

"Do you want me to tell Sieur Verlin? About Janat's unreliability?"

Gods— "No."

Rennika frowned.

"We're magiels, Rennika. We barely have permission to be here. The instant a sewing needle goes missing we'll be out on our ear."

"But—"

"She's our sister. We can watch her."

A new understanding came into Rennika's eyes.

"I know it's harsh." A touch of bitterness soured Meg's mouth. "But after you've been taken for a fool a few times, you learn."

Rennika pursed her lips and nodded reluctantly.

Meg rose. She was restless. Janat was safe, at least for now. Meg needed to get out of the confines of this house, this apartment.

"Will you sleep?" Rennika asked.

Meg shook herself a little. "I slept all day." But Rennika would need an excuse. "I need to buy some black-market ingredients." She jingled her purse. "For Dream Incense."

"Meg, don't go out."

Meg turned in surprise.

"The more you go out, the more you risk getting caught."

But she hadn't come to Highglen to hide. To stay imprisoned behind safe walls. And . . . there was a chance—a *chance*—to follow the rumor of the Amber. Nose about, look for Gweddien or the merchant he'd followed. In case. "I'll be careful."

"Meg . . ."

Meg put her blanket on the chair and plucked her cloak from its peg. "I'll be back late. Sleep, Rennika. Take care of Janat."

༆

Raef Gramaret pulled back from the eyepiece of his telescope and, by the light of his candle lantern, he recorded the time on his sand clock and the position of Ranuat's merchant star on his ledger. He compared his observation to his star chart.

Yes. Within minutes of his astronomer's prediction. Raef sat back in his furs and blew on chilled fingers, letting the glory of the River of Stars wash over him. The One God's firmament moved precisely, like a machine.

Men understood so much more of God's plan than when Raef was a boy; how nature enacted it in predictable ways. Raef had commissioned engineers to build him a model of wheels and gears to move miniature stars through a replica of the Heavens, and already it foretold the progression of celestial bodies. Not precisely enough, though; not yet. The machine was not sufficiently accurate for his astrologers to anticipate the details of the future. But it was coming. It was coming.

His astronomers had already predicted his success, but they were sycophants.

Raef *must* be crowned King of Gramarye. He must.

Everything had been in alignment. He'd endeared himself to the masses by bringing in new business, more employment. Allied with powerful families, enriching them by improving the textile industry. And the name, Gramaret, for God's sake, should have sealed the bargain.

He'd had enemies disposed of; even disposed of some himself, despite being a cripple. And wasn't he actively searching for an outstanding magiel, one of pure heritage—or the purest he could find in this beggared situation—as a gift to Huwen for his Marigold venture? A business made more difficult by Hada's sudden scheme of evicting every magiel she could unearth.

Hada might think she could take his crown, but the little princess was not as secure in her position as she thought. Still, he could not underestimate a Delarcan. He would annex the land next to the thread factory for the textile mill. He would widen the road to Arcan, and beyond, to Pagoras. He would make this country so wealthy that Huwen, with the debts he'd incurred in this endless civil war, would come to *him* for assistance.

His spies in Holderford assured him of this. And once his celestial prophesy machine was enhanced, so would his astrologers.

CHAPTER 14

The outside stair to the Three Corners Alehouse, a small post-and-wattle room above a distillery, was slick with yesterday's snow-turned-ice in the crisp, clear cold. It had no railing, and Meg was surprised she saw no broken bodies in the alley below.

She caught a movement in the corner of her eye. An upriser, following her? No, a blur. This place drew ghosts.

Inside, tallow candles beat back the shadows beyond the tavern's occupants. Two men, cloaked against drafts sifting through the waxed linen windows, sat on a bench warming their hands at a brazier in the middle of the room. A skinny grandmother sat on a stool. All three raised their heads when Meg entered.

The woman, iron in her eyes as well as her hair, nodded to a chair, and Meg drew it into the circle of warmth. "Ale or whiskey?" the woman said. "It's all we got."

"Ale." A corridor led to back rooms and the moans of someone making love. Alehouse and brothel?

The woman waited expectantly. Meg fished a chetram from her purse. The woman snatched it and disappeared behind a bar in the gloom. Both men eyeing her were worldlings. One was a youth with some bulk to him and a raised scar across his cheek and mouth. The other was older than Meg, with an unshaved jaw and red, puffy eyes. Both looked as though they hadn't prayed since the outbreak of the war.

"I was told I might find Vellefair here." She spoke in a baseborn Pagoran accent. Foreign enough to explain her quest, and humble enough to encourage amicability.

"He just left," the boy said. "But I could take a message. Two chetra. It's a bargain."

The woman brought Meg a tankard and resumed her seat. Someone cried out, faintly, from down the corridor.

"I'll give him the message myself," Meg said dryly.

"Might wait a while," the boy said.

She shrugged and tasted the ale. Bitter stuff, doctored with worldling magic to boost its alcohol content. The barkeeper would attract customers with this, and no doubt find it easier to separate them from their money. "I was told he knows who comes and goes in Highglen. I can wait."

"A long while."

She lifted her mug in a toast. "To good company and good drink, then."

The woman chuckled and drank. "You been to a few taverns looking for a magiel man."

Meg's glance riveted on her. They knew?

"Lost him, did you?" The barkeeper and the men laughed at this.

But no. This was a tight community, was all. She covered her alarm with a drink. Rumor of her quest had traveled within the thieves' network, as she'd intended. "Him, or the one he's following," she said easily. "Any new free traders this past week? The kind who deal in interesting goods?"

"Traders come and go," the woman said. "Though when this rain turns to snow, not so much."

The men nodded at this wisdom. "You got magics for sale?" the older one asked.

Meg gave a half shrug. "Always got magics."

"Hey!" the woman snapped, her jovial mood vanishing. "You buy from me."

The older man spat on the floor.

"Xadria, you don't do magiel magic," the boy said.

Meg held up her free hand before Xadria could jump to her feet. "I'm not here to steal your business."

The man lifted his jaw. "What you got?"

"No? Looks like you are."

"You got Heartspeed?" the man asked, ignoring the barkeeper.

"Sure."

"Dream Incense?"

"I got ganja," Xadria put in.

"Everyone's got ganja," the boy said.

Meg nodded. "Enough for a lark. I have healing herbs too. Other things."

"Xadria don't have incense." The man grinned at the old woman. "She's got love potions and curses. And they don't much work."

"Targeted curses work better," Meg offered.

"Haven't had good magiel magic for a while, ever since that Delarcan woman come. Magiels ain't exiled or fled are too scared to cure a hangover," the boy grumbled.

The man fixed his rheumy eyes on her. "How much you want for a Heartspeed?"

"I just want to find Sieur Vellefair, or someone else as can tell me what I want to know." She reached into a pocket in her robe and withdrew a corked glass vial. "The magiel man would've come here four, five days ago. The free trader would've come ahead of the magiel."

Xadria smiled nastily and nodded at the old man. "You found Vellefair."

With a grin, no doubt intended to be charming, Vellefair held out his hand for the Heartspeed.

Meg wrapped her fingers around the vial, concealing it. "The magiel I'm looking for. Or the free trader."

Vellefair glowered at the barkeeper.

"Well?"

"No magiel like you say has come to Highglen," he growled. "Come back tomorrow and I'll see what I can find out about the trader."

Vellefair was lying. He didn't need to nose about for information. It'd become clear to Meg in a few short days, the thieves' network in Highglen was small enough any newcomer—and their business—was well known by all. She'd described Gweddien two nights ago in a different tavern, but her quest had preceded her here tonight. No, Vellefair knew if there was a new free trader in town. He angled for for some advantage. She slipped the vial back into her robe. Xadria grinned.

"You better give it to him," the boy said, rising. "If you know what's good for you."

"Sit down, Idiot Stick," Xadria said.

Meg looked up at the boy. "I'm a magiel. I didn't come here unprepared."

The threat hung in the air for a moment.

"Listen," Vellefair said. "I can give you money."

"I got money. I want to know about the free trader."

"I can give you other information."

"As I said." She put her half-finished tankard on the table and rose. "Not interested."

"Wait." He put a hand on her arm.

She looked at the hand, and then at Vellefair.

He pulled his hand back. "One of the princess's spies come in here earlier today. Stopped at the brothel after reporting to Hada."

So. He truly didn't have information on the free trader. Or the free trader had something on him. But Meg might seed a connection with Vellefair in a different transaction. "And you know this because . . . ?"

"My sister did him."

Hmm. Drabs were as reliable a source as the thieves' network could usually produce.

"This is news," Vellefair said. "Not more than three, four days old. The spy come from Coldridge."

Coldridge. "All right. If you speak true, and the information is news. Real news." She fished the Heartspeed out of her pocket again. "I'll bring you another tomorrow for information on the trader."

"Huwen's retaken Coldridge." Vellefair delivered this disclosure with a smirk of satisfaction.

"What? But, this summer, the uprisers . . ."

Vellefair held out his palm. "Uprisers haven't held it longer than five weeks," Vellefair said.

Piss! She gave him the Heartspeed.

"And here's something for free," the older man said with a flourish. "King of Elsen routed a nest of uprisers at Glenfast."

Rennika lay in the dark, curled in Yon's arms, staring through the window at the arch of the stars. Wishes and worries, too many to pin down, swirled in her thoughts.

Verlin had not called for her.

He was busy, to be sure. Details of the contract, meeting with other masters in the textile business, touring the thread mill to examine the machines, sending watchers and listeners to see what they could find out about the plans for the new mechanical looms, calculating thread production, fabric volumes and quality based on changing assumptions—he didn't have time to confirm Rennika's role. He was just assuming Rennika would be his master dyer, a detail he could confirm later.

Or he delayed. Consulted other dyers, calculated costs of hiring a master. Negotiated terms. Weighed the cost of keeping a mere journeyman on, unrecognized by the guild. Inexperienced. A woman.

"Go to sleep," Yon murmured in her ear.

She let out a breath. Sleep was not going to come. "I should go back to my bed."

His arms tightened. "No. Stay here."

She smiled. It was this way every time. He knew she couldn't stay.

"What is it?" he whispered.

She rolled over in his arms. "Everything. I don't know how you sleep."

He opened an eye. "I can't. You wiggle too much."

She stifled a snort.

"I've been working my tail off," he said, closing his eyes again, as if this explained everything.

"So have I."

"And making love with you is *very* relaxing." He stroked her breast and she squirmed. He grinned at her and ran a finger down the side of her face. "Come. Tell me."

She sighed. "The contract."

He played with a strand of her hair.

"It will change things."

"Father'll keep you on. You know he will. He just needs to find a way to legitimize your station."

She breathed. She needed to hear that. "What about you?"

His head shifted on the pillow. "What about me?"

This was a harder question to broach. "Ide's family. The Naids are the biggest weavers in Highglen. We've been allied with them since . . ." Since before Rennika came to live with Yon's family.

Yon's hand fell back to her shoulder.

"Will Lord Raef put them in charge of the new mill? Or will they lose their livelihood? Not as many weavers will be needed, once machines do the work."

"Don't know."

"Will your father be urging Lord Raef to give them a good position?"

She felt him shrug in the dark. "I would imagine. As long as it doesn't interfere with his contract. It's not yet signed."

Not until the ceremony. And even if it was, aristocracy could always find loopholes.

"Is that what's worrying you?"

No. Not everything.

She tucked her head into his shoulder, and he draped his arm over her, his body relaxing.

She couldn't ask him. *Might Verlin ask Yon to marry Ide? To join the families?*

She rolled over.

"Rennika."

She shook her head and slipped from the bed. "I'd better go."

He did not argue this time. She let herself from the room.

But another question was still not answered; the question she'd never asked him in four years together.

Why had he never asked her to marry?

Sun struggled to glow through gauzy cloud as Meg made her way among beggars and traders, bleating sheep and yapping dogs, to peruse herbs and oddments in the tent-roofed stalls of Chetram Common. Three-day-old snow had melted into icy crusts creating inconsistent patches of slick cobbles, crystalline mounds, and here below the river, frozen mud.

She'd told Sieura Verlin that morning she must go to the market for the draper, which was true; he wanted more Dream Incense. But she'd also taken time to haunt the poorer neighborhoods with which she was becoming familiar, where she could sell her own spells—curses, love potions, fertility amulets, the usual—for contingency money. And to query anyone who might connect her to a free trader with exotic objects for sale. Sometimes she gave a chetram to a beggar in the name of Kyaju, whispering that more Gods than just the One would listen to prayers.

And if Meg strengthened a potion to help a local magiel look like a worldling, well, that was her own business; the charm cost her little if she made it along with her work for Verlin. It angered her to see a magiel roughed in the street, forced to *donate* to a royal *charity*, told he'd be "tried" as a child molester if he didn't. Sometimes it was best to seem to be a worldling.

But she couldn't make such spells for every magiel every day. She couldn't return land stolen from those lords who'd once encouraged councils of guildsmen to advise them on the needs of the common people. She could not make kings agree to be constrained by rule of law. Not without the Amber. No, this small charity might help one man or one woman through a day, or perhaps a week, but it did nothing to change what was.

The watery sun emerged from the clouds, doing nothing to warm the air. She shook her head, dispirited. She departed the common, following a narrow lane between overhanging shops.

—the sound she'd listened for since leaving Glenfast.

Rhythmic crunching snow. Footsteps tracing her path.

She paused by a bushel of apples at a grocer's and chanced a glimpse behind her. A man, far back in the crowd. Catching her eye.

Meg dropped the apple she fingered and pushed her way through a cluster of shoppers. Not a soldier. Upriser, then.

She turned a corner, wishing she knew the geography of the city better. She'd intended to return to The Three Corners to follow up with Vellefair, but it was in a grimy, isolated district.

No. Time to change direction. She touched the vials in her pockets as she splashed through icy puddles and elbowed past shoppers. A Fever Suppressant, a Serenity, and a Luck Charm. Nothing to make into much of a weapon; she'd used her last Memory Loss avoiding a handful of worldlings bent on abducting her for some kind of work crew.

She took an abrupt turn around a corner.

Bad move. The alley was plugged by a cumbersome hay cart that seemed to have got itself stuck.

She turned—

And the man was there, blocking her way.

"Excuse me." She side-stepped, keeping her face obscured.

"Sieura Falconer?" He spoke in the southern highland accent of Gramarye.

Her glance flicked up reflexively to the man's face. *Ranuat.* "Sieur?" She did her best to cover the gaffe, appear confused. She'd given no one in Highglen that name.

"Might I take you to a rice house? Perhaps, for a midday meal? There's one I know, not too far from here."

Meg took the lay of the street. Though three men down the lane argued over the hay cart, this man appeared to have no companions. It was broad day, but no one would intervene if a worldling decided to drag away a magiel.

The man didn't look the type to use force, though appearance could be deceiving. He was well enough dressed. There was a faint stink about him that suggested, like Rennika, he worked in a noisome profession. He had a pale complexion that contrasted with ruddy spots on his cheeks and a quirky, handsome face. She'd never seen him before.

"Your sister is Rennika Falconer?" he asked earnestly.

Rennika—again, Meg's surprise betrayed her. Piss, even after eight years of being hunted, she was behaving like an amateur. Was she being overly wary?

No, she cautioned herself. Colm had threatened her, said Janat couldn't be trusted to keep their activities secret. But even Meg was a liability if she were captured by royals and tortured. If Colm couldn't recapture them, he was fully capable of sending an assassin.

"I'm sorry, I've completely lost my manners. My name is Miach." The young man held out a hand. "Journeyman tanner. I just heard you were in Highglen."

She touched his fingertips in the Gramaryan fashion. "You . . . heard . . . ?" She was a long way from where anyone knew her. Halfway across Shangril.

He nodded back toward the common. "I saw Rennika yesterday. She mentioned her sisters were visiting."

Meg would wring Rennika's neck. "I'm sorry, Sieur." She had to get the situation back under control, extract herself. There was still no one near enough to appeal to for help, if any would give it. "You have me at a disadvantage."

"I know certain people," he said with modest importance. "Rennika never said anything, but I put pieces together." He gave her a tiny nod of admiration.

She stared at him, nonplussed.

He leaned fractionally closer and murmured, though there was no one but her near enough to hear his words. "It's said you were responsible for the death of High King Huwen's magiel, Wenid of Holderford." He pressed his lips together, and his eyes glowed with wonder and respect. "Eight years ago. And the Ruby Prayer Stone has not been used against the people of Shangril since. Every man, woman, and child in the seven nations owes you more than they can say for that act of bravery." He gestured, pleasantly enough, toward the street from which she'd momentarily stepped.

Well. The tale was specific, and accurate as far as it went. Miach was an upriser; he must be. He knew who she was—at least, her rebel identity. It would be difficult for her to deny the story. Was he Colm's man? If so, he was a very good actor.

"Thank you, Sieur," she said by way of buying time to decide what to do. Guardedly, she accompanied him back into the street and to a reassuring scatter of oblivious pedestrians. If the rice house was public and crowded, she would be as safe as she could be, anywhere outside of Verlin's courtyard. And what choices did she have? She would not outrun him: he, with strong legs and knowledge of his own city. She was far from the draper's house and, in any case, would not want to lead him there.

No, she was best off to bluff until she knew more.

The rice house was close by and comfortably occupied with a handful of midafternoon diners scattered at a half-dozen tables. Miach—who'd given her no last name—chattered at her with easy small talk, selecting an out-of-the-way table.

Once their rice was served, he turned to her and spoke in a grim voice. "Are you here to help?" he whispered.

She stopped blowing on the steaming rice. Help?

For what? Military action? She'd been suspicious of his idle chatter and innocent questions. She was not about to answer this one. "Tell me your situation."

"I sent word by way of a wool trader I know to upriser contacts in Cataract Crag last summer." He cast a quick glance at the sparsely occupied tables. No patron was near enough to hear his low words. "You know him, I think. Yon Verlin."

The facts clicked into place. *This* was her source?

"I've heard nothing back. Now—better yet, midsummer—would have been time to strike. A third of this city would rise up, if called."

Miach was the reason she'd petitioned Colm to give her permission to approach Dwyn for men? *Yon* had brought his message to the uprisers. *Of course.*

"Have you come with a reply?" he pressed. "It's almost too late now. Winter comes early in the mountains. Heavy snow can block the roads anytime. Unless you're here to tell me the king-in-exile has men approaching as we speak."

"I wish I could give you reassurance." She dipped her chopsticks into the rice bowl.

He leaned closer, his voice barely audible. "There will never be a better time. Courtiers don't know whose authority is stronger, the Delarcan princess or the regent appointed by the High King. And he isn't much older than Hada. Huwen's too distant to give a decision—maybe even unaware."

Meg waved Miach's words aside. "I understand the politics." She put her bowl down. "I'm frustrated, Sieur, on your behalf."

"So, our pleas go . . . what? Unanswered?" He sat back in bafflement. "Raef makes himself out to be the Gramaret hero of the masses, but he sold himself out the instant Gramarye fell to the High King, pledging allegiance to the One God to save his skin. The Delarcan woman deserves the ax, but Raef merits it just as much."

"Believe me." Meg leaned in. "I did what I could."

"So, no help is coming." He snorted in disgust. "The fiend takes our right to pray to the Gods of our choice. Takes our masters' lands. Takes our magiels who bring us death tokens." He shook his head, inarticulate. "And the king-in-exile says nothing."

"I'm as outraged as you." She scooped the last of the rice from the bowl with a bit of bread. "But I'm no longer working with the uprisers."

Miach's lips parted as though he might speak, yet he held himself in check, studying her in surprise. "Why are you here?"

"I've come here to . . ." She considered. There was no reason to mention Janat. Or the Amber, which likely didn't exist. And even if it did, she had no reason to give this stranger her trust. "To live quietly. I'm as ill-served by rebellion as you."

CHAPTER 15

It was a game, watching the rats. Gweddien lolled against the brick wall, eyes slits, his limbs sprawled on the cold clay, his flesh almost as cold. The rats were thin enough to want a taste of him, but not so thin as to be incautious.

He'd survived. That was surprising.

The ghosts. He remembered the smudges, blurs crowding him. Ghosts attracted to death. Or maybe that had only been a figment, his inability to focus, to control any part of his heaving body. Disordered mind.

How long had he been here? That was a laugh.

Hada, clearly, had not sent for him. Perhaps he'd been given that whipping by his guard. He really didn't know.

A rat nosed along his boot. He wasn't sure what he'd do if he caught one. Wring its neck and throw it to its companions to watch the feast, he supposed. He was conscious enough, now, to be bored. And it wasn't like he was going to go anywhere higher than the First Heaven when he died; the sphere of Ranuat, Goddess of Murders and Thieves. That was, unless his executioner denied him his death token, in which case he'd become a ghost, which he probably deserved.

Now that he was awake, he might unlock his shackles. But he was too weak to go anywhere.

The shock of a kick racked his body, waking him from a stupor. "Get up." A jangle of rattling. Chains? No, iron keys on a ring. His guard looming over him. Two more, behind. Funny. Was he that dangerous?

Well, he was a magiel, so he supposed they thought so.

Steps. Wide, fitted, smooth; stone glazed with a slick verglas of crushed snow up to a terrace before imposing gilt doors. Gweddien knew these steps, these doors. Highglen Castle had been home, as a child.

Soldiers, one on either side of him and a step behind, held his chains, prodding him to follow the guard into the Great Hall.

Within, the bones of the building were the same: sweeping marble steps directly ahead to the throne room. Doors to either side of the steps leading to library, meeting rooms, the chancellor's offices, his father's workrooms. Father. Royal magiel of Gramarye's Chrysochola Prayer Stone, before the war.

But details differed. Unfamiliar tapestries, paintings, carpets. Curious servants and courtiers. Reminders everywhere that this was a royal seat of the Delarcans. A soldier poked him again, and he climbed the steps. But they didn't enter the court. Instead, they turned to the right, passed down a long corridor lit by bright sunshine through glass-paned windows opening onto the bailey. At length, they stopped at an office. Guards waiting there announced them.

Gweddien remembered the suite. It had been used by a tax collector and his scribe; a room Gweddien had barely visited. Now it was softened with hangings, carpets, and cushioned chairs. A scribe sat at a desk to one side, writing by the light of a single candelabra. A courtier dressed in silk stockings, breeches, and a velvet doublet stood by the fireplace, cold, now. Hada lounged on a couch.

She'd grown. Her blonde curls had darkened to a soft brown. The pudgy cheeks were sleek now, and the defiance in her gray eyes was hooded and direct; more confident. She pierced him with those eyes, searching for the truth in his claim. That he was Gweddien, Huwen's childhood playfellow and confidante.

He knew he looked nothing like his former self. He'd aged. Thinned. Was ill, shivering, ragged and unwashed.

She rose slowly from her place on the couch, eyes never leaving him. The courtier watched. "Leave us," she said, flicking her fingers at the young lord, scribe, and guards.

The courtier, by his expression, was loath to go, but he went with the others even so. The page remained, closing the door behind them.

"Gweddien?" Hada's voice was soft, wondering. She stepped out from behind the low table before her couch. "Is it you? Truly?"

He bowed his head.

She peered at him in the dim light, doubts flicking through her eyes. "I have enemies. Tell me. Is it you?"

"I can show you."

She gave a small nod.

He approached the candelabra. "I'll need darkness."

She fluttered a hand in assent, and he blew out all but one candle. Then, blocking this only source of light with his body, he turned to her. He found a calm space in his mind, an instant of stillness in time, allowing the depths of his magic to manifest itself. The shimmer of tiny moments of past and future that blurred his skin ceased. In their place, the velvet void of the Gods' firmament spangled with a glitter of infinitesimally small sparks of light. The Heavens, visible through his skin. He heard the page gasp, and he let the veil of time resume.

Wonder transformed Hada's countenance. "Oh, Gweddien." She reached a gentle finger to brush his cheek.

He let out a breath, weak.

"Come," she said, leading him to a chair by her couch. "Rest." She turned to the page. "Go to the kitchens. Bring meats and bread and wine."

Bread. Arcanian food.

"And, boy." Hada halted the servant with her voice. "You will not reveal what you've seen here today. To anyone."

The boy hastened a frightened bow and scurried from the room.

She sat on the end of her couch, leaning forward, taking him in with her eyes. "Oh, Gweddien, I am so sorry. I only just learned you were here."

He shook his head. "No need, Your Highness. Things have changed since we were children."

Her face darkened, but she made no excuses for the decrees of her father or her brother. The massacres. Gweddien's family. "What am I going to do with you?"

There were constraints, even for a princess. But Gweddien's mind was clear; clearer, he reflected, than it had been for . . . well. And if it had dulled from his abuses, that couldn't be helped now. "Use me," he answered. If he could persuade her to cast her protection around him, he might yet live.

Her eyes sharpened in the dim light.

"May I speak?"

"Do."

"It's said the governance of Highglen has come into question since your arrival."

She stilled. "Tell me what you've heard. And—I don't need sycophants. I have plenty who would tell me what they think I want to hear, who avoid my direct questions, and who try to manipulate me into doing what they think a royal woman should do. Marry, not govern."

Yes. The spoiled little Hada who chased after him and Huwen in Holderford all those years ago, railing at being shoved aside during fencing lessons or made to sit sidesaddle in skirts, had not changed all that much. "Even in prison I heard you came here without Huwen's knowledge or blessing." He leaned close in the dark, spoke in a low voice.

"Father left Gramarye to me."

"That you defied your regent, Raef Gramaret, by defining the country's borders with a gate on its most important highway."

"I never defied him. There is no need for a princess to ask permission of a regent."

"That you're too young to govern. You have no experience."

"Only nineteen years watching my father and my brother. Huwen botches everything he touches."

"And that you are a woman."

She took in a breath. This, she could not argue.

"All of this is superficial," he concluded. "Rumor and gossip. What the underlying truths are, I don't know, but I assume there are politics within politics."

She gave a slow, silent assent.

"I suspect you could use an ally. One without lands or wealth to lose. One who only gains when you gain. One with . . . a certain level of power."

A knock, and the boy arrived with servants bearing food and drink. Hada nodded, and they laid the dainties out on a low table before them, lit the candles, and withdrew.

She took a honeyed pastry and, drawing back on her divan, gestured for him to eat. "What's your proposal?"

"I can make you spells. Not just intoxicants and healing potions, but curses to help you control key individuals."

"So could any magiel I pick up in the lower town. It's against Huwen's decrees."

"Is it?"

She quirked her head.

"Magiels are vilified." He filled a bowl with steaming black rice. "Their homes and possessions are taken. They are imprisoned on false charges and forced into ghettos." Stuffed meats in sauce. Crisp autumn vegetables. "But Huwen has a magiel advisor. As does your brother Eamon."

She lifted her chin, studying him.

"I am a full magiel." He raised the bowl to his lips, blowing on the steam. "My magics are not of the same quality as those made by a ghetto wretch."

She waved this aside, a given.

"I am skilled enough to make subtle hexes to influence, poison, or slow your enemies without easy detection. I can also offer you personal wards. Again, delicate ones." He tasted the food. Ambrosia.

She nodded thoughtfully, and he knew she understood. Raef Gramaret.

"What do you want, Hada?" A risk, using her given name. "Whatever it is, I can help."

"Only what is mine," she said. "Rule of Gramarye."

"Under your brother's direction."

"Of course."

Gweddien poured himself a glass of wine.

"Huwen is hunting for you." She watched him curiously from her place on the divan.

Ah. So, there it was.

"There will be consequences to my harboring you in Gramarye."

His gaze flicked to hers. *My harboring you.* She didn't deflect the decision to the captain, blame him.

"I will consider your proposal."

Huwen Delarcan dismounted and strode into Coldridge Castle, Igua at his heels. Though the sun shone in a cloudless sky, the brisk, poplar-scented air had not yet warmed to the honey glow promised by the last days of summer. He'd toured his siege lines and found them solid. Uprisers would not retake the city. Not now.

He entered the throne room and took his seat in the ornate chair that served as a symbol of power in this hinterland court. Igua took his place, a step behind. A young lord-in-waiting, son of a Coldridge landowner, stood next to a messenger.

The emissary, likely older than Huwen by ten years, knelt, greasy hair falling over his eyes. He had a straggle of beard, a weathered face, and the lean look of a man who had pushed hard over difficult roads at some cost. His travel cloak was stained with mud and brambles.

"Have provisions been made for this man to eat, bathe, and rest?" Huwen asked the young lord.

"They have, Majesty." The courtier handed him a written report.

Huwen nodded. One thing his father had taught him before his untimely death was to care for his men. "Corporal," he addressed the soldier. "At your ease. Deliver your news." God grant the information did not concern the queen, or their newborn child.

The man rose slowly to his feet and spoke in a low, gravelly voice. "The magiel who escaped your prison here in Coldridge, two years ago, has been located."

Huwen's attention snapped to the messenger's face. *Gweddien. Friend.* Huwen steeled himself. He couldn't afford sentiment. The loss of this magiel had been a crippling blow to the Marigold scheme. "Where is he now?"

The man's eyes hooded, warning Huwen not to let his mind leap beyond the statement. "Arrested by troops from Gramarye."

Gramarye? Hada had authorized this?

"A request to release him to Arcanian custody was denied," the soldier continued. "Gramaryan defenses and strength exceeded our own on their land, so we withdrew. Your lieutenant dispatched this report." He nodded at the scroll in Huwen's hand.

Huwen tapped the roll on his knee, digesting the courier's words. He glanced at Igua, and his chancellor looked troubled. Huwen turned to the young lord and flicked his hand, dismissing the messenger. "See that this man is looked after."

The messenger bowed and followed the courtier from the court.

"Leave us," Huwen commanded his other attendants. "I will speak with Igua alone."

The servants and courtiers bowed perfunctorily and left. Igua, now in his mid-thirties, was a stooped man, pale from much writing by candlelight. Second cousin to an influential Elsen duke, with extensive family wealth from coal and iron mines, he'd never been a warrior. Huwen's father had begun cultivating Igua as a youth, apprenticing him in Treasury and Law. Though Igua was only a few years older than him—and though Huwen personally disliked him—he depended on his chancellor's sharp mind, more so than even the advice of his seasoned advisers.

Huwen pushed himself restlessly from his chair, catching Igua's eye as he drifted to a table laden with breakfast meats. God, he wished he was home in Holderford, with Ychelle. Beautiful, unquestioning, Ychelle. But Coldridge had to be well secured before he could consider going home. "Well?"

"He took the south road, through Ubica and Grassy Bluff to get here," Igua said, following him. "Managed the ride in ten days."

Through Midell, Eamon's stronghold. "Credit to him." Huwen slumped into a chair at the table. "And to the lieutenant who sent him. He saw the importance of the message."

"The lieutenant had seen the drawing of Gweddien's likeness."

Huwen nodded reflectively. This was all due to the machine he'd seen in Cataract Crag three years ago, when he visited his younger brother, Jace, now ruler of Pagoras. Father's third son was loyal enough, though he lacked ambition. But he certainly had a talent for making money.

Igua sat as well, perusing the breads and fruits and cheeses. "Your printing press from Aadi was a good investment."

Jace had shown him the contraption, hauled—in pieces—from the valley of the foreigners. At first, Huwen thought such a thing would be too expensive for its utility. But after seeing what Aadian steam and black powder could do, Huwen was careful not to dismiss it out of hand. Now, he was glad he hadn't. Intaglio prints of the sketch of Gweddien taken from life had been copied and distributed widely.

Huwen hunched back in his chair, rubbing his thumbs on its arms, too agitated to eat. "Your analysis?"

Igua sat back as well. "It is impossible to see this act as anything other than a direct challenge to your authority as High King."

Treason. Hada had left Holderford without permission while he was embroiled in battle in Coldridge. Gramarye, a politically unimportant backwater but a good source of leather and wool for trade to Aadi, was governed by a regent—a local man with ties to the country, but loyal. Hada's move smacked of duplicity, though technically, the country was hers—to be ruled under his authority, of course. "Arresting and imprisoning the magiel is not precisely treason. It's what she's supposed to do."

"Failing to turn him over to you when requested *is*."

Huwen drew in a long breath. So was refusal to turn over the Ruby Prayer Stone, as Eamon had done. Continued to do. So, for that matter, was growing fat on high-priced spices and silks and coveted new technologies, as Jace was doing, while Huwen's armies stretched to their limits combatting one uprising after another. "Given our resources and the issues we face, I'm not clear that this . . . misunderstanding . . . is our first concern."

"Send a diplomat, then." Igua said. "Clear up any misunderstanding and ask plainly for the magiel to be delivered. The Marigold scheme is crippled without him. This summer you lost—what?—four mothers, fifteen children? Four of them promising exceptional ability?"

"We recovered two mothers and four children. We're hunting down the rest."

"The women are no use without a trueborn magiel to sire children on them."

Huwen set his lips in a line and breathed out his disgust, pouring himself a glass of ale. His father's scheme—Wenid's scheme—was— He shook his head.

He'd seen Gweddien once—only once—after his incarceration at Coldridge. He wasn't the same. His wit, gone. His tall, firm body, sloppy. His grin silly. But the magiel had seen through his magical shackles, even then, and looked at him. Helpless. Despairing. Huwen had made a point never to see him again. "The plan is beyond barbaric."

Igua bit into an apple. "And yet, you need it."

Huwen waved a hand and drank his chalice back.

"When you get the Ruby, you'll need a magiel to wield it with you."

Huwen slapped the mug onto the table. "We'll never get the Ruby. Eamon will never give it up. He's crippled himself, can't live without it."

"The Ruby's *your* birthright."

Huwen shot Igua a black look. "I keep you on as chancellor for your advice, Igua. Unless you can come up with a *way* to obtain the Ruby, telling me why I need it is of no help. The Ruby protects my brother and the entire kingdom of Midell. Our armies, even with cannons, have proved they can't stand against his magic. Our assassins can't penetrate his defenses. He must decide he wants to give me the Ruby. He can't be compelled."

Igua leaned forward across the table. "Now. Think of this. Hada bears royal blood. She has a full-blood magiel. What happens if she gets the Ruby?"

Huwen snorted a mirthless laugh. "Eamon is giving that prayer stone to no one."

Igua lifted a brow.

A possibility tumbled. "You mean they might work together?"

Igua gave a half-shrug. "Eamon's magiel is only part-blooded."

"No." Huwen shook his head. "Eamon would never share. Anything."

Igua continued to hold him with his stare.

But. What if?

CHAPTER 16

Rennika banked the fire and snuggled onto her small raised bed, pulling the down quilt up to her chin. She loved the opportunities to stay overnight at the dyeing compound in the mountains, in the silence of the wind and the breath of the fire, with only the stableman across the bailey and his beloved horses.

Today, she'd made dyes for the fabrics they would use for the contract signing's formal clothing. No one questioned her need to sleep at the compound at such times. Quennell had done the same. And a dyer's art was mysterious. Her results rivaled, even exceeded, dyes from anywhere else in Gramarye.

Alone in this small mountain hut, she didn't mind living other parts of her life. She was safe, and if she spent the night awake trudging as a refugee or playing in her mother's garden or glimpsing cryptic bits of a quiet country life—or the odd moment of some inexplicable future event—she didn't mind.

For a long time, she floated in her own thoughts, listening to the snow-muted night, breathing in the scent of woodsmoke and leather oils, until she finally drifted into sleep.

She was standing in a dark stable, warm with the dregs of high summer heat. A candle ensconced over a stall cast a warm light on her sisters cooing and laughing and weeping for the joy of a fresh-born colt, wobbling on unsure legs, nuzzling its dam for milk. Gods, she remembered this night. Fleeing the dangers of overstaying their home in Silvermeadow, the last night the three of them would be together before the battle of Coldridge.

Meg touched Janat's arm, and Janat turned. "Rennika?" she asked in wonder.

Rennika had used magic that night to help the mare birth her colt. She'd been, maybe, twelve at the time.

"When are you from?" Janat asked.

Gods, they were so young. They knew nothing of what would befall them. "You're strong," she said to Janat, her eyes still bright and clear. "Remember," she said to both of them. "You're sisters. Hold on to that."

"What do we need to know?" Janat persisted.

"Cherish each other." Her moment with them would be gone abruptly. "Remember tonight." It was all she could think of to say. "Remember Kandenton." All she could think of, to keep them safe. "Remember this gift."

And then she was gone.

A smell. Somewhere near a fragrant poplar forest. The drip, drip, drip of rain beyond the open doorway of a wooden shack. She sat on a hard earth floor, Meg cross-legged beside her. She remembered this day, this past. *An array of herbs, insect parts, and other ingredients were arranged on a cloth before them, and Meg held a piece of parchment up to the thin light.*

"It says, grind the sorrel in a mortar until it's sore." Meg giggled and nudged her.

Rennika's cheeks ached, as if she'd laughed too hard for too long. "It does not say that! Let me see."

Meg held the recipe up and away from her, taunting, and laughed all the harder.

Sieura Barcley had been teaching them magic. Rennika had purchased the precious, imported silkworm cocoon with money she'd earned begging. And thieving.

The image flickered—

Pain cracked against her cheek.

She lay on a feather bed, she didn't know where, but she'd lived a snippet of this future before. The fresh bruise throbbed, and a furious nobleman sat astride her, gripping her upper arms, her elaborate robe torn. Her heart beat against her ribs like a trapped falcon and sweat drenched her armpits and back. She struggled against his strength.

A bad one. If only she could wrench herself out of it. But, no. A few moments, and it would end—

But not yet. She cast about the candlelit chamber paneled with gold and amber, strewn with brilliant cushions, glass panes in the inky windows. Her hair had fallen, disheveled, over her face. Her arms and legs ached with more than one injury, and liquid streamed down her face from a tender nose. She struggled to get out, get away—

Gods, what future would bring her to a nobleman's bed? She tried to see his face in the dark.

And the moment passed.

⚜

Tyg rushed, pink-faced and cloak flying, into the laundry. "Janat!"

Janat blinked from her reverie. A fancy of a sunny summer day, of slipping away from Highglen with Gweddien. Basking by a creek in a high mountain glen with a drink of wine. And glim.

The girl hopped on one foot. "Come quick! Grandmamma wants you."

Janat smiled at the girl, for whom everything seemed to demand a response immediately, and let her long wooden paddle rest in the simmering clothing. She pulled her cloak from its peg and crunched behind the child to the courtyard. The day was brilliant, if cold. Snow which had not melted squeaked under foot. With only two days remaining before the signing of the contract, likely whatever Sieura Verlin wanted her for was urgent.

Ide's family, tailors all, had been sewing up a flurry of new dresses for all and sundry, and at least two of Yon's sisters were with them, hemming and having last fittings. Yon and his father were at the wine merchant's, selecting the wines for the meal. Rennika was at her workshop in the country, dyeing decorative ribbons. Meg had eschewed breakfast and gone out. Just out, no explanation given. Janat, idly watching the laundry, was undoubtedly the least busy person in the household.

She followed Tyg to the kitchen, then hovered outside in the snow. Half a dozen neighbors were helping with various preparations for the banquet, all up to their elbows in flour or boiling jars or chopping vegetables. It would not do for Janat to be seen.

Sieura Verlin emerged into the sunshine. "The jam for our dessert is not nearly sweet enough, and it's not setting properly." The heavy woman led the way back to the main building that housed the family living quarters and shop, where her son-in-law was examining skeins of spun wool brought on offer from a family of herders. She thrust Janat quickly into her office. "Do you know what sugar is?"

"I tasted it, once." In Cataract Crag, a slice of pear dipped in a sugar sauce. It had tingled her tongue like ambrosia, and was frightfully expensive, coming as it did from Aadi-of-the-Valley.

Sieura Verlin produced a purse. "Ide tried to buy some at market yesterday, but the vendor had none. We thought we could get away without it, but—" Sieura Verlin counted a large number of coins into a second pouch. "We need it now. Today, for the jam. I'm not sure where in Highglen you might find some. You might have to go to the lower town."

Sieura Verlin was sending her out of the quadrangle? In broad daylight? To . . . trade on the black market?

"Leave here by way of the servants' gate and be discreet. If you are caught with this money, we'll have to say it was stolen. You understand."

Janat eyed her. This was dangerous. Her heart thumped in anticipation. An intrigue, a game of wits. Gods, *freedom*.

"I've heard there are free traders," Sieura Verlin said in a low voice, "who deal in more exotic goods. For a price." She gave Janat a look that suggested a magiel might be acquainted with shadier characters.

Perhaps she should feel insulted. And perhaps, Sieura Verlin would not be unhappy to have one of her inconvenient guests disappear, either.

Still, Janat felt alive.

The matron pushed the two pouches into Janat's hands. "Haggle if you can. Only open the second purse if you must. Sieur Verlin did not build his position by being overly free with his money. But we must have a pound of sugar, or the desserts will not be fit to serve."

Janat gave a short nod. She'd been a refugee, pickpurse, and dealer in charms long enough to understand the subtleties of navigating a bargain, and the sorts of rogues who might deal in hard-to-obtain items. And, to be released from the mind-numbing tedium of the laundry . . . to actually contribute something necessary to the household . . . She smiled in appreciation of the errand.

Sieura Verlin came close then. "And you needn't tell anyone. My son. Anyone."

Janat was loath to question her. But clarity seemed abruptly critical. ". . . that you sent . . . me?"

"That, or what I sent you for."

Sugar.

"Or how much."

And Janat understood.

Sieura Verlin grasped her hand on the pouch a moment longer. "There are over a hundred gultra in the two purses."

Janat returned her hard look. "I understand." If there was no good accounting for the money, she—and Meg—would be held to reckoning.

If Ide, the tailor's daughter, could not find sugar at any of the markets in the upper town, Janat knew better than to risk showing her hard-to-perceive skin here. Raising her hood with gloved hands against the cold—and unfriendly eyes—she crossed the river, making her way down to the narrow streets of the lower town. Here, shops spilled from the lanes into tiny plazas crammed with farmers' and guildsmen's flimsy booths.

Twice, Janat spotted soldiers. The hubris that made the Delarcans, with their big, impersonal armies, decree that their men should dress identically in distinct, colorful uniforms, made spotting them easy. Each time, she turned down other streets, whiling her way back after a comfortable length of time.

Janat let herself wander, seeking the free traders, whose only taxes were paid to highwaymen prowling the countryside. They would be found in alleys where games of dice or cups enticed the idle; where vagrants sat, blue and glassy-eyed, or roamed, agitated and seeking; where watchers marked the clientele to let pass unmolested, to follow, or to approach. Out-of-work spinners, displaced by the thread factory, imbibed cheap gin from the distillery. She found a likely corner and drifted to one side to become one of the watchers.

A woman with a brazier cried the virtues of her skewers of dried yak meat—more likely rat, at that price—her voice puffing white into the air. Another, conveniently located next to a potter with small bowls for purchase, heated wild rice. A third told fortunes with stacks of illustrated cards. Here the wares ran to the cheap and practical, though it was still possible to buy marigold-scented soaps, incense for the shrine, and exorbitant bottles of Aadian wine.

A hawker of lewd drawings at the mouth of the lane did a good business, and a man with a cask of Teshian whiskey sat on a stool in front of a leather man's stall discounting his samples for anyone who bought whips. A fully cloaked woman in a doorway undulated to flute music, tempting passersby to enter and sample whatever delights awaited inside.

During a lull in the flow of customers, the whiskey seller poured an aromatic dram and held out the small cup to her. "Only five chetra. Keeps back the cold."

Janat's mouth dried, but she shook her head, her hood still pulled far forward. She was beginning to shiver.

"Selling, then? Not buying?" he asked. The calculations in his eyes shifted as his gaze landed on her face. He'd seen the shimmer of her skin.

"Buying," she said. "But nothing so common."

The whiskey man set the dram aside. "All the way from Teshe. Good highland whiskey, better than Gramaryan gin. Be hard to get, once snow closes the roads."

She lifted a shoulder, and he held out the glass to a pair making their way down from the cheese shop.

"More unusual than whiskey from Teshe?" A child she hadn't noticed—a boy too young for the eyes he used to appraise her—squatted on the dirty ice at her side, repeatedly catching a ring on a stick. He was not richly dressed, but the cloth of his small cloak was thick. "Perhaps you want something curious from Aadi?"

She dismissed him with a tiny frown, then went back to watching for a likely trader.

"Silk? Pepper? Ganja?" he asked, never missing his catch.

Ganja. It had been so long since she'd breathed in the calming, dizzying vapors. But— "Sugar," she said. Sugar came from Aadi.

"My father has sugar." Still, the boy, a good-looking worldling with a tousle of brown curls and an engaging smile under a freckled nose, clacked repeatedly with his game. The ties on his cloak were loose, and she saw his soft inner collar. He wore a death token. Most children, these days, had none.

Janat cast a quick glance into the street. Another knot of shoppers ambled past the leather seller's, one hanging back to talk to the whiskey merchant. The dancer had disappeared. No one close enough to overhear. "Where's your master?"

The boy caught his ring and tossed it again, nodding down the lane. "Not far. He has a shop. Below the chandler's."

The sky was still bright, but it was well past midday. Perhaps three chimes. Sieura Verlin would want her back. "Very well."

The boy caught his ring and trotted off, surefooted on the slick frozen ground. "My father has lots of strange things."

Janat did not reply. Her business was her own.

"Spell books."

He'd seen her wavering skin beneath her hood, then.

He dodged a flock of sheep and darted around a corner, waiting for her as she followed. "Animal parts. Herbs. Amulets. Other things."

Potions? The boy was too wily to say so. "Is your father an apothecary?"

"No." He turned and led her through a dark passageway that steepened to form a stair opening out into a small courtyard with a well. A stable stood along one side and a rice shop on the far corner. A handful of artisans and free traders had tables and booths in the center, and children and dogs played among them.

A wooden sign swung above the chandler's shop, and the boy entered a door next to it, unmarked. Abrupt steps led down to a cramped room lined with shelves, lit by a single small opening, high up, occluded from time to time by the shadows of pedestrians' feet. A single candle, and the glow of coals on a small hearth, augmented the dim light.

"I'll get my father," the boy said, scampering behind a table and through a curtained arch.

Janat lowered her hood. Despite the open window, the room was warm enough. As promised, the shelves were crammed with jars of murky liquid containing uncertain beasts that might have been lizards or lampreys, fingers or fetuses. Pestles, powders, vials, some labeled, some not; dried herbs, well-worn books and scrolls, drawings, diagrams, maps, rat skulls, dolls, amulets, jewelry, and other more dubious objects spilled onto the rush-strewn floor and lined small tables. Intermixed with spell ingredients were various foods, bits of clothing, boots. The place looked like the lifetime amalgamations of a dozen disorganized village magiels.

"All very useful for magiel magic." A man, perhaps a few years older than Janat, stood in the arch, the hanging pushed aside. He was well dressed in a combination of traditional robe and Aadian-style vest and breeches, with trimmed hair and beard. His brow was high and wide in a well-fed face, and his eyes were pale as ice. He spoke in a refined accent, slightly Arcanian, and smiled disarmingly.

Well. No need for pretense. He knew she was a magiel.

He came out from behind the clutter of tables and shelves and held out his hand. "Sieura."

Surprised, she touched his fingertips. Few worldlings offered such social niceties to magiels these days. "Sieur."

"You may call me Yaquob." A tiny frown creased his brow momentarily, as if arrested by a flash of vague recognition, though she was sure she had never seen him before. She'd traveled many places with Meg and the uprisers, and she had to admit, she didn't remember every man she'd met. But, no. In this dim light, she saw nothing familiar in his features.

"Please. Be at ease. If I cared to torment village magiels, I'd have no customers."

She eyed him, then relaxed, turning back to the shelves. "You're not a magiel. Do you keep these herbs to work worldling magic?" She was being polite. For a worldling to follow recipes in a spell book was hardly magic.

"No." An amused smile spread across his face. "I'll tell you truly, I barely know what each item is."

She cocked her head at him.

He rearranged a vial or two, lining them for better visibility. "I've only been in this shop a few days, won't likely stay more than a week or two. Have to get down to the valley before the snow gets too deep for my cart."

"You are a trader in . . . curios?"

Yaquob sighed. "I confess, I am a rascal. War, Sieura, is not good for business. I used to trade in fine wines." He shook his head. "Stock smashed, stolen, or appropriated by the army. Or by uprisers. I've found a better niche. High King Huwen's decree against magiels."

She did not follow.

He leaned closer. "When soldiers find a magiel and arrest him, I . . . acquire . . . his inventory."

Indignation heated her cheeks.

"Better it be sold to someone who can use it than smashed by soldiers or looters. You get a bargain." He pulled a bottle of fine white powder from the shelf and uncorked it. "To be honest, I hardly know what to charge." He took a sniff, then blinked and straightened. "Whatever this is, it's potent."

A waft of vitality, like a bracing spring air, touched her. A powdered form of Heartspeed? By Kyaju, what she would give for just a taste.

No. She couldn't. She wouldn't. She shoved the thought back.

He capped the vial and replaced it on the shelf, eyes sparkling with animation. "I must remember to charge a good price for that one."

The acquisitions of multiple magiels. Could he have glim? Again, she pushed the thought back. "My mistress sent me to buy sugar. Two pounds, if you have it."

"Ah, yes. Raoul told me." He grinned and called out. "Raoul! Bring two pounds of sugar." He turned back to her and his eyes danced over her features. Did he flirt? "All the way from Aadi. They charge a fortune. I can't part with it for less than a hundred and fifty gultra."

"I, myself, have just come up from Cataract Crag." She hadn't bought sugar there and had no idea of its price. But the day just became interesting. "I could get this much for forty gultra."

His lips quirked in amusement. "Then you should've brought some with you. But," he held up a hand against her leaving, "I could spare two pounds for you, for . . . a hundred and twenty."

"My mistress allowed me to go as high as seventy." Ranuat, she wanted to grin, but she schooled her face.

"There is none to be had in the upper districts," he argued. "You have no choice but to purchase in the lower town. One hundred, and I make no profit."

At this statement, she could not keep the grin from her face. "My mistress would never let me carry so much money to this part of the city. I'll have to find another free trader." She turned to leave.

Yaquob put a hand on her arm. "Ninety, then, and a promise to come back and purchase a magiel powder."

She hesitated, then. "Done."

But she would not be back.

CHAPTER 17

Hada stood at the glass-paned doors to the balcony of her receiving room, her gaze soaring past the distant blue peaks rimming Gramarye's upper valley, to the indigo of encroaching night. Days were getting shorter.

She'd arranged for a casual dinner, here in her suite, and the small table next to her was set for two. Her page had just refilled her glass when an attendant reported Gweddien's arrival. She smiled. "Bid him enter."

The transformation made by a bath, shave, and proper clothing led her gaze to linger on him. "You look almost human." She skewed her lips. "Or magiel, should I say?"

He inclined his head with a rakish grin. "I thank you for the gifts. But particularly for the improved lodging."

"You look more rested." She nodded to the page, and the boy poured a glass of wine for her guest.

Gweddien joined her at the window and lifted his glass to her, drinking deeply. "And, my proposal?"

To the point. She liked that.

Yes. She found herself nodding softly to him. This could work.

She indicated the table, and the two of them sat as her page lit the candles, then withdrew to the shadows. She pushed a small package across the table to him. "Your freedom will be restricted to this floor and this wing of the keep. There's no need for others, especially the Regent, to know I consult a magiel. The fewer people who see you, the better."

He nodded his understanding and unwrapped the paper. "A gift?"

Not exactly. "A new collar for your death token. You will wear it as long as you are in my service."

He held up the golden collar and looked at her sharply. A thin golden chain hung from it.

Symbolic, but she needed him—and anyone who saw him in the castle—to understand his position. "Your title will be Secretary, but you will attend on me as a chancellor does."

"Handle everything." He removed his collar and transferred his death token to its new holder.

She suppressed a smile at his audacity. "Not quite. To begin, I want my listeners to report to you. I prefer some small distance from them, and you can formulate advice based on unfiltered information."

He refreshed her glass, sending the page to the shadows. "Where do we stand at the moment?"

"I'm rethinking my strategy." Her left hand fisted on the table and she studied its tension. "When I arrived, I began reordering the ministries for more logical and efficient operation. But there's been resistance. No outright defiance, but slow response and misinterpretation. I can see now, some of the bureaucrats either think I lack competence or assume my brother will not legitimize my crown."

"Betting on Raef."

She drank. "Just so."

He nodded, studying his glass.

"My listeners tell me Raef is buying the support of the landholders. Not that they matter, ultimately—"

"They matter."

She shot him a look.

Gweddien caressed the stem of his glass. "Everything matters. The rich, the traders. Rebel factions. Even the poor. Even the magiels." He leaned forward. "You may have the One God and the law on your side. Even your own household guards. Maybe other things. But until you are crowned, Raef has legitimization from Huwen. And he has the army."

"We're not talking civil war." Her new adviser's mind leapt too far.

"No? Where will you stop, then, if your politicking is ineffective?"

She stared at him. "Not civil war."

He reached across the table and grasped her hand where it rested on the stem of her wineglass. He pulled it toward himself and topped up her glass. "Then you need to take into account every faction. Large or small. *Ensure* events cascade your way."

She smiled. He was smart. She liked that, too.

He lifted his glass, drained it, and, emptying the bottle, signaled the page. "Bring whatever sustenance my queen has arranged," he said, turning back to her. "And another bottle of wine. We have work to do."

Hada laughed. She'd chosen well.

※

Meg trudged up the stairs to Rennika's apartment, drying her hands on her apron, and flopped into the armchair. Janat and Rennika sat at the small table by the brazier, bent over mounds of fabric as they embroidered the Verlin family's dresses, talking idly.

The distraction of the celebration had been a boon to Meg. She had no trouble slipping away, unnoticed, each evening, once work was done. But the locals were a tight-lipped bunch, and it would take time to gain their confidence.

The delay was frustrating. Why wouldn't a free trader want to announce he was open for business?

Rennika held up a child's skirt. "Want to do Tyg's ribbons, Meg?" she asked. "All the women are going to wear skirts with bodices, like they do in Aadi."

Meg took the fabric. Neither Rennika nor Sieura Verlin—none of them—actually knew the fashion in Aadi, and Meg certainly didn't care, but she could help out. She pulled a length of thread from a bobbin and bit it off. She was too tired and too discouraged to go back to the lower town tonight. Besides, the wind had picked up outside, and the air was bitter.

"So," Janat said in a lull in the conversation, grinning at them both as though she'd been waiting for the moment to speak. "Shall I tell you what I did today?"

Laundry. At least, that was what she'd set out to do this morning.

"Sieura Verlin sent me out to buy sugar."

Meg's attention snapped up.

"She gave me a purse. Over a hundred gultra."

Rennika shot a glance at Meg.

"There were no merchants in the upper town with sugar. I finally found one on the other side of the river. I talked him down from a hundred and fifty gultra to ninety. For *two* pounds." Janat shifted her fabric. "Sieura Verlin was thrilled."

"Two pounds. That's a lot." Rennika bit a thread. "Janat, maybe you should know. Sieur Verlin doesn't tell people, but he usually won't let anyone in the house buy more than a few ounces."

"Well, it's for the desserts." Janat sat back on her chair. "You know, I don't remember the last time I just walked down a street by myself. Must have been—" She blushed a little and flashed a fleeting look at Meg. Then, reconsidering, she let her hands fall into her lap and let her eyes linger on Meg. "I'm . . . all right," she said softly.

Rennika's eyes lingered on the two of them for a moment, then returned to her sewing as if she'd intruded on something personal.

Meg gave Janat a nod and smile. *She was*, Meg reflected, recognizing in herself a small sense of cautious relief. Janat was all right.

Janat returned her smile, took a deep breath, and went back to work, chattering on to Rennika.

Janat *was* doing well. Her eyes were brighter, she seemed to have more energy, to be able to laugh, to notice others besides herself. Her natural loveliness shone through. Meg should be happy for her. *Was* happy for her.

And . . . Meg had deferred her own wishes to help Janat. So perhaps, now, Meg wouldn't be as constrained to sit idly by as the world moved without her.

Not that she would do anything. No, she'd promised herself.

But Sieur Vellefair had told her—according to Hada's spy—Huwen's armies had retaken Coldridge from the uprisers. After only a few weeks' possession. *And* Glenfast had fallen to the king of Elsen. If this was true, it was the end to the dreams of those who would see the High King release his iron grip on the seven nations. An end to their cause.

But, was it true? Or did Vellefair simply feed her unconfirmable lies to bilk her out of potions?

If the uprisers had been routed, the strategic importance of Highglen was even more critical.

If . . .

. . . something Rennika had said . . .

"Rennika."

Her sister lifted her head.

"Did you say your work sometimes takes you to Hada's castle?"

"Sometimes. Not routinely. Why?"

What had Vellefair said? The spy had reported to Hada. It would have been five days ago? Six? Would he still be at the castle?

"Meg?"

Meg put her sewing into her lap and spoke in a low voice, aware that voices traveled between floors. But sounds of the family singing now drifted up from below, so the music would mask her words. "Can you . . . keep your ears open. While you're there?"

Rennika looked from Meg to Janat.

Janat turned to her warily. "Meg? Are there upriser plots in Highglen?"

"Nothing like that." By Ranuat, one query and Janat thought she'd abandoned her. "I heard a rumor that Coldridge fell to King Huwen. I just want to know if it's true."

"Coldridge?" Janat asked, puzzled. "So soon? The uprisers just took it this summer."

"And Glenfast."

Janat drew quiet. They'd lived in Glenfast for three years. They had friends there.

Rennika buried herself in her embroidery.

"Rennika?"

"I'm no good at that kind of thing, Meg."

Meg rolled her eyes. "As I recall, you were the best pickpocket of the three of us when we were on the run."

"A hundred years ago," Rennika quipped.

Meg bit her lip. Gods, the atrocities the Delarcans performed. Breeding *magiels*, for Ranuat's sake. Rennika had no idea. None. Meg shook off her disgust. "It's only—"

"That's your calling, Meg. Not Rennika's," Janat said. "And you told me you'd stopped."

The lawful ruler of Gramarye, Lord Regent Raef Gramaret, had come down to Verlin's house, *himself*, with a coterie of retainers, to perform the signing ceremony. The regent prided himself on being one of the people. Janat was impressed.

And, despite the panic of preparation, the house and shop were clean and decked with fragrant juniper boughs and mistletoe. The Verlin family and all the esteemed guests—including a number of aristocrats, guild masters, and wealthy landowners—were resplendent in quickly finalized garments. The food was rich, varied, and plentiful. Especially, Janat was delighted to note, the desserts.

More people than Janat thought possible crammed themselves into the house's various rooms and spilled into the shop below the Verlins' living quarters, despite being unable to directly view the ceremony from there. Janat listened to the chatter, out of sight at the top of the attic stairs, along with the three youngest Verlin children.

Rennika had planned to join her, but Tyg whisked Rennika off to stand in some place of honor at the last minute. The tenor, flautist, and cithren player were exquisite, and the Holder's words of binding were strong and clear. Then, there was an explosion of applause, a drummer and two singers joined the musicians, and food and wine flowed. When Lord Gramaret left in the middle of the evening, the more illustrious guests departed as well, but dancing swept the rest of the assembly away into the candle-lit dark of night.

The only flaw in the day came, Tyg told Janat later, when Sieura Verlin found out a trader's boy had stolen a purse of money. Yon'd had to have the boy and his master, protesting, ejected, and the purse was not recovered. Janat was glad she'd been able to account for the vast sum of money the matron had entrusted to her.

Janat sat on a cushion on the stair just below Rennika's attic, with a cup of mulled cider Tyg had brought her, listening to the musicians. She wanted another cup, but there were too many people who might see her magiel skin if she crept down the stairs. Maybe in the night, when they were gone, if she couldn't sleep. Below her, the last guests, unwilling to break the enchantment of the night, joined in soft ballads. The faint breathing of the three youngest daughters sleeping on makeshift pallets in Rennika's gathering room—the children's bedroom had been reassigned to a cousin's family from Zellora—was barely audible. Meg had made herself scarce, even before the ceremony began, and had not yet returned. Rennika, Janat suspected, was one of the singers below.

A quiet melancholy had crept up on Janat during the ceremony, as she realized the whirl of excitement of the past two weeks was about to come to an end. Winter would set in with dark days, cold, and the imprisonment of snow. She'd spent the last ten years in the lower countries of Elsen and Teshe where winters were deep but travel was not impossible. Minstrels came, and some free traders. The uprisers went on a few raids, returning with food or goods or stories.

No, winter in Gramarye would be much more like the winters of her childhood in the high country of Orumon. She remembered them. Dull, long, and frigid. And she had been not only privileged, living as she did in King Ean's castle, but she'd had tutors to entertain her. Here, she looked forward to laundry and house cleaning and cooking. Meg didn't even want her working on the Dream Incense they made for Sieur Verlin.

If only she could ease the time. A little Dream Incense for herself would not go amiss. Even an occasional glass of ale.

Or, if there were glim. But there wasn't.

No. She had to put such thoughts from her mind. Thoughts of glim brought with them thoughts of Wenid. His corruption. Her corruption.

She shook herself, abruptly aware her face was wet. Sitting here, alone in the dark, was the worst thing for her right now. The children didn't need her. She could slip down, join the singers, if she stayed in the shadows. Couldn't she? Perhaps take a glass of wine—just one—

Footsteps on the stair, flicker of candlelight approaching.

She turned away, found a handkerchief and swiped at her eyes, then blew her nose.

"Janat? There you are." It was Rennika. She sounded tired.

"I was just looking for a shawl." Janat turned toward the darkened bedrooms in Rennika's suite. "I thought I might come down and join you."

Rennika set the candle on the table and slumped into the easy chair. "Most of them are going home. I think there are only two or three left." She rubbed her forehead between her eyes. "You can take my shawl if you're cold. It's in my room on the bed."

Janat felt a chill, just then, as though her excuse to turn away had made her realize she was cool. She stepped around the sleeping girls and into Rennika's room to dab at her eyes one last time and find the shawl.

It wasn't on the bed but had slipped to the floor next to a small table. A drawer stood ajar and the corner of a small leather purse protruded. She pushed the bag into the drawer and, fetching the mantle, returned to wrap herself and join Rennika next to the warmth and soft music drifting up the stairs.

Rennika's finger traced the bowl of the candlestick absently. "Well," she said softly, "it's done."

"Everyone seems happy." Janat sat in the other chair next to the brazier.

Rennika's gaze flicked to the sleeping girls, all three dead with exhaustion. "Maybe." She slipped back into thoughtfulness. "The family's new status. It will change things."

"Has Sieur Verlin confirmed you as master?"

"Not yet." She dipped her finger in a bit of melted wax. "He says he's working on it." She stared intently at the hot film on her skin. "There's pressure from the dyers' guild."

"Do they have the power to deny you?"

Rennika lifted her head. "They couldn't do anything if Lord Raef decreed my status."

"And would he do that?"

Rennika shrugged. "He might. If I was truly a part of the family. Part of the contract."

"What do you mean?"

"If I was married to Yon."

Janat peered at her sister's face, lit in warm tones against the dark. "You'd marry, just for your situation?"

Rennika rubbed at the slick wax on her finger. "We're lovers."

Really? Her little sister? Not so little.

"It's not that, Janat." Rennika cleaned her finger on the edge of the candle holder. "I'm sure Verlin knows about us, and likely Sieura Verlin. It can hardly be a secret after all this time." She lifted her head. "I don't think Yon has asked him."

"For you."

Rennika's eyes closed in frustrated confirmation.

"Maybe he doesn't—"

Rennika's eyes snapped open in a glare.

"I mean . . ." Janat shrugged. "Love doesn't last, Rennika."

Her sister's face stiffened.

"Lots of men, rebels, admired me. That first year after the battle at Coldridge? You remember?"

Rennika managed a tight nod. "On Dwyn's farm."

"They thought I was pretty, and I was a strong magiel, helped with uprisings. I was fun. But it didn't last."

Rennika swallowed, her nose reddening.

"I know you think your situation is different, and in some ways it is, but . . ." Janat wasn't sure what words to use to help her sister. "You can't rely on others. You have to be able to take care of yourself."

"I have a trade."

That wasn't what Janat meant.

"It's not for money or security." Rennika hunched closer to the brazier. "And I don't care what Meg says about prayer and serving the people. I want to be married." She gestured at the space around them. "I'm smart enough. Pleasant enough. I could be a good wife."

Janat peered at her in the dark of the candle flame. "But do you love him?"

"*Yes.*"

One of the girls shifted in her sleep, and Janat sat back in her chair, letting the silence of the crackling brazier envelop them. The singing below had stopped, and the house made only the sounds of wind and scurrying rats that buildings always made.

"Did I make the wrong choices, Janat?" Rennika asked softly from the darkness. "Mama made me the strongest of the three of us. She wanted me to be magiel of the Amber, not Meg." Rennika picked at the bits of dried wax that still clung to her finger, letting the flakes fall to the floor.

"It doesn't matter. The Amber's gone."

"But should I have done as Meg said? Forget what I wanted and stayed with the uprisers?" Her sister clasped her hands in her lap. "Given myself for the people?"

Janat shook her head slowly. "It doesn't matter."

Rennika was silent for a long moment. The coals on the brazier flickered and sighed. "It might," Rennika said slowly. "Meg wants something. She wants me to spy for her."

"Meg's obsessed. It's not your concern."

Again, Rennika poked a drip of wax on the side of the candle. The stub had almost burnt down. "But what if Meg is right? If Mama was right? I should be thinking of more than just myself. Thinking of all the people with no death tokens, who'll never go to Heaven."

Janat couldn't answer this question. One could only survive. Janat touched her own death token.

And ease the long, long wait until death. However, one could.

CHAPTER 18

As he was accepting a glass flute of wine from the servant's silver tray, Raef saw the man who should've been dead.

He was conversing with Lydon, lord of extensive lands west of Highglen, at the lord's gathering of fifty or so of the city's landowners, influential merchants, guild masters, and their mistresses. The number of guests attending the soirees at Lydon's town home had grown since spring, as the older man—still hale—cultivated conversations in support of tradition and Gramaryan pride.

As a Gramaret, Raef could hardly decline the invitation, not that he would want to. He'd be damned if he was going to slide mildly into the background as that Delarcan girl, barely out of diapers, asserted herself queen. So he made himself available. At court, and at these gatherings, in the factories, even with the guildsmen. He was Raef the Good, a man who could be approached. And Lydon, though he had his own reasons for opening his home to men of influence, was a man who made Raef visible.

Hada had attended tonight's gathering, too, but, thank the One God, she was as distant to him as he was to her. *Damn her for coming to Gramarye and drawing political attention to his quiet home.* This realm had been operating quite nicely for years with no interference.

Raef's spies and influencers would ensure Huwen recognized his sister's bald ambition for what it was. Treason, but a petty situation Raef could manage himself, with no armies marching in.

Tonight, as always, the food was exceptional. Delicacies were casually laid out on tables or served by unobtrusive servants in the Aadian style—or so Raef assumed, as no one had ever been to Aadi. Traditional melodies, delicately and capably played on flute and harp, accompanied the steps of fashionably but conservatively dressed young people oblivious to the political implications of the guest list. They flirted and vied for one another's attention.

In one of the rooms, its walls covered with pale silk, a crowd gathered around a table to watch someone from Pagoras showing a game from Aadi, played with stiffened paper cards, painted on one side with scenes like fortune cards, but used for gambling. In another room, conversation grew languid as its occupants eschewed wine for Dream Incense. Tomorrow, none of the participants would be good for anything requiring thought, but they'd congratulate each other on the amusement they'd had, and praise Lydon in whispers for laying hands on black market spells banned for lesser people. From another salon, laughter spilled into the corridors as puppets spewed political satires.

Raef had drifted to the card game where he hoped to speak with Andred, a man with rich yak herds, who'd been overheard praising the princess. Sincerely, or not? That was what Raef hoped to discover, and if necessary, to influence.

Raef stood to one side of a doorway, leaning on his cane and craning over the heads of those sitting at the table, trying to see if Andred was here. Raef was not a tall man, and the infirmity in his leg gave him a crooked stance, though his shoulders and arms were strong. The man from Pagoras dealt the cards to each player so each held a unique combination invisible to the others, and upon which they made various wagers.

His gaze caught a man on the far side of the room, a bystander like himself, watching him. Abruptly, the man turned back to a conversation with Lydon, feigning interest. Raef withdrew his glance.

Familiar. A few years older than himself. Trimmed hair and beard. Clothing conservative but of excellent quality.

Raef's gaze flicked back. He knew the man.

The stranger was again studying him, coolly, now. His gaze flicked to a doorway midway about the room between them, then back. He murmured something to Lydon, then made his way to the door. An invitation.

Pulse thumping, Raef followed.

The man paused in the corridor—a servant's hallway, apparently—to address a butler coming from the back stair with a tray of wine goblets. "My good fellow, is there a quiet room where my friend and I could speak, uninterrupted?"

Ah.

The butler nodded and led them to a small room with a cheery fire. The servant checked to ensure it was not occupied by lovers or private discussions, offered them each a glass of wine, then left, closing the door behind him.

The stranger did not sit by the fire but turned to address him. "My name is Yaquob," he said pointedly. "I am a merchant from Pagoras."

Raef took in the man's militant stance and direct gaze. So, this was how . . . *Yaquob* . . . wished things to be. Raef had known him, when they were children, under a different name. He would not openly acknowledge what they both knew. Well, Raef could match him. "I am Lord Raef, Regent of Gramarye."

The other nodded slowly, accepting. "It is an honor to meet you." The words, carefully polite, and the direct gaze said Yaquob understood precisely the deception.

Raef waited, leaning on his cane, masking his uncertainty. Was the man here to blackmail him? He would not get far. *Yaquob* hid something; he would not have changed his name and spread a lie that he was dead. What he was hiding, Raef didn't know, but he could have unobtrusive inquiries made. Perhaps this man could be made into a lever.

So, why had the man lured him into this room?

"Sieur, I wonder if we might work together on a transaction that would benefit us both?"

Raef doubted it. But he would wait to hear what the man had to say.

Yaquob paced the opulently furnished room, eyes roaming as he moved. Spies in the tapestries? "I have a message for Princess Hada."

"There are protocols," Raef said mildly. "Petitions. Court." Of course, the man knew this. If he thought Raef would intervene on his behalf, he was mad. For old times' sake? The thought was ludicrous.

Yaquob stopped. "A private message."

"I could send my man to your place. I would see any message you send by him personally delivered." A letter was different. At the least, incriminating, and possibly enlightening. And Raef would be more than happy for this man to hand him his address.

"No." Yaquob continued his circuit.

Raef spread his hand in helplessness, conveying no regret.

"As much as I can hearten you that we have common interests, I understand you cannot act without assurances," Yaquob said. "Trust is so fragile these days."

"Anything else is folly." Very well, the man was not about to fall into a simple trap. Raef would have to work harder.

"Agreed." Yaquob returned to his initial position, his back to the fire and his face in silhouette, cupping his untouched wine. "Well, for my part, I can demonstrate my trustworthiness through—" he toasted Raef "—silence." He drank.

Raef regarded him, hoping his face retained its impassivity despite his turmoil. A bald threat. Well, Raef would return the man no such assurances. He gave a curt nod. "Thank you, Sieur, for your petition. However, as I indicated, I cannot circumvent court protocols. Good evening."

"I am disappointed."

Raef turned and let himself from the room.

Gods. He must find his footman and have him follow this *Yaquob*. Immediately. Tonight. Before dawn, a small party of his personal guards must ensure the man had no opportunity to prove—or disprove—his vow of silence.

<hr>

"Your Highness." The servant bowed, holding a silver tray with a folded paper. A message.

Lydon's party, a tedious affair, was finally over. Hada had been looking forward to a hot bath, a glass of wine, and a good book by her fire, with no sycophants and no politics until morning. But the note was from Gweddien. She considered ignoring it.

But no. She read the contents. Nothing important. Still. "Fetch him."

She eschewed the bath but had changed into a traditional robe and was sitting by the fire with a glass of Aadian white when he arrived. She bade the servant bring him a chair and a glass, then depart.

Gweddien accepted the wine and stretched out in the chair, still wearing his breeches, chemise and vest from earlier in the day. And the golden collar. "First, how was your evening?" he asked.

She rolled her eyes. "Boring."

"But you were witty and engaging." His comment was a reminder of his instruction to her before she left.

"Yes, of course." Maybe. She might have to try harder next time.

"Were you able to get Andred on side?"

"He flatters very well. It's hard to say what he intends." Time to question him. "You received the spell ingredients I sent?"

He brightened. "Yes. Made a few basic potions so they're ready if you need them."

"Already." She peered at him with a sardonic smile. "Such as?"

"Confusions, Memory Losses, Heartspeeds, Dream Incense—"

"Dream Incense? What possible use could I have for that?"

He raised his brows in mock innocence. "Even a queen must relax sometimes."

She held up her glass. "I do."

He gave her a knowing look.

"I don't need Dream Incense."

"Have you ever tried it?"

No. Why would she? She sipped her wine and leaned back in her chair.

He gave a half-shrug and, reaching into his vest pocket, held up a small vial.

Really? "I've seen people. At the party tonight, for instance. They look entirely stupid when they breathe that potion in."

He tilted his head in disinterest. "No one's watching."

She had to smile. "You've tried it, I trust?"

He gave her a wicked grin and opened the vial.

Huwen reined in his horse and gazed out over Coldridge from the brow of a hill. Behind him, mountains rose, rank on rank, north and west to the wild lands, south to the cursed lands of Orumon. East, beyond the recaptured border city, spread wide rolling hills of Teshe and in the distance, the flat lands of Midell. Beyond sight, many days' ride, were the rich, gently sloping farmlands of Arcan, and home. Holderford.

By the One, he wished he was there. With Ychelle and their miraculous Shalire.

Igua pulled up by his side, and a handful of retainers gathered to gaze out on the view.

"Looks peaceful," Huwen said to his chancellor.

He heard, rather than saw, his adviser shift on his horse. "It is."

"The uprisers are well-controlled."

"Our best information tells us they've withdrawn," Igua said. "For now."

That was crap. "And that Dwyn Gramaret is mortally wounded."

"We have no way of knowing if the rebel king's wounds are mortal," Igua cautioned.

Huwen turned in his saddle.

"Majesty, we can't withdraw your armies. Not yet."

"Then, when?"

Igua gazed south and east, toward the curve of mountains that marched south of Midell as far as the eye could see. Beyond the horizon, the distant realm of Gramarye. "When Teshe is stable, there is still the matter of Hada's treason."

"Unconfirmed."

"When our emissary returns," Igua said mildly, "we will know more."

Huwen turned away in frustration. Igua was right. But damn it, he was tired of war.

"Majesty—"

"Send an elite squad, then. Even a division under our best general. Sort the mess out."

Igua turned to him patiently. "Majesty."

Huwen let out a long breath.

"You don't know what this border wall means. You would have to send the greater part of your forces. And *yourself*, as High King, to speak with your sister and assess the situation. We cannot raise war against her without your direct leadership."

War? Gods, no. Not against another Delarcan.

CHAPTER 19

In one of the outer rooms of Princess Hada's suite, Rennika spread the blue fabrics on one end of the broad low table, and reds at the other. The yellow and green samples, reportedly the princess's favorite colors, Ide arranged across the center of the table. Tyg, suitably silent and still, stood well back with sacks of other samples. As one of her first acts upon arriving in Highglen, Princess Hada had announced a festival in honor of the One God, a day of prayer and celebration on the autumn equinox. The equinox was racing upon them in nine more days, and the princess had only just called to have a new dress made for the occasion.

Several large candelabras scented the room with honey, and a bright fire crackled on the hearth. Wearing the dress Ide's sister had made from her masterpiece fabrics for the signing, Rennika perspired in the warmth of the overheated room.

"There isn't enough light to show off the colors properly." Sieur Verlin, also dressed in his best, surveyed the room, then stepped around the table to make minute adjustments to the display. "Pull back the drapes."

Rennika and Ide twitched the heavy hangings from a tall, glass-paned window looking out over the castle bailey. The vague gleam from the overcast day shed a surprising amount of light, but it was dull and failed to bring out Rennika's hard-won colors.

Below, moving purposefully on their errands, a handful of servants and soldiers, as well as two courtiers, were visible in the crushed snow. A large cart pulled by two horses was entering through the servants' gate. Jack, the collier. "Sieur Verlin."

Her master straightened from his fussing.

"Did you pay the collier's bill? I mentioned it a fortnight—"

"Not now, Rennika. It slipped my mind with the contract, but the man will get his money."

The handle clicked, and the four of them hastened to the side of the chamber to bow their respects.

"No, no, come in. We can do both at once." The voice, the princess's, was high and dulcet. She swept into the room in a loose-fitting gown patterned after the style of Aadi, but without the structuring supports that gave such clothing its stiff elegance. Her hair, too, hung softly about her face, pale brown curls held partially back with inefficient combs. The entire effect of gentility was at odds with her quick, decisive words and movements. "Rise," she said absently, seating herself on the cushioned couch before the display of fabrics.

Rennika and Ide relaxed from their stiff postures, and Tyg stepped back into the shadows.

"Raef has influence, but you will be queen. Don't underestimate what I can do." A man, well-dressed and well-groomed, had entered behind the princess and, at her nod, sat on a chair beside her. A collar of gold gleamed at his neck, covering his death token. A fine chain hung from it to his knees, neglected.

His skin. He was a magiel.

Gods.

It was Gweddien.

"I won't rest until it's accomplished. There are those who would rewrite my father's will." Hada flicked her hand at the page by the door. "Leave us," she said. "Attend without."

Rennika blinked, momentarily gasping, trying to make sense of what she saw. *Gweddien?* Thinner than when she'd seen him as a child. Aged badly, for one only a few years older than her. But it looked like Gweddien. Shackled? But . . . not.

Sieur Verlin shot her a sharp look. Rennika dropped her gaze, taking up her position with slate and chalk.

"The dress must be spectacular," Princess Hada said to Verlin, perusing the fabrics. "None of this dull stuff." She waved at the yellows and greens. Ide pulled the disfavored samples from the table.

Yes. Rennika was certain. It *was* Gweddien. But how . . .

"These." The princess poked her finger into the array of crimsons and fuchsias. The brilliance of the fabrics would do nothing for the princess's pale complexion.

Sieur Verlin snapped his fingers and Tyg pulled out a bundle of red fabrics and dyed yarns. Ide arranged them on the table.

"Raef said nothing about evicting the magiels from the districts above the river," Gweddien said. Rennika listened hard to his words. They were muddied, as if he'd been drinking and was trying to mask it.

"Yet. He's biding his time. He's a cripple, and he counterbalances his infirmity with cunning." The princess examined the new display. "Show me the styles," she said to Verlin.

Verlin produced a sheaf of drawings, all faceless women in various dresses. He tapped three. "I viewed these styles this summer in Cataract Crag."

"Aadian?" She asked Gweddien. "Or traditional?"

Gweddien was *advising* the princess. And she was listening.

Hada looked up suddenly at Rennika. "Stand. Take off the over robe."

Rennika set her slate and chalk aside and did as she was bid. Her skirt and bodice were of the latest Aadian design, a stiff brocade robe over a full skirt and fitted bodice.

"Turn."

Rennika turned.

"It looks tight. Can you move in it?"

"It's structured, but not uncomfortable." Rennika demonstrated walking and bending forward. "There is less movement than in a robe." She caught Gweddien watching her gestures.

But he did not look at her face. Did not recognize her. "The Aadian fashion'll be too foreign," he said to the princess, almost lazily. Yes, Rennika could swear he was actually drunk. His color was high. "You want to win these people over. That is the whole point of this festival."

Not prayer?

Hada darted a smile at him. "Be strong. Be soft. Make up your mind."

"Be soft where it doesn't matter. Be strong where you need to."

Rennika marveled. How could Gweddien not recognize her? They'd traveled together in the same band of refugees for weeks. She'd been taught her first lessons in magic by him and his mother. It was years ago, and she'd been only a child, but . . . had she changed that much? That Hada had never recognized her was no surprise. Hada had been a toddler the last time they met.

"Bring me the robe, then," Hada said, holding out her hand.

Rennika gave her the robe.

"And my advisers?" The princess turned the brocade over to examine the contrasting lining.

"Bron, when pressed, will say a woman can rule. And Oliver." Gweddien's attention was on Hada. Yet . . . that didn't explain it. "The others . . ." He toyed with the chain hanging from his golden collar. "Await the result of the struggle."

Hada bit her lip and studied Gweddien.

He spread his hands, and the chain tinkled. "Shape everyone. Trust no one."

Gweddien had looked at Rennika . . . but hadn't seen her. She was a servant. Invisible.

Hada turned back to Verlin and pointed to a drawing. "Traditional robe." Then, she selected a handful of the red fabrics: silk, wool, leather, and—drat—linen. "When can you have a sample?"

Rennika recorded her choices.

"Three days for a linen version for fittings." Sieur Verlin bowed.

She stood. "Three days?" she asked the magiel. "Will that give us enough time?"

He nodded.

Hada turned to Verlin. "See my steward to schedule an appointment." She swept out the door, Gweddien trailing.

※

Beyond the tiny attic window, dull cloud hung low over Highglen. It obscured the mountains, smearing the grays of the nearest houses so they merged, one into the other. Janat stared out at nothing, waiting for . . . what? She didn't know. A flake to fall from the sky. A raven to appear, a dog in the street. Something. Anything.

A brown leaf flicked erratically, frozen to the snow, its quarrel with the breeze the only movement in the whole dreary scene.

Rennika had gone to her workshop to make dyes and wouldn't be back until evening, while Ide and Sieur Verlin were at the palace fitting Hada's sample dress. Meg had made Dream Incense earlier, and now slept behind her closed door. Yon and a friend had gone to the tavern. The women of the household had spent all day yesterday and this morning reestablishing their work routine after the signing, and now, napped. Sieura Verlin—who'd startled when Janat, searching out her next task, had found her in Verlin's office—made it plain to Janat that she was not to be visible. So, she was here. Listening to the creak of the house in the wind. Trying not to think of the purse in Rennika's drawer.

Trying not to see the memories again. Trying to forget Coldridge castle.

Impossible.

She tried to focus her thoughts on something else. Anything else.

Sulwyn. The night he told her he no longer loved her. No.

The war. Bodies, blood—

She shook her head. Something pleasant. A tavern.

Meg. Disappointed in her.

Ranuat, was there nothing she could do to drag herself out of this miasma of circular thoughts? She was worthless, an obstruction to Meg's calling to help the people of Shangril.

Gods, couldn't she just stay out of everyone's way?

She wrenched herself from the window, paced. Lay on her bed. Stared at the book of political poetry on the floor, read. Read twice, in fact.

The memories came back.

Coldridge. The robe the servants had dressed her in. The room they'd led her to, warmed by a fragrant fire after her long stay in the cold prison. The steaming, scented bath they'd given her. The wonderful meal of meat and bread and turnips and carrots. Wine. Tarts made with jam. The patiently waiting canopied bed.

Janat didn't take Rennika's purse. She left it in the drawer. Only a few coins, not enough to be missed. And only borrowed, after all, until she could earn something from Sieura Verlin.

She slipped from the house by way of the servants' gate.

The room was dark when the sound of footsteps in her sister's sitting area woke Meg. She lay for a few moments on her pallet, groggy and disoriented, thinking back to the places she'd been—pasts and futures. Nothing stood out. She was, for the most part, careful to plan her use of magic so she might rest in an unobtrusive location during the reverberations of her time stream. So, when she lived bits of her life out of order, the times she lived tended to be lying on straw in the back of a barn or under a bush, or, like today, on a pallet in a nondescript room.

She was hungry. She must have slept away the entire afternoon. She rose and wrapped a shawl over her sleeping clothes and slipped out. Rennika, immersed in a blanket, sat by the brazier staring intently into the flame of a candle, a book fallen to her lap. A pot of tea and two mugs, one steaming, sat on the table beside her. Rennika roused herself and looked up at Meg.

"You're back from the dye compound," Meg observed.

A brief look of tenderness flicked across her sister's face. Then, with an affectionate smile, she gestured toward the second cup. "Yes. Tea?"

Perfect. Meg sat, shaking off the chill, and poured. "I must have missed supper."

"There's yogurt and honey in the pantry."

Meg nodded and blew on her hot tea. "You went to your workshop in such haste, I didn't get a chance to hear how your visit to the castle went."

Whatever reminiscence had engulfed Rennika slipped away, and she became her quietly efficient self again. "Odd. You won't guess who was there."

Meg was certain she wouldn't.

"Gweddien."

By the Gods.

Rennika shook her head in mystification. "I hadn't seen him since we were on the road. Remember? He disappeared from Silvermeadow when I was about, eleven? I think you or Janat said he'd been caught by the High King's guards. What he's doing in Highglen, I have no idea."

"You're sure it was him?"

"As sure as I see you. I was this far from him."

"What did he say?"

Rennika lifted a shoulder and set her book on the table. "He didn't recognize me. And he seemed to be on good terms with Princess Hada, giving her advice as if they were of the same station. I had no chance to say anything."

Gweddien. So, he *had* come here. But . . . how had he arranged to rendezvous with Hada? He'd been following some unnamed merchant, one who'd bought an amulet Gweddien was convinced was the Amber Prayer Stone. "Did he say anything to Hada? Anything that might explain why he's here?"

Rennika twisted her lips, staring intently at nothing. "He was giving her advice. Or that's what I gathered."

"Advising her on what?"

Rennika pursed her lips. "He said she shouldn't wear an Aadian dress for the festival. It's too foreign. He told her she wanted the people of Gramarye to accept her."

As queen. She would want some support among the people if she didn't want to provoke an uprising. Civil war. "Anything else? Anything about Coldridge?"

"Nothing."

"And Gweddien?"

"He was telling her not to listen to her advisers. Hada expects some kind of confrontation, but it was unclear." Rennika shook her head. "That's all."

Confrontation with Raef, that was obvious. "Thank you," Meg said, still trying to make sense of it. "I'm not sure how this can help, but . . ." *Gweddien.*

"Help with what?" Rennika asked. "I thought you were through working with the uprisers. That Janat needed you."

Yes, of course. It was just . . . "Old habits."

Rennika's eyes narrowed. "Meg."

"Gods, Rennika." Meg didn't mean to snap, but she didn't need Rennika's implication. Meg was not getting enticed back into politics. But— "You know Mama sacrificed everything—"

"Yes—"

"She wanted to give the world hope when the prayer stones were gone." Was that such a terrible thing?

Rennika's color heightened. "Mama sent us away to save *us*. Because she loved *us*."

"She sent us to restore the people's access to Heaven."

"Our lives are to *live*," Rennika whispered. "To love, Meg. Marry. Raise children. Care for each other."

"And when you die?" Meg countered. "*You* have a death token. But what about your children? What will happen to them?"

Rennika breathed harshly, mouth snapped closed. Finally, she spoke. "The king's brother has the Ruby. He and his magiel go to Heaven. There are death tokens in Midell."

"So, your solution is to move to Midell?" Meg snorted. "What, maybe curry favor with an aristocrat, one of King Eamon's friends, who might be able to get you one?"

"Don't be stupid."

"Everyone can't move to Midell."

Rennika glared, as if she'd decided not to argue.

It was attitudes like Rennika's that made Meg's task impossible. "No hope of building a world where kings are subject to the rule of law. Ever," she muttered. "Where the law applies equally to everyone."

"I don't object to those things," Rennika said at last, her voice lowered. "No sane person would. But that battle's over, Meg. It's done. Leave it."

"And Huwen's magiel breeding scheme?" She knew her words were biting. "Let that run?"

Rennika's brows lowered.

Gods, her sister didn't— "You don't know?"

Rennika tilted her head at her in confusion. "What is that?"

Meg stared at her. "The Delaracans control the Ruby."

"Yes."

"But they can't use it without a magiel." Rennika began to argue, but Meg held her hand up. "Once in Heaven, the royal has no role but to protect the magiel, ensure she or he returns to earth safely. The Gods can only hear the *magiel*."

"I know—"

Meg leaned across the table and took Rennika's hand. "The Delarcans don't dare use any magiel they can't completely control." She waited a moment to let this sink in. "Or the magiel would simply ask the Gods to take all power from them."

She had Rennika's attention now.

"Huwen is breeding magiel *babies*, Rennika." She couldn't keep the disgust from her voice. "The babies are taken from their mothers to raise in a cloister. To believe only what the Delarcans tell them."

Rennika paled. "That's . . ." She shook her head in disbelief. "That's inhuman."

"The purer, the more powerful the breeding stock, the better. Gweddien is the last male magiel who can trace his line directly to the One God and one of the Goddesses." She didn't need to finish the thought. That she, Janat, and Rennika were the last women descended directly from the One God and Kyaju of the Amber.

Rennika let out a long breath as she made the connection.

"You, with your worldling skin, might hide from Huwen. Janat and I—" Meg shrugged. "The myth that we're dead is all that's keeping us from being hunted down."

Rennika's eyes bored into her, her face set in horror.

"If you could do something, Rennika?" Meg had to make her see. "If you could stop Huwen with the Amber? Wouldn't you?"

Rennika pulled her hand away.

Meg let her tone soften. "Rennika, I don't know what I intend to do. I did come here to get away from the uprisers. I did come for Janat. But . . ." She didn't want to say, *if the Amber exists. If it wasn't smashed.* Such a thought was madness.

Rennika let out a long breath. She lowered her head, sipped her tea.

"I don't want to hurt you or Janat." But Meg had to find out. What was Gweddien up to?

Rennika looked up suddenly. "Where's Janat?"

Meg looked around the empty apartment. Janat's door was closed. "She didn't come to supper?" Maybe it was just as well to let the subject drop. Meg had given Rennika something to think about.

"No."

"Did she go to bed early?"

"I checked. She's not in her room. I thought you'd know where she was. But it's getting late."

A sick feeling crawled into Meg's stomach. *Not again.*

"I could go down and ask if anyone's seen her," Rennika said.

Meg cast her thoughts back to the morning. Janat had risen, perhaps a little later than usual, though after the flurry of activity in the past days, the entire household had slowed its pace. She'd been quiet, but then, she was often quiet in the mornings. Janat hadn't said much when Meg told her she'd be making spells for Sieur Verlin. Floors were being washed, as Meg recalled, so she assumed that was Janat's work for the day. Then Meg had lain down. Janat had said she was going to eat.

Meg set her cup down.

Rennika stood. "Do you want me to check?"

"Yes. I'll get dressed."

Rennika returned her book to her chamber but came back a moment later. "Meg."

Meg poked her head from her room, tying her under robe over her chemise and smallclothes.

Rennika held up her purse. "I had over five gultra. Now there are three chetra."

"Piss." Meg hurried back to her room to throw on the rest of her clothes. "Stay here in case she comes back."

"Where will you look?" Rennika stood in her doorway.

Meg had no idea. "Rennika." She threw her cloak on. "I'll get your money back."

"Just find Janat."

CHAPTER 20

Raoul recognized the hooded figure hurrying across the common. The one who'd come for sugar. He detached himself from the gloom and stepped in her way. "Do you seek Master Yaquob?"

The woman hesitated. "Yes."

He recognized her voice. "Come." Raoul led the way across the square. The woman hesitated, then followed. She'd told him her name, but he'd forgotten it.

At the opening to a lane crammed with sagging shanties was a small rice cookery, vacant of customers. "I'm hungry," Raoul told her. "Buy me a bowl of rice."

The woman scowled. "Where's your father?"

Janat. The name popped into his head. He shivered despite his cloak. "I'll tell you, but first, give me something to eat."

She eyed him, then told the shopkeeper to bring two bowls of rice with nuts and lentils, as he knew she would. He chose a table next to the window, lifting its curtain, and carefully loosened the waxed linen covering to peer back into the common. He crammed down the rice, not minding that the food was scalding.

"Where's your father?" she repeated.

He nodded beyond the window. "Do you have an appointment?"

"No, I—" She stopped. "He's a shopkeeper. Shopkeepers don't take appointments."

Raoul shrugged at her objection. "My father does." He shoved rice into his mouth, watching through the hole he'd made. "He's meeting someone important. I have to keep watch, so he's not disturbed. You can see him after."

Janat blew out a breath of annoyance and slumped back in her chair.

Raoul shoved the empty bowl toward her.

She stared at him.

"I'll let you know when the man goes."

Reluctantly, she bought him a second bowl of rice, this time with only lentils, but he attacked it with as much appetite as the first. Then, across the common, a coach arrived in the falling snow and a cloaked man disappeared into it. His father's patron. He let the curtain drop. "The man is leaving."

Janat nudged him aside and put her eye to the hole Raoul had made.

Raoul licked the bottom of his bowl and tightened his cloak. "I'll take you now."

"First, give me back my purse."

Raoul gave her an innocent stare.

She held out her hand. "You should know better than to steal from a magiel."

"You didn't feel anything," he reasoned, handing back her purse.

"We're born knowing how to pinch."

He grinned, shrugging, and led the way back through the accumulating snow to his father's shop. "The magiel's back," he announced, skirting past his father and through the hangings into the back room.

Janat hung back in the doorway, soaking up the warmth within the chamber, her heart suddenly racing, her purse heavy.

Yaquob, who'd been bent over a table writing a note, straightened, his gaze flicking from the boy to her. "Ah," the free trader said heartily, though something in his eyes belied the joviality. "The sugar magiel. Sieura, you drive a hard bargain."

She licked her lips and eased into the room, closing the door behind her. "Well," she said softly, "part of our bargain was that I would come back. We might make another trade, perhaps more to your liking."

He slid his pen into the inkwell. "At your service."

Now that it came to it, she had a hard time saying the word. "Glim," she whispered.

He leaned forward, tilting his ear. "Glim?" She sickened as nothing in his expression betrayed any recognition of the word. "What is glim?"

The basement cell in Coldridge castle. She, dressed like a lady. Wenid. Gweddien. The bed. The table. The two goblets.

The winter chill ran down her back. This free trader didn't know the potions he sold. Or so he said. "A powder," she whispered. "Green."

Yaquob spread his hands to indicate the room and again, though his voice was hearty, the depths of his eyes hid the kind of disapproval—disgust—she saw in landlords and barkeepers. "I've seen nothing with such label in all these wares. And I *have* been making an inventory."

Disappointment pierced her unreasonably, stripping her of the last traces of her strength. No one had glim, save Wenid, and he was dead. No one even knew what it was, save Gweddien. She'd had no reason to expect this trader, any more than the others, would have glim. *Trader in exotic magics.* She'd have to laugh. "Dream Incense, then," she said, but she had no energy to speak above a murmur.

Dreams, yes. Not Heartspeed, not manic dancing and laughter, no. Dreams. And maybe, find some young man and augment its floating delight with the bliss of touch.

"Dream Incense. Ah. I have a little left." He let his fingers walk along the edge of a shelf, pushing vials aside. "You're in luck. I have two."

So few.

He continued to search the shelf. "You have to know, now that most of the magiels are gone and can't replenish stock, I've sold out of most of the spells of reverie or sensory delight. I could sell you the ingredients. And I could sell such potions to customers on commission, too, if you can make them."

"No. No." She had no desire, no strength. Not just now.

They agreed on a price, and Janat paid, discovering belatedly that the purse Raoul had returned to her jingled only with chetra. No gultra.

Clutching the two vials, she escaped into the night.

※

Meg trudged through light falling snow. Where had Janat had gone? When? She could waste candlemarks, even days, in the search. Janat was good at losing herself. Every interminable moment spent seeking her was an age in which Meg second-guessed herself, berated herself, imagined herself finding Janat broken, violated, or worse.

Except.

Except this was not the first time Janat had disappeared. There were places Meg might predict. She began with the tavern they'd eaten at, their first day in Highglen. Then other taverns and public houses nearby. Then the less reputable places Meg had come to know in her quest for Gweddien's elusive free trader.

No one would admit to having seen her.

Meg trudged up the steps to The Three Corners, part of her hoping she would not find Janat here, another part wondering where she would look if her sister was not. The small, bare room was livelier than it had been the last few times Meg had stopped by. Tallow candles pushed back the gloom, and the brazier had been moved to one side of the room. A number of ripe yak wool cloaks steamed on hooks above it. A lutist played a lively tune in one corner and a half-dozen patrons, well into their cups, sang loudly over him. Xadria, the alehouse proprietor, was busy behind the bar, and a girl bustled between half-full trestle tables with a tray of tankards. The place smelled of beer and sweat and yak hide.

Meg scanned the room. Janat was not here.

She drew in a breath and let it out. She could try the stables.

But she needed a mouthful of ale and a moment by the brazier before she returned to the swirling snow. There was a seat by the bar. Vellefair was there, deep in conversation with a man Meg didn't know.

She sat and laid a chetram on the bar.

Xadria was busy at the barrel, filling a half-dozen tankards. Meg waited.

She recognized the man, boy really, on the other side of her. Belden. He'd been here the first time she'd come.

"Them as I know would take Lord Raef as *king*. Not regent," the man on the far side of Vellefair argued vehemently. He took Vellefair's arm and leaned into him. "There was a magiel, yesterday? Falling down with the blood cough? Soldiers whipped him."

Vellefair shrugged. "So?"

"They think if he's a magiel, he has to be drunk."

Belden stared into space, neither acknowledging her, nor seeming to notice Xadria or the infernally loud singers.

"The Delarcan doesn't care a chetram for what the people of Gramarye want," Vellefair agreed.

Gods—the boy. Belden had a small sore, open but crusted over with a dull yellow paste, peeking out just above his death token collar. Had that deadly curse—she forgot its name—migrated beyond Pagoras?

Boneblood. Itch. That's what they'd called it.

The serving girl pushed Meg into Vellefair, setting her tray on the bar, unloading it.

"If Lord Raef was king," Vellefair said, "there's plenty here who'd help him fend off the High King *and* his cannons." He wobbled around to see who bumped him.

You've never seen cannons, Meg thought. *Or what they can do.*

Xadria plunked tankards on the girl's tray, shooting Meg a scowl.

The man noticed Meg. "Didn't think your place could get much lower, Xadria," he said. "Guess I'll take my business elsewhere, if you're serving magiels, now."

Xadria shoved Meg's chetram back at her. "Got business enough. You can drink somewhere else."

Meg felt her face heat.

"You heard me," Xadria said. "Stop gawking. Get out, unless you want to work in one of the back rooms."

Meg's muscles bunched as her fingers curled around her coin. Gods, this woman, this . . . *ass* . . . had no clue what Meg had done for her. Done for all of them, fighting. Killing *Wenid*, for piss sake—

"Get!"

She slid from her chair.

"Don't listen to her." A hand steadied Meg's arm.

She looked up. Vellefair.

He steered her to the far end of a trestle table where a bench had space for two. "People don't like magiels. So what." He grabbed two tankards from the dozen on the table and shoved one in front of Meg. "You have more Heartspeeds?"

She let air fill her lungs. "I can get it."

He nodded, a confirmation.

She breathed again and took a sip of the beer, letting her racing heart calm. "Thank you."

He shrugged and quaffed his beer. "I don't much care one way or the other about the vibration of someone's skin. You got magic.

You can make me good spells, good curses. Better than Xadria." He lowered the tankard. "And I like the rates you charge."

She knit her brow at him.

"Information." He grinned and played with the handle of his tankard. "You wanted to know if a trader come to town. Dealer in special merchandise."

She gave a barely perceptible nod, her mouth dry.

He leaned into her. "Name's Yaquob Tagel. What's that worth to you?"

"Where?" Her word was a whisper, inaudible beneath the din. "Where?" she repeated.

He kicked something beneath the table. She felt with her foot. There was someone—small—on the floor. Asleep? She peered into the shadows by their feet. A child?

"That's his boy, a little pickpurse. Followed another magiel here. The boy'll take you to him." Vellefair put his hand flat on the table in front of her. "What's it worth?"

"I'll bring you a Heartspeed. Tomorrow."

"Make that three. I bought you a beer." He grinned.

"Two." He'd just saved her from making a fool of herself, and likely, a beating. "A third when I meet Yaquob." Vellefair's words filtered through her tumult. "The boy . . . what? Followed a magiel here?" *Janat.*

Vellefair grinned. "Pretty one."

Meg scrambled to the floor and shook the boy, pulling him to a sitting position among all the legs. "Boy!"

The boy blinked, then braced himself in a crouch.

"The magiel you followed."

He licked his lips, gaze darting to gauge the cage of legs surrounding him.

"Looks like me?" *But prettier.*

The fear transmuted in the boy's eyes from fear of her, to fear of . . . something more distant. He nodded.

"Why?" Meg wanted to shake him, though she knew it was nonsensical. "Where did you follow her from?"

"From my father's shop. He told me to."

"Why?"

"To be sure she's safe."

Meg stilled in surprise, staring at him in incomprehension. "Safe? Why?"

He shrugged thin shoulders. "I don't know. I don't talk back or he whumps me."

"Where's she now?"

The boy nodded toward the back of the bar.

Meg half rose. The rooms?

She turned back to the boy. "You stay here."

One look at his face told her he wouldn't.

"I need you to take me to your father."

Then she understood the hidden fear in his eyes. Right. She wouldn't get him to go back to his father. Not after giving away information.

Meg climbed to her feet. "Vellefair. Three Heartspeeds. Hold the boy. Don't let him go 'til I come back."

Vellefair reached a long arm under the table and clamped the boy's arm in one huge claw. "Where're you going?"

She gestured with her chin. "Back there."

There were four rooms in the back of The Three Corners. Two were empty, their doors ajar; a third thumped with lovers. Meg slammed the fourth door open.

The tiny chamber was dark but for dim light spilling around her onto the floor. But Meg made out a pallet against the wall. A figure shifted on the pallet. Alive, then.

Dread battled her relief. "Janat?" Meg lowered herself to a crouch, felt for the edge of the pallet, found a foot beneath a blanket. "Janat."

The person—woman, the ankle was slender—moaned.

Meg moved closer, gauging where to reach for a shoulder. "Janat."

The figure twitched away as though burned, then rose abruptly to a crouch. "Get out of here!" she screamed. Janat's voice, slurred with drink or charm. Janat's form in the dark. "By Ranuat! Meg! What do I have to do to get a moment's peace from you?"

Meg's mind flashed, white, blank. *A moment's—*

After all she'd done? Got Janat—

Meg's voice was low, hoarse with fury. "You get yourself home."

Janat leapt to her feet, fell into the wall. "No."

Meg stood, power rising through her. "You get yourself home. Get into your room and stay there—"

Janat bent over, her arms windmilling, clawing up clothing. "I'm staying here."

It was all Meg could do not to slap her. "You're not."

Janat straightened, wobbling, a bundle of clothes and blankets in her arms, her hair wild, face savage in the dim light. "These people like me. These people . . . they look out for me. They're my friends."

"I look out for you. I—"

"And they don't criticize me and try to run my life." Tears streamed down her face.

A shadow fell on the room. "Get out." Xadria's voice.

Meg turned. "Stay out of this, Xadria. Janat's—"

Janat darted past her, out the door.

"Janat!" Meg pushed to follow, but Xadria blocked the door. The pub owner grabbed Meg's arms, tripping her to the floor. Meg screamed, shoving at the woman's weight as it descended on her.

And there was a blade at her throat. Meg stilled.

"You don't come in here and start a fuss in my house." Xadria's voice was low and clipped.

Meg held herself rigid. A sting on her neck told her the blade was sharp. By Kyaju, she ached to find a time when the woman's trachea was at a different angle. Hold it there. Give the woman a fright. In these last years of war, she'd learned such subtle tricks of magiel killing.

But Meg needed these people. She couldn't undermine the trust she'd been building. Reveal the strength of her pure heritage, her ability to do magic without charms or potions. Especially when Janat only fought her. Xadria clearly believed Meg was a common half-breed magiel who could do nothing without potions, or she'd never have attacked so heedlessly.

"Why do you care?" Meg whispered.

"I don't like you. You take my business."

Vellefair's Heartspeed. And . . . did the woman have designs on Janat? Meg sickened. The line between habituation and harlotry, she suspected, might be no more substantial than the line between want and need. And there was nothing Meg could do, if Janat refused to come. "I'll leave."

Xadria eased back, her knife still pointed at Meg's throat. "And I don't want you coming back."

Meg ran a thumb over the drop of sticky warmth above her death token collar. It galled her to back down, but she bowed her head and scrambled back, pulling her cloak around her.

Xadria followed her into the tavern.

The lutist continued to play, the singers to sing, and the patrons to enjoy the ambience. Apparently, a few screams from the back rooms was no reason to stop drinking. Vellefair still clutched the boy, wriggling, by the upper arm. It was as if the altercation had taken only a minute. Which, Meg reflected, it probably had.

She took the boy's arm—he jerked, strong for his size, but she held him—and made for the door.

Vellefair put a hand on her wrist. "Three Heartspeeds."

She shoved her hand into her satchel and produced two spells. "The third when I meet Yaquob." She pushed the vials into his hand, then drove past him and out the door.

"Tomorrow!" he called after her.

The door closed behind them, and the boy renewed his wriggles.

"Stop that, or we'll both fall to our deaths," she said, easing him down the icy steps. The snow had only thickened while she was inside.

"I'll tell my father! I was supposed to follow that magiel. Now she's gone."

Meg stopped at the bottom of the steps and, holding him by the upper arms, peered hard into his face. "That magiel is my sister. Your father doesn't need to care for her." Meg had no idea what kind of interest this boy's father—Yaquob—had in Janat, but Meg had a hard time thinking he meant her well. "In fact, why don't we both tell your father, together? Hmm? I'm sure he will be happier knowing his son is at home with him on such a cold night."

At this, the boy stilled. "Don't take me there."

The stricken look on his face twisted something inside Meg. She knew better than to be a dupe. Still, she could see no feigning in his fear. "Why?" she said softly, though she knew the answer.

"He'll be drunk. He'll wallop me around the shop for coming back."

She considered him in the translucent light of the snowy night, flakes accumulating on his shoulders. He was a comely boy, and his clothing had some weight to it. She caught a glimpse, even in this light, of a collar at his throat beneath the top of his cloak.

Did he have a death token? Such a treasure, for one so young. "I'll strike a bargain with you," she said. "You show me your father's shop, and I'll let you go where you will. I'll tell him nothing of this encounter."

"You chased the magiel away. I can't follow her. He'll still beat me."

True. She straightened but knew better than to let go of his arm. Still, he was worth nothing to her if she couldn't gain his trust. He could tell her any shop was his father's, and she'd have to believe him. "All right, then," she said, thinking. "You show me your father's shop, and I'll tell him I was responsible for your misadventure."

He eyed her as if judging whether to trust her. Finally, he gave a short, sharp nod.

CHAPTER 21

Gweddien knew the door open before him was the door to Hada's suite. Yet it wavered, a hazy green-blue, reminding him of a pond he'd swum in as a boy in Holderford.

He wrenched his thoughts back. Hada sat at a desk, perusing papers, dressed in a night robe. Yes, sat at a desk. Not floated behind it. Gods, he never expected to be called after the chimes of midnight. A taste, a whiff of Dream Incense . . . in his own chamber. A heady dose. He should've been safe from interruption.

". . . Gweddien."

He didn't trust himself to speak intelligibly. He smiled at her with interest. He hoped.

"Huwen's ambassador came, demanding your release."

He spread the fingers of one hand to equivocate, then fisted, so as not to distract himself with the beauty of that motion. He had to talk to her about the Amber. But not now. Not now.

"I thought we might appease my brother with a good captive magiel for his Marigold scheme. I told his emissary I won't let you go." She drifted to a couch and hovered into it. So graceful, with no feet. Or, no, he reminded himself. Her feet merely glided invisibly beneath her gown. Ha.

He followed her, slipping into a chair.

"There must be some good magiels in the lower town, but they're in hiding." She stared at the flames on the brazier, bit her finger. "I'll send Raef to find them."

He nodded sagely, enjoying the motion of his head oscillating on his neck.

"It will give the Regent something to focus on, other than palace intrigues."

Gweddien cleared his throat. "I . . . could . . ." He lost his train of thought.

Hada shook her head. "No. We have to control him, but I don't want him bewitched. Too easily traceable back to you. No accident, no assassination."

Gods, she was going to notice. How wrecked he was. She would throw him back in the dungeon.

". . . lull him by cooperating. What do you think?"

Gweddien lifted a shoulder. "I . . ."

She turned in her seat, and the sudden motion made the room swirl disconcertingly. "Can you give him some kind of spell to control the magiel he's arresting? Or a ward to keep him safe from their spells?"

Gweddien nodded. "Oh, yes. Without a doubt." Gods, it was funny.

<hr>

The cellar was dark when Raoul took Janat's sister down the narrow stairs to his father's shop. He opened the door with no sound. The shop was gray in the dim overcast from glassless window. Snow dusted the shelves and formed a small pile on the floor beneath it.

"There." Raoul turned without entering the room. "He's asleep." He kept his voice low in the silence peculiar to snow and night. He'd kept his end of the bargain, and he wasn't going to spend the night here and wake up to the mercy of a hungover father. Some doorway or stairwell, hiding under his cloak, would have to do. Right now, they had to leave.

Finally, the woman turned and climbed the stairs. He followed on her heels.

She stopped out of earshot of the shop.

"You have to come," he reminded her, stamping his feet and shivering. "Tomorrow. You promised." Take the blame for his failure.

She nodded.

"At dawn."

"Your father wakes so early?"

He lifted a shoulder. "You need to tell him before he starts looking for me. It might be early; it might be late."

"Very well. I'll be here." She nodded her affirmation and turning, trudged across the common.

Raoul nudged up against a recessed doorway in a stone wall and crouched in the snow, wrapping his cloak about him, covering his face with his hood.

The snow fell, quiet ticks of sound striking his cloak.

A crunch of footsteps in the snow stopped in front of him, and he looked up from under his hood.

"Raoul." The woman—Janat's sister—nudged him with her foot. "Come on. I'll find you a place out of the snow."

Meg woke up to brilliant morning sunshine streaming through the inn's window. Though the attic room was freezing, the sun had a cheering effect, scintillating off the snow. The irritated innkeeper had charged steeply for being woken to admit her and the boy. Still, Meg couldn't be unhappy. Raoul would've been dead by morning, frozen, otherwise.

Janat. Meg hadn't slept for worry until the sky began to gray with dawn. She was sick with knowing there was nothing she could do.

She sat up. The boy sat cross-legged, dressed, on the end of her bed, watching her as though trying to puzzle out something he found exotic about her.

She sat up in her chemise and underskirt, irritated he'd caught her defenseless.

"Why'd you help me?"

Meg shrugged and put her feet on the cold boards, pulling her dress from the heap on the floor. "I don't know. Didn't want to see you freeze." She laced her boots.

"But it cost you money. You said you had a place to stay."

She rose and pulled the garment over her head, lacing the loops. Taking him to the draper's home would be as good as proclaiming to Sieura Verlin she wished to be tossed into the streets. "I may not, after today." She broke the skim of ice on the pitcher and poured water into the basin to splash on her face.

Raoul watched her silently.

Unnerved, she stepped behind the screen to use the chamber pot. When she emerged, he was still watching her. "What?"

The boy hopped from the bed, came up to her, and solemnly handed her the purse.

"What?" she cried.

He flinched, throwing up an arm to take the brunt of whatever blow he expected to fall.

Gods, she was stupid. Vellefair had told her the boy was a pickpurse. She let out an annoyed breath and shoved the purse into her pocket. "I guess I deserved that." Then she rounded on him. "But don't do it again!"

The smile was completely disarming in its charm. "We have a pact." He held out his hand, and she touched his fingertips.

6

Meg—that was the woman's name—bought Raoul a bowl of rice at the rice house across the common from his father's shop. Raoul kept an eye out for sign that his *father* had woken.

They were the rice monger's only customers, and when they showed no sign of leaving or ordering more rice—after he'd had eaten three bowls—and no further customers were forthcoming, the owner disappeared into a back room, leaving them alone.

Raoul picked the last of the rice from his bowl, watching the common.

"You told me last night your father loots magiels' homes after they've been arrested and sells their potions," she said.

He had. "Yes."

"I'm looking for an amulet. Maybe you've seen it amongst your father's things."

"Maybe." This was interesting. When people wanted something, things happened.

"It's a large orange stone, smooth and round." She made a circle of her thumb and forefinger. "The setting is gold, with seven rays, rippling like snakes. It might be on a chain, to be worn around the neck."

He thought for a moment. "No." He licked his bowl.

"Are you sure? He might have just bought it in Cataract Crag before you came to Highglen."

Raoul lowered the bowl. "How do you know we were in Cataract Crag?"

"I'm interested in the amulet."

"You want to buy it?"

"Yes." But she was lying. He could tell. She wanted to steal it. Still, whatever happened, it could be entertaining. Even exciting. "I could look in his shop."

"He might not have it displayed on a shelf. Does he have places he keeps . . . special things?" He'd bet a beating she'd stopped herself from saying, "valuable."

Raoul nodded. "It's harder for me to look there. If he catches me—" He turned sharply to peek out the window. The stable door was open and farmers were setting out tables of fall vegetables. "Father's awake."

Meg eased the door open and hesitated in the entrance to Yaquob's shop. The day's radiance did not beam directly into the space from the room's tiny window, but the light which filtered in gave a soft, bright glow to a hover of golden motes. She doubted if the Amber was hidden in plain sight, though the shelves were heaped with enough paraphernalia to mask such an object. No. The jewel's political and religious value precluded such a strategy. The Prayer Stone would be on the merchant's person or locked in a snared puzzle box, warded and chained.

The hanging over a doorway opposite the window fluttered, and a man emerged. His clothing was of good quality, though he appeared hastily put together and his brow was furrowed, as though he battled light or waking or worries. He forced a smile, however. "Yes, good morning," he greeted her. "How may I help you?"

"I've come to apologize to you." She removed her hood. "I believe you are Yaquob Tagel?"

His eyes flicked briefly in some quick recognition, then masked. Likely, a reflex identification of her magiel skin, veiled. "I'm not sure I—"

She stepped aside, and let Raoul, head lowered, step into the space. "I waylaid your son last night, very late. I was informed by one of the locals that this boy could lead me to a man who trades in unusual magiel magics. Your boy was intent on some errand for you, I believe, and I prevented him from carrying it out. For that, I apologize." This man knew Janat. Had an interest in her. She watched him for any hint that could lead her to her sister.

A trace of black anger touched the man's cheek, so fleeting, Meg was not sure she'd seen it. But, again, he recovered. "No need for apology. The boy has chores." He tapped a finger. "Pack that satchel like I told you."

Raoul darted through the curtain into the private room.

Yaquob turned to her. "You have an interest in unusual amulets or ingredients?"

"A precious stone." Such a glaring request from one whose complexion proclaimed the purity of her magiel heritage was reckless—and she had no idea who might be loitering just beyond the open window—but Meg's patience was exhausted. "Perhaps you acquired one from a jeweler from Orumon recently in Cataract Crag?"

A hint of a smile quirked across his face and a fleeting sense of familiarity touched her. Had she seen him before?

He perched on the edge of the only table that was not laden—likely a small space for the writing of receipts—and the sensation vanished. No. Maybe she'd once met someone who had a similar smile.

"Please. Feel free to peruse my wares. I purchase, and otherwise procure, curiosities of all kinds from craftsmen and magiels." He waved a hand. "The irony of my situation is that those with the greatest interest in my specialized commodities are magiels, and in recent years, magiels have been the least able to afford what I have to sell."

Not a denial. No hint he knew Janat.

His eyes lidded as he observed her. "Do you have a special interest?"

Did he guess who she was? She couldn't hunt down rumor of the Amber without risk. "There's no one in all of Shangril who would not be interested in the recovery of an amulet once thought lost," she murmured.

"You refer to the Prayer Stone of Orumon." Yaquob sighed but matched her murmured tone. "People of the seven nations would rejoice if such a powerful amulet could be made whole again." He shook his head. "And I would be a wealthy man if I had such a jewel to sell. I'm sorry to disappoint you."

Of course, he could not admit to having it, even if he did; not unless he was prepared to sell it to her, and clearly, she did not have that kind of money. He'd just said so. He would give it to her, if he supported the cause of the uprisers. But a merchant who pursued only his own gain was safest to sell such a thing to a Delarcan. Or with some risk, to a royal intent on cutting a piece of Shangril out for him—or her—self, in defiance of the High King. Raef Gramaret? Hada, defying her brother?

And Hada had a magiel to use it with.

Gweddien would certainly—if he hadn't already—convince Hada to have her spies find this shop and send a servant to obtain the jewel. Meg would have to act fast, if she wanted to steal it. If it wasn't already too late.

Raoul.

He was her key.

CHAPTER 22

The man before Raef was tall and haggard, his hangdog look summing up a bundle of troubles from poverty to drink to dullness of mind. The man was a scullion Raef's servant had caught thieving—good table leavings meant to strengthen the hunting dogs. A petty crime, but one that could lead to dismissal, if brought to the chamberlain's notice. However, Raef had a reputation among the citizens: Raef the Good, true heir to the throne of Gramarye.

He was more than happy not just to overlook the misdemeanor but to give the scullion a second wage—for a second job. Reporting on the magiel picked up during a jurisdictional kerfuffle between the puppet border guards set up for Hada's amusement, and an Arcanian patrol. Raef's spies reported a handful of Marigolds had escaped during the botch at Coldridge, so this could be one of them; one Huwen might appreciate having returned. And there was a whiff of talk Hada was using this magiel for some, undoubtedly corrupt, purpose.

The scullion accepted his first payment, and Raef dismissed him.

Raef leaned on the closed door and let his gaze wander over his room. The morning sun threw the small space into blocks of brilliance and dark.

Too many questions had no answer. The magiel of interest to Huwen had been, apparently, trying to *enter* the country when he was arrested. Why?

Hada had been actively ejecting magiels from the country, yet she approved her border captain's decision to take this man in. Again, why?

Finally, and most pointedly, could this mysterious magiel be the Barcley heir, Gweddien? Son of the royal magiel of the Chrysocholla of Gramarye before the outbreak of civil war, and perhaps the only remaining full-blooded magiel? Who else would be of such interest to both Huwen and Hada?

If so, Raef had not seen him since they were both boys. Gweddien had been too old, when Raef was a child, for the magiel to pay attention to him. And Gweddien had spent much of his youth with Huwen in Holderford, so really, they'd barely known each other.

But the world was too uncertain to depend on anyone but one's self. Raef could not gamble on Gweddien's memory of him. If the scullion's report confirmed his identity, Raef must work out a mechanism for the magiel to meet with a slim blade to the ribs or, better, a plausible poison or curse. But the planning had to be exquisite. Raef could not afford such an intrigue to be traceable back to him.

In the meantime, he'd be careful to ensure their paths did not cross.

He hobbled to the far side of the room, leaned his cane in its holder, and sat at his desk.

One thing, at least, Raef could guess. The magiel had worked a spell on Hada. Promises from a honeyed tongue, a love potion, or some type of obedience spell, perhaps. Hada had freed the man, given him autonomy within her private wing, given him clothing and rooms, *and a servant*. And she'd begun to listen to his flattery over the advice of her courtiers.

Perhaps it was the magiel's influence, but Hada was increasingly overstepping her role. She had the vexatious propensity to instigate action—frivolously and with silly non-apologies after the fact—without Raef's approval. Or foreknowledge.

Such as the festival for the One God. A day of charity, marked by a few of the devout. Now—spending her personal wealth, so he could not censure her for public excess—she'd declared it a day of prayer and celebration, with singers and jugglers and puppet troupes hired to entertain in the castle and in all the town commons. And the woman was handing out free bread and ale for all. It had been publicly announced, so Raef could do nothing but watch as the city's merchants and artisans and businesses lose a day's wages.

Raef had not been happy, but the woman—girl—was a Delarcan. Without Huwen's guidance, Raef was uncertain how far he could push his jurisdiction, and Raef did *not* want to draw Huwen to Gramarye over such a silly issue. A silly issue that could—would—win the girl the hearts of Gramaryans.

He picked up one of the scattered small vials on his writing table. Now, this.

A page had delivered the potions, with a note from the princess. Half were magical perfumes which, used according to instruction, could overpower a person—worldling or magiel. The rest were personal wards which, when smeared over one's self, were a protection against all but the most powerful magiel spells. Hada had sent them for Raef's use in reining in the city's magiels. Or so she said.

If they weren't poisons, made by her new magiel, intended to rein *him* in.

Yet . . . he wasn't certain. Such a potion, if real, could be beyond value. At the least the gesture put him off balance.

He turned the vial over in his hand, read the tiny lettering on the container. He would have his captain try one. See if the princess was honest.

Meg should return to the brothel for Janat. Yet, how could she?

She trudged through mounds of fresh snow, brilliant in the morning sun, making her way back toward Verlin's house. She kept a vigilant eye out for soldiers.

Going to The Three Corners today would result in the same outcome as yesterday. A battle. Insults—mostly hurled by Janat, though Meg's patience could be broken. She might succeed in bringing Janat home or might not. Either way, she would find herself afterward, shaking with rage, or shaking in fear for her sister. Or both.

The image of Janat perched on the Glenfast town wall darted back, unbidden.

Had Meg done the right thing? Loosing that stone beneath the soldier's feet? He'd been crazed with drink and frustration. He'd already attacked Janat—torn her dress—and seemed bent on finishing what he'd started.

Yet . . .

Had Janat provoked him? Maybe stolen from him? Ran her mouth off at him?

She might have, but that was no excuse.

Had the soldier been enraged that Janat's spells had failed them in battle? Perhaps he'd lost a friend. A brother. The situation might've been more complex than it appeared. Still, no excuse for . . . whatever he'd intended to do to Janat.

But death? Should Meg have found a different way to save her sister?

What other options had she had? And how could she have weighed each in the heat of that moment? No, she'd had no other choice.

And, yet . . .

She brushed the worry aside. There was nothing she could do about it, not now. She had to look out for Janat *today*.

But what could she do? It tore Meg apart to leave her sister with those who would hurt her and take advantage, especially while Janat was too compromised to defend herself.

If only Janat would tell her what was wrong, why she was so driven to hurt herself.

Gods.

Meg reached the river and made her way across the bridge through the throng of shoppers and merchants. The steam engine's noise was loudest here.

Meg must make an accounting of herself to Sieur Verlin. Her place in his house depended on feeding his clients' habits for spells of dreaming and bliss, and on being invisible in the process. Her stock of Dream Incenses was getting low, and she and Janat had disappeared last night with no explanation. They were not proving themselves reliable business partners.

She sighed and wove through the morning traffic into the upper districts, doubly careful to be discreet. A woman leading a donkey, a scatter of dogs and children. A man ducking into a shop.

Hastily.

Reflexively, she turned the other direction. When was the last time she'd worried about Colm's threats? Had this man been watching her? Likely not, but nevertheless. She shouldn't be daydreaming as she walked. Colm might still—though it had been some time—want her hauled back to Glenfast or wherever he was hiding now.

She stopped at a ragpicker's stall and casually looked back. Nothing. Her imagination. She moved on.

Her thoughts returned to the Amber.

Raoul was the only one who could tell her where Yaquob kept it. He could tell her his father's habits so she could carry out the theft when Yaquob was absent.

Meg stopped on a street corner.

She'd wasted too much time. The Amber, if it were in Yaquob's possession, could be disposed of at any moment. She must hound Raoul until she got the information she needed. She shouldn't be heading up the hill, she should be heading down.

She turned and retraced her steps, eyes sharp for anyone who might have been following her. Anyone who also reversed direction.

Tonight, she'd craft the spells she'd need to ensure she—and Janat—could escape the merchant's wrath. Her sack of belongings in Verlin's house contained, what? Two or three Confusions? Yes, and a Memory Loss. Really, all they'd need was food, money, and travel gear. And a few Heartspeeds.

By Kyaju, what a time for Janat to disappear.

And what a time for fresh snowfall. Clouds were gathering overhead. There would be more snow tonight.

Right now, though, she needed a disguise.

Below the river, she purchased a used yak herder's cloak, patched and stinking of animal. She smeared disguises—a Time Shimmer Erasure and an Aging Cream—on her hands, face, and hair. No disguise was perfect, but she would pass for a yak herder's wife or widow to the casual observer, at least for a few candlemarks.

Then she returned to Yaquob's shop. Raoul was not in evidence, so she settled herself by the unbarred window and listened for Yaquob to send Raoul on some errand. She set out a cup in the snow before her, seeded with a few chetra. In the busy market plaza, she was only one of half a dozen beggars.

Yaquob entertained only three customers before midafternoon, though the common bustled with good foot traffic and Meg actually attracted some much needed money to her cup. But nothing she heard through the merchant's window was particularly instructive, nor did Raoul emerge. She was getting chilled despite the second cloak she wore and the grudging warmth of the sun.

But as the afternoon light was thinning, everything changed.

Two men, well-dressed but heavily cloaked, arrived on horseback. They dismounted, and one—a servant, by his deference—pointed to the door to Yaquob's basement shop. His master entered, and the groom tended the horses.

"Sieur." Yaquob's melodious voice drifted up through the open window. There was a mumbled response and then, "Ah. I met your servant yesterday." A pause. "Raoul!"

A moment later, Raoul appeared, but he did not trot off on some errand. Instead, he loitered casually near the door.

A guard?

Abducting the child in front of this groom might be possible, but chancy. She waited where she was. In any case, she was intrigued by Yaquob's customer. His livery bore no sigil, but both it and the horses were of exquisite quality. The visitor had to be from the castle; in which case, the Amber might come to light within the next few minutes, making its theft simultaneously easier—revealing its location—and harder. She listened.

"I do appreciate your coming in person."

"You told my man—" Meg knew the voice.

"Glim. Yes." Yaquob's voice was low, and Meg had to listen hard to hear him below the crunch of snow and chatter drifting over the common, and the distant chug of the steam engines.

But the word—glim.

Raoul swaggered over and nudged her with his toe. "Can't beg here. This is my spot."

Meg lifted her hood and glared at him. His eye was blackened, and his lip was cut and swollen. What—

He backed from her in sudden fright, then stopped himself and peered at her.

Exasperated, she beckoned him out of range of the window. "It's me. Meg."

He cast a hasty glance over the common, then peered again under her hood. He gave a short laugh. "What happened to you?"

"A small potion. A disguise."

He looked at her more closely. "That's ugly. And you smell."

She nodded at his bruise. "What happened to you?" But she knew. Her apology had only gone so far.

"You saved me from a good beating," he said cheerfully. "Only this one wallop. A bruise on the face can be good for begging."

"Let me listen." She indicated the open window.

His lip curled up in a growing smile and nodded appreciatively. "All right."

She hobbled back to her place and tried to gather the thread of the conversation.

"No. I tell you, they're lost," Yaquob said, and again, his voice was so low, she could barely make out the words. "They're not written down where they might be discovered. I've not deceived you."

Glim. Meg remembered. Mama had told her to beware of it. Glim was the one seduction no magiel could resist.

"What do you mean by telling my man you can procure it, then? But *only* if I attend you in person?" Meg scoured her memory for the identity of the visitor's voice.

"Sieur, you are aware of the lost jewel."

There was a sudden stillness below, and Meg, head bowed, strained to hear any whisper above the whuffle and stamping of the horses. *Yaquob* had introduced this topic?

A growl of indistinguishable words.

"Only to Hada," the merchant was saying.

"The princess won't come to this rat hole." That voice—

Gweddien. *Yes. Finally. Gweddien.* She'd found him.

As Rennika reported, raised up for some reason by Hada as her adviser. With a servant, and—independence to leave his mistress's side? Or magiel magic, making escape a mere matter of desperation and subtlety?

And . . . he was here, in the lower town. Looking for . . . glim. But—Gods. *The Amber.*

"I am willing to come to her," Yaquob said quietly.

Then the merchant *did* have it. And unless he gave it to Gweddien immediately, Meg had a chance to steal it.

A burst of laughter from a group of men leaving the stable obscured Gweddien's reply.

"No. Only to her. I will not trust another with it."

"It's no secret to say the woman who'll one day be Gramarye's queen has enemies." Gweddien's words were thick. Meg could swear he'd been into the drink. "She won't admit a stranger into her presence. Even if I were to advise her to do so."

Yaquob's voice became regretful. "As her magiel, I can only say you would be well advised to encourage her to admit me."

"She can have you arrested. She can have your premises searched."

"And her soldiers can fall prey to traps. And she can have me killed and lose forever the secret of the gem's location."

"Sieur, I can attest that torture can be effective in loosening tongues." Gweddien's voice raised, clearly audible.

Yaquob responded by lowering his own voice, and Meg had to work to hear. "And you, Sieur, disappoint me. I have offered you the most precious and sought-after gift in all of Shangril, for no more than the price of mere *money*. And you reject it on your princess's behalf. Such folly could earn you a place at the end of a hangman's noose."

"Sieur, I don't reject you." Gweddien must not be so far gone into his cups that he couldn't recognize the merchant's caution and lowered his voice as well. "I simply inform you. What you ask is impossible," he said in a harsh whisper. "You must entrust me as your intermediary."

A shadow touched Meg. Piss! She lifted her cup. A passerby dropped a noisy coin into its jingle.

Gweddien was speaking again. "If money's all you want, you've no need for a private audience with the princess."

"Ah. Sieur, you have me. I desire money, yes. But I want to see this object reaches the hands of the princess. Not the High King. Not another king, by way of some middleman's money-making scheme. Not the uprisers. The princess is the only one to whom I will give the gift of this opportunity."

Meg eased her back against the wall beside the window, suddenly aware that she was pushing herself to hear.

Yaquob's voice drifted up to her, faint but clear. "I await your arrangements."

CHAPTER 23

Footsteps sounded on the stairs to his father's shop, and Raoul hissed at Meg, but she had already covered her face with her hood. He slipped into a doorway as the courtier and his servant rode away.

Yaquob emerged from the shop, locking the door. Raoul stepped from his spot, and his father gave him instructions: lure Meg away, then play cups in the common before the castle—out of sight of the soldiers—until he was evicted. Watch who came and went. Then Yaquob crossed the common, going to the tavern.

Raoul made his way up a lane. Shoppers and artisans and workmen of various kinds were filling the streets, mostly going home for the day.

Meg caught up to him by the time he'd reached the next crossing. "Raoul."

He turned and grinned at her, walking backward up the alley.

"Where's your father?" She picked up her pace to stay with him.

"Where he always goes." He tripped a little in the snow and turned to walk forward. "You still stink."

Meg took the yak herder's cloak off and left it on a rubbish heap and wrapped her own, better cloak more closely around her. "Did you find out where your father keeps that necklace? The one I told you about?"

"Yep. He lied to you this morning when he said he didn't have it."

He reached another square, this one larger and louder, closer to the factory, and Meg was still with him. This common had better shops and a half-dozen tents in the center selling goat dumplings, goose sausage, pork intestine on a stick, and rice noodles. "He keeps it around his neck, like you thought." He eyed her curiously. "Do you have enough money to buy it? Father said you don't."

"I'll have to do what I can."

He watched her face. "Can you pick locks?"

"I'm a magiel."

Raoul studied her for a long moment, deciding. "All right. He drinks until he falls asleep. Every night. He'll sleep from when the taverns close until, maybe the rise of the star of Sashcarnala. Then he dreams and wakes up a lot. But for two candlemarks, nothing can wake him."

She nodded slowly. There was a hunger in her eyes. Then she indicated his black eye. "Raoul . . ."

He didn't want her to follow him to the castle, so he sat in the snow by the wall and put out his cup. "You can start my money."

Meg threw a handful of chetra into his cup. "One more thing. What interest does your father have in Janat?"

Yaquob had told him how to answer this question. "What do you think?"

She ran her tongue over her teeth, and he knew she'd drawn the right conclusion. "If this bruise is your payment for not following Janat . . ." Meg hesitated, as if she was loath to involve herself. But he waited. She would take the bait. "What will you suffer for telling me about the necklace?"

He took his stick and hoop out of his satchel and began the tossing and skewering game. "If he catches me?" Raoul grinned. "He isn't going to catch me."

"How do you know?"

"Because I'm going to kill him."

Meg made her way through narrower streets toward the back of the draper's house, turning Raoul's words over in her mind. She couldn't be distracted, let sentiment deflect her from her purpose.

And Yaquob. Raoul hadn't been explicit, but Yaquob must be working with Xadria, setting Janat up for money. Or sex.

By Kyaju, how many people had to be hurt before justice was restored? She couldn't let worry for Raoul or speculation over his father's motives keep her from recovering the Amber.

She reached the twisting path between the lesser artisan shops and the better-off servants' homes. A corner at the steeper part of

Highglen, below Highmarket Common, brought her suddenly upon two soldiers leaning over a lentil vendor's open-air brazier. One glanced her way, his grin replaced by surprise, and then alarm.

Her disguise. Applied this morning. Long gone.

His grip fastened on her arm before she could withdraw. "Magiel." His word was a muttered reflex.

Fear sank through her stomach. She tugged back, but his grasp tightened, and the other soldier, bowl in hand, turned. The scatter of passers-by flowed around them, heedless.

A Confusion. Did she have any left in a pocket? Maybe, but not to hand.

The second soldier shoved his bowl back at the vendor.

She twisted soundlessly, avoiding a second trapping hand, and blindly stabbed thought into the first soldier's skin, yanking at any source of warmth—a fever only a few weeks ago. She brought it to *now*, concentrated into the flesh of his fingers. It was shock, more than any sudden heat or pain that made him release her.

Then she pelted back the way she'd come, throwing magic behind her, finding a time when a stone or cobble had lain loose or projected from its place, to trip and slow her shouting pursuers.

But Meg couldn't run long or far. Some helpful citizen was certain to grab her.

The Confusion. She fished it out of her bag as she ran.

She turned a corner and unstoppered it, releasing its gentle aroma into the air and ducking to avoid breathing it in. She scuttled beneath the expanding cloud, holding her breath, then slowly straightened. Turning another corner, she forced herself to slow down to browse the steel needles at a tool maker's stall.

She shook her head, *no*, at the peddler, then turned a third corner to breathe in fresher air.

No one was behind her.

She breathed again, this time, from relief.

Heart and breath racing, she ambled downhill toward the noise of the engines, and districts whose inhabitants were more sympathetic. She listened, alert to any sign her hunters had failed to inhale the puff of gentle magic.

No. Nothing. They were gone, at least for now.

She meandered to the lower town to find some quiet nook to hide. She'd used magic and would need to conceal herself while she lived bits of her life out of sequence.

Eventually, in full dark and by a different path, she made her way back to Verlin's house, watching for a quiet moment in the street with few to observe her, before slipping into the narrow passage to the servants' entrance. Home.

She smiled a little to herself. Not her home, but still. Meg was happy Rennika had found a safe and warm place. Found a family.

The gate was locked but it took a moment only to place her finger on the handle, move the tumblers through time to their open position, and enter. A small magic, and one—she hoped—that would not disturb her time stream much or interfere with her plans for later tonight.

No one was in the tiny courtyard. At this time of evening, the family would all be at dinner in their dwelling above the shop. She eased the gate closed and, as was her wont, hugged the wall of the wool warehouse as she passed to the back door of Verlin's shop.

The warehouse door opened, spilling light onto the skiff of snow, and a silent shape stepped out to bar her way.

She halted.

The man's hand darted out, grabbed her shoulder and roughly propelled her into the warehouse. The door clicked. "What are you doing?" The voice was Yon's.

"None of your business," she snapped, startled by the unexpectedness of being waylaid. Gods, would the day never end?

A half-dozen candles glimmered on the fabric inspection table, illuminating scattered mounds of brightly colored textiles. Floor-to-ceiling shelves lined the walls, some laden with bolts of cloth, others with bins of fleece or yarn, others dark openings waiting to be filled.

"I know my father's business with you." Yon leaned both fists on the table, bright-lit against the shadows behind him. "I'm not proud of it, and neither is he, truth be told. The only reason he lets you stay here is for Rennika. You know that."

"Your father profits. In gultra, and in his clients' favor." Meg's contract was with Verlin, not with Yon. But Yon, as the family heir, undoubtedly had his father's ear. She needed to be careful not to be too prickly with him.

"Your agreement also specified discretion about being seen coming and going from this house."

"I am vigilant." She disliked being accused groundlessly.

"Frequent use of that gate, when it was never used before, draws attention. Coming after dark when it is locked raises questions." He tilted his head. "How many days in a row do you require additional ingredients for the same spell? The one my father has only so many uses for?"

"Have you been challenged?"

"No." He straightened, his breath puffing a faint white cloud in the candlelight. "Answer the question."

"I make spells and sell them for money." There was no reason to lie.

"And work with the uprisers to provoke unrest in preparation for war?"

"No!" She glared at him.

"No? I was talking to Miach."

She thumped her hands on the table. "Then you will know I refused his offer."

"You're an upriser from Elsen. You've been working with them since the outbreak of the civil war."

"Miach approached *me*," she corrected. "He asked for *my* help. I told him, and I'm telling you, now, I am here to be *away* from the uprisers. To be with my sisters." The Amber was not a fact. Not yet. She might not acquire it.

"So, you are not involving yourself with anything that will implicate my father? My family? Rennika?"

"I told you, no."

He gave her a long probing look.

She returned it. "Miach told me you're not innocent of upriser politics."

His eyes hooded.

"He said you delivered messages for him in Cataract Crag." She scrutinized him. "Requests for uprisers to come to Highglen and free your country from Delarcan occupation."

"That's my business."

She straightened. "You can work for the uprisers, but I can't?"

Yon studied her for a long moment, then let out a deep breath. "I helped him out. Miach is militant."

"I gathered."

"His family, all but his brother, were killed when the High King first marched in," Yon said. "He thinks Gramarye can return to

Gramaret hands. He doesn't see that the world is fundamentally changed." Yon frowned and looked down. "Miach brushes away the cost of war. The death." He raised his head. "I don't."

The cost of war. Raoul. Children like him. Homeless thieves.

Yon's face closed. "I will not see my family hurt. My grandmother, my father, my sisters."

"Nor would I." And yet, if the world were to be restored, people would be hurt.

"Or Rennika."

The last people on earth Meg wanted to hurt were Janat and Rennika.

Hada lay back on Gweddien's shoulder on the cushioned couch, watching clouds through the window drift past the stars. Their light was pearly pale. So lovely.

Gweddien played with a strand of her hair, wrapping and unwrapping it around his finger. "Because the power looms will put your weavers out of business. Just like the thread factory did to the spinners."

She marveled that her magiel could keep his thoughts clear and ordered. He was used to Dream Incense, she supposed. She felt as if she was moving in a bubble through time, each instant clear in her mind, but disconnected from all moments before and after. "But Raef says the factories are making us wealthy. There's more trade than ever."

"Factories line the pockets of the landowners who sell wool. The guild masters who do the dyeing. The merchants clamoring for a wider road for their carts."

"And the drapers and seamstresses, and the food vendors," she added, amazed that she followed his train of thought. "The commons are full of markets, and not just one day a week, but . . ." Her attention was caught by the crackle of flames leaping on the hearth. Their flicker so delicate and ephemeral. Like her thoughts.

"But what about all the spinners who came for work when the carding machines created a glut of fiber?" he was saying.

What were she and Gweddien talking about?

"Only one in ten can work in the spinning factory. The rest become beggars, thieves, and indigents." He shifted a little beneath her. "Are you defending Raef?"

No. "I'm . . ." What was she trying to do? "I'm trying to understand him. If he's making the lords wealthy, they'll support him, not me. You said we need to get the aristocrats onside."

"We do. But not at the cost of your people."

His finger stroked the side of her cheek, and a sudden thrill astonished her body. "Then, what do I do?"

His finger paused. "There is a possibility."

She ached for his caress to continue.

"Something has come to light. An opportunity."

The topic had changed, but she wasn't sure anymore what Gweddien was talking about.

"There's a man I think you should meet. Privately."

Again, confusing. "What man? No one's come to my apartments. How could you have met him?"

The caress resumed. "A listener told me."

Oh, well. Too nebulous a connection to be concerned about. The warmth of the fire, the warmth of Gweddien's body, the tingle of his touch, the floating sensation that infused her, all distracting. She rolled over to face him, watching the firelight dance across his shimmering skin. She placed her fingers on his cheek, as if she could steady its flickers.

His chin lifted and his lips touched hers, a long soft kiss, bursting slow intense explosions of bliss across her skin, through her breasts and groin. Rapture immersed her, and time stopped.

His lips pulled away and she panted, echoes of pleasure coursing through her.

His eyes widened, and he let out a long breath, shifting a little beneath her. "Oh." He blinked. "I'm sorry. Your Highness, I—"

"I'm not."

He struggled a moment, then straightened on the couch, and she had to sit up. He ran his fingers through his hair and looked over his shoulder toward the door.

Was someone coming? No one would interrupt.

"It's late."

Why this change? "Not that late."

He turned back to her, his aspect suddenly sober. "Highness, I should go."

"Call me Hada," she whispered, bewildered and bereft.

His eyes softened, then, and he turned in his seat, grasping both her shoulders in his hands. "I'm . . ." He shook his head. "I'm . . . not good. For you."

She searched his face. "What do you . . ."

He bit his lip. Taking her head in his hands, he leaned in and kissed her forehead. "I have to go."

Rennika's steps slowed as she climbed the stair to her chambers. Candlelight.

It was Meg, sitting in the easy chair by the brazier. She looked up as Rennika topped the stair, but she said nothing.

Rennika cast about the room. Empty. "Where's Janat? Did you find her?" Rennika kept her voice low, in case Sieura Verlin or one of the others was below and could hear.

"I found her." Meg's gaze drifted back to the floor. "I'm sorry, Rennika. I tried to bring her back."

What did that mean?

By the goodness of Kyaju, Rennika had been worried sick, praying all last night, when neither of them returned. She'd woken late this morning, still in her chair, and tried to put on a good face for Sieura Verlin who, thankfully, didn't question the fact that the two sisters would not be helping with the house today. And for Sieur Verlin, who also didn't ask. She'd canceled dye inspection at the workshop, leaving everything to Xoran's judgment, and made work for herself here, despite the fact that Princess Hada's dress was needed within the week, and the seamstresses had not yet cut the pattern.

"She doesn't want to come back. I can't make her."

"Doesn't want to?" Rennika tried to parse her meaning.

Meg pressed her lips together and said nothing.

"Gods, Meg." How had Janat turned so suddenly from working quietly for two weeks in Verlin's house, with never a peep of dissatisfaction, to . . . refusing to come back? Something had happened.

Still, Meg only stared at the floor.

Rennika glared at her, perplexed. "Well, perhaps we should talk to her again."

Meg sighed. "She has people . . . protecting her."

"*Protecting* her? From what?" Meg was not telling her everything, not by a long shot.

Meg licked her lips. "Protecting their interest in her, I suspect." She lifted her head. "Rennika, until Janat wants to come back, we won't see her."

"But you told me she doesn't make good decisions." Meg was back far too soon for a thorough search of even the lower town.

"There's no point—"

Rennika stepped past her to her room and grabbed her cloak. She had to do everything. "Where do I go?"

"Rennika, no."

"You told me she's a spell-eater." She wrapped her cloak around herself. "I don't know much about this, Meg, but that means she can't stop, doesn't it? It means she *can't* come back. It means she could be somewhere dangerous. She could have been picked up by Hada's soldiers, imprisoned, ejected from Gramarye—out on the road, in the snow—"

"It's night. The people with her will be drunk and belligerent. There's no point in going before morning."

The danger of what Rennika might face became suddenly real. Her hands fell from the cloak ties at her throat.

"Come. Sit."

There had to be something. Something.

"Rennika." Meg's voice was gentle. "Come."

Rennika slumped onto the hard-backed chair opposite the brazier from Meg. How could Meg have driven Janat off? Janat, who was so delicate? Who never hurt a spider?

Meg sat in the armchair. "She'll come around." But her voice sounded far from certain.

Meg had no idea how turning up here with Janat had sent Rennika's world into a spin. No idea. Plunged her back into memories of her childhood, the precariousness of being a refugee, on the run, hiding. Had the life she'd lived in the past six years since she'd come to Verlin's house become her new reality, or was it just a sham, a hiding place that had lasted longer than most? Did her sisters' return signal a resumption of her life as a fugitive from the High King's justice?

She must ask Sieur Verlin to give her a portion of her savings. Keep it close to her, in case Meg's antics—or her own complicit spying—led to a sudden need to flee.

Sieura Verlin didn't like Meg or Janat. The old woman said nothing, but she'd made it perfectly clear to Rennika. Sieur Verlin knew the arrangement would come crashing down. He'd been honest, though; he would disavow them at the first hint of a problem and make Rennika choose sides. She could see it, plainer than the snippets she lived from other parts of her lifetime. The Verlin girls—all except perhaps Tyg and the little ones—were nervous and uncertain about harboring magiels. One of them could unintentionally say something. Tell a friend. Yon was deeply uncomfortable; he probably knew his father had stretched the city's unspoken expectations. All for Rennika's sake.

And Meg, from the first, had traipsed in and out at all times of day, oblivious.

Now, this. Rennika had no idea how she was going to explain Janat's vulnerability—liability—to Sieur Verlin. Or to Sieura Verlin.

"You're worried you'll lose your position at the castle," Meg said softly.

"Yes!" Was that petty? To want to maintain her work, her reputation? Her . . . *family*? "Or Sieur Verlin will. Or worse."

Meg gave a tiny tilt to her head. She rose and walked to her room, returning with a purse she placed on the table. "Here's the money Janat took."

Meg recovered the money from Janat?

"I hope it's enough." Meg looked her in the eye. "I'll leave tonight. I'll do my best to be sure Janat doesn't come back here to bother you."

The words cut. "What do you want from me?" Rennika whispered, unable to hold back her fear and anger and frustration. "Nothing I do is good enough, is it? I secured this place for you and Janat to live. When we were refugees on the road to Silvermeadow, it was my begging that supported the three of us. Whenever the two of you need something or want something, it's me you come to."

"Then we're both in the same valley, aren't we?" Meg said calmly. "Because nothing I do is good enough for you, either."

"What do you mean?" Rennika couldn't believe this. Meg could be so cruel.

"When Nanna grabbed us that night in Archwood and smuggled us out of the castle, I was seventeen," Meg said.

The blackness of that night crashed around Rennika. The bright candlelight and dancing and music in King Ean's court. The last time she ever saw Mama. The cold and the wind and the rocks and the fear, running from the castle. Into the dark, into the mountains. "And I was eleven. What's your point?"

"When that orum killed Nanna, it was left to me, Rennika." Meg left the sentence unexplained.

Rennika gave her head a small shake, as if doing so could rattle some sense out of the non sequiturs.

"To find a way to get you and Janat off the mountain," Meg said. "To keep you safe and fed. To keep you from being captured as political prisoners. *Seventeen.*"

Seventeen.

Four years ago, when Rennika had been seventeen, she'd had a home, here with Sieur Verlin's family. An apprenticeship with Master Quennell. Her rooms. Food. Clothing.

"Mama told me," Meg said softly, *"take care of your sisters.* I might not have done a good job, but you're alive."

It hadn't been Meg's job to care for two sisters. But she'd done it. "So, you're saying it is time for me to take care of you?"

Meg reached out and took her hand. "Rennika—"

A soft tread sounded on the stair. They both turned.

Janat leaned on the railing at the top of the stair.

CHAPTER 24

Janat let her gaze roam over Rennika's sitting room. The table her sister used, to study dye recipes and fabrics, had not changed. The doorways to three rooms, two standing open and dark. The small table lit by a single candle. Her sisters, both here, staring at her.

The same room. Not the same room. Janat leaned on the banister, easing the hurt in her left leg.

The twist of revulsion on Rennika's face confirmed for Janat what the pain in her jaw and cheek and head had already told her. Xadria had done a good job of emphasizing her meaning of the word, "loyalty."

Her sisters rose, and Rennika led her with soothing words to sit in the padded armchair.

Janat tried to protest. Gods knew, she wasn't worth their sympathy.

Rennika hurried to bring a basin of water and a soft cloth.

Meg knelt by her knee and took her hands. "Where are you hurt?"

By Ranuat's Murderers, almost anything would be better than this sympathy, this pity, this humiliation. *Wasn't that a party?* she wanted to joke.

No. Not this time. She couldn't pay her debt to Xadria the way Xadria wanted to be paid. Working on her back. With no money, no place to go . . .

She'd had no choice but to crawl back here. Take their pity and "understanding."

Meg's carefully neutral expression in the candlelight pinched her brow, tightened her lips, turned to liquid in her dark eyes.

Gods, Janat had been unfair. What had she said to Meg? She couldn't remember. A venom had come bubbling out of her, spilling poison everywhere, and Meg had collapsed, even before Xadria detained her. Now, her sister was at the end of her rope, running out of ways to cope. And Janat was to blame.

"Janat?" Meg repeated. "Where are you hurt?"

Rennika set the cloth and basin on the small table. Then she brought a blanket and tucked it around Janat's shoulders.

Meg wrung out the cloth and laid its cool softness, stinging, on Janat's forehead, her cheek.

"I'm going to check you for bleeding and for broken bones," Meg murmured, and her hands were gentle, though the pain that responded to her touch was not.

When Meg was done, Rennika wrapped the blanket more firmly around her.

"Bruises." Meg smiled. "A few scratches. You'll be all right."

Be all right. Janat would have barked a harsh laugh at that, had her jaw not hurt so much. She was not *all right*. She would not *be all right*. She inhaled raggedly, trying not to expand her ribs. Piss, something had to change. She had to do something different. She couldn't keep hurting Meg. Now Rennika, too. Everything she touched was infected.

"Meg." It was hard to form the word. Her lips had swollen on one side. *Ranuat, give her strength.* "I'm going to change," she managed. She must change. She must gather all her will and use it. Every day. Push aside memory. Put others first. Do as Meg told her to do. More, help Meg with *her* ambitions.

Meg nodded, but there was no belief in her eyes. "Yes, Janat. Do that."

A spark of hate flared in her for an instant.

"Don't be condescending, Meg," Rennika said.

Meg turned her penetrating gaze on Rennika for a moment. Then she turned it on Janat. "What's different?" she asked. "What makes this time different from before?"

The panic clawed in her chest then, raking her stomach and heart and ribs. A flash of memory. Of Wenid and Gweddien. The wine. The glim.

Gods. How could she be so weak, so fragile, to promise one minute to put the memories behind her and the very next have them flood her mind, engulf her, sweep her back, and drown her?

Drown. Soft. Sleep.

Wouldn't that be best for everyone, if she could just slip away, just . . .

"Come." Rennika was urging her from the chair. "Come to bed."

Sleep. Escape. She wouldn't sleep.

She felt Rennika smooth back her hair, tangled and dirty, and touch that spot, that pinprick beneath her death token collar, awry, now. Rennika rubbed the scab and Janat felt it dissolve to dust.

And Meg's eye caught hers.

Janat's stomach turned sick.

Accusation.

And pity.

Meg stood, fixed to the floor. Rennika took Janat, limping, to her room.

No. Kyaju. By all that was good, no.

It had been a trick of the light. A single candle threw more shadows than illumination.

Itch. Boneblood. Meg's mind shied away from the words. From the image of Kirst. From the man's words. *Might not be dead now, but they're as good as.*

She had to get Janat out of Highglen.

Kyaju help her.

Meg went to her room. Her hands moved of their own accord, finding her sack. Stuffing her clothes inside.

And go, where? Not Cataract Crag.

She cleared her shelf of stoppered vials, filling a small bag.

West, perhaps. Not Coldridge.

Some place in the far north of Teshe, some village no one had ever heard of. If Janat could travel that far. If Janat *would* travel that far, come morning.

She had so few possessions. Just as well, though. They had to carry everything on their backs.

Piss on it. Why should Meg work *so damn hard* for someone who didn't even care if she was there to pick up the pieces? Nothing she did helped. She was incompetent. Powerless.

More than one person had told her. Let Janat go.

Meg's arms fell to her sides—the mouth of her sack, loose in one hand. And what about the Amber?

Tonight. She'd planned to get it tonight.

If it was the Prayer Stone, *if*— Piss, she wasn't going to second guess it again.

The uprisers had lost Coldridge. They'd lost their toehold in Glenfast. If they had no base of operations, no sanctuary . . .

Children with no death tokens would be fated, when they died, to walk the cold earth forever as ghosts denied Heaven. No revolution could create a paradise on earth—Meg was not so naive as to believe this—but the Amber could make a world in which the people could at least have a right to their death tokens. In which there were voices to influence the kings. In which the rule of law presided over the rule of tyranny.

Could Meg leave Janat to whatever fate held in store for her?

Janat, once she decided to be contrite, would be quiet. At least, for a few days. Maybe a season. Maybe longer. Janat . . . when she was doing well . . . worked very hard at being agreeable.

And Meg was so close. *So close.*

She felt, more than heard, a presence behind her. She turned.

Rennika stood in the doorway, face contorted in grief, tears on her cheeks. "You don't have to go."

Meg felt the sack in her hand. Had she been packing to take Janat away or to escape Highglen once she had the Amber?

"You and Janat," Rennika whispered. "Stay. Please. I want us to stop fighting."

Meg bit her lip, unsure how to respond.

"I'll help you, Meg. Whatever it is you're doing, I'll help."

Cloud had moved in, and it now obscured the Gods' constellations, deepening the murk within the city streets. Still, the whiteness of the remaining snow magnified what little light there was, muting the world to blurs of gray. The neverending, rhythmic wheeze of the steam engines at the factory seemed clearer in the mist.

Meg had sat by Janat's pallet, stroking her hair in the dark, waiting for her to sleep. When she rose from Janat's bedside, Rennika's door was closed. No one saw her slip from the house and across the tiny courtyard. Meg watched at Verlin's servants' gate to be sure she saw no movement among the shadows before sliding along the buildings and into a side street. Especially here, in the upper town, Hada's soldiers would be alert to suspicious stirring at this time of night.

Part way toward her goal, she spied two soldiers conferring at an intersection, and she hovered in the gloom of a doorway until they parted ways and patrolled out of sight. In the lower town, a scatter of people drifted through the streets, making their way home from the taverns, or scavenging. There were fewer meddling military.

The snow-trodden space before Yaquob's shop was empty, and she saw no movement in the shanty town by the rice cookery. The chandler's shop and home were dark, as were the stable and all but perhaps two dwellings looking out onto the now empty common. Meg slipped into the shadow of Yaquob's doorway.

Heart thumping and breath speeding, she placed her hands on the knob and lock, feeling for the tumblers within. The door eased open with a faint creak. She stepped inside and closed it, almost soundlessly, behind her.

The shop, a pitfall of delicate, precariously balanced glass poised on obscured shelves, waited for the faintest touch of her cloak to shatter the silence. Holding her breath, she edged among them, halting and easing herself away from the slightest nudge against a table or chest.

A shift in the shadows set her heart racing and she stilled, her hand slipping onto a vial of Confusion in her pocket.

The splotch of darkness rose—the shape of the boy.

Meg breathed, strength coursing through her body.

Raoul approached her on cat feet and beckoned her close. His words were a breath in her ear. "I'll help."

The disorientation, momentarily, was hers. Why should he help? Revenge. Of course.

She nodded. Less chance she would have to use any more magic and handicap herself later with its cost.

He beckoned to her again, and she lowered her head. "I'll do the pinch. You be ready with a potion. In case."

His fingers were small and light, and he knew, presumably, where and how his father wore the pendant at night. Again, she nodded, the vial in her hand ready.

Raoul turned and slipped soundlessly through the gloom, and through the curtained doorway. Meg followed.

The darkness within was absolute. A closeness, a warmth in the air, and the heavy breathing of the sleeping man gave Meg the sense of a small space. If any light seeped through the drape at her back, she could not detect it.

But . . . she listened. Did Yaquob breathe deeply? Truly? Or feign?

Raoul paused, perhaps orienting himself or reaching out a hand or foot as a guide. Then he moved forward. Hands splayed and feet tentative, Meg followed him, stopping when her outstretched fingers brushed the boy's clothing. She checked the tension of the cork on her Confusion. Should she need to use it, she'd have no choice but to fling its contents into the air and dash for the doorway, escaping before its magic enveloped her.

The moment in the darkness stretched, infinite, marked only by the rhythm of the man's breathing and sound of the distant machine. The sense of tension in the small body so close to her only magnified her own.

Then she felt the tap on her elbow and the boy squeezed past her. Was it done? With no need for magic? Well, if so, it had certainly been easy.

Meg followed Raoul through the hanging into the relative light of the murky shop and let the curtain drop behind her. Raoul held his hand up, and she opened her palm beneath it. The pendant, like a large multi-rayed stone sunburst, dribbled from his fingers on a chain until it rested on her hand.

The clouds had broken up and were drifting across the constellations as Meg climbed the road toward Highmarket Common. A greenish glow fluttered in ribbons above her—the Gods' Light. It was not seen often. A sign of blessing. It filled her with awe.

Though the streets were empty, she stayed in the shadows, a hand on her vial of Confusion, conscious with every step of the weight of the pendant beneath her robes.

Gods, she wanted to dance her way up the streets, giddy with an ache to slip her fingers beneath her cloak and bring the jewel out to inspect it, to see if it was, truly, the prayer stone that once belonged to her mother. The prayer stone Huwen claimed to have smashed. The savior of the people.

She calmed her racing heart. Such an act would be the height of folly.

When she was seventeen and the High King's troops marched on Castle Archwood, Meg and her sisters had lost their home, their religion, and their freedom, and so had the people of Orumon.

By the Gods, with the Amber in her possession, Meg was going to get those freedoms back. She'd made this vow when she first ran from royal swords. Now, she would do it.

When Sieur Verlin's gate closed behind her, she allowed herself to breathe.

The house was dark, the draper's quadrangle silent but for an occasional snuffle or movement from the barn or henhouse, and the faint whistle of the wind above the distant chunking of the steam engines. Rising above the shrine to the One God and the courtiers' chateaus, the castle that had once belonged to Dwyn Gramaret emerged in fitful starlight, haloed in rippling green. Meg let her hand slide beneath her cloak to touch the Amber, feel its outlines, recall its shape as she had seen it resting on her mother's pale robes.

Mama at court. Sitting on her high back chair beside King Ean and Queen Elana. Beautiful, regal, untouchable. Her shimmering skin against the simple, unbleached linen of her magiel robes, so different from the woad blues and madder scarlets and marigold yellows of the aristocrats. The reverence with which everyone—*everyone*—treated the great magiel.

Mama's calling, to bear a prayer stone, was the highest pursuit for a magiel, reserved only for those born of pure lines traceable to the One God. To use the Amber under the protection of her king; to ascend to the seven Heavens to petition the Gods themselves; to bring back the everlasting life of death tokens for the people.

A life that should have belonged to Meg.

That *would* belong to her, once she and Janat removed the Amber safely from Highglen. Took it to King Dwyn.

The constellation Kanden appeared, bright in the sky, twinkling through the Gods' Light.

Something stirred on the castle's parapet.

Not a soldier. Someone in grand robes, color washed away by night. A man.

A courtier, perhaps. Maybe even Raef Gramaret with his cane, awake at this candlemark to look at the spectacular sky. Someone.

The figure was too far away to make out. The man peered through a telescope.

The words of the innkeeper's wife, in Cataract Crag, came back to Meg. *A rich man's mistress.* Gods, she'd have to be desperate.

Had Mama been King Ean's mistress? Meg knew who her father was: Kraae, magiel to the Ruby of Arcan. She'd met him once, just before the outbreak of the civil war, and he'd touched her hair, proud of her as-yet-unproven talent. But though he and Mama seemed friendly, Meg could see they weren't lovers. No. But there was a closeness between Mama and King Ean; a closeness even Meg, even at seventeen, understood. A closeness not evident between the king and his queen, though their love was manifest.

Mama needed no lover. The glory of communing with the Gods brought a joy so abundant, nothing, not even a consort, could ease the burden of returning to the lowest sphere of earth. Of returning to a world drained of animation, of life.

The maids had hushed Meg, hustled her ashamedly from Mama's chamber. But she'd seen Mama toss with restless dreams for days after visiting Heaven with King Ean, sit in a darkened room bereft but for the visions in her head. Spend brief moments with her children before listlessness overtook her again. The price of devoting herself to her people was high. But Meg had grown up prepared to assume this role at the proper time. To be the Magiel of the Amber.

Meg closed her eyes. Soon. She had the Amber now.

The draper's yard darkened as clouds covered the stars and the fading green glow. It was late. She must wake Janat before dawn, before Yaquob discovered the theft. Raoul might want to kill him, and Meg might want to bring the boy with her, but neither was practical. Meg had emptied a pouch into Vellefair's hand and asked him to hide the boy, for all she might be able to trust the Heartspeed user.

Before more snow came and escape with the Amber became impossible, she and Janat must slip away like ghosts in the dark, manage the steep, cliffy gullies to the long valley that led to the lower lands of Shangril, and find King Dwyn, wherever he might be.

A daunting task. The snow would slow them, their trail obvious, Janat a handicap. In addition to Yaquob and any mercenaries he might hire, Hada's soldiers guarded the new border crossing. Meg could only use so many Disguises, Confusions, and curses. And the Amber was no more magical than a rock without a person of royal blood to touch it with her and transport them both to Heaven. To be captured by royals would deliver the prayer stone to those who would smash it forever—or use it for personal power.

Did she . . . *need* to escape?

Meg's hand on the doorknob to Verlin's house stilled.

She'd thought immediate escape, once the Amber was in her possession, would be paramount. But . . .

She didn't *have* to take the Amber to the uprisers.

She needed no king's—or prince's—cooperation to use the Amber. Only their royal touch.

Once the three were joined—magiel, prayer stone, and royal—the transport to Heaven, or so Mama had instructed her, followed. And in Heaven, the royal had no dominion. He—or she—would be Meg's servant. His or her only role was to remain detached from the glories of paradise and bring her safely home. Meg could pray for anything she wanted, and whichever royal traveled with her had no power to change that prayer.

She only needed to touch Princess Hada.

Gods' Light, green and shimmering. Hada lay on her stomach on a cushioned divan pulled up against her open window. She nestled in a fur robe, moved to awe by the waving curtains of light above the stars. A fire blazed on the hearth behind her—a harpist brushed the air with splashes of arpeggios—as she danced with the lights in a swirl of Dream Incense.

A part of her wondered where Gweddien was, and if the Gods spoke to him through their light as well.

Raef threw on his thick woolen cloak and hobbled out to his balcony.

Gods, yes.

There, blazing above him, the glory of the Heavens. God's Light. A sign.

Change. Hope. Fulfillment.

Now. Now was the time for action. For the realization of accomplishment.

Raef let his cane drop to the flags and leaned both hands on the stone baluster, gazing out over the rooftops and mountain peaks and arch of stars to the shimmering firmament. It was time to stop this cautious, waiting and watching. Time to take matters into his own hands.

⁂

"My Lord."

Huwen woke slowly, groggily, to peer into the dark and cold of his foreign bedroom. The candlelit face of his manservant hovered over him.

Ychelle. Bad news? Shalire?

"I'm sorry to disturb you, Majesty," the man said, "but there is a display of Gods' Light."

Huwen blinked past the man at the pale light drifting through his open curtains.

Gods' Light. He mumbled a thanks and pushed back his quilts, donning the slippers and robe his man held.

So, no misfortune. No concern about Ychelle. He breathed.

Pulling his robe closed, he stepped out onto the balcony, his man a pace behind him.

The skies blazed with curtains of green light. Huwen stared, struck dumb at the expanse of luminescence soaring above the river of stars.

A sign of promise.

Yes. His emissary to Highglen had returned two days ago. Hada had been gracious but slippery. She had not given up the magiel.

Huwen nodded. And now, a sign from the One God. *Go. Do. Act.*

He would ride to Gramarye tomorrow.

CHAPTER 25

Clouds weighed on Gramarye's mountains, a ceiling of gray almost close enough to touch, and a gale whipped up sharp crystals of snow. Meg huddled out of the blast in a corner of the leatherworks compound where Miach was the journeyman. The fingers of her left hand clutched a handkerchief over her nose and mouth, numbed in the bite of the icy morning air. She wondered if Yaquob had been murdered. Whether Vellefair had been able to protect Raoul.

The foreman had looked at her askance when she arrived just after dawn but admitted her to the compound. He was not about to let a magiel wait in the master's workshop. He claimed tersely not to know when to expect Miach, so she marked time, cloak wrapped about her, until the gate opened and the fair young man strode in.

"Miach." Meg darted from her niche to intercept him before he reached his office.

He stopped in surprised affront before recognizing her. With a deepening expression of puzzlement, he led her into the workshop and closed the door.

The smell of urine, feces, and fermentation within was overpowering, and Meg gagged into her handkerchief. She turned away, hood up against the curiosity of a handful of workers at the vats.

Miach led her up a narrow stair to a dim, orderly room centered on a table and two chairs, with shelves containing an impressive number of rough-bound books and scrolls along the walls. He found a splinter and lit a candle from embers on the hearth. "So." The upriser set the candle on the table. Slates and chalk, an ink well and quills covered its surface in neat lines. "News?"

"Where's your master?"

"The slaughterhouse, haggling for hides. But he sympathizes."

She closed the door behind them. "Nothing from Dwyn's uprisers. But there's been a development."

He flipped his cloak back and knelt to build up the fire. "Good news?"

"Possibly. Would your people fight for Highglen? Hold it, against the High King's armies? If there were a chance we could take it?" She drew the Amber from beneath her robes and laid it on an open book of accounts. She'd promised Yon she would not involve herself, but everything had changed now.

Miach's glance riveted to the prayer stone and the log he was holding slipped from his fingers. He rose, his eyes never leaving the jewel. "What is it?" he whispered.

As soon as she'd come home the night before, Meg had hurried to her room to study the gem by candlelight. To the best of her memory, the talisman was perfect. The smooth, rounded stone, a deep, lustrous orange, was polished to a flawless oval. A golden ring framed it, radiating seven snaking rays reminiscent of orum necks, to the size of her palm. The candle's radiance had passed through the stone, unobstructed by even the tiniest stain or fault, casting a warm gleam on her pillow. And now, in the new day's light of the leather master's office, the stone—incredibly—remained just as unblemished. Study as she would, Meg could find no sign of forgery.

Miach approached the table and reached out a finger toward the stone. He stared at her. "This can't be . . ." His throat worked, as if his words dried in his mouth.

She let her head move slowly from side to side. "No." She matched his muted tone. "It can't be."

He lifted a brow in question, and she gave a slight nod. Reverently, he took up the pendant. "I've seen drawings. A painting, once. I would have no way of knowing how close this is to the real prayer stone."

"Few people would."

He turned. "How can it help us? Where did you get it?"

"The story I'm given is that this is the true Amber."

His face dissolved in incredulity. Then skepticism.

She sighed and sat. "After the siege of Archwood, when the fortress fell, the High King marched into a dead city."

Miach stood beside the small waxed-linen window, examining the amulet. "I know the story. Everyone knows it."

Meg pushed on. "Talanda—" her mother "—cast a curse on the entire country of Orumon. The occupying force was compelled to leave."

Miach turned back from the window. "That's where the story begins to sound like myth. No magiel, I'm sorry Meg, is that strong."

True. It was hard to conceive of a curse so powerful it could drive all people from an entire country, erase it from all maps. Yet even now, eight years later, the country remained an uninhabited valley filled with orums. "Huwen's father was assassinated by the city's last archer, and Huwen became High King. Those who were with him swear he found the Amber and smashed it, just as his father smashed the other five prayer stones. But there's another story."

Miach set the Amber on the table. "That Huwen smashed a fake. Every upriser since the start of the civil war has pinned his hopes on that story. You're saying it's true?"

She shrugged. "This is what I know. Gweddien, magiel heir to Gramarye—"

"I know. He was captured and killed."

"No," she corrected him. "He was imprisoned in Coldridge but not killed."

Miach knit his brows.

"He escaped two years ago. This summer, he came to Cataract Crag, which was where I saw him."

"He had the Amber?"

She held up a hand. "He met a jeweler from Archwood, one who claimed to have created an exact duplicate of the Prayer Stone for Huwen to destroy."

Miach's eyes narrowed. "The jeweler smuggled the original out of Orumon?"

"So, it would seem. If he can be believed."

Miach shook his head. "Too dubious. Sounds like some jeweler trying to make money from people's hopes."

Meg picked up the amulet. "I have to say, I agree with you. As much as neither of us can spot this as an obvious fake, the chances of it being the true Amber are vanishingly small. Still, it could be of use. A dupe, to hoax our way into a better position. Or at the very least, a symbol around which people might rally."

Miach ran his tongue over his teeth, studying her.

She fingered the prayer stone and watched him.

"And . . . if it's real?"

"I'm a magiel. I wear it, concealed in my clothes. I touch anyone of royal heritage—"

"Princess Hada."

"—Princess Hada," she confirmed. "We go to Heaven where the Gods will grant any prayer I make."

※

Despite the drafts and cold floor of the inordinately large salon, Rennika had stripped away her cloak and outer robe to give herself more room to maneuver as she alternately stood, knelt and bent, with Ide, to fit the ceremonial robes to Hada's servant.

For loose-flowing traditional garments, the adjustments were surprisingly intricate, as layers had to sit upon layers in precise, significant positions. Even minor variance could lead to unintended symbolism, and the serving girl assigned to the task of standing in for Hada had the wrong posture. The girl had no idea how to correct it, even when Verlin positioned her. The result was a time-consuming resewing of all the basting stitches.

"Rennika, for God's sake. Pay attention," Verlin snapped. The girl had slumped and Rennika dropped the shoulder folds.

Ide sat back on her heels, sighed, and removed the pins on the hem.

Rennika readjusted the yoke and tried to focus, but it was hard. Today, as she entered the castle, she'd tallied the guards and their positions, and for the first time—as near as she knew—they watched her back. Coldly. Even eyeing the number of doors and turnings made Rennika feel conspicuous as she, Ide, and Verlin were escorted through the Great Hall. Meg wouldn't admit she was back working with uprisers, but why else could she want such information? Still, Rennika had promised, and now she'd identified Hada's suite, Raef's suite, and all-important servants' passages. For what it was worth.

The door at the far end of the chamber burst open, and the princess marched down its length. She glared at Verlin first, and then at the girl standing on the stool. "Get her out of that dress," she snapped. "God!"

The girl scrambled from the stool, and Rennika had to hold her still as Ide snipped the basting threads holding the gown together so she could slither out of it.

The door thumped closed, and unhurried footsteps echoed on stone, accompanied by a clicking of light chain.

"Are you mad?" Hada glared over Rennika's shoulder as she climbed onto the stool. "Or drunk?"

"Neither. The festival's on the equinox." The words reflecting from the marble walls slurred, but only a little. "The star of the One God'll be in his own house, and Kyaju approaches the constellation of Kanden. It's propitious."

Rennika peered over her shoulder. Gweddien.

Verlin snapped his fingers, and she turned back to her work. The girl, red-faced and casting glances at the princess's secretary, darted for her clothes. Rennika snipped the threads holding Hada's robe in place, and it cascaded to the floor around her, so she stood in only her shift. There was no hint of blush on the princess's cheeks.

"Will the dress be ready?" She lifted her arms, and Ide draped the inner robe in place as Rennika gathered up the princess's clothing and carefully folded it.

"Absolutely, Your Highness," Verlin said. They'd be working day and night to finish for the festival.

"Gweddien? Is three days enough time to make the announcement?"

"It is."

Rennika watched Verlin's fingers for silent guidance and took a small tuck in the collar of the princess's inner sheath. The festival had already been proclaimed. A different announcement?

The princess stood very straight for Ide's needle. "I still don't like it."

"It solves the problem." Gweddien's voice came from much closer, and Rennika sensed he leaned against the mantle. "And as your consort, *he'd* bring all those dissenting voices under your rule, without the need to resort to heavy-handed tactics."

Rennika's fingers stiffened. Consort. Marriage? This was stuff Meg would want to know. Verlin twitched a frown at her and she adjusted the undergarment.

"But will he agree?" Hada fidgeted in her position of regal stillness as Rennika and Ide composed the drape of the gown under Verlin's scrutiny.

"I've arranged an appointment for you this afternoon," Gweddien said. "I suggest a simple business meeting, with one or two high-placed advisers to witness, that leaves the details vague. With only three days until the festival, you can press for an immediate answer."

Hada turned to face Gweddien. "But *will he agree*?" Ide pulled back, lest her needle touch royal flesh, and Rennika fumbled with the folds.

"As long as he thinks he'll rule," Gweddien replied. "I can arrange for you to have another appointment scheduled immediately following, so the meeting does not drag out."

Marriage. Hada and Raef?

Verlin nodded, and Rennika and Ide slipped the outer gown onto their patron. Rennika marveled at how the princess's hand responded, cooperated, yet the woman, herself, seemed completely oblivious to their presence.

Servants were invisible. And Verlin had warned her, the first time he'd brought her here, and repeatedly, they were deaf and dumb as well. To repeat even a word was a betrayal of that trust.

"If he doesn't agree, word of my proposal will be everywhere. Raef and half the people of Gramarye are waiting for me to do something frivolous so he can call me stupid and impractical."

"He'll agree," Gweddien assured her with an overlarge gesture. "You're offering him what he has slavered for since the fall of his father's kingdom."

Rennika adjusted the collar and sleeve of the outer robe to Verlin's silent specifications, and Ide tacked them in place. Informing Meg, for whatever her hidden purposes, could only damage Rennika's position here. And Verlin's.

"How?" Hada pinned him. "How will you do it? Exactly?"

"Best you're not too closely tied to the details." Gweddien flicked a glance at Verlin.

Hada stood stock still, looking straight ahead.

"Shall I make the appointment?"

Hada's left hand fisted. "I still don't like it."

Verlin nodded, and Rennika and Ide tacked the final layer in place. Verlin stood back to admire the work.

Hada released a long breath through her nose. "Do it."

Rennika peeked into the darkened room. Starlight barely penetrated the covering on the windows. There was no sound. Yon must be asleep. She should go.

"Rennika?" Yon's whisper was drowsy.

She let herself in and eased the door closed behind her. "Do you want me to leave?"

"No." There was a rustling of bedclothes and she could just barely make him out, raising himself onto an elbow. He flung back a corner of the duvet. "Come. I wanted to talk to you, anyway."

Was there rumor about her position as dye master? Or the contract with Ide's family? She discarded her overrobe on a chair. "What is it?"

He let out a breath and leaned against the wall. "I need to talk to you about your sisters."

Oh, no. She'd been dreading this. "Has your father said something? Or your grandmother?"

"No," he said. "But they've been completely unreliable caring for the house. And Meg comes and goes at any hour. That was not the agreement."

Could Yon—possibly—think she was a Falkyn? No, that was too preposterous an idea.

"If we're found harboring magiels, her antics could get the contract with Lord Raef reassigned to another family."

A drooping feeling sank through Rennika's belly. "I'll talk to them." She threw her under robe over the stockings on the chair and scurried, chilled, to the bed.

"How well do you know these half-sisters, anyway?" he asked, covering her with the duvet.

She nestled into him and shrugged. "I haven't seen them for years. You know that."

"Did you know they are uprisers?"

She stilled. "What do you mean?"

"Meg's famous among those who know such things."

It was best to say as little as possible.

"Rennika, you might think this is a fabrication, but your sister killed a man."

"What?" Wenid.

"She infiltrated a castle and assassinated a nobleman. She's not what you think."

Gods. How had he found out? What if he told someone, told his father? "That can't be Meg."

"She's just using you, Rennika. Using us."

That remark was not as far from the truth. Meg wasn't free of her involvement in politics, whatever she said. And Rennika had promised to help her. *Was* helping her. Meg had asked for a layout of Highglen Castle's Great Hall and a route to Hada's apartments.

"It would be a kindness to your sisters if you encourage them to move on. Before one of them does something stupid and gets us all arrested."

CHAPTER 26

For the second night in a row, Meg returned to the draper's home after dark, and after having been absent an entire day. She could not guess how thinly she'd worn Sieur Verlin's—or his mother's—patience. She must replenish his stock of Dream Incense tonight in recompense.

The first thing she must do once she was alone was check the locked puzzle box hidden in her clothing in the attic room. Where to keep the Amber until it could be used had been a problem since she'd acquired it. She'd taken Yaquob's example at first and worn it, even at night. But she was no worldling, able to walk with impunity through the streets, and a close encounter with a soldier and a body search had given her a sharp fright. She didn't like leaving the thing in her room but had no better place.

In the afternoon she'd left the city, still amazed the Yak Herders' Gate was unguarded. There were herbs and other ingredients that could be gathered despite the snow, up on the high, wind-blown ridges; some, even, that must be collected under wintry conditions. She and Miach had spent the morning running scenarios: using the dubious prayer stone as a rallying point to inspire masses of peasants; using it to seduce Princess Hada into defiance of High King Huwen. *If* that was a goal Hada desired.

They even considered how they would use the stone if it was real.

But every eventuality carried enormous risk of discovery and death—or plunging the country into war, and the people of Shangril still enslaved to the whims of the High King.

Almost every eventuality took Meg away from Janat's side.

The crisp, cold air and her day in the sparse alpine forests—even the wintry blasts of wind—had refreshed her, cleared her head. But it had not brought her any closer to knowing what they must do.

So, Miach would consult with two of his closest organizers and come up with a plan. Meg didn't like this decision, but by the end of the morning she and the tanner had arrived at nothing concrete. They could not wait for Dwyn's uprisers to march into Highglen in the spring—if he would even do so. By then, Gramarye would be in the grip of a firmly entrenched monarch. So, Meg grudgingly conceded that Miach might consult two tacticians sworn to secrecy.

She climbed the stairs to Rennika's apartment.

Rennika and Janat sat at the small table by the brazier, looking at slates in the light of two candles. A scatter of fabric swatches and yarns had been pushed to the side. When Meg entered, Janat looked up and smiled. "Have you had supper?"

She hadn't been hungry until Janat spoke. "No, actually."

Janat waved at Rennika's worktable. "We thought not. We brought you up a plate of cold mutton sausage, some cheese, and yogurt."

"And there's a pot of tea," Rennika said.

"Pull up the stool and come and see these." Janat turned back to the drawings Rennika was showing her.

Meg poured tea into a mug and brought the stool close to the brazier, setting her plate on her lap. Janat looked better—the bruises on her lip and forehead were yellow in the candlelight, with much of the purple already faded. She tried discreetly to catch a glimpse of the tiny sore on Janat's neck, but her death token band covered the spot. *Kyaju, make me wrong.* A trick of the light. A deception.

"Look!" Janat said, hunting through the stack of slates and pulling one out.

But no. The image was clear in her mind. A small scratch covered in yellow paste.

Meg looked at the slate.

It was a skillful drawing created with remarkably fine chalk lines, of a woman in an elaborate traditional gown. "This is Verlin's drawing. Ide has already made most of the robes and done a first fitting." She pulled out a second slate showing a sleeve with a detailed design. "This is the embroidery. I'm allowed to help, because there is so much to do, and the dress has to be ready in three days."

"Whose dress?" Meg balanced the plate on her knees as she cut the sausage.

Janat turned to her in exasperated, delighted surprise. "Princess Hada's."

Rennika smiled and nodded, tentatively proud.

"Show her the embroidery silk," Janat cried.

If Janat had slipped . . .

Rennika brought out three skeins of silk in varying shades of burgundy and violet, a snip of leather dyed deep crimson, and a swatch of magenta wool. "This is the belt and the trim," Rennika explained. "The underdress is linen, and I don't have a sample of that. Linen takes longer to dye."

"Will it be ready on time for Ide's sister to begin the sewing?" Janat asked. She turned back to Meg. "You've been away so much, you've missed everything."

Meg shook the worry from her head and ate a slice of yak sausage. "What?"

Rennika put a hand on Janat's fingers.

Janat rolled her eyes. "You tell her, then."

Rennika sighed.

"What?" Meg asked again.

"Verlin thought the family should know because we're all working on the gown Hada will wear, but we're sworn to secrecy." Rennika looked at her doubtfully. "Meg, you have to promise not to do anything to hurt Verlin's place in Highglen."

"*Rennika.*"

"I mean it."

Meg was insulted. "I promise." Anything she did would be for the good of merchants and artisans like Verlin.

"Hada is planning her marriage." Rennika let the slate in her hands slide to her lap.

By Kyaju. Marriage.

Rennika schooled her face. "I was at the great hall yesterday with Verlin, doing fittings for the gown. We overheard Hada talking to Gweddien. If it's confirmed, they'll perform the ceremony during the festival."

"Who's she going to marry?" Three days. This would not be a secret for long. But, perhaps long enough for plans to be made. Events to be set in motion before locks snapped closed.

Rennika gave a half-shrug. "Hada hasn't even confirmed it with him. He might say no."

"Who?" But there was only one candidate.

"Lord Raef."

Sleep was impossible.

Meg huddled under her blankets, her room unilluminated but for a faint rectangle, the tiny window looking out onto a starless night.

Marriage. An alliance clamping down all possibilities and political uncertainty. City and country fastened hard against change. Against any whisper of rebellion.

Gods! She was so close.

All she needed was to *brush* against Hada. But though the castle stood visible just above Verlin's house, it might as well be halfway across Shangril, for all Meg could get into it.

Piss on it.

Meg threw back her quilt and tossed her robe over her night clothes. She stumbled on feet of ice to the door, feeling for the handle in the dark.

The central room of the apartment was marginally warmer, and marginally brighter from the glow of banked coals on the brazier. She found a splinter, lit a candle, and then tapped on Rennika's door.

The house was silent at this mark. The hush of the charcoal in the brazier, the faint skitter of a rat, the flutter of the candle. The ever-present thrum of the engines. Meg heard nothing from within Rennika's room, so she eased the door open. "Rennika," she whispered.

There was a muffled, questioning moan from the dark shapelessness that was the bed and its contents. Then a sudden intake of breath, and Rennika's head lifted slightly. "Meg?" she mumbled. "Why are you up?"

Meg set the candle on the floor by the door and scurried across the short space to her sister's bed and sat on the end, tucking her feet up under her. "Can you get me into the castle?"

Rennika pulled herself up on one elbow, her hair a mass of tangles around her head, half of her face now lit by the flickering light. "What? No. What are you talking about?"

Meg leaned forward, tugging her robe more closely around herself. "I could be your servant."

Rennika squinted at her in the feeble brightness of the candlelight. "No, you couldn't."

Her sister was still mostly asleep. "A ruse," she said impatiently.

"And I said, I can't," Rennika retorted. "I don't have a servant. They all know that. I'm Verlin's servant, his apprentice, when he goes. He takes Ide. Or Tyg, if he needs more help. He'd never take you. You're a magiel."

Meg sat back. "I can assume a disguise."

Rennika pulled her covers up to her ears and put her head back on the pillow, turning away from the candle. "Do you even think these things through?"

Piss. "There has to be a way. We just have to think of it."

"You're a magiel," Rennika muttered. "They'll arrest you."

"I can make a potion to hide my shimmer."

Rennika made an inarticulate grunt. "How often do you do that?"

She ignored her sister's goad. Gods, she couldn't let a little thing like Rennika's reticence get in her way. Rennika was always like that, afraid of her own shadow. "Rennika—"

"No. Listen, I've helped you. I got you information. That's all I can do. Go to bed."

"Listen—"

Rennika rolled over and lifted her head again. "Why do you want to get in? Another assassination attempt?"

"What?" Meg's neck warmed at the implication. Infiltrating a castle during the battle for Coldridge eight years ago, and killing the High King's magiel, was no small feat. And she'd paid with nightmares and blind-siding attacks of anxious guilt. And her deed had been a key action of the battle. Rennika had no cause—*no* cause—to be dismissive.

"I said I'd help, but I told you. I won't do anything to hurt the family," Rennika mumbled into her covers. "Go to bed."

"I have the Amber."

Rennika's face popped up and her eyes drilled into her for a long moment. Then the head flopped back on the pillow. "No, you don't."

Meg returned to her room and came back with the puzzle box. She opened it and held up the lustrous jewel in its glimmering setting. Marigold beams bobbed over the walls, reflecting candlelight.

Rennika raised herself onto her elbows, staring at the thing with a fierce frown. "Gods, Meg," she whispered. "You don't quit."

The words stabbed.

"Is it real?"

"Sometimes you have to make sacrifices. Some things are more important than one—"

"Sacrifice? Sacrifice Janat? Me? Verlin? Anyone but you, you mean."

"Rennika!"

Her sister was silent for a long moment. She held out her hand.

Meg gave her the amulet.

"Is it real?" Rennika repeated.

"I don't know."

"Then it isn't."

Gods, her sister—sisters—could be so aggravating.

Rennika turned toward the candlelight and studied the jewel, stroking its smooth curve with a thumb. "I never touched it," she said quietly.

Meg hadn't, either. It had always been locked away, or around Mama's neck beneath her robes.

A tiny frown marred Rennika's brow. Memory. Sadness. Loss. "It's a curse."

"It kept Mama alive during the siege of Archwood," Meg whispered. "For a year and a half."

Rennika stretched out her arm and gave the amulet back. "What are you going to do with it?"

Meg put the chain around her neck and slipped the amulet under her night clothes. "Find out if it's real."

Rennika put her head back on the pillow, pulling her blankets again up to her ears, but watching Meg in the candlelight. "How?"

"Touch Hada."

Rennika barked a mirthless laugh. "Go to Heaven with Hada? Chance that she won't leave you there?"

"Murder me?"

"If she thinks you've taken her kingdom, what would she have to lose?"

Meg had considered this. "My prayer would be to help Gramarye and to return here. The Gods would protect me." She put a hand on Rennika's arm. "Rennika. Take me to her."

"I can't get you into her presence. I can't. Really."

She could, though. Meg didn't know how, but it must be possible.

"And what happens if you drag Hada off to Heaven with you?" Rennika asked.

"I pray. I ask the Gods—the One God, if I can reach the Seventh Heaven—I ask for peace in Shangril under King Dwyn."

Her sister snorted. "And if you fail? Taking one grain of Shangril will aim Huwen's army on Highglen. His cannons."

"Do this, Rennika," Meg urged. "One risk. One chance."

"Huwen'll besiege Highglen like his father besieged Archwood. We know how that ended. With the High King marching in once Mama and King Ean were dead. The Amber couldn't save them."

"The situations aren't the same. Archwood was ambushed. Here, *we* have the advantage of surprise. Hada's put a gate at Gramarye's border, and we can reinforce it. The population is self-sufficient within its borders, not dependent on whatever food exists in limited warehouses. Huwen can't use the Ruby, as long as his brother has it. *And* we have goods—superior wool and furs—the free traders of Pagoras want to send to Aadi. Huwen's coffers are depleted after years of war."

Rennika did not drop her gaze.

"Huwen is not his father. A peace can be negotiated."

Her sister closed her eyes. "And if you touch the princess and your amulet is false, then what?"

Meg was silent. Miach's plans were still too rough, too full of holes, too debated. But the festival, the marriage, was coming up in two days. Did they wait and miss their chance? Or infiltrate the castle during the chaos, even with a half-formed plan?

"You have no plan. You're too seduced by the hope the Amber is real. I'll tell you what's going to happen. You'll be arrested and jailed—*if* you're lucky. Tortured and killed. Maybe sent to that magiel breeding scheme you told me about. I'm jailed, or killed, or tortured. So is Verlin and his family. And if, by any chance, Janat escapes, who is there to care for her? Hmm?" Rennika squeezed her eyes closed as if she would will Meg away. "You're supposed to be my smarter older sister."

"Rennika—"

Rennika sat up abruptly. "Meg, you're my family. I love you. If there were some way to help you, I would. Please. I want you to believe me."

"But—"

"But not like this."

※

Meg's voice—yes, and Rennika's—filtered through the wall. Janat rolled over. Gods, it was the middle of the night. What was Meg doing, talking to Rennika at this mark? Janat rubbed her shoulders against the rough linen sheet. Her back was itchy, just *there*, just where she couldn't reach.

"How?"

"Touch Hada."

What were they talking about? Meg had said—

"I can't get you into her presence." Rennika was telling Meg—

The Amber. Did she hear Meg say . . .

The *Amber*? Meg had— No. She couldn't.

Meg had—

—said they came to Highglen to see Rennika. To find a place *out* of politics.

Janat rubbed her eyes, pushed at them with her fingertips. If only she didn't *itch*!

Meg had betrayed her. She'd come here for the uprisers. To do something with the Amber.

Meg had the Amber and she hadn't told her. *Gods*.

What a dupe Janat had been. What a dupe. She'd believed Meg. Believed she was only making incense for Verlin. Each day, Meg had disappeared, gone to the market for kitten livers. Gone to the apothecary for winter marigold, or for milk of poppy, or for a new pestle. Gone to the hills to collect frozen toads.

. . . the day Janat met Gweddien in Cataract Crag. No, the day after. She and Meg had been cleaning rooms at the inn. Meg had been adamant they would not budge from Pagoras, not leave such a good position. Then—

Janat tried to follow the chain of logic. What had happened first?

Janat told Meg Gweddien was going to Highglen. Janat left to follow him, and Meg caught up to her on the road. But Meg hadn't dragged her back to Cataract Crag.

Why?

Gweddien had asked Janat, in the tavern, if she'd heard any rumors about the Amber.

Had Meg spoken with Gweddien? Had he told Meg something? Gods, Janat had been such an idiot, thinking she was so smart, getting Gweddien to buy her a beer. And another. And a whiskey. The rest of the night was no more than a blur.

So, Meg had come here for politics. She'd lied. That was her reason, all along.

Gods, why did Janat even try? Meg had no idea, *no idea* how hard it was . . .

And she *itched*.

Janat listened. There was mumbling, but she couldn't make it out . . . No, Meg's voice, raised a little. The war. Over.

Meg only wanted to help.

It was true. She wanted to help people regain their death tokens. She wanted to help Janat. Every night, Meg made her a potion to help her sleep, help her stay calm.

Janat didn't want Meg to give up on her hopes and dreams. Janat should make more of an effort to help her sister. Yes. She would, first chance Meg gave her. Gods, if Meg could stop the madness, Janat could forgive her anything.

But nothing was going to stop the Marigolds.

And her back was driving her wild.

She threw back the covers and scrambled to her sack in the corner. She pulled out her knife, its dull gleam almost invisible in the non-existent light from the tiny window.

Why not? Why not just slice that knife a bit deeper this time? Would it get her out of Meg's way? So Meg could do the work the Gods meant her to do? Or just foul her sister up more?

God, she *itched*!

She made a tiny prick, oh, so tiny, on the inside of her arm, high up next to the others, where no one could see.

CHAPTER 27

The corridor was dark but for a glimmer from an ensconced candle at its far end, where the sentry stood guard. Hada, wrapped in a long shawl against the cold, hesitated before the closed door. Her feet were bare and, despite the short distance she'd come, already icy cold. She tapped lightly on the door.

There was a moment of silence, then, "Come."

She let herself in.

Gweddien's outer chamber was small but comfortable, a two-room suite designed for retainers of guests from the queen's personal invitation list. At present, it was lit only by a single candle and a small fire on the hearth. Gweddien sat in the sphere of the embers' warmth with a book now closed on his lap, a glass of wine in one hand, and a puzzled expression on his face. He stood. "Your Highness?"

Her lips pressed into a tiny grin. "I thought we'd already established what you may call me when we are alone."

He returned the impish smile. Then, tearing himself from her gaze, he indicated a second chair by the fire. "Glass of wine? I think a celebration is in order. I understand Lord Raef accepted your offer of marriage." He held up the bottle.

She stepped closer to him. "Or something more adventurous?"

He lifted a brow and enumerated as she slipped her arms around his waist. "Well, you've tried Teshian whiskey, and Dream Incense, and poppy tea. I don't recommend Heartspeed at this time of night. Perhaps a mushroom? Do you have to get up early?"

She lifted a shoulder. "Just whiskey this time."

He made to move, but she held him momentarily. "And, perhaps we can relax somewhere more comfortable than separate chairs?" She looked through the doorway to his private chamber.

His muscles tightened in her embrace, and he looked down on her, abruptly serious.

This was wrong. She peered into his face, questioning.

He lifted a hand to caress her cheek, and the touch was gentle and loving, arousing her body. "Hada," he said softly. "You are so beautiful."

She lifted her chin, her lids drifting closed.

"I am not of your station," he said simply, reaching behind him to her wrists.

"And I am to be married," she responded, gently resisting his fingers. "We've had this conversation. No one is watching."

His hand fell back. "I . . ." He grimaced, as if in pain.

She tried to read his face, read his thoughts.

"I can't love. A woman."

She shook her head minutely back and forth. What . . . ? He was handsome enough, he—

She would not have guessed— "Your taste runs to men?" She had heard of such a trait. There were boys in Holderford. People whispered.

His breathing became faster, shallower, and she let him pull back from her a little. "No."

She could see his distress mounting. "Here." She led him back to his chair, put his glass of wine in his hand, and pulled the second chair closer, that she might still hold his hand. "Tell me."

He finished his wine and set the glass on the table, pale and staring. "I . . . When I was a boy . . . young man, not fully grown . . ." His words stopped, strangled.

"Something happened?" she whispered. "Someone . . . hurt you? Misused you?"

Abruptly, he stood. He let out an explosive breath and went to a side table and pulled a heavy bottle from the cupboard. He returned with two glasses. "You said whiskey? This is a very good year. From the high glens of North Teshe." He slapped the glasses on the table and splashed a generous amount into each. Without sitting, he took one and downed its contents, squeezing his eyes closed at the effect.

She took her glass and pulled back into her chair, startled by the intensity of his sudden movements. "All right," she said. "You don't have to—"

"It was your father's magiel. Wenid, not Kraae. He wanted children born of my line. I wasn't given a choice in the matter."

She riveted on him. "What do you mean? He—"

"He put me in a room. Every night, every three nights, a different woman. Sometimes the same one. The women had no choice, either. They struggled. They wept. They gouged at me with their fingers. They endured like stone." He slammed the glass on the table and poured again. "Seven years."

"My father was assassinated before then," she whispered.

He glanced at her. "Your brother carried on when your father died."

What? "Why?"

He tossed back the whiskey. "Ask him."

"Oh, Gweddien."

He looked down on her, and there was nothing in his eyes.

What could she say?

Then the moment passed. "You're not like either of them." He softened, sat. "You're strong, like your father and your brother. But you have . . ." He gave a small, half-shrug. "Something. Compassion. Humanity."

She held his gaze for a long moment.

Then he poured into his glass a third time. "I think tonight I shall be very drunk."

She put her hand on his before he could lift the glass. "Let me stay with you."

He tilted his head in annoyance. "I told you."

"Just stay. Just be with you. That's all."

He touched her chin in wonderment, and a small smile returned. Then he lifted his goblet, and hers in her hand, clinking glasses. "Only if you don't mind being with a man who is very, very drunk."

When Meg found Janat unable to wake at dawn the next morning, she knew the signs to look for.

And she found them. Tiny sores, a half-dozen of them, smeared with yellow paste, on the insides of her sister's arm. The blur on the edge of vision. Ghosts hovering.

Meg knelt, eyes closed, one hand on the back of Janat's head, the other on her stomach, searching, probing, for the poison that was Boneblood, finding each mote, manipulating it, pulling it apart, finding a time when it was innocent, when it had been its harmless, constituent parts. Each one. Searching, finding, releasing. Searching . . .

A hand on her shoulder. "Meg."

With a great effort, she opened her eyes. A brightness. A blanket pressed on her forehead. No . . . Her forehead bore her head's weight. She lay face down, on . . .

Beneath her, someone moved.

Meg pushed herself up, back to a painful position on her knees. She knelt on the floor beside Janat's pallet. Janat, before her, rolled over, retching.

Rennika's hand warmed her shoulder. "Meg. I think you fell asleep."

She tried to keep her eyes open. The light slanted from somewhere behind her.

"You've done as much as you can." Rennika pulled on her shoulder, and Meg stumbled to her feet. Janat vomited on the floor in the dim grayness of the late fall morning. "Her body will have to do the work now," Rennika said. She led her from the room.

"She's getting worse."

Rennika guided Meg to her own room. "I'll clean her up. I'll watch her today. You sleep."

"This can't continue." Gods, if Janat had been deeper . . . It had taken two of them to pull the Boneblood from Kirst. Meg felt her head move slowly from side to side . . . no. If Janat had been more in that spell's grip, Meg could have—would have?—had to plunge herself so far into the ripples of time . . . she might have been lost for days. Longer.

And, what if—

Meg put a hand on Rennika's arm. "Janat's vomiting. She'll get dehydrated."

"I'll take care of her." Rennika pulled back Meg's quilt. "You've used a lot of magic. You won't be able to do anything today but sleep."

Meg could not fight her exhaustion. She slipped off her shoes and outer robe. Rennika was right. And Rennika was a skilled magiel. She could care for Janat.

"I have to find a way." *There is no cure.* Wasn't that what the man in Cataract Crag had said? "I have to—"

"Not today." Rennika took her hand, guiding her to lie down. She covered her with the quilt.

Meg had told Miach she'd meet him at midday. Miach was to have a plan. But she had to help Janat. Find a cure.

There *was* a cure.

A plea to the One God in Heaven. With the Amber.

Tears came, and Meg slept.

A wagon bedecked with colorful ribbons. The entertainers.

Had Meg woken? Probably not. Probably she'd left her body sleeping, to come to this part of her life.

Janat was getting a boost onto the platform that lowered from the side of the wain, to improvise with the gypsies. Meg remembered this day. Players had come to Fairdell, and the streets were packed with people from miles around. A handful of Dwyn's folk had come down from the hills. *Meg blinked and scanned the crowd. Tonore was there, beside her, slipping his arm through hers. "You won't believe what the tavern is charging for beer," he whispered in her ear.*

One of the actors gave Janat a mask, while another in elaborate parody of Aadian dress was spouting off in a bad highborn accent. Meg had never laughed so hard.

And darkness, chill with autumn, engulfed her.

She raced on horseback through the woods—which woods, she had no idea—in the company of a dozen riders, maybe more. The jolting terror of the beast beneath her, stumbling over rocks and roots, veering to avoid low branches, almost unseated her. Gods, wherever she was, whatever was happening, she prayed to Ranuat all that was required of her was to stay on the horse.

Without warning, the race was gone.

She sat on a polished marble bench in a fragrant wood. Midsummer heat pressed on her with the drowsy hum of insects, desultory with afternoon sun. She smiled. She'd traveled here before—wherever "here" was. This was a moment from her future.

Graceful arches and polished, broken walls surrounded her, the roof tumbled down and open to the sky. A shrine to the Many Gods. This one was dedicated to Kyaju. The sigil of the Sixth Heaven, a dove, was carved in marble on the keystone.

Summer, and deliciously warm. She wore only her shift, but her cloak was close by, and her sack. She assumed it was hers.

She looked to her left and knew what she would see. Rennika sitting next to her, washing her feet in a bowl of cooling water. She smiled at Meg. "I hope the others get here soon. I'm hungry."

A bird trilled in a tree, and somewhere nearby, a stream gushed over falls.

Midday was well past when Meg returned, finally, to her own time. Battling fatigue, she rose, found her clothing, and made her way from her room. Rennika was not there. She checked Janat's room. Janat slept.

Where was Rennika? She should be watching.

But the sound of conversation drifted up the stairs. Rennika's voice, and Tyg's. Meg let out her breath. Very well.

Janat's floor had been washed, and the bedding changed. The stink of vomit lingered faintly. All of Janat's possessions appeared to have been removed. Likely just as well. Meg withdrew.

A cure.

Meg was still too fuzzy to think.

There was no cure, short of traveling to Heaven with the Amber. Meg touched the smooth hardness of the Amber beneath her robe. The Gods could grant any prayer.

There had to be a cure, despite what Hane had said. A cure on this sphere.

There were libraries of spell books. Great cities had had such libraries, once, not that long ago. But of course, High King Huwen would've pillaged them, as he'd pillaged the homes and shops of all the magiels he'd had executed or dragged off to—

Yaquob.

He'd made it his profession to rob magiels of their potions and paraphernalia—including spell books—when they were arrested. If anyone had a spell book, it would be Yaquob.

CHAPTER 28

Something—Meg couldn't tell just what—was wrong with Yaquob's shop.

She stood in the mouth of an alley, hood raised, still unsure that reverberations in her time stream might not affect her again. Exhaustion dragged at her shoulders and legs.

As she watched, passersby made their way, hurrying in the cold gale, across the common to the rice monger's stall, or a tavern, or home for the evening. Only a scatter of artisans' tents remained stubbornly in the plaza, and the stable's door was closed. Meg lowered her head and pushed into the bitter breeze to cross the common to the merchant's shop.

The door was open. The lock was intact but the wooden frame around it was splintered. Meg scuttled down the steps and into his display room. It had been demolished.

Shelves were overturned, vials strewn on the floor, their contents smeared. A faint, sickly smell from one of the vials reminded her of a worldling potion for sudden sleep. Crockery was broken and sacks of herbs spilled. Books and scrolls had been heaped in a corner and apparently set to burn, though mostly only covers and the edges of pages were singed. Clothing huddled in heaps like the dead.

The scatter of food was frozen. So. The shop had been like this for more than a day, at least.

She shuffled into the back room. It was still dark, but lighter with the hangings torn down. The straw pallet had been shredded. Clothing ripped. A bottle of wine lay broken in a corner, some rice had been flung over the floor. There was no sign of Yaquob. Thank Kyaju she'd given Raoul to Vellefair to care for—for what that was worth.

There was no indication of where the free trader had gone, or why his shop had been ransacked. But she saw no blood; that was good.

Meg had brought a sack. She gathered up the books, then hunted among the vials for anything remotely useful and intact, completed potions or promising ingredients, taking anything of use. She still had to make Dream Incense for Verlin, at least for now.

A shadow touched the floor. She turned, pulse skipping.

A man, cloaked against the cold, stood in the doorway.

Meg tensed, gripped her sack.

The man revealed his face and prematurely balding head. A scar where his left ear should have been . . . it was Tonore. *Gods*. She breathed.

But—Colm had to have sent him. He was here to bring her back.

"Tonore." She eyed the distance between him and the shop's entrance, the space between her and freedom.

"Meg." He entered the ruined shop, taking in the destruction with his eyes, not nearly cautious enough. Good.

Her heartbeat thumped. "Fancy finding you here."

He moved from the doorway. Mistake. "I need to talk to you."

She shifted slightly closer to the door, gripping her sack. Could she dart past him? "Oh?"

No, he'd be too quick. "You know I do," he said. "Colm—"

She sprinted.

He lunged, arm outstretched, snagging on her cloak—

But she was out the door and up the stairs.

A flock of three sheep and their shepherdess meandered from a side street, and she raced past them.

"Meg!" His voice, behind her.

She was too far away. She'd learned these streets.

♀

Meg slipped into the rice house near The Three Corners tavern, the one where Miach had first taken her. The place was crowded, despite the early candlemark, with no unoccupied seat, no ledge to rest a tankard or bowl. The stink of wool drying in the heat of so many closely packed bodies was overpowering. She'd squeezed with her book-laden sack through two circuits of the room, trying to remain inconspicuous while scanning for Miach, before squeezing behind a mostly full table in a dark corner near the stair to the rented rooms. Miach wasn't here.

Tonore. So, Colm hadn't given up his hunt for her. She should've expected as much. And who better than Tonore to send? Colm knew they'd been lovers, once, and counted on Tonore being able to anticipate her actions.

The first time Tonore had made love to her was in the summer, in a mountain valley south of Fairdell. She'd been doing laundry at Dwyn's farm and Tonore had come back, overheated, from a hunt. He'd taken her hand and led her through the woods along crisscrossing animal trails to a cavern he'd found by almost falling through its roof. When he brought Meg there, he shoved a log into the hole, and the two of them climbed down its truncated branches into a grotto with an underground pool of sulfurous water. She remembered her wonder and amazement at the dancing reflections over pale flowstone walls and stalactites, from the shaft of light streaming down through the ceiling, the crisp echoes of every drip and lap of water and shuffle of their feet. He'd taken her clothes off, and his, and pulled her into the warm pool with him.

She'd been frightened, at first. She'd courted men, before and since, but he'd been her only lover. For three seasons. Less than a year.

"Meg?" It was Miach.

Meg shook off the remembrance. "Miach."

"You're late. By a good two candlemarks." He wrapped his cloak more tightly around himself and led her into the street.

"Something came up." She matched his stride, marching into the wind. "Is there somewhere we can go?"

He gestured at the empty lane. "No one will hear us here."

True. "What's the plan?"

Miach shoved his hands beneath his cloak, putting his head down against the weather. "Still a lot of unknowns," he growled under the blast.

Like yesterday.

"We came up with several ideas. But it's hard to foresee all the complications that could arise with each action," he said. "So many things can turn on a whim."

"So, no," she summarized. "No plan."

"Yet."

The street turned uphill and the going was harder, though the work warmed her. "Hada intends to marry Raef, if he'll have her," Meg said. "At the Festival of The One God."

He glanced sharply at her. "Where did you hear that?"

"My sister. She listens for me when she's in the castle. It won't be a secret for long. If we want to put contingencies in place, we have to do it now."

"Two days." He lifted his head at a splitting of the road and gestured toward the higher street. "Once Huwen is confident his capture of Coldridge is secure, he'll look again to his empire. Hada may worry her brother isn't too happy about her cutting out a piece of it for herself."

"Agreed. She's rushing things in case he comes. Could bungle it and create opportunities."

Their boots squeaked in the snow, and the wind gusted grains of ice into their faces. Meg's sack was awkward and heavy, and she wanted to get back to the draper's to go through the spell books. At least, they were climbing in the right direction.

"We've eliminated two possibilities," Miach said at last. "We won't use the—item—as a symbol for rallying dissent. We haven't unearthed any good outcomes with that plan. We'd be forced into a one-sided war we don't have the troops or armaments to win. Also, it could become a target for theft. Second possibility, we don't want to simply keep it secret. We may as well not have it."

Meg nodded. She hadn't taken the Amber to do nothing with it.

"And I doubt we want to take it to Dwyn, even if we did know where to find him, now that Coldridge and Glenfast have both gone to royal hands. The time frame is just too long to be effective. We can send him a coded message."

"Then that leaves touching Hada." With enough brute magic—Disguises, Confusions, Poisons—Meg *might* be able to bypass one or two of the barriers to make her way into the princess's presence, but—from her experience eight years ago infiltrating Wenid's suite—there were far too many unknowns. Factors that could go awry. The chances of success were vanishingly small.

"We need to get into the castle, which is impossible," Miach summed up. "Which is why we still have no plan."

As they came to the street below Highglen Common, the wind was beginning to lessen. Meg stopped, scanning the lane, hoping to slip into the quadrangle before the gate was locked. Here, as below, only a few market stalls had been erected in the bitter weather, but a crowd had gathered, milling. "Rennika says she can't get me in," she said surreptitiously to Miach. "But she can, I'm sure of it. She's just afraid I'll botch something, and Verlin's family will be disgraced."

Miach turned to her. "You think?"

Meg shrugged. "It's the only hope. She knows the layout inside the castle and could move efficiently, and find niches to hide in, if need be." Not to mention the magic of two magiels.

Miach bit his lip. He looked curiously at the growing press.

Someone rushed past, heading downhill, and Meg averted her face. "The princess is to be wed!" he cried. "Long live King Raef!"

Gweddien pushed back his plate. Something was wrong. He couldn't put his finger on what.

He and Hada had eaten a good meal with a fine wine in his suite, lingering over yogurt and sugared apples as he worked very hard to point out the advantages of bringing together magiel, royal, and Amber to secure Hada's rule of Gramarye. But Hada was cool. Withdrawn.

"It is not the Amber." Hada cut him off, leaning back in her chair. She sucked the sugar from a slice of fruit held in delicate fingers, her eyes smoldering.

Yesterday, she'd offered herself to him, but though he wanted her, anxiety had flooded his senses at the thought of physical love.

"Certainly," he responded. "It's likely the stone is a fake. But can you take that chance?"

"This man you speak of, Yaquob. You only have your servant's word for what transpired." Her robe was of a casual style, cut low enough to reveal an enticing cleavage.

Gweddien hadn't told Hada he'd slipped through her flimsy locks to deal with the free trader, himself.

She dipped a slice of apple in yogurt. "This man refuses to deal with an intermediary. Doesn't that seem suspicious to you? That he won't present his proposal at court but must see me in private?"

"Those are his terms."

"Subjects do not make terms."

"He fears duplicity as much as you." Gweddien tried to be patient, but—*Gods*—he was so close feeling the touch of the jewel in his hand, the exhilaration of leaving his body, the flight to Heaven in prayer. Like glim. *Better* than glim, if tales were true.

"Delarcans have enemies," she retorted. "Gweddien. Which explanation is more plausible? That my father never smashed the Amber? Or that some zealot would give his life for the chance to assassinate a Delarcan?"

"I would be here with you," he argued. "Your guards would search him. He would remain across the room." He leaned forward, his hands fisting. "I can give you a personal ward to shield your body, like I did for Raef."

Her eyes smoldered. "You would make *my* health and happiness your most important consideration."

"Yes! Highness, I have searched for the prayer stone every waking moment since my release from your brother's bastille. I've followed the jeweler who—"

"You told me." Her fury seemed out of proportion to his explanation.

Words tumbled out, faster. "If we know the Amber is in Highglen, others could, too." Gods, could she not see? "We must secure the merchant before—"

She stood.

Gweddien stared at her, perplexed.

She turned, as if she would leave, then stopped herself. Then she lifted her hands, fingers spread, as if to grasp something. Tears filled her eyes.

He rose. "Hada . . ."

She shook her head, mute, and the tears spilled onto her cheeks.

He came to her, engulfed her. "What . . ."

She trembled, shuddered with silent sobs.

He held her, rocked her, buried his head in her hair. "Shh, shh."

After a long while, her shaking eased, and she took a long hitching breath. "I . . . love you," she said in a small voice.

He took a deep breath in and closed his eyes. Gods, what had he done?

Still, he held her. Warm, soft, precious.

He was not drunk enough to manage this.

She pulled back a little, found a handkerchief and wiped her nose. "I love you," she said again, and made him look at her.

He grimaced against his own sorrow. *Piss on it.* "I love you, too. But—" he put a finger on her lips to quell the rising joy in her eyes "—I can't."

"You can." She tugged at the strings on his chemise.

He shook his head, trying to swallow back the hardness in his throat. "I want to." He grasped her fingers, stilling them. "Please. You have to know. I want to."

He could see in her eyes she did not understand.

How could he explain? He blinked, his mouth open, words not coming. He squeezed her hands within his and pushed himself back.

The flash of anger.

"You're a Delarcan," he said inadequately. "You're going to be a queen. I will do anything for you. But I . . ." He took a deep breath. "I can't do that."

She searched his face. And then, she drew back. "You're right. I'm going to be a queen." She straightened, and a mantle of dignity sheathed her. Bitterness sharpened her tongue. "And royals are not permitted to love. Not where their hearts lie."

With time . . . He wanted to ask for her patience, but such a demand was unfair. He didn't know if he could heal, not with any amount of time.

And then the moment passed. She closed her eyes with a sigh and stepped back. "Send men to fetch your free trader." She wiped her face and blew her nose on her handkerchief.

Gods, yes. "Thank you."

She straightened her skirts. "Secure him in a cell. I will see him at my convenience."

Gweddien gave her a small nod, emptiness and regret filling him.

She left the room.

He sat at the table for a long while with the bottle of wine.

Rennika inspected the last of the fabric—the linen—for the princess's dress. The color of the fabric was good, some of her best. Now the lengths were packed into her saddle bags along with several skeins of embroidery silk, ribbons, and sewing thread. She'd checked every item against her list to ensure she wouldn't have to come out here again before the festival. She had her cloak on and was closing up her workshop as Wynn saddled her mare, when Yon arrived. Her fingers stopped on the workshop lock.

He dismounted in the courtyard and led his gelding to the railing.

Rennika hadn't asked Meg and Janat to leave, and things had been cool between her and Yon for the past few days, neither of them willing to be the first to make things right. She locked the workshop and stepped into the compound.

"Rennika." He cast a quick glance around the enclosure. His hair tumbled about his freckled face in soft curls.

Her voice dried. "Everyone's gone except Wynn."

Yon gave a small shrug and smile. "That's all right. It's you I wanted to see."

His words flashed simultaneous heat and cold through her. "I was just leaving. Ide needs the fabric."

"We can ride back to Highglen together."

He'd ridden all the way out here, just to ride back? She said nothing but went to the stable where Wynn was cinching her mare. She thanked him and mounted, guiding the horse into the courtyard. Wynn closed the gate behind the two of them, and they rode side by side on the cart track down the mountain.

Out of habit, both scanned the skies for orums. There were none. The breeze was just enough to carry away the stench of the dyes, and the westering sun shone over high blue mountains, easing the bite of cold earlier in the day. The rush of the creek and the rattle of bare deer-browsed bushes sang a ceaseless melody. Under other circumstances, the ride would've been idyllic.

"The announcement is out," Yon said. "Hada had criers proclaim her marriage, to be held at the festival. When I left, the streets were filling with people."

"So Lord Raef must have agreed. Some will be happy."

"Some." But he didn't continue the conversation, and clearly, he had more on his mind. "Rennika, I've come to tell you something."

A sinking sensation descended through her stomach. "What?" she asked slowly.

Again, he was silent for a long moment. "The details of the contract have been settled."

So. Not about Meg and Janat. She gave him a sharp look. Information about the contract should be good news, but he was speaking as though trying to cushion her from a blow. Dread rose in her. "Tell me."

He looked straight ahead, down the valley. "Lord Raef was adamant. He wants a master dyer, not a journeyman." He paused. "And he wants a man."

She thought she'd been prepared, but she was not. A ball of iron bloomed in her stomach.

He glanced sidelong at her. "There's no appeal."

Rennika kept her gaze on her mare's shoulders, alternating as the beast walked placidly down the path curving across the mountainside.

Oh, Gods. All she'd worked for.

He let out a deep exhalation. "There's more."

There couldn't be more. She could barely breathe.

"Father has been working to be sure the Naid family is guaranteed the first consideration for the operation of the new power looms."

Ide's family.

"Lord Raef wanted to put the offer out for patronage. Sell the post to the wealthiest bidder."

The road descended into a gully, and the air became sharper. She couldn't concentrate on his words. She squeezed her knees in the saddle like a novice afraid to fall from her horse.

"Father convinced him. He . . ."

Ide.

Yon reined in his gelding and turned in his saddle. "He wants me to marry Ide."

Her perception shrank to a globe no larger than the two of them. Within it was no room for understanding. For breath.

"Make them family," he added, unhelpfully.

But Yon was supposed to marry *her. Rennika.*

"A small, quick ceremony. In two days."

She looked up sharply, and the sudden movement made her mare snort. "The festival," she murmured. The day of Hada's wedding.

"He's practical." Yon's tone suggested a funeral more than a wedding. "We'll be dressed. There'll be feasting."

Her heart pounded in her chest. "And . . . what did you say to your father?"

"What could I say?" Yon frowned querulously. "He's my father."

He could have said no. She stared at him. *He could have said no.*

His gaze broke off, and he nudged his mount.

He was a trader, for Gods' sake! He could have *negotiated.*

Her mare resumed walking alongside the other horse. ". . . and me?"

"There'll be a place for you in the dyer's compound."

"Journeyman?" she asked bitterly.

He looked away. "Apprentice."

"Apprentice?" She turned in her saddle.

Yon looked at her obliquely. "Lord Raef doesn't want the master dyer to feel awkward." He clarified. "Rivaled."

She snorted. "He doesn't?" Her mare, confused, picked up her pace. "There's some who thought *I* might be as good as a master?"

Yon blinked in helplessness, his horse spurting to match hers.

"And what about you and me?"

He reddened. "Father knows."

"Of course, he knows. Everyone *knows.*" That was not her question. "We have to stop."

She pulled back on her poor mare's mouth.

His gelding came to a halt, and he turned. "Out of respect for Ide. Surely you can see—"

Ranuat! "Not that I would *ever* be your mistress." Though—she realized belatedly—she already was.

Eyes stinging, she kicked the unfortunate horse and flew to the city at a gallop.

CHAPTER 29

For some time, Rennika had sat by the brazier, embroidery blurring and faltering in her fingers. Meg had disappeared into her room almost as soon as they'd trooped up from dinner. Janat, poking at her embroidery in a desultory fashion without speaking much, had similarly retired early.

Rennika had thought—hoped—when she saw Yon, he might've come to say he'd told his father he wanted to marry her.

Of course not. When had he ever shown courage, ever stood up to his father? All at once she could not think of a time.

And . . . no position in the dye works.

She could not go back to being an apprentice. The new dye master, whoever it was—Gods, she hoped it wasn't Charl—would make it his mission to find fault with every piece she made, belittle her, make her redo every swatch. Make her spend her days crushing mordants.

Had Verlin offered her this position, knowing she was too proud to accept it? As a way of forcing her out? No. He was a father to her.

So she'd thought.

But the odd thing was, she found herself running over in her mind again and again, the pain of losing her position. Not Yon.

Had she loved him? Or was hers an infatuation?

He was the only man she'd ever lain with. He had his spoiled ways, but she'd always worked around them, placating. One had to give, when one loved. Yet . . . how had Yon given to her, other than the occasional trinket?

Rennika wanted to be married. To have children. Be to them what Nanna had been to her. Be mistress of her own house, her own tiny kingdom. This was a certainty. But . . .

Was Yon the only man who could love her? And did he love her?

Not enough. Clearly.

Rennika rose and tapped on Meg's door, then opened it without waiting for a response.

Meg lay on her pallet, dark hair arrayed in long, thick bunches on her pillow, her large, brown eyes like shiny buttons in the light from her candle. A book was folded closed over her finger. Meg looked up at her entrance. "Is Janat all right?"

Rennika closed Meg's door. "She's fine. She went to bed right after you." There was nothing for it but to be direct. "I'm going to the castle with Verlin tomorrow. I'll try to find out about any upcoming opportunities. Work out a way to get you in."

She would have to ask Verlin for the money he held for her in his office. In case she found herself suddenly on the run.

A look of wonder spread on Meg's face, with glimmers of puzzlement and relief. She nodded slowly. "Thank you," she said. She opened her mouth as if she would say more, then closed it again.

Rennika gave her a brief nod, then went to bed to ponder what she had just done.

Meg lay on her pallet, combing through Yaquob's charred and stinking spell books for some enlightenment on how to fight Janat's frailty. The leather bindings, once beautiful, hand-tooled works of art, had kept the contents mostly intact.

It was late. Or early. Dawn would come soon.

But Rennika's words rattled around Meg's mind, distracting her from the tedium of parsing entries smudged or written in a cramped, idiosyncratic hand, or in obscure or ancient dialects. Rennika would help. Get her in. *Thank Ranuat.*

Meg buckled down to the book in her hand.

She made note of the occasional spell that was new to her or suggested an improved variation of a healing charm. But she found no reference to Bloodbone, Itch, or any potion resembling it. There were few spells for treating dependencies, and what were there were mostly annotated as failures. There were three references to glim, all warnings.

She needed sleep. But she had work to do first. She dog-eared a bound book and added it to the stack of those she'd scanned. If there was no cure, at least she'd done her best.

She caught herself.

Ranuat, was she making excuses? Justifying her own failures? The thought was unworthy.

She rose wearily and shook her head. She didn't know. She was too tired, too discouraged to know anything, anymore.

Mechanically, she took stock of her potions and ingredients and, going out to Rennika's sitting room, prepared a handful of brews over the small brazier. Miach was pinning his hopes on her. The hopes—and lives—of so many in Highglen. All of Gramarye. All of Shangril. And Rennika had finally come to trust her with her fears for the safety of that good and loving family she'd adopted. Meg had to come through.

Before sunup, she sealed a message for Miach. Then she slept away the bulk of the day.

Raef brought his horse to a halt just within a common that had been cleared of market stalls, and the cheering of the crowds following him and his entourage from the castle to the lower town quieted. His captain arranged a straggle of young girls, both magiel and worldling, before him. A couple of young men had been rounded up as well. The day was crisp and cold, and many of them shivered in thin cloaks.

"Marriage." Lord Lydon smiled and nodded at the mass of onlookers in the common but pitched his voice so only Raef and Vael could hear. His blue eyes stood out brilliantly from his white hair and beard above his ermine collar. "Not a bad plan. I'm surprised the woman was astute enough to come to you with it."

Vael, mounted on Lydon's far side, spoke in an equally quiet voice. "She sees it as a way to bolster her precarious position," he said dismissively. "She wants to be queen. What better way to ensure her station?"

"The girl will be easier to manage until the coronation as long as she thinks marriage will allow her to rule." Lydon chuckled at the absurdity.

Raef smirked. He disliked the Delarcan girl, but he could put up with her for the crown. And for control over her accursed propensity to initiate boneheaded maneuvers to ruin trade. The little snip had suddenly taken to inventorying carts bringing trade goods through her border gate, holding them up for hours. *Hours!*

Vael shrugged. "You'll put her in her place," the rich landowner said to Raef. "The wedding night will serve for that."

Indeed. He would.

"But arrange for the investiture as soon as possible," Lydon advised.

The crowd in the common hushed as the captain raised his hand and spoke. "People of Highglen. Lord Raef, protector of the people, your regent and soon-to-be king—"

The assembly broke out in cheers.

"—on the occasion of his wedding, wishes to increase his household by one carefully selected servant. This position is open to any young, unmarried person in Highglen, regardless of station or heritage. Worldling or magiel."

A buzz of wonder shook the crowd.

Raef was here to choose a magiel. Hada had proved that hunting and arresting them resulted in the capture of a handful of only village half-breeds that barely shimmered and could make a spell no stronger than a worldling's. No, he was Raef the Good. He would entice one.

Maybe forty dirty, ragged candidates had assembled. Soldiers prodded them into an approximation of ranks, and of course, pushed the worldlings to the front row.

Raef made a show of examining them from his mount. With his useless leg, it was impractical to dismount; besides, he cut a much more imposing figure on horseback. He pointed to two to be brought forward, then called for the second row to be presented.

"None too likely," Lydon commented.

Raef called for the third row. Here were some magiels, but again, the soldiers had chosen those with the least blur in their skins to place near the front. Still, Raef included one in his selection. A murmur reverberated through the throng.

"That one won't make you a poison subtle enough to deal with Hada's magiel," Lydon said under his breath. Rumor had spread that the Delarcan's magiel was none other than the Barcley heir, and evidence presented by Raef's own spy had confirmed it.

"Gweddien?" Vael dismissed the remark with a wave of a pudgy hand. "The man's a sot. He's no threat."

Oh, but he was. And Raef had been frustrated in his attempts to insinuate an assassin into Hada's entourage. Her servants were maddeningly loyal. Raef had to try harder.

"Hada's magiel could make magic enough to quietly execute her new husband," Lydon said dryly, "and who would there be to accuse her?"

"She's chosen marriage. A woman's manipulation," Vael scoffed. "The girl is like her brother. She has no stomach to be decisive." He added, "Besides, assassinating a beloved regent would make too much trouble for her with her people. And Huwen."

"I won't find a magiel powerful enough to cast a spell on Gweddien," Raef clarified. Though the creature he chose might make a charm sufficient rid him of the free trader who called himself Yaquob. The day after Lydon's soiree, Raef sent a spy to follow the merchant. The spy lost the man within three turnings of Lydon's house. It had taken four days—four *days*—for his men to locate Yaquob's rooms, in a basement below a chandler's shop in the lower city.

Yaquob knew Raef's skeletons, and Raef had no idea what he was intending to do with the information. The man had to be silenced. Yesterday, a contingent of Raef's household guards, dressed as thugs, had gone to steal the man away, to be hidden in one of the castle's unused storage rooms below ground. But the merchant, who'd been busy in his shop in the morning, was gone before Raef's men could kidnap him at midday.

But Raef was nothing if not persistent. He would find the man. "Next row," he called to his captain.

Finally, magiels with some capriciousness to their skins came forward. He chose one magiel. "Bring my selections forward," he said to the captain. "Release the rest."

Five candidates remained in the circle left vacant by the rabble. Two worldlings and three magiels. Several in the crowd appeared to be making wagers on Raef's preference. He smiled to think of the gamblers who'd assume his choice must be a worldling.

"The one on the right," Lydon opined in an undertone. "She has the most magiel in her. And she's not hard to look at. Females are less trouble."

"If you don't want to charm Gweddien, why choose a magiel at all?" Vael asked.

"Tribute." A small grin touched Lydon's lips, and he leaned in to Raef. "And if you want, you can have your way with her a bit before you have to give her up. I understand you have wards to protect yourself against magiel magic."

From Gweddien. Odd, that. A clever, counterintuitive move meant to unbalance Raef, sabotage his doubt. But his captain had tested one. It worked. "The woman on the right," Raef said to his captain. "Have her washed and brought to the castle. Find a suitable clothing, and lodge her with the servants until I call for her."

Vael quirked a frown. "Tribute?"

"For Huwen," Lydon spelled out. "To maintain good relations. For some reason, he's collecting magiels."

The afternoon was waning when the potter and the baker's man, separately, left Miach's room above his master's home. Meg plucked her cloak from the peg by the door. "Your team has made a remarkable response for just two days' planning time. Neither Colm nor Fearghus could have done as much."

"We have a common commitment." Miach took the used mugs to the sideboard. "Have had, ever since the first days when Sulwyn Cordal came to us, saying Dwyn Gramaret was king-in-exile."

She pulled the cloak over her robe. "If the men and weapons you enumerated today come through, we'll be in good shape."

"Here's hoping Kyaju answers your prayer and we won't need them. That Hada relinquishes all authority to Dwyn Gramaret."

Hope. Yes. "And your man—"

"Gurd."

"Gurd, the potter—" Meg fixed the face in her mind. "Who was here today—he'll be waiting across the common from the main gate?"

"Yes, you have it. He'll be waiting in case there's a problem."

If the Amber failed. If Meg found herself running for her life from the castle. "And we only have a two-minute run to where the packs and snowshoes and your guide will be."

He offered her the last cheese dumpling and when she declined it, he popped it into his mouth. "Our men will be in hiding about the castle common, the main gate, and the upper gate, and half a dozen other places," he reassured her. "If there's a pursuit, and if distractions don't suffice, we can take to arms. Don't worry about that part. Once you're out of the castle, our group will have quite a reasonable influence on events."

And within the castle she'd have potions of Disguise and Confusion and Memory Loss. And Rennika.

CHAPTER 30

Brilliant silk thread, marigold and amber and magenta, shone in the candlelight. Janat's embroidery needle wove in and out of the rich, fine-spun linen of Hada's middle robe, a scallop pattern along the hem, following the faint trace of the pattern.

She'd performed magic. Last night.

Meg would've been frustrated with her, if she knew, but Janat had a room to herself here, so Meg didn't need to know. It'd been an experiment. She'd touched a handful of straw from her mattress and taken each stalk back to a time when it was a young, green shoot. Then waited for her time stream to rebound, hoping to find a past.

Before she met Wenid.

It was an imprecise experiment. She had no control over which part of her life she entered. Then, she had mere moments to make a change. In this case, to take her own life.

But, no. There was no time. No time. The seconds or minutes she needed weren't enough to do more than make those around her look at her oddly. The crazy woman.

She tried again. And again.

She could have averted so much pain. For herself, for Meg, for others, if she had never met the High King's magiel.

But she could do nothing to change, *really* change, events that had passed.

She sighed and readjusted the embroidery. She was a mass of failures.

Beside her, Meg worked inattentively, stopping frequently, at the other end of the same garment, edging its neckline. Janat owed Meg so much. She wished . . . there was some way to repay her, even a little of what she'd given.

Beyond the window, from the common below, Janat could hear music and singing. The festival and wedding, tomorrow. Times for celebration. She snipped her thread and pulled another from the skein.

This robe, a pastel contrast to the deep red upper layer and the crimson under layer Hada would wear, would peek out beneath the leather-trimmed vestment. Ide's sister had decorated the vestment with a series of whimsical, long-tailed birds, sigil of Kanden the Good, drawn by Sieur Verlin.

Rennika, on the far side of the brazier, worked on the inner layer, a sleeve that would, like the birds, show beyond the rolled back sleeve of the outer vestment. "The festival will open with prayers to the One God at the third candlemark," Rennika was saying. "Hada's Holder of Histories will perform the rites in the castle shrine. Every shrine in the city will have a Holder perform festival rites at the same candlemark."

Meg adjusted her grip on the dress. "And after the ceremony?"

"Hada and her retinue will cross the bailey to the Great Hall, where there'll be a feast for invited guests. The bailey will be open to anyone from the city. There's to be free bread and ale given out there, as well as in the city plazas."

It had been a good day. Janat had tended the laundry, made several beds—she couldn't really remember how many—and helped chop vegetables before dinner. Sieura Verlin had sent her to market as well, though that might have been yesterday. She was very good with Sieura Verlin's money, though she knew she owed money to someone at Xadria's ale house. Not much. Nothing she couldn't handle. It was awkward that Meg didn't trust her with money. But, then . . .

"No," Rennika was shaking her head at some question Meg had asked. "You'd never get near her then. Too public. She'll be surrounded by guards. She's terrified of assassination." Rennika shrugged. "Not without cause. A Delarcan in a foreign country."

Meg rested her hands in her lap, apparently accepting this. "Is that everything? Anything else?"

Rennika held up her embroidery and studied it critically. "Hada said her soldiers failed to capture some free trader with a shop full of magiel supplies. Gweddien was infuriated," she recalled. "That's all I can think of."

Janat let her embroidery slide to her lap. The embroidery thread was so lovely, the way it gleamed in the candlelight, against the peach color of the linen.

She'd seen that room, filled with magiel amulets and spell books and herbs. Met the free trader. But just now, she only wanted to listen to the flights of marigolds inside her head.

The conversation lapsed, which suited Meg. Rennika had to have the dress finished tonight, and Meg had no idea how much sewing was still required. Time until the wedding was now measured in candlemarks. Beyond the walls of Verlin's house, the sounds of revelry were a distant echo. For once, the steam engines seemed to have stopped.

Janat was good-naturedly quiet, sewing steadily, but dreamily. This was a bad sign, but if only her sister could hold on for another day, Meg would petition Kyaju on her behalf. Free her of her dependencies, then get her out of Highglen. Perhaps as fugitives, but at least they could hide in some distant part of Shangril where no one had ever heard of Boneblood.

Gweddien's presence in Hada's court bothered Meg, though. He was like a wild tarot, full of too many possibilities. Had he come here to obtain the Amber from Yaquob and use it with Hada? Or had things come together for him serendipitously? If Gweddien had the Amber, he and Hada would be in a position to obtain anything the Gods could grant. Which was . . . anything. If Hada understood this, she'd be as fervent as Gweddien to obtain the Amber. Yet Rennika's description of the botched arrest of the free trader suggested the queen was ambivalent. She must think the stone was counterfeit.

If the stone was fraudulent, though, that answered a key question. Why had Yaquob not pursued Meg after she stole it? No resources? No clue as to who had taken it? Her stomach twisted. Because he'd already determined who the thief was. Raoul. In which case, she would not give a chetrum for the boy's life.

If it was a fake, it might be one of several. Why waste energy trying to get hers back, if he had a drawer full of them? That could explain the lack of pursuit.

Or, Raoul—or someone else—had succeeded in slipping a knife between his ribs.

Meg adjusted the sewing on her lap, held it up to the candlelight to see the pattern better.

In all likelihood, by this time, the day after tomorrow, she and Janat would be on the road, running for their lives. Unless, of course, Meg came to her senses and quit her madness.

She could.

Miach would be upset with her. Oh, well. She would not cry over him.

Tonore, whom she'd seen at the abandoned shop, though. Meg would still have to watch out for him. Find a way to send him on a goose chase.

But Rennika and everyone associated with her, whether they were privy to what was happening under their noses or not, would be relieved if Meg backed down. Even Colm and Fearghus could hardly be upset, as they had no idea she'd even contemplated such a crackpot plan.

And she could care for Janat. Really care for her. Maybe Meg could live quietly somewhere, build a life. Have a family.

The voices floating up from Verlin's rooms had ceased some time ago. The brazier crackled a little as the embers shifted.

Janat lifted her head from her sewing and looked at Meg with unsettlingly calm eyes. "You have the Amber."

Meg stilled and Rennika's gaze snapped up, wary.

"You are going into Hada's castle with it to touch her and go to Heaven to save us."

Gods. What had she said in Janat's presence?

She'd become complacent, thinking Janat unaware.

"Do it." Janat nodded and resumed her sewing. "I want to help in any way I can. You're going during the wedding?"

Meg turned to Rennika.

Rennika looked from Meg to Janat. Then she said softly, "The wedding night."

Meg felt the blood drain from her face. If Janat knew, it was no secret. "Rennika."

"A candlemark before dawn."

"With all those opportunities of chaos, you want to wait until the silence of night?" Janat asked.

"The guards will be on high alert right up to the wedding and during it," Rennika said. "If there's going to be a problem, that's when they'll expect it. No one without strict authorization will come or go from the castle. After the revelry—when it's quiet—they'll be fatigued."

The reasoning wasn't bad, but— "No one can know this, Janat."

"You'll have to use magic to enter," Janat pointed out. "To break the wards."

"I can do the magic," Rennika said. She turned to Meg. "I'll attend you," she said. "Get you in, and to the correct room. I can ride out the reverberations of the magic, afterward, and you can stay alert and in the present."

Meg would have to get herself out, if necessary—which was fair enough. "Janat? Did you hear me? No one can know."

"I know." Janat returned to her sewing.

"I'll need to be back here before Verlin catches on," Rennika said.

"Hada won't be alone in her chamber," Janat pointed out.

Meg tried to swallow. Janat knew. Gods, how could Meg have been so stupid as to speak in front of her?

"I thought of that," Rennika said. "But I don't think you need to worry. It's a political marriage. By morning, Lord Raef will have left her bed. Neither of them likes the other. "

Meg sewed steadily, thinking furiously. The wedding was tomorrow. She had over a day to wait for Rennika to get her into the castle. Too much could happen in that space of time.

And then the dress was done, and Rennika had taken it away and Janat went to bed, leaving Meg to pace and stew. When Rennika returned, Meg stopped her at the top of the stairs. "Janat knows too much," she hissed. "The whole thing could blow up in our faces."

Rennika's eyes widened. "I thought she knew. I thought you told her."

"No!"

Rennika blinked.

Meg bit her lip. She couldn't explode at Rennika. It had been an honest mistake.

"What do you want me to do?"

Meg licked her lips. "I've been trying to come up with something, but I can't."

"I'm sorry, Meg—"

"No, it's not your fault. It's mine. I've been wracking my brain to think of what I said in front of her, and I think I've said far too much for far too long."

"She's not stupid."

"No. Exactly."

Rennika cast a quick glance down the stairs. "I'll be busy from dawn until after the wedding. You'll just have to watch her."

Meg nodded. "I have to tell Miach. In case he wants to call everything off."

Rennika bit her lip. "It's late."

Meg shrugged. "I've got to."

Rennika nodded. "All right. I'll be here until you get back."

Meg took an easier breath and fetched her cloak. "I won't be long."

Miach approved Rennika's plan for smuggling Meg into the castle. He listened hard to Meg's admission of the risk Janat posed. Finally, he shook his head. "Nothing we can do about it. Watch her, as Rennika said."

Meg pressed her lips together. She would get no sleep.

"Call on me. If you need help, I can come or send someone."

That made her feel better. "You don't want to call it off?"

He shook his head, and she closed her eyes in relief.

"Go," he said. "Get back safely."

It was past midnight when Meg left Miach, but the streets were still as busy as they might be for a midwinter festival. Harps, mandolins, flutes, and voices competed in a rainbow of discord as she made her way along the street among clumps of merrymakers and debaters, now animated with drink. For good or ill, time rolled onward, unrelenting: sweeping the great events of nations along with it, or quietly nudging each man or woman forward along her own journey. Inexorable.

The wedding would happen. She was reassured by Miach's confidence. Night would deepen, and Meg would enter the castle. And then, who was to—

A hand shot out from a narrow alley and gripped her wrist, pulling her off balance into the darkness. A second hand clamped over her mouth before she could scream.

She thrashed out wildly, squeaking muffled shrieks as her face hit the snow. Several sets of hands quickly and efficiently bound her wrists behind her and wrapped a sickly-smelling gag over her mouth. Her squirming did her no good as a sack was shoved over her head, and she was wrapped in a blanket, then lifted, shifted slightly and dropped into what she could only imagine was a straw-lined box. She redoubled her efforts, but a scrape of wood on wood sounded above her, and her voice was drowned by the ringing of a hammer. Her prison shook with rhythmic blows, and the music and laughter and talk from the street abruptly faded.

The potion her kidnappers had spilled on her gag was not strong. Likely it was only worldling magic, but it was confined with her in the small space of the bag on her head. A lightness and a pleasurable spinning sensation eased her alarm. She jostled as the box containing her was hoisted. A jerky, rocking motion. She was being carried.

Carried.

Somewhere. Set down. A jerk—a horse-drawn wagon? The muffled sounds of the street celebration faded, and all she could hear was her own breathing, and the music and colors in her own mind.

She slept.

CHAPTER 31

The faintest hint of gray filtered in through Rennika's window. She'd been restless for some time, uneasiness prodding at her from somewhere unseen. Now she let her eyes open a slit. Too early to rise. But sleep had gone.

Kyaju. Rennika should never have made those promises to Meg. Take her to Hada's apartment in the keep. What was she thinking? Meg's mission was insane. She would be captured, imprisoned, doubtless tortured before she was put to death. People under torture talked.

Today was the festival and Hada's wedding. Yon and Ide's wedding.

Rennika rose. She moved restlessly into the common room, hoping her footsteps didn't waken anyone.

Janat was there, wrapped in blankets against the chill, staring at the cold brazier from the armchair.

"Janat?" Gods. She'd promised Meg she'd watch her.

Janat turned. She was hollow-eyed this morning, and pale. But . . . more alert? No, she looked . . . hunted. Haunted.

"I couldn't sleep." Rennika pulled tinder and kindling from the stack of stove-lengths.

Janat shifted in her blankets. "Same." She scrubbed the rough blanket back and forth across the back of her neck. "Today's the day. Will you renege?"

Rennika looked up from her flint and steel, startled. But she had no reply.

"I thought about it," Janat said.

Rennika blew on the glowing tinder. "And?"

Her sister drew in a deep breath. "Mama died in the siege of Archwood, promising to deliver the Amber to us." She was silent a long moment. Rennika fed twigs to the tiny flames. "She wanted one of us to become the Magiel of the Amber and save the souls of everyone with no death token. I can't go back on my word to Meg."

Rennika nodded. All of this was true. But did the world's problems need to fall on their shoulders?

"And . . ." Janat curled tighter into her chair. "I owe it to Meg."

Rennika sat back and queried her with a frown.

"All the things Meg's done for me," she said softly. "No one could have been better to me. And I've treated her—" Janat shook her head and sank deeper into her blanket rubbing the rough wool along her arms. She shrugged. "This is something I have to do."

Rennika bit the inside of her lip. She wished she was as certain as Janat seemed, now. Wish as she might, she could see no realistic way Meg's plan could work. They'd all be dead. Or running.

Rennika had lain awake, seeing it in her mind. If forced to flee, the best life she could predict would be to survive as a refugee. Maybe—years from now—begin working as a dyer again, if she dared. The worst, she didn't want to contemplate. She would ask Sieur Verlin for the money he held for her. She wouldn't tell him how her complicity in Meg's plan would betray him.

Rennika straightened. "I'm making tea." Anything to change the subject. "Do you want to wake Meg?"

Janat rose from the armchair and padded, barefoot, to Meg's room and tapped on the door. "Meg?"

Rennika added charcoal to the fire and rose to fill the kettle.

Janat turned in Meg's open doorway. "She's not here." Her voice quivered. "Hasn't been here all night."

Piss. Rennika wished Meg would keep them informed of her comings and goings. Especially, now.

Janat went to her room. "I'm going to look for her."

Rennika looked up sharply. Janat's concern seemed to come on suddenly. "She'll be back," Rennika hushed. Janat couldn't leave. Rennika had to watch her.

Janat reappeared, tying the strings to her robe, fingers flying in panic. "She was telling us the uprisers have everything in place. It's tonight or never."

"The raid tonight is Meg's reason for existing. She won't miss it. Janat, you can't go flying off—"

"What if she's hurt? Imprisoned? Can't come?" Janat grabbed her cloak from its hook.

Rennika blocked the top of the stairs. "You're a bit dramatic, don't you think?"

Janat's face was pale, her hair disheveled. Something was not right. She stared hard at Rennika, her eyes blank. "Let me go."

"Why the rush? Give her time to get back."

"No danger? Really?" Janat's voice filled with sarcasm. "A magiel? Full blood?" She pushed past Rennika.

"Janat—"

But she was gone, feet tapping a tattoo down the stairs.

Rennika grabbed her cloak to cover her nightclothes and ran down the stairs, hoping her scuffle of slippers on the steps would not disturb the family. She rushed out into the biting dark and looked wildly around the compound. No Janat. Gods, she was quick.

Rennika ran to the servants' gate. It stood open, but Janat was not in the alley. Rennika hurried as fast as the icy path allowed, to the end of the lane, and looked out onto the street. The shops were still closed, the street empty. No movement. No sound, not even the steam engine. Only the wind in the rooftops.

Rennika darted through the common to the mouths of intersecting lanes, then downhill in the direction of the river. But it was no use. There were too many niches to check, too many alleys and streets. And she was nearly barefoot in the snow and half-naked. She wheezed as she climbed back up the lane under a lightening sky.

Janat was gone.

Ranuat, Janat itched!

She'd slipped ungracefully from Rennika, only to find herself in a bit of a chase when some random soldier happened to spot her.

But she had to get out of Verlin's house. If she stayed any longer, she was going to go into her room and take a knife to her itching places. She couldn't do that anymore. She'd seen Kirst. It would kill her.

She needed Meg. Needed her strength.

Meg would be with the uprisers. Janat knew Meg's contact was Miach, and it was only the work of a half a candlemark to learn where to find him.

Of course, Rennika was right. Meg would come back.

Janat wouldn't approach Miach, not yet. She knew where the Amber was—Meg had hidden it in a puzzle box in her room—but Janat wouldn't take it, not unless it was clear there was no other choice. Rennika thought the infiltration tonight wouldn't work without Meg, but Janat and Rennika were Falkyns, too. Mama's heirs.

Meg had given up everything for Janat and, by the Gods, Janat vowed for once she would make things right for her sister, make sure nothing stood in Meg's way. The quest had to be completed, regardless of Janat's personal outcome. Janat had promised herself before that she would help Meg. This time she meant to go through with it.

For Meg. For Shangril.

And until the designated time, Janat would stay clean. No Bloodbone. She turned to the lower city, to Xadria's.

Only a little Heartspeed, to keep her awake and alert.

⁂

Sieur Verlin closed the door to his accounting room, and Rennika waited in the dim, crowded space, her stomach churning. Verlin had betrayed her. Abandoned her for the price of a royal contract.

"This can't wait? Even until we've broken fast?" Sieur Verlin wore only his morning robe over his night clothes, most unusual for him. He would be bathed and dressed before going to the castle, as would Rennika, Ide, and Tyg. Even contracted tradesmen, attending the ceremony from the back of a high balcony, would be dressed in their best.

"Please, Sieur," she said, trying not to disclose the turmoil she felt. "You told me I could come to you at any time." And she *had to* look for Janat.

"Yes, of course, but—" He sighed. There were no demands on him, other than to pace and second guess himself, until at least midmorning. "Very well, Rennika, but please be brief." He fingered the edge of the table where he drew his designs.

She steeled herself. "Sieur, I'm asking you to write a letter of my competence, to whom it may concern, conferring my mastership. And to release the money you saved for me." His letter would not carry the weight of a master of the dyers' guild, but it would be something.

Verlin jerked back as if stung. "Now?"

"Yes, Sieur." Before she was set back to the status of *apprentice*. Before she had to stand by and watch Yon marry her best friend.

"You're planning to leave us?" She had his full attention, and the shock and surprise in his eyes turned to distress.

He'd actually thought she would stay on, with her demotion? "Sieur, I must." Whether with Meg and Janat, or not.

He squinted at her in disbelief. "Not before you can have a proper farewell. Not before you can judge Xoran's journeymanship."

The new master could do that. "Sieur, the weather could change at any time."

"You would leave Highglen?" The concept of leaving the place of one's birth—though she knew he was aware she'd come from away, many years ago—seemed a foreign one to him, despite his travels as a merchant. "Before winter? And go where?"

"My father's family is from Zellora," she reminded him. She'd had time as she'd lain awake in the night to review the story she'd told when she'd first come to Highglen.

He shook his head and stared at her. "Has someone in my household offended you?"

Sudden warmth, traitor to her composure, flooded her neck and cheeks.

He heaved a heavy sigh and nodded. "I am sorry. I want you to know that I value your work. That you're . . ." He shrugged and opened his mouth, then closed it, then pushed on. "Like one of my daughters." He pressed his lips together and nodded, stepping back.

Her eyes closed involuntarily. Gods. She had hurt him more deeply than she could likely ever know. But his falseness had hurt her as well. Still hurt her.

"As much as that's true," he said softly, "you know I'll support you." He turned to leave.

"Sieur—" She stepped forward. "A letter will take only a moment."

"Tomorrow, Rennika. After the wedding."

"I . . . will fulfill my commitment to your house at today's fitting, of course." She had to force the words through a rough throat. "But Sieur, if the letter is complete and my money is in my purse, the time of my departure can be my own."

Verlin looked sharply at her.

She lowered her gaze. He knew Yon was her lover. He must know Yon's wedding must grieve her.

He let out a long breath. Then he moved to his chair and found a piece of precious vellum.

"Thank you, Sieur." She kept her head down.

There was a moment of scratching of quill on paper, then he rose to take the dipper of melted wax from its place over the candle and, returning to the desk, dropped a puddle of red beneath his signature. She replaced it for him as he pressed his seal into the wax.

"All of us will miss you, Rennika," he said as he handed her the letter.

She nodded, an excuse to turn away her face against threatening tears and, folding the letter without looking at it, put it into her purse. Gods, she needed to get her money and go after Janat.

Verlin cleared his throat and stepped behind his desk, opening his book of accounts. He turned to the page he kept for her and traced his finger along the last entry. "A goodly sum," he said. "Fifty-four gultra."

Fifty-four. She'd kept a rough tally in her head, and thought the sum might be as much as forty . . . She'd have to be careful, carry it in several purses.

He turned his back to her, and she took a discreet step away as he opened the puzzle box chained to its place against the wall. He rummaged among the nested boxes within. Then he turned, perplexed, holding up a large, deflated bag. "Rennika, I'm not sure how to say this. There are only three gultra here."

※

Who had access to Sieur Verlin's locked box? Sieur Verlin, of course, and Yon, for the merchant trade. No one else.

Rennika slumped back into a chair. Verlin had already sold her position for royal favors. What possible reason could he have for taking her money as well? The idea felt false.

Without waiting for her to speak, Verlin strode to the door and opened it. "Tyg." The girl must have been nearby. "Call Yon. Tell him I need to speak with him."

Rennika breathed. The money was not gone, just misplaced.

It took only a minute before Yon arrived. Rennika rose to her feet, unable to look directly at him.

"Close the door," Sieur Verlin said.

Yon did so, also avoiding her gaze. He took in the open box, and his face drew serious. Pale.

Verlin nodded to the box. "I was keeping Rennika's money safe," he said, "but it's gone missing."

A flutter of comprehension touched Yon's eyes. "You're leaving?"

"I may." He'd given her no reason to stay.

His eyes grew cold.

Something deep inside her curled. He would let her leave. Not say a word to stop her.

And why not? She had no hold on him. He'd let his father and his grandmother marry him to Ide for the sake of family wealth and standing, and never a word of argument. She must do the same, find marriage and children with someone else. Someone more worthy.

"You know nothing of what could have happened to it?" Verlin asked. "No one has access to my puzzle box beyond us two."

Rennika blinked, trying to focus on Yon. It was true. If Verlin didn't know where the money was, Yon had to. She chafed to get on with it.

"Officially," Yon said carefully.

Verlin tilted his head. "What do you mean?"

Yon came more fully into the room, looking at the box. "The puzzle lock would keep any worldling out. But we have two magiels in the house now." He said the word as if it were dirty.

Rennika's face flashed, hot. She bit back a retort. He thought *Meg* had taken the money? Or Janat?

Verlin cast a worried look at Rennika, then turned his back, rummaging in the box.

Rennika glared at Yon, but he looked down, not meeting her gaze. Sullen.

Verlin pivoted. "Money is gone from other compartments as well."

"My sister did not take your money!" Rennika said in a low, choked voice. Though, what Yon said was true. Either of them would be able to. Easily. And Janat—and Meg—were both missing.

Verlin looked at her in dismay. He said nothing but slumped back onto the corner of his table. Gods—her mentor, her master . . . the only man who'd been a father to her . . .

"The money is gone, and now you would leave us," Yon said softly.

She slumped to her knees before Verlin. "Sieur," she whispered. "I promise you. I know nothing of this. But my sisters did not take this money."

He blinked and placed a hand on the side of her head. "You are a good woman, Rennika." He pressed his lips together for a moment. "You see nothing but good in others."

No! He could not believe her sisters would betray his trust.

But, Janat. Midnight prowlings. Her illness. Meg's warning.

She stared up at him, breathing hard.

Behind her, Yon shuffled.

She gathered her racing pulse, trying to calm herself. Trying to think logically. "They didn't do it," she said with soft intensity. "But I will ask." She put her hand on the arm of a chair to help herself rise, her stomach turning. Janat. And Meg.

CHAPTER 32

Gweddien paced the corridor outside Hada's suite in the predawn gray. Sweat soaked his shirt beneath his doublet, his head pounded, and his stomach twisted. Besides the two guards, a page waited for the princess's maid to come from her rooms with instruction to fetch the royal bath and breakfast and hairdressers. The boy eyed him surreptitiously, as the only diversion—and possible threat—in the silent hallway.

Gods, he'd had no drink, no Serenity or anodyne, nothing since last night. He'd promised Hada. But the need for glim was on him, stronger than ever, and neither drink, nor Heartspeed, nor Dream Incense could lessen his need of it. Once the wedding was over, he'd indulge.

The door opened. Gweddien turned.

Hada's maid. She nodded to the boy who scampered to him with a carefully neutral face. "Her Highness will see you now."

Gweddien wrapped the golden chain in his left hand to keep it from flying about and bolted past the girl before the words were out of the page's mouth.

He closed the door behind him, his back to its panels. Hands shaking, he loosened the golden collar.

Hada stood in the door to her bed chamber in a casual robe, her hair disheveled and her brows knit in querulous concern. "What is it?"

He nodded in a cursory bow. He'd donned his clothes hastily, and he knew he looked rumpled. His mouth was dry as late summer grass. "Highness, the opportunity of which I spoke. It is upon us."

"What—"

"The Amber."

She squinted at him briefly, then her expression cooled. "Gweddien—"

She could not deny him now. She could *not*. He flung his hand free of the chain and strode to her side, sinking to his knees before her. "The men you promised me. We must bring the merchant into the castle. *Keep him safe.*"

"I sent men. His shop was ransacked, and he was gone."

"Yaquob has been located. I've spoken with his emissary."

"Not today." Her eyes snapped open. "Today is the festival. For God's sake, Gweddien. The wedding."

But she would do it. He hung on her silence, waiting.

"Tomorrow," she conceded.

A flood of relief and panic shot through him simultaneously. "Sieur Yaquob could be dead by tomorrow." He could be dead, now. The stone lost. "There are empty cells in the castle." Safe cells. Locked cells. "I told his messenger I would send a letter to him this morning." The urchin.

Hada's jaw tensed.

A timid knock came at the door, and her gaze twitched away. Her bath.

She sighed. "Very well." She rose. "I will send soldiers to arrest him. Will three be enough?" She added irritably.

A lightness suffused him, and he would have wept. "May I attend with them? Your Highness? To be sure the merchant doesn't bolt?"

She flicked her hand, dismissing him. "You may. But cover yourself. And be back here and bathed in good time. I want you at the ceremony. And not drunk."

☙

Rennika halted in the doorway to the dining room. The family sat at the table, animated with conversation. Sieura Verlin, Tyg, the sisters and brothers by marriage, and her own usual place with its untouched bowl. Meg's and Janat's, also pristine. Yon and Verlin, just seating themselves.

Tyg noticed her hesitancy. "Rennika, come eat! We've almost finished the cheese dumplings. Where are your sisters?"

Yon and Verlin lifted their heads, letting the rest of the conversation swirl around them.

"They went out early," she said carefully, fastening the brooch on her own cloak, her voice sounding false in her own ears. "I just came to say I have to run an errand. I'll be back in plenty of time."

"Today?" Sieura Verlin asked in disbelief.

"You're not having breakfast?" Tyg cried.

"Be back before noon," Verlin warned.

Rennika could not help but look at Yon, but he had averted his eyes. "I will," she said.

Meg woke, nauseated, head pounding in the cold. Spruce and fir branches huddled over her, a faint glow flickering on their undersides. The straw and hard boards beneath her had done little to keep the snow from stealing her warmth. At least the lid of her prison was gone, and the cloying gag removed. The bag over her head had been taken away, as well as the ropes binding her wrists. She could move.

The straw under her rustled as she shifted to peer over the edge of the box. Under a heavy gray sky, it was full day. Gods, how late was it?

A cloaked man at a small crackling campfire in the snow, tending something in a pot, sprang up.

Tonore.

Gods, he was still as handsome as he had been the night she'd first seen him through new eyes.

They'd captured a rich chest of gold that day—Dwyn's farm had grown to seven buildings, just to house people who'd flocked to him to fight the Arcanian invaders. A group of them had held up a Delarcan toadie's coach on the King's Road and captured treasure: almost fifty swords and bows, and seven muskets—even Meg got practice firing one. That night, the singing, the camaraderie, the wine. She'd had too much drink—they all had. When she left the campfire looking for her bed, Tonore accompanied her. That was when she realized he'd been captivated by her, afraid to approach. And realized she was smitten with him.

Meg had never wanted another lover after Tonore. It was easier to throw herself into work, to spend her unoccupied moments reading about religion, or politics, or history, than to let herself love someone, anyone, who could cause so deep and unrelenting a grief.

Now, Tonore pushed back his hood from his balding head. He'd changed since those days. And yet, not.

She disentangled herself from the confines of the box, her stomach heaving. They were camped in a small clearing. No one else was in the glade.

"Meg." He held out his hand to help her from the box, his grip like an iron band. She might escape with magic, but not by choosing to suddenly run.

She blinked at the black trees surrounding her, sentinels in white snow. A tangle of footprints disappeared uphill, several sets. He must have hired locals to carry her this far. "I won't try to bolt," she said. For now. Her head still spun.

He released her. "I have porridge."

Her stomach roiled. "Maybe a little tea." She shuffled to a stump by the fire.

Tonore sprinkled a few dried leaves into a mug. She watched his quick, efficient movements. He was looking good. Lean. Fit. The scar where his ear had been was no detraction.

But grief for the loss of his lover still haunted his eyes. It had only been a short time since the failed raid in Glenfast, she reflected. The night Colm had brought the ragged looting party back almost empty-handed. Tonore had blamed Colm for the rout, for his lover's death, but Fearghus's stinginess and Janat's sickness had been responsible, too. And Huwen's guns. Too many factors to parse.

"So," she said. "Uprisers really aren't going to let Janat and I alone to live our lives."

"Colm and Fearghus sent me," Tonore said.

"Looks like I managed to put them in agreement, for once."

This drew a smile. "I'm not sure King Dwyn even knows you fled. I doubt Fearghus told him." He poured from the steaming pot into her mug. "I didn't want to hire those bandits to grab you. I only wanted to talk to you."

A grim compliment. "How did you know I was here?"

He passed her the mug. "Cataract Crag was an obvious choice, Meg. You didn't really try very hard."

Gods, had she been that transparent? Worry about Janat had distracted her. A deadly stupidity.

"Colm sent searchers in different directions." He spooned porridge into a bowl. "I happened to find a woman called Kirst."

Of course. Tonore guessed where to hunt. In the districts of spell-eaters. Meg might as well have left him a map. But— "How did Kirst know where we went?"

"Janat told her."

Gods, Meg would never understand her sister.

She checked the position of the sun, too high behind low cloud. Gods, she hoped Rennika, Miach, *someone* was watching Janat.

She had to go. Still, she wouldn't get far just now. Her stomach still seethed. "You're alone?" She let her gaze flick about the campsite, though there was no evidence anyone was with him. The kidnappers were locals, hired and gone.

Tonore ate his porridge. "I left Peate with our horses below the headwall. The horses couldn't make it up the road from there."

"The snow." Of course.

"Meg, I wanted to be the one to talk to you. I thought . . ." He gestured helplessly with one hand. "We have an understanding." He caught her gaze and held it. There was still love for her—of a kind—in his eyes.

She gave a soft shrug. She'd had to work by his side this last few months since his company had been assigned to Glenfast, but with his lover there, she'd kept her distance.

"I was never good enough for you, Meg," he said. "I'm sorry."

Ah. Confessions. "A bit more to it than that." Catching him with Vonte. *That* had broken her. Tonore could love women, but it turned out, he loved men more.

He tilted his head in acknowledgment of her unspoken thought. "The heart wants what the heart wants."

She nodded.

"But I can never be sorry about my years with Vonte." He lowered his spoon. "I never got a chance to tell you. It was never about loving you. It was about loving Vonte . . . differently."

She straightened and sipped her tea. Enough of the past. "You know I can't go back with you to Fearghus."

"Why not? Meg, I can't let Shangril down. I can't leave the mission. I can't let the people lose faith in their Gods."

"You think I can?"

"If you'd only work with us. You were more passionate than anyone." He frowned. "What's changed?"

"Colm and Fearghus." She huddled close to the fire, trying to drive back the cold that still chilled her from a night in the snow. "We're getting nowhere."

"You're more effective here?" He gestured to the woods and the mountain.

"There are uprisers in Highglen," she said. "They have plans to take back their country. It does our common cause no good if you take me out of those plans."

He lowered his bowl and scrutinized her. "An action?" He tilted his head, absorbing her news. "When?"

"Soon." Today.

"Huwen's army is on the march," Tonore said at last. "He's coming to Highglen. *With* cannons and muskets. Not more than a day behind me."

She looked up sharply. That would cut their plans close. If the prayer stone was real, she and Miach and the others could be ready for Huwen's arrival.

Or she might be unconscious alongside princess Hada, recuperating from a journey to the Heavens, when the army arrived. Meg's mother had languished in a darkened room for days after praying with King Ean.

But if she was on the run, Huwen's march into Highglen could be a fortuitous distraction, drawing attention from her flight. Though, the risks of bolting in the midst of a battle multiplied many-fold. And if it came to leaving Gramarye, could she get a self-charmed, uncooperative Janat out of a city besieged by a formidable army? She quailed at the idea.

Tonore appeared to take her silence for resistance. "You may calculate the risk of being captured worth this military action, whatever it is, but King Dwyn has an interest in keeping your knowledge of his plans and resources secret. The war's not over, Meg. Not for King Dwyn, and not for those loyal to the freedom and equality he represents."

Platitudes. Meg could scream. "Will King Dwyn support Highglen's bid for independence? Has he sent fighters to help?"

"Highglen has never asked for support."

"Gods, Tonore, how bungling can Dwyn's generals be? I heard about Highglen's request when I was in Glenfast, for Ranuat's sake, and I told both Colm and Tonore. I met the merchant—right here in Highglen—who carried the message."

Tonore shook his head. "No such plea made it to King Dwyn."

"So, no. The uprisers are too disorganized. There's too much in-fighting. Can't you see why I need to be more effective elsewhere?"

"Whatever the reason—Highglen's messenger or King Dwyn's generals, it's impossible for him to send men now. Huwen's riding here because he's smashed the uprisers. They're scattered in four countries in hidden camps, tending their wounded. Including Dwyn."

"Dwyn?" She shook her head in sympathy. But. She would not be drawn in. It was time to leave.

The tea had had a reviving effect, and she blinked the last of her grogginess away. Exercise was likely her best medicine, and she had to warn Miach about the army. And the cannons. She stood. "I have to go."

"Meg." He stood as well, and his look said he'd kidnapped her once and he could do it again.

"Give me a day," she entreated.

"You know I can't. By then Huwen will be here." But his denial of her request was empty. If she really wanted to leave him, he could not stop her.

"I wouldn't ask if I didn't think there was a possibility of success." She wanted to go without worrying about him following. Interfering. And go, knowing she could return and rely on his horses to get her and her sisters out of the country.

His eyes narrowed. "What have you got planned?"

"I can't tell you." But she had to give him something if she wanted him to free her without a fight. "But there's a chance we can take Highglen. If so, the uprisers have hope again."

He let out a breath, shaking his head. "All right. One day."

She took his shoulders and kissed him on the cheek.

"Just guarantee you won't get caught and tortured by Huwen."

CHAPTER 33

Rennika hurried through streets crowded with roisterers and celebrants. She knew Meg could take care of herself, and that nothing short of a calamity would prevent her sister from returning to keep her rendezvous by midnight.

But Janat, gone. The money, gone. And . . . *could* Meg be part of a planned theft?

Rennika's stomach twisted. She had no idea where to look. Highglen was a large city and filled with secret corners. She'd lived here for years but rarely went to the lower town. And she'd never asked Meg—or Janat—where they went when they left Verlin's house. Rennika hadn't wanted to know.

But there was one person who might know. Miach.

Miach put his hand on Rennika's arm, and they halted below a wooden stair tacked onto the outside of a tall building at the end of a narrow alley. He'd told her he was glad she'd contacted him. She didn't tell him about her missing money.

The stench of vomit and piss and feces turned Rennika's stomach, and she could not step anywhere without dragging the hem of her cloak in stinking muck.

Miach pointed to a doorway giving out onto a landing at the top of the stair. Light snow fell from the gray sky above. "You might want to wait out here and let me see if they're inside."

He was treating her like a flower. Rennika had lived as a refugee those first years of the war. She'd seen ugliness. And she hadn't come all this way to wait outside. "No."

"It isn't the nicest of places."

And then she registered his intent. She might not want to see what her sister had come to. Rennika hardened her stomach. "I'll come," she said quietly.

He gave a tiny shake of his head. "Your sister might want . . . some dignity."

Again, her perception of the situation altered. But, no. "What is, is. It won't improve by being hidden."

Miach ran his tongue around his mouth. He led the way up the stairs.

The common room of The Three Corners was like any number of cheap taverns Rennika had seen as a girl hiding with the refugees from the High King's soldiers. Bare trestle tables and benches crowded the plain room, its floor filthy with spills and half-cleaned vomit. There was no fire in the brazier, and the room was cold. A small wooden bar stood at one end where the tavernkeeper could serve spirits, and a doorway led deeper within. The place was quiet, but for an occasional murmur from the rooms down the corridor, and someone snored. A young boy played some type of ring toss game at one of the tables.

A wiry, gray-haired woman entered from the back hall. She stopped when she saw Rennika and Miach, as though she'd been expecting someone else.

"Xadria," Miach said.

"What do you want?" The woman's gaze flicked from Rennika to Miach.

"I want to see my sister," Rennika said.

The older woman eyed her, pointedly looking at her fine clothes. "You're Master Verlin's dyer. What an honor." She shrugged and turned back to the corridor. "Your sister's not here."

"Janat Hawkins," Rennika said. She tried to look past the woman into the darkness.

"Janat? She was," the boy said. He lifted his attention from his game. "She left."

"Your sister owes me money," Xadria said, turning back. "You can pay her bill."

"How much?" Foolish question to ask, considering Rennika's money was gone. "A night's rent?" Such a derelict inn could hardly cost a chetra.

Again, Xadria measured Rennika's worth with a look. "You *might* be able to pay it. Sixty gultra."

"What?" Miach sputtered. "How?"

Sixty? A debt rung up in—two fortnights? Less?

"She can pay it herself," Xadria murmured. "A half-magiel. Some customers dream of a magical experience. I was hoping it was her coming now, to begin work."

The marrow in Rennika's bones chilled. "No."

The woman shrugged. "I suppose the likes of you can afford to look down on the likes of us." She held out her palm.

"Don't," Miach said to Rennika. "Do you *have* sixty gultra?"

Gods, no. "My money was stolen," she admitted. "From Verlin's locked box."

And—Janat *hadn't* taken Rennika's money. That was clear. She'd never have run up such an exorbitant debt if she'd had Rennika's gultra. Or, if she'd only just taken the money a day ago, the debt would be repaid, no need to sell herself.

No, the thief wasn't Janat. This time. Rennika breathed. Thank the Gods.

So . . . who?

"You didn't answer the question," Miach said. "How did she run up such a debt?"

"You have to ask?" Xadria sneered. "She's a spell-eater."

"You let her build up this debt to make her your chattel," Rennika accused.

"Your sister's vices are hardly my fault," Xadria said in mild surprise. "She was shackled before she came to me."

It was true. Rennika could make no response.

Xadria sighed and shook her head. "Look. I'm a businesswoman. Janat and I have a contract. I can give her what she needs in order to work. But either way, I'm owed sixty gultra. And . . ." The woman rolled her eyes. "I shouldn't stick my neck out and tell you this, but if you want to find your money, the one you should be talking to is Vellefair."

Vellefair? Rennika looked to Miach for clarity.

"Why would Vellefair have Rennika's money?" Miach asked.

Xadria lifted a shoulder noncommittally. "I'm not saying he has it. I'm saying he might know where it is." She turned to Rennika. "There. Information for free, and see what good it does you. I don't know why I'm so generous."

To get rid of me.

"Rennika?" Miach spoke softly. "The wedding."

But she still hadn't found Janat. Or Meg.

He held out his hand to her. "We'll look for Vellefair. Then you have to get changed and go to the castle. There are a lot of people depending on you."

"That's right," Xadria echoed. "You need to clean up. Go to the castle. You're important."

Rennika glared at her, rage curling helplessly in her stomach. But there was nothing for it. She followed Miach from the room.

The sun was rising toward noon behind inconsistent high cloud and flurries before Rennika, following Miach, saw Vellefair. The villain sat in a back booth of a nondescript tavern—the fifth Miach had led her to since leaving The Three Corners—nursing a tankard of beer and what looked like a demon headache. The place was almost empty.

Miach slid onto the bench opposite the old man and Rennika followed suit. She'd promised to be back at Verlin's home by now. Verlin—Yon, all of them—would be crawling the walls, wondering where she'd gone. And she couldn't shake her worry for Janat.

"Vellefair." Miach signaled the serving girl and lifted three fingers in the air.

Vellefair straightened a little and gave Miach a small grin. Miach seemed well connected among the reprobates of Highglen.

"I don't have time to waste," Miach said, leaning forward and speaking in a low voice. He nodded at Rennika. "This woman's master is Sieur Verlin."

Vellefair stared at him and then at Rennika. His eyes were sunk into deep pockets of flesh, making up for the lack of flesh everywhere else on his body. They sharpened to a rheumy alertness at this news.

"Her money's gone missing. Xadria said you might know something."

The serving girl brought three tankards of beer, and Miach paid her, for which Rennika was grateful. Vellefair looked grateful as well, quaffing the remainder of his first—or perhaps, "previous" was the better descriptor—tankard. "I would," Vellefair said. "What do I get?"

Miach indicated the beer with a waggle of his eyebrows.

"And?" He reached for the handle.

Rennika pushed her tankard toward him.

"Our everlasting gratitude." Miach put a hand on Vellefair's wrist before he could sip the second beer. "What do you know?"

Vellefair took in a breath and let it out, sitting back on his bench. "I know who took it. I take packages to and from Verlin's house all the time." He shrugged.

Rennika didn't understand.

"Gambling?" Miach said.

Vellefair shook his head. "Sugar."

Rennika cocked her head, confused. "Who do you exchange money with?" she asked.

"His son. Yon."

Rennika stared at him. This was impossible. Xadria and Vellefair had concocted an elaborate ruse to mislead her. "But . . . to what possible end?"

"His grandmother can't eat enough sugar."

Though Meg followed fresh tracks through the snow, the going was hard. The group burdened with her coffin had been able to manage a steeper path going downhill than she could manage, ploughing through the snow, going uphill. At one point, it appeared the porters carrying her had rested her box on the slope and skidded it directly downhill. Not too fast, she hoped. The crystals churned by the men's feet was easier to climb than the fresh drifts, but even so, she halted, panting, as she struggled up the steep treed slopes and icy cliff bands.

Rennika stood at the back of a dark, crowded balcony box peering between a florist and his assistant, and ahead of them, a group of clerks responsible for copying out wedding invitations. Below, on the main floor, Rennika estimated well over a hundred people had been packed into Castle Highglen's shrine. Every member, it seemed, of the half-dozen families that made up the yak herding estates of the upper valley were there. Representatives of most of the families whose lands below the valley supplemented Gramarye's wealth with forestry and quarry products, were in attendance, as well. Even some lesser lords and highly placed artisans and guildsmen who curried favor were present. Two aisles meeting below the central skylight where the Holder of Histories waited, had been kept clear.

Most of the artisans and craftsmen who'd contributed to the wedding had already found their places on the balcony when Verlin, Ide, Tyg, and Rennika, having sewn the final stitches on Hada's gown, wormed their way up the stairs. Rennika, exhausted by the events of the morning and by Verlin's anxious perfectionism, had let them squeeze into a crammed gallery and found another for herself, further along the corridor. She had no strength to be with Yon—the lying bastard, the lying *thief*—or Ide. Or Verlin.

And she was sick with concern over Janat. She'd returned to Verlin's house, sneaking in beneath the glares of her worried, pacing master. She dashed into her clothes and left in Verlin's entourage minutes later, sitting in the back of his coach in the tense silence of his disapproval, Yon's mistrust, Ide's anxiety, and Tyg's wary confusion. They'd arrived at the castle on time, but that made no difference.

Rennika hadn't had time to look in Meg's room, into the warded puzzle box, to reassure herself that the Amber was safe. Of course it had to be there.

Or Meg could have it. Probably Meg had it.

But it's worth was untold. And Janat had debts.

Rennika shouldn't be here. She should be looking for her sister. Both of them.

Meg would be all right, Rennika reassured herself. Meg would defy any obstacle to meet her tonight. The absurd prize was within her grasp.

Unless . . .

Unless whatever diverted Meg—and kept her from helping Janat as well—was no mere *distraction*.

By Kanden, Rennika should be anywhere but here. She chafed and shifted her weight again to the other foot. If only—

But the ceremony began. Soft music, lost under the weight of Rennika's circular fears, shifted to a familiar wedding melody. The murmurs of the gathering died. It would be impossible for Rennika to leave now, even if she tried.

Doors at either end of the great hall opened, and Princess Hada and Lord Raef entered from their respective places. Rennika could not help but crane to see how her fabrics shimmered in the light of hundreds of candles. Rennika's colors with Verlin's design and Ide's deft stitching were luminous, compared to the dull shades of the observers. Raef, too, had hired admirable tailors, and his robes blazoned the traditions of his royal Gramaryan lineage. His cane had been leafed in gold.

Pomp. Politics. When Rennika should be with Janat. Helping Meg.

The two figures met and stepped onto the dais before the Holder. The words he spoke and the couple's vows rang out clearly over the still crowd, traditional pledges that most could recite by rote. A sigh of approval—relief?—percolated through the assemblage. Though the joining of these two was not without its detractors, Rennika had heard many express the opinion that a Gramaret uniting with a Delarcan would bring stability to the country's future.

Then the final words. "The One God," the Holder intoned in a deep, carrying voice, "binds His Grace, Lord Raef of Gramarye and Her Highness, Princess Hada of Arcan, as one, henceforth and forever."

Cheers erupted from the gathering.

At last. Rennika shifted toward the door, anticipating throngs impossible to navigate, as she tried to free herself to search out her sisters.

A hush fell.

Rennika turned back to the pageant below. The Holder of Histories now held a jeweled crown in both hands.

A coronation? On the day of the wedding?

The princess stood very still, her gaze fixed on the Holder, while a look of alarm flashed in Raef's eyes and his hand slipped up to his throat.

"And on this glorious occasion, may it further please the One God to bless and sanctify the true queen's coming of age and ascension to her throne of Gramarye."

Hada knelt.

The court held its breath. Raef's vision seemed to shift to some internal concern. An attendant gestured, and the Regent took himself awkwardly to his knees as well, further back from the Holder, turned away now from Rennika's vantage.

The Holder of Histories lowered the crown onto Hada's head. "Equally, may it please the One God to bless and sanctify the true queen's husband and consort." A page produced a smaller, jeweled circlet and the Holder placed it on Raef's head.

Consort.

Murmurs rumbled through the gathering.

"Rise, Queen and Consort!"

With a renewed cheer—was it more hesitant than before?—the royal couple rose and turned to face the assemblage. Hada beamed confidence and pride.

Raef's throat worked, and he glared at his wife.

CHAPTER 34

Rennika moved with the crush down the stairs of the shrine as the animated throng made its way toward feasting tables laid out in the rooms and corridors of the Great Hall, beyond the royal dining room. She caught sight of Verlin and Ide disappearing somewhere in the crowd ahead of her. She worked her way toward the anteroom where her cloak and sewing bag hung. Then she inched into the bailey where several bonfires had been lit and common folk from the city poured through the main gates.

And—there was Yon.

A coal of anger flared in her stomach. He'd lied. To her. To *his father*. Stolen her money to feed his grandmother's craving for sugar. She thrust through the rabble to clap a hand on his elbow. "I found out who took my money," she shot at him.

He pivoted, a flash of shock paling his face. Then he pulled his arm from her and spoke without inflection. "Good." He nodded curtly and shouldered toward the Great Hall. "I can arrange to have them arrested."

She took his arm a second time. "A runner for expensive goods by the name of Vellefair told me money bleeds from your household to cover your grandmother's taste for sugar. And that you facilitate it."

"Then this scoundrel is a liar." Again, he pulled his arm from her grip and shoved through the press. "I'll have him arrested as well."

"Janat didn't take the money." Rennika pushed to keep up with him.

"A *magiel*—" he dismissed her "—can spout nothing but lies."

The coal erupted. "My sisters!" Gods, hers was a family with the stature of *royalty*. Descended from the One God!

"And you are a yak herder's niece." He stopped and looked down at her. "The Verlin family reputation is spotless. You won't blacken our name with slanders from such rogues."

Sieur Verlin contracted Meg to make the Dream Incenses.

Yon reached into his purse. He pulled out a scattering of coins and, taking Rennika's hand, pushed them onto her palm. "There. This is my charity. When my father and Ide and I come home tonight for our own wedding ceremony, I expect you, your possessions, and all trace of your sisters to be gone."

Rennika stared at him, her mind exploding with wordless retorts as he turned and disappeared into the masses.

An ugly man. She could not fathom how she'd ever thought him beautiful.

Gods, Janat did not know what to do. She'd headed through gathering crowds to Xadria's to find someone with Heartspeed or poppy or a Serenity. But Ranuat, that sly goddess, was with her, and she had seen Vellefair before she arrived.

He had nothing to help her, but he had information. Xadria had sent the hulking boy, Belden, to find Janat and bring her to The Three Corners to pay her debt. Janat wasn't sure how much she owed, but if Xadria was willing to hire a bully to find her, she wasn't about to go there to find out.

She nosed about and found a magiel willing to swap her Heartspeed and poppy for the cloak Rennika had given her, and within a few minutes she'd regained an approximation of normalcy. Then she slipped out through the city's untended Yak Herders' Gate, fighting streams of country peasants arriving for the festival, to follow a snowy track toward the herdsmen's scattered hovels, knowing Belden would not think to look for her there. Twice, she thought she'd been followed, but both times turned out to be delusions from the Heartspeed. She still itched, and the cold bit her thinly clad body, but she didn't care. It was best not to go back to Verlin's quadrangle during all the fuss and flurry of wedding preparations, but she'd returned after the summoning wedding bells had ceased.

No one was in the house. All undoubtedly were at the castle or in the mob at Highmarket Common, celebrating with the city's revelers.

And Meg was not there. By Ranuat, where was she?

Janat checked the puzzle box. Still in place. She worked the locks. A worldling would not know the box opened, and most magiels would become confused by its twistings and turnings. But Janat knew Meg, and after a few false starts, sprang the final catch. The Amber gleamed within.

She remembered Mama, on her throne in white ceremonial robes with the Amber gleaming on her chest. The image made Janat smile. Wealthy nobles, landowners, guildsmen, and their ladies. The reverence given to Mama. Mama kept the orums from devastating their far-flung mountainous country. She brought death tokens and carried the petitioners' prayers to the Gods. Abated the curse of disease and brought prosperity.

Meg was right. It had been a golden time. A time, a life, that the Amber had the power to restore. This Amber. Here, in her hand.

She fingered the amulet's soft gold, its polished stone. She could imagine Meg on that throne.

But, Ranuat, where was Meg? Janat cast her gaze around the empty room, silent but for the filtered shouts and singing from the square below.

There was no explanation. Meg would move the very Heavens to be here. Every obstacle.

Meg must be hurt.

Yes. Had to be. That was the only thing that could keep her away. Or . . . arrested. Or worse.

A hardness settled in Janat's chest.

She rummaged among Meg's things and found a handful of potions, then crept down to the Verlins' living quarters and clothed herself in finery. She stole a good cloak. She draped the chain around her neck and, sliding the Amber beneath her robe, she slipped into the night.

The kidnappers had managed to carry Meg a surprising distance from the castle, and her return slog through unconsolidated snow had been exhausting. She'd taken a wrong turning that cost her good daylight. As a result, evening had melted into darkness before Meg made her way back to Highglen, and the gates above the city were closed.

But in her hidden pocket she still had one or two potions. She smeared a cream on her hands and face to calm the time vibrations shimmering her skin and pounded on the unguarded Yak Herder's Gate. She told the attendant her sister had given birth, making her late in joining her husband for the wedding celebrations. The attendant reeked of rice wine and cheerfully admitted her. She wormed her way through the teeming streets to the noise and shoving and smells of Highmarket Common.

She had to find out if Rennika had been able to watch Janat.

"Meg!"

She turned, searched the crowd.

Rennika pushed through the clusters of merrymakers, carrying a heavy sack. "I almost didn't recognize you. Where *were* you? Things have changed."

A pang of concern jabbed her. "Not important. I'm back. What's happened? What are you doing out here?"

Her sister's face in the flicker of braziers and torches was grim and pale. "I was waiting by Verlin's to be sure you didn't try to go in."

"What's wrong?" *Janat?*

Rennika led the way downhill, in the direction of the river. "I had money with Sieur Verlin, and it was stolen. Yon accused Janat. She didn't take it—Yon did." Her voice faltered for a moment, but not with grief. With fury. "And all the other money Yon took from his father . . . it'll all be blamed on us. We have no place."

"Oh, Rennika. I'm so . . ." What could she say? ". . . so sorry. I've been so caught up in my own problems."

Rennika shrugged. "This whole thing showed me what kind of a man Yon is. You saved me from throwing my life at that vile blackguard."

Meg bumped through the crush of revelers. "Where's Janat?"

"I don't know. She ran off this morning and I still haven't found her."

"Oh, no."

"Miach has people looking for her. So far, there's no indication she's been captured or spread information. But that's no guarantee." Rennika stopped, then, like a rock creating eddies in the flow of the throng. "Also, we need a place to stay. I've taken everything that belongs to us from our rooms. And the stone is missing."

Cold chilled Meg. *No.*

Rennika must've read her face. "I don't think it's gone. I don't think."

"What do you mean?" She could barely whisper the words.

"The box is still there, and it was locked when I saw it. I think Janat has it, wherever she is. That's the only explanation. No one else would've known to look in the box or to be able to open it. Or would have left it undisturbed, with your things."

Meg listened hard. Branching possibilities. Implications.

"I don't think she's sold it to pay her debts. I saw Miach again after the ceremony, and he says thugs are looking for her."

"Debts?" *Looking* for Janat? Thugs?

Hadn't captured her. Meg breathed. There was far too much to comprehend. But— "Then . . . where is she?"

Rennika bit her lip with a shrug.

Someone bumped Meg hard enough to send her into Rennika.

"We need to go someplace," Rennika repeated. "Figure out what to do. Before someone sees you're a magiel."

Meg's mind clicked through possibilities. "Yaquob's shop."

Rennika shook her head in incomprehension.

"It's vacant. Someone broke in and smashed what was there. It should work for us until tonight, as long as the landlord or squatters haven't taken it." She shot a glance at her sister. "We're still going in tonight?"

"If . . ." Rennika closed her eyes. "What's the point, if we don't have—it? And what about Janat?"

Meg breathed. "Tell me. Everything," she said, leading the way to the lower town.

⚜

Raoul was earning money. He'd come to the castle bailey for the free food and for once in his life had eaten his fill. Then he made friends with some of the frolicking urchins and engaged them in a game of cups. As the ale flowed, older children and adults formed a circle around him, intrigued by his fast hands. They began to gamble, and Raoul was clever enough to let them win, only skimming enough coin to make the night worth his while.

And all the while, he was alert, as was his habit. Soldiers, brutes, drunken hotheads. No one of any interest. But good conditions for whiling away the evening. Yaquob had been arrested that morning, as arranged. Then, Raoul thanked Vellefair for his hospitality and departed. He had no more need of him; the old rogue had nothing worth stealing, and Raoul would sleep in the shop tonight.

Raoul wondered where Meg had got to. She was nice. He wondered if she needed a lookout or thief for a bit.

But drink had worked its way through the throng, and the crowd was passing from exuberant to maudlin. Many had left the bailey, and the rest were huddled by the braziers, singing sentimental songs or rolling up in their cloaks to sleep. The gamblers had drifted from his game.

"Janat!" He saw her as she entered the gate, and scrambled over to her. She was dressed in a thick woolen cloak and had covered her face with some kind of spell to make her look like a worldling.

She peered at him, as if she thought him familiar but couldn't quite place him.

"I'm Raoul."

She smiled vaguely and nodded.

He wilted a little. Like most adults, she had no use for him.

He gave her back her satchel. She had no money anyway. Only vials of spells.

Rennika sat on a pallet and leaned against the wall in the back room of the merchant's shop. Verlin's letter, tucked into her bodice, was the most valuable thing she owned now. If, or when, Meg's gambit disintegrated and they were running, it was the only thing that would stand between her and destitution. Her dreams of marriage had slipped away.

The shop was a mess of broken glass and spilled powders and potions. She was still unclear about whose shop this was, or what connection it had to Meg, or why the landlord who lived overhead had not cleaned it up. But thieves had not taken everything. There was a brazier and charcoal, candles, and some food—frozen—that had not spoiled in the time since the occupants had left. There was a blanket to hang over a rod in the doorway to hold the warmth in the back room and to keep their fire from being seen through the high window in the shop.

Meg had gone out to touch base with her compatriots, whoever they were, and see if she could find news of Janat, but it was getting late and the roisterers were growing still. Part of Rennika was anxious with not knowing where her sisters were or what was going to happen, but part of her clung to the hope that the night would pass uneventfully. The three of them would, like as not, slip out of town in the morning to look for work and lodging down valley.

The curtain twitched.

Rennika was going to call out Meg's name in greeting, but a small face appeared, as startled as hers must've appeared.

The big eyes took in the situation. "This is my father's shop," the boy asserted.

Rennika blinked. "I'm sorry. We thought it was vacant."

The boy slipped through the curtain. "Do you have food?" His cloak was warm enough, but the night had become bitterly cold and his nose and fingers were pinched and reddened. He appeared not to mind that she was camped in his home.

"Only what we found here." She pulled a cup from the array of unbroken pottery she'd assembled. "Would you like some tea?"

The boy sat on the pallet beside her and nodded, his bead eyes missing nothing. "Who's 'we'?"

"My sister." She sprinkled the leaves into the cup and poured hot water on them.

He nodded again and took the cup she offered. "You look like Meg."

She stared at him. "You know her?"

"That's your sister." He gave a short, sharp nod of confirmation to himself and blew on the surface of the tea. "You have another sister, too, don't you? And she's a magiel, like Meg. But you're not." His brow clouded with the puzzle.

Again, she stared, astounded. "How do you know all this? Who are you?"

He looked at the pallets, warming his hands on the mug. "Are all of you sleeping here tonight? Because I need a place."

Two pallets. But the boy was small. Smaller than his eyes suggested he should be. "Meg will be here."

"Not Janat?" He pressed his lips together and frowned. "Is she staying in the castle, then?"

This conversation was making less and less sense. "Why would she stay in the castle?"

He shrugged. "I saw her there, a candlemark ago. She had a pretty dress on, and she didn't look magiel at all."

It had taken pissing long enough, but Raef finally shut the door to Hada's private chamber and eased the lock closed behind him. She had wandered toward the window.

Too far. He closed the gap.

She turned, chin high and eyes cold, about to make some announcement, but flinched at his proximity. He dropped his cane and pounced.

He might be crippled, but his arms and shoulders were powerful. He slapped one hand over her mouth and the other on the back of her head, using the momentum of the assault to swing her toward the bed. He missed, and they tumbled to the floor. He almost lost his grip as she fought, scratching and trying to kick.

He held her, pinned under his weight, holding her mouth and nose until asphyxiation weakened her struggles. He pinched only enough to diminish her strength. He did not want to harm her, only to school her. When her blows became feeble, he shifted his hand to free her nostrils.

She took a deep, ragged gasp of air, and her eyes flew open.

Raef still could not speak, or not above a whisper. That snake, Gweddien, had done something to him. Raef didn't know how, but the magiel must have managed to administer some subtle potion. "You have not won," he mouthed, unable to tell if she heard him. She needed his cooperation, his connections, and his influence. Stealing his crown did not coerce his cooperation.

And he would demonstrate in their marriage bed, exactly who was in charge.

CHAPTER 35

If Highglen Castle was laid out like Archwood Castle, Janat reasoned, Hada's apartments would be found in the keep. Her heart raced at the thought of the game ahead, and her skin itched. The entrance to the keep, of course, was barred and guarded; there was no alternate approach. Janat was good at releasing locks, but a draw bar was too heavy for her to lift, either manually or magically. And a Confusion or a Memory Loss would not compel a soldier to open a door.

Celebrants in the bailey were mostly gone, now, except for a few that had passed out on the ground.

The guards eyed her as she approached. They looked stupid and slow.

She dipped a curtsey. "Sieura with no name to see Lord Andred." She'd heard Verlin speak of him and hoped the courtier lived far enough away to be staying in the castle for the night. She gripped her fingers to keep them from trembling.

The taller guard frowned. "This was not told to us."

"Is it usually?" She quipped, letting a sly grin creep to her lips. She sashayed a little frisk. "I was just called to come . . . urgently."

"With no escort? Who called you?"

The second guard spoke. "We could check."

"Yes, check," Janat agreed sweetly.

The taller one eyed her skeptically, but the other slid the bolt back in its cradle, and she followed him, dancing, within.

☙

Gweddien removed the golden collar covering the soft band that held his death token and leaned an elbow on the mantle before the hearth in his bedchamber. The laces of his shirt were open, and a delicate wineglass stood empty beside its companion bottle on the table. The gold of the collar glinted in the red light of the embers. He fingered its embossing.

Hada would be in Raef's bed now. She was queen, and queens needed political alliances. Royals never married their magiels. That didn't matter. The intimacy a royal and her magiel experienced when they traveled to Heaven was of an entirely different, and far deeper nature than physical or even emotional bonding. So he'd been told, and so he had observed in the days of his youth. And, if his sensation of hovering magically just outside the borders of Heaven with glim was any indication, true flight to Heaven with a prayer stone was a rapture of exquisite bliss.

He slapped the collar down on the mantle. By Ranuat, he was so close.

The boy, Rayle, Raleigh . . . Yaquob's son.

The child had been hanging about the castle gates as much as three days—*three days*—trying to find some way to get a message to him, trying not to get picked up by the guards on suspicion of vagrancy. Someone, and Gweddien had not found out who—possibly Raef—had come hunting for Yaquob, and the trader and his boy had barely escaped. The merchant had found some expensive hole to shiver in and sent the boy. It was only late yesterday that the boy had been able to pass his father's letter along.

Gweddien breathed, calming himself. Yaquob was here, now, in the castle. Safe. Locked and guarded in the best room Gweddien had been able to arrange in the chaos of the wedding. He wished he'd had the authority to have the merchant searched, the Amber seized. Gods, if he only had it in his hands *now*.

But no. It was best the merchant hand it over willingly. Best that no guards' searching fingers touch what the man carried. After all, if the merchant wanted to sell it and make a bit of money, what was wrong with that? Tread gently, gently, until the thing was in his hand.

The fire had burned itself almost to nothing. Gweddien wasn't cold, and his eyes had grown accustomed to the dark. He groped his way to the table, found the bottle, poured the last of the wine into his glass. If only he could sleep, pass the candlemarks until morning, until Hada was awake, the marriage consummated, and she could be rid of her leech. If only Gweddien could gain her ear, bring in the merchant and secure the transaction.

He tossed back the last swallow of wine. He should have the page bring another bottle.

No, best not to be fog-headed in the morning. Better to pace the entire night away rather than—

His door burst open. "Gweddien!" Hada, silhouetted against faint candlelight.

He sprang forward, catching her as she stumbled into his room. His page and two or three other figures—guards come running at the disturbance—hovered in the background. She clutched at him, her weight causing him to stagger momentarily. "My queen."

"Shut the door," she screamed, turning on the servants.

Hastily, they obeyed.

She cast her arms about his shoulders and buried her head in his chest, heaving with spent breath.

"Hush, hush," he whispered, holding her, calming her instinctively, with no other hint to guide him. Was she hurt? Or was there devastating news—the Amber? Had something—

No, not that.

Huwen. Could he be on their doorstep with an army?

"Shh." He led her to the chair before the coals. She was shivering violently.

He took her upper arms. "You're cold. I'm going to stoke the fire." He looked more closely. A bruise was forming below her left eye. "Gods, Hada," he whispered.

Swallowing, she pulled herself into a ball.

He added kindling and a log, and blew on the flames to nurse them, then returned with a blanket from his bed. He crouched at her feet, cradling her arms. "Now," he whispered. "Tell me."

She swallowed again, nodding intensely but not speaking. Her shivers lessened, but her body trembled with hiccupped breaths. She swiped at tears.

Muffled voices broke out from beyond the door. Hada straightened in the chair, shrinking into him. The sound of a brief altercation, then a fist pounded on his door.

Before he could do more, the door opened a second time, and a man with a cane halted, silhouetted in its frame, wild fury animating every gesture.

"Go no further." Gweddien stood. He had not the authority of blood, nor stature, nor magic, and yet the man—some courtier attending for the wedding?—stopped. As before, the page and a small crowd of onlookers lingered. Curious, afraid, or concerned, it didn't matter.

The man flexed his fingers at his side as if he twitched to fist them, hit something. He raised his cane, but only halfway.

Cane. Raef? Whoever it was, he threatened brutality.

Gweddien had no weapon, no way to defend himself or his queen, no spells at hand. But there were guards close by. They could take him.

"So, she comes to you. A magiel." The courtier's strained whisper dripped with scorn. The man pointed to his throat, the movement black with fury.

Gweddien's spell. To silence—Raef . . . He peered at him in the dim light of the fire. Raef? The man had changed since they were children. No matter. Gweddien pointed to the guards. "You three. Ensure the safety of your queen."

The man—Raef—shot a glance at the guards, then turned back to Gweddien. "The two of you." Raef scraped. "Yes. This is your plan."

"Delarcans rule in Shangril," Gweddien said, still trying to see the boy in the man.

"You cast a spell on me. Today, during the ceremony. I couldn't speak."

The three drops of a beautifully concocted mixture. A candlemark of silence, but only after a delay so carefully calculated, and keyed to elements in his target's blood. Administered by a trusted servant days ago. One of Gweddien's subtler charms. "I thought you had a poison taster. Is he affected?"

Raef eyed him and ran his tongue around his teeth.

"A magiel can only perform magic through objects or elixirs." Not quite true, but Gweddien did not want to emphasize his abilities. "Perhaps you were nervous. Anxiety at the greatness of the ceremony could tie your tongue."

Raef gripped his cane and pointed to his throat. "Don't try to dupe me." He nodded at Hada. "I'm no rutting *consort*. I was Huwen's appointed regent, and I married a queen. I am the *king*."

"Noooo," Gweddien said slowly, as if to a child.

Raef fisted and stepped forward. "You, pissing—"

The guards separated to either side of him.

Hada stood. "I am the queen and ruler," she said. "You are my husband. You have power *when* and *if* I delegate it to you."

Raef drew back. "I'm not your husband."

The man's abrupt coolness was wrong. "You were married today," Gweddien said. "In the eyes of the One God and the people of Gramarye."

"The marriage isn't consummated."

"It is!" Hada cried.

"There's no blood on the sheets." Raef's jaw flexed, an unborn smile. "You came here. You gave your union to—" he flicked a finger at them "—a *magiel*."

A lie. But one difficult to argue. Appearance was everything.

"Declare me king."

Gweddien snorted a humorless laugh

"No." Hada's voice strengthened.

"Then there will be war."

Hada stepped in front of Gweddien. "Delarcans have the Ruby. We have cannons. We have the One God on our side."

Raef clumped to the door and placing his hand on the knob, turned. "All true. And Huwen will bring it to bear against a treasonous sister."

Janat sat in a stone stairwell in the tenuous light from some distant window, piecing together flashes of memory, unsure how she'd come to be there. Once she was inside the keep . . . yes, she'd used a Confusion to rid herself of the guard. She must've breathed in some of the spell.

Her robe was hitched up and she was scratching at a bleeding sore on her inner thigh. Piss, what a time for the poppy to wear off. In the thin light from some window, she emptied her satchel on the step beside her and poked through the vials she'd taken from Meg.

Nothing. By the shapes of the bottles, one was likely her last Confusion. Two Memory Losses, and one—something else, likely some sort of disguise. That was all. Nothing she could identify in the dark as poppy or Serenity or Heartspeed or even Dream Incense. *Nothing.*

Livid, she swept the satchel and vials down the stairs. Glass shattered.

Rennika studied Meg's face in the light of the brazier. It was deep night in the merchant's demolished shop. The boy slept with a soft snore. "The last thing Janat said to me this morning was how much she owes you," she said.

Meg eyed her, askance, gnawing on an apple. She'd returned only a few minutes ago from reporting to Miach on the imminent approach of Huwen's army. Miach's listeners had no news of Janat. Meg had not told him that the Amber was... misplaced. "Owes *me*? It was your purse she took."

Rennika and Meg had been trying to piece together what might have happened. "For caring for her," she clarified. "How determined she was to ensure the Amber is used to restore the people's access to their Gods. She must have it."

Meg shook her head, studying the fire. "Janat changes her mind on a whim."

Rennika shrugged. "Raoul saw her in the castle. Dressed as a lady."

Meg studied her, her head shaking imperceptively in the negative. "The fool."

But there was no other explanation that fit what they knew. "It's mad. But I don't know what else could have happened."

"We have to go in." Meg's eyes riveted on Rennika, her face set, determined.

To her own surprise, Rennika agreed. They couldn't let Janat bumble about on her own to be captured and sent to Coldridge. For the Amber to be confiscated. For Janat to be interrogated. "And do what?"

"Find her. Keep her safe."

Janat came to a parquet landing midway up a set of wide stairs. A broad corridor led to her right. Another led to her left. Both were lit dimly through windows looking out onto a starlit courtyard and by widely spaced ensconced candles. To her right, far down the hall, a drowsing sentry and a sleepy page stood before a door.

She fisted her hands to keep from scratching. Excitement coursed through her like Heartspeed, exciting and nauseating her at how far she'd come.

The door must be Hada's. Or some other aristocrat's. Janat gripped a vial in one hand. She wasn't sure what it contained. It was the only one she'd been able to find in the stairwell after her fit of pique. If it was a Confusion or a Memory Loss, it would get her past the guards. Her lock picking would get her into the room.

She was almost there. She hoped the vibrations of her skin were still masked.

She would salvage Meg's plan.

The cloud cover had thinned by the time Rennika led Meg from the ruined shop, and patches of constellations were visible. A few celebrants remained in the streets, murmuring around braziers or drifting homeward, but their way to the castle wound through increasingly deserted streets.

Rennika had given her sister her loose, finely dyed over robe, made from the fabrics of her masterpiece, and Rennika wore the Aadian-fashioned gown she'd worn beneath it. Meg had covered her hands and face earlier with a magic to calm the temporal shimmer that marked her a magiel, but Rennika gave her another vial in case she needed it later, as well as a handful of potions she'd brought from Meg's room in Verlin's house.

It was the work of half a candlemark to worm their way with patience and magic through the castle's outer defences to the keep. Guards were more alert than Rennika expected, which again would be explained if Janat had befuddled them already. Twice, Rennika was certain they would be found out, but bluffing, knowledge of castle routines, and the subtle use of a spell or two brought them, finally to Hada's wing.

Raef stormed down the corridor, frustrated beyond belief. That sot, Gweddien. He'd sidestepped the curses Raef'd had his new magiel make. She was useless, a part-blood, no better than a worldling for conjuring charms.

An assassin's knife. And soon. Even if Raef came under suspicion, he could ride out any accusations. He was Raef the Good.

He'd bluffed. Just now, to Hada. He'd composed letters to Huwen, yes. But with no intention of sending them, of bringing the High King here. That was the last thing he wanted.

No, he must separate the Delarcan girl from her magiel. That would be enough. She could be crushed. Perhaps not tonight, but he would find a way.

As he approached his suite, his steps slowed. Where was the sentry he'd left at the door?

The page saw him and came scampering. "Your grace." He bowed. "A magiel tried to enter your chambers."

A magiel? He squinted at the boy. Not Gweddien. Raef had just left him with Hada.

"She tried to charm the guard and me, but her spell didn't work, and she's caught in your rooms. Your guard just sent me to call the captain."

His magiel? The one he'd taken on as a servant? Why would she come to him now?

She knew he was trying to assassinate Gweddien. Information he would prefer not be disclosed if she decided to undermine him. "Wait."

The boy bowed, staying on his command.

"Where is she?"

"Your guard lured her into your private bedchamber, Your Grace. Then he locked the door."

"When?"

"Moments ago."

Good. That would hold her for the moment. Raef bade the boy to remain outside his door, and he entered his suite.

CHAPTER 36

Rennika stilled inside the servants' access to the royal apartments, Meg just behind her. If Janat *was* trying to test the Amber, she would be trying to come here.

Flickers from far more candlelight than was warranted for deep night danced in the passageway from the main hall. Too many voices holding urgent conversations filtered down the corridor, and too many sounds of moving bodies. Something was going on.

The stir hamstrung them, but it might be a sign they'd located Janat—if it was Janat's presence causing the disturbance.

Heart beating, Rennika crept forward to listen. She peered into the main corridor.

Some distance down, a knot of servants and soldiers peered through an open doorway into what, from her observations, Rennika knew to be Gweddien's outer chamber. She checked the other direction and immediately drew her head back.

Meg frowned a question at her.

She pulled her sister further into the servants' passage. "Hada's chamber doors are open and her guards are gaping down the corridor at Gweddien's chamber," she whispered.

Meg's brows knit deeper. "Did you see Janat?"

"No." Rennika bit her lip. "You won't get into Hada's rooms tonight. I don't think she's even there."

"Where, then?"

Rennika didn't know. "With Gweddien? No. There aren't a lot of soldiers, like you'd expect if Janat had been caught."

Meg put a fist to her lips. "So, whatever is happening has nothing to do with Janat."

"Maybe. I don't know. That's a bit of a leap."

Meg's gaze shot up with a flash of inspiration. "*I know.*"

"What?"

"Where she went. I'll wager my death token."

Rennika squinted at her. "Where?"

"Raef Gramaret. He has royal blood." Meg's words tumbled out. "She's gone to his room to wait until he comes back from his wedding night. He'll return for a bath and a change of clothes before morning."

Raef. Son of King Dwyn Gramaret of Gramarye before the war. Royal to the Chrysocolla Prayer Stone. Of course.

"We can't do anything here," Meg whispered. "It's worth a try while there's a distraction. Where are his chambers?"

"Down a floor."

Meg nodded.

Silently, Rennika turned and led the way. The floor set aside for Raef and his retinue was dark and still, but for the faint light of an occasional well-spaced, sconced candle.

Rennika peered into the vacant hallway. No movement. Lord Raef's chamber door was guarded by an alert sentry and a page. Meg came up beside her, and Rennika nodded at the doorway.

Meg squeezed her arm in thanks.

Rennika pulled a Confusion from her satchel and led the way forward.

※

Raef leaned his cane against the wall next to his desk. The guard attended in the corridor, awaiting his command. Raef wanted no listeners when he confronted his new magiel servant.

He opened the drawer in his desk. The last two potions Gweddien had given him rolled there, loose. His captain had tested them and found them effective.

Raef examined the labels in the candlelight. One was a ward: light, invisible, scentless. He undressed and smeared it over his body, then donned a night robe.

The second, a perfume, was a potent sleep draught. If for some reason this magiel he'd taken on decided to turn on him, he would be prepared. He slipped it into a pocket in his robe along with a knife. He closed his desk drawer.

He checked that the door to the corridor was closed. Then, taking up his cane, he unlocked his bedchamber door.

The room was dark and stank of vomit. He took a candle from the table and entered, closing the door to his outer chamber behind him. Someone was indeed within, crouched on the floor near the bed. A woman, but she was too well-dressed to be his magiel.

He hobbled across the room to cast the candlelight over her. She was a magiel. He frowned. Who was she? "Stand up."

The woman retched again, then rolled onto one side, pushed her hair back, and lifted dull eyes to meet his.

She was familiar . . . He took a step closer, holding the candle high.

Thin. Her skin was pocked with bleeding sores. Yet . . .

Before the war. Talanda Falkyn, the magiel of the Amber, had come to Highglen to meet with King Dwyn; she and her retinue, including her three daughters. Raef scrutinized the intruder. Could this be . . . one of the daughters?

No. Not possible. Talanda and her daughters had died in the siege of Archwood.

But, despite the woman's debilitating illness—Raef took a step back and leaned his cane against the bed to make a sign to ward the curse—she was the best specimen of magiel he'd seen on his search. Falkyn? Maybe. But in any case, a worthy tribute to the High King, of sufficient value to make Huwen overlook Raef's small crimes.

He set his candle on the table and pulled Gweddien's perfume for overpowering a magiel from his pocket. If she was a Falkyn, he could take no chances. He sprinkled the potion liberally on his handkerchief and tossed the empty bottle aside.

A click sounded in his outer chamber. A door, opening. Muffled voices.

※

Meg found Raef Gramaret's outer chamber curiously empty of personality. In the scant light of a single candle, she could see the furnishings were of good quality, but plain. Draped windows flanked a fireplace, banked and devoid of warmth, and the little art present favored military scenes from antiquity.

Rennika moved quietly to a door, presumably leading to a private chamber, on the far wall. She tried the handle.

Candlelight. Meg screamed a warning.

The door tore from Rennika's hand. A young man in a rich robe dropped a stick and threw an arm around Rennika's neck. He shoved a cloth over Rennika's face, pressing it onto her mouth and nose as she shrieked and wriggled.

Ranuat!

The man—Raef?—stared at her as he squeezed Rennika's head in his arms, suffocating her with his gag. Rennika squirmed violently, buffeting him, but could not dislodge her face from his embrace. A faint, sweet smell scented the air. His potion—was it the one Tonore had used on Meg? She recognized the scent. Yes. The sleep spell, but by its perfume, stronger than the one Tonore had had. This one was Magiel made.

In the bed chamber, beyond the struggling pair, someone lay on the floor.

Meg uncorked a vial and flung its contents onto the man holding Rennika. A Confusion. A direct hit. She backed away from its widening effects.

Raef, staggering a little in the tussle, held Rennika's head in an enveloping clinch, but though she bucked spasmodically, he didn't let go.

The charm—what was wrong? It had no effect.

Rennika's scuffling weakened. Still, Raef held the cloth over her mouth.

Piss. Meg scrambled for another vial. Rennika grew heavy in the man's arms, batting at him now without conviction. He lowered her to the floor, crouching to hold the charmed cloth over her face. Her fight abated to a few twitches.

Meg uncorked . . . a liquid. She rushed forward and splashed it directly in his face. A Serenity. It should at least slow him down.

Raef dragged Rennika back into the bedchamber.

No effect! What was happening to Meg's spells?

Rennika went abruptly limp. Gods, her spells were working . . . but not on Raef? What had he done? How was he immune to her magic?

He was warded. A potion protected him against curses.

"Back away," Raef said, his voice low and rough.

It was Janat who lay on the floor beside the bed. Her eyes were glassy, her skin pale and damp, and she gagged by a pool of vomit.

Gods, she looked bad. Meg darted to Janat's side before Raef could extract himself from Rennika and bar Meg to the outer chamber.

"Get away from her," he warned.

Raef had both her sisters in his power, and by extension, herself. By Ranuat, how? "She's ill!" Meg shouted over her shoulder. It was the Bloodbone. Meg felt Janat's head, her neck, her torso. Beneath her bodice, she wore the Amber.

The poison was deep. But the *want* of the Bloodbone was drowning her. Janat's body had become intertwined with the spell, no longer able to be separate from it.

"I'll break this one's neck."

Rennika. But no ward could protect Raef from the Amber, if Meg could just—

"Back away."

Meg's body screened Janat from his view. She lifted the Amber from Janat's neck and slipped it into her own pocket.

"I tell you—"

All Meg had to do was touch him. She jerked back, falling into him, her free hand out to clutch at his legs, the other gripping the Amber in her pocket. *Gods, set Janat free—*

"Get away from me!" he screeched.

She stared up into his surprised face. Nothing . . . had happened. No transport to Heaven.

Panic, like the weight of a great thick stone, dropped through her. No . . . no! *No!* This could not be *happening*.

She sprawled, staring up at his shocked, disapproving face, her heart fluttering wildly in her chest. No magiel ward he wore could block the prayer stone. None.

The Amber *was false.* An imitation. Yaquob's swindle.

Gods, she'd known this. Hadn't she? Within her heart? She'd ignored every scrap of evidence that didn't support her ambition.

"Get up."

She had to think of something.

"Get up!"

She obeyed, scuttling back to a crouch by the door.

Raef extracted himself from the tangle with Rennika, and she lay where she'd fallen, awkward and asleep.

Meg's breath trembled. "I can help you." First, calm his fears.

Raef retrieved his cane and straightened his night robe. "How did you get in here?"

She tried to get her own terror under control, make her brain think. "You need magic." Everyone needed magic, whether they knew it or not. "I can help you attain . . ." What? ". . . whatever you desire." Not true, but—

His eyes focused on her. Good.

Her heart slowed to a deep, painful throb. Political life. Yes, of course. "You must have enemies. People who forestall your goals." Gods, was this the wrong thing to say? Imply he was not the powerful man he might think? She kicked herself.

But he'd stilled. He leaned on his cane, breathing hard, and stared at her as if he'd taken in something she said. Digested it.

She could kill him. Meg could close Raef's throat. Even from here, from across the room, she could do it. Hold it until he would never breathe again. Save them.

And then what? Run? With Janat ill to death and Rennika asleep? How would she drag them from the castle? Pursued? How would she get them out of Highglen?

There had to be another way. "I can do magic for you." She was repeating herself, buying time. She had to think of something.

That woman. In Cataract Crag. The innkeeper's wife. Her words popped into Meg's head . . . *a rich man's mistress*. Dread sank through her stomach. "I can hurt your enemies, so they don't even know . . ." And sell herself, and everything she'd ever fought for. To a *royal*.

Gods, no. But what choices were left? Kill, again? Like Wenid?

She forced the words. "Be your mistress."

Raef ran his tongue around the inside of his mouth. If he'd panicked before, he was in control now. "Like Gweddien," he said softly, looking at her but speaking to himself.

Gweddien and Hada. Yes.

Cool appraisal came over Raef's face. His gaze traveled over her expensive clothing. "Who *are* you? Some half-magiel village witch? Or—" His eyes narrowed. "Talanda's daughter," he whispered.

Her identity, kept safe, hidden all these years.

His attention flicked to Janat and then to Rennika. *"Three of you."* His head nodded faintly. "Talanda's daughters."

Raef had guessed.

A faint cynical smile touched his lips. "Magiels. *Falkyns. Here.*" He shook his head in incredulity. "I thought I recognized that one." He nodded at Janat. "But, yes. I saw you once, when we were children."

When Mama had taken them to visit the seven realms. But . . . Meg didn't remember him.

Doubt crept into his eyes. "Talanda's daughters died in the siege of Archwood."

Which answer would save their lives? Keep him from bargaining them to Huwen for his breeding scheme?

His brows knit. "But, no. This one." He touched Rennika's arm with his cane. "She's no magiel." Misgiving deepened on his face.

Meg took in a cautious breath. "I can cast all the spells you need. Be your magiel. Let the others go." She would never achieve Mama's dream of restoring the people to their Gods, but as this man's magiel, she might finally be able to take care of her sisters. Keep her family safe. That was something, wasn't it?

Gods, let Raef contract with her.

He stared at her for a long moment, calculating her offer. "You tempt me." Then his posture relaxed. "But no. I can have what I need of you without bargaining away the others. You, and that one," he indicated Janat," are worth more to me as tribute to the High King."

No.

He lifted his cane slightly. "I don't want to smash this girl's face," he said of Rennika, "But you have more potions hidden in your secret magiel pockets." He nodded toward her hands. "Strip down to you shift, so I don't have to worry about your magic if my ward wears off."

A ward. As she'd thought.

"Then you can tie up your sisters." He raised his voice. "Guard!"

She stopped his heart on the word.

His eyes snapped wide.

He should have believed her. *Wenid, choking on the floor from her poison.* She pushed the image back. Gods, she never wanted to kill again. Not like this. Violent. Intimate. Raw.

The man dropped his cane and his fingers clawed at his chest. His left arm crumpled.

Hers was no worldling spell, no village witchery, no *potion*. Hers was true magic. Magiel magic. Holding the muscle of his heart still in time, she found a Heartspeed in her pocket and knelt by Janat's side. She opened the vial, wafting it under her nose. Janat stirred, tried to leap up, and then retched again.

Raef's eyes bulged in pain.

Rennika lay as one dead. Meg tossed the man's cane aside and waved the Heartspeed under Rennika's nose. Janat stared wildly around the room.

"Come on, Rennika," Meg murmured. Rennika made no move.

This wasn't right. Meg checked the pulse in her neck. It was weak and fluttery. "Rennika!" She slapped her face. Rennika moaned but didn't waken.

"Meg." The voice, hoarse, was Janat's. She'd dragged herself to her feet and leaned on the bed. "Someone's . . ."

Raef had crumpled to his knees, gasping for breath.

Gods, why wasn't Rennika waking? Meg scrambled in her pocket for another Heartspeed.

The door opened. The guard.

She found one and her fingers felt like sausages, trying to uncork it. *Come on, Rennika!*

"Meg!" Janat lunged past her toward the intrusion.

The guard blinked in the doorway, a look of surprise on his face.

Meg spilled the Heartspeed powder directly onto Rennika's face.

Janat charged sloppily at the guard, and he caught her arms, shoving her into the door frame.

Meg launched herself into him, bowling him to the floor as Janat recovered and staggered past him.

Behind, she heard Raef gulp a huge indrawn breath.

The guard grappled for her, but she was on top of him and she stomped her boots into his knee and groin and jaw, propelling herself from his grasp and into the outer chamber. "Rennika!" she screamed.

Janat grabbed her elbow. "Get out! They're coming!"

The guard picked himself up in the doorway, and she could see nothing in the candle-lit dark behind him.

"Meg! They're coming!"

And then, she and Janat were beyond the second door and into the corridor. The page ran toward the main staircase, screaming, and the tramp of boots echoed from below.

CHAPTER 37

Rennika woke muzzily to pain. A hideous ache circled the base of her skull, pressed on the top of her head and temples, and lodged behind her eyes. The stink of vomit made her want to gag.

Someone nudged her thigh. She opened her eyes.

Candlelight. A room in the castle.

She lay on a floor. Hard. Wood. Her arms and legs were splayed at awkward angles and she drew them in to release some of the discomfort, though the action jarred the misery in her head.

The nudge again. A stick? Cane. Raef. She and Meg had come to Raef's room and someone had grabbed her. She remembered struggling. Meg's horrified face.

"Get her up." Raef's voice. Yes.

Hands on her upper arms pulled her to her feet. A soldier on either side of her. An armchair shoved under her, and she sat with a thump, a spasm shooting through her head.

Lord Raef—Prince Consort Raef, now—was seated before her in a cushioned chair in the light of half-a-dozen candles. His leg was propped on a stool, cane by his side, and his face was gray, ill. He leaned slightly forward, resting one forearm on the arms of his chair, the other massaging his chest as if he was starved for breath.

What time was it? Almost a candlemark since she'd used magic at the first gate. Only a small magic. She might vacate this part of her life. But she might not.

"Rennika Falconer." He studied her. "I'm told you are a local dyer and draper."

She lowered her eyes in assent. "Your Grace."

"I was just attacked by someone claiming to be your sister."

Her eyes flicked about the room. Meg wasn't here. Part of Rennika felt relief. Part of her tightened, wondering if Meg was imprisoned, maybe fleeing soldiers. Or dead.

But . . . Meg had attacked Raef? And . . . Janat. They still hadn't found Janat.

"Two sisters, in fact. They ran off. We'll catch them." He regarded her. "Left you behind, it seems."

Her head pounded. Two sisters? Janat? Rennika had come here with Meg, looking for Janat. Something had happened. Raef had caught her, administered a spell. And Meg had attacked him and run off? With Janat? And what about the Amber?

If Janat had brought the Amber here. *If* Meg had had a chance to try it . . . then the Amber was . . . oh, Gods.

False.

It had to be. If the Amber had worked, Meg would not have left. Meg and Janat would not have run away. Rennika would not be Raef's prisoner.

All Meg's hopes. Gone. Oh . . .

But that was a string of *if*s. Rennika lifted her eyes. Raef regarded her like a curiosity, a dangerous intensity smoldering under his sickly mien. She would be . . . what? Imprisoned? Flayed?

Rennika heaved, but nothing came up.

"Who are you?" The prince rasped. He rubbed his left arm. "Really?"

She tensed.

"Rennikala Falkyn?"

Her heart caught, frozen.

"Your sisters? Meghra? Janatelle?"

Just before the war. She'd been about ten. Mama had brought the three of them on a tour of the countries of Shangril. They'd come to Highglen. She'd met Raef.

That was ten years ago. Surely, he didn't recognize her. She would never have recognized him.

"One of the most powerful magiels in Shangril?" he croaked. "Powerful enough to mask your skin? Or no one? A yak herder's niece?"

Her heart freed itself, racing.

With two hands, he lowered his leg from its resting place and leaned forward to peer at her. "Worthy tribute to the High King, perhaps." In the light of the candles, she wondered if the color was returning to his cheeks.

"No, Your Grace."

"What?" he snapped.

She shook her head, numb. Marigolds. What had Meg told her? Something awful. "No, Your Grace," she mumbled.

He prodded her belly with his cane. "You escaped the siege at Archwood. Somehow. Your sister—not a candlemark ago—stopped my heart. *From across the room.*"

She felt the blood drain from her face.

"No magiel can do that. None. But she did." The guards' hands tightened on her arms as Raef leaned forward, panting, propped on his cane.

She worked her throat, trying to generate moisture, trying to speak. She could not give in to him, admit who she was, who they were. But—clearly, one of them had used powerful magic. Inexplicable magic. How was she to talk her way out of this? "My half-sisters are magiels," she conceded. "Not me."

He jerked back.

"My mother was old when I was born. Feeble."

A frown—black anger flashed across his face. "You lie."

She cringed. "Look at me," she whimpered, dropping her gaze.

There was a long silence. She could hear him breathing furiously through his nose.

He gave a gesture and the guards let go of her arms. In a single move, he dropped his cane, rose from his chair and grabbed her shoulders. He shook her.

She pulled back, averting her face, made herself as limp as she could.

He dropped her back into the chair. A guard scrambled to return his cane to him. "What?" he said softly, looming over her, his breath ragged. "You don't lash out with magic? To protect yourself?"

"I can't." She wept.

"*God!*" he growled. He made to move, then stopped.

With no warning, he walloped her, backhanded, across the face, knocking her across the arm of the chair.

She stared at the floor, dazed. Liquids—blood, snot—streamed in her nose and lips.

"The *prizes*? Are gone? And you're *worthless*?" he bellowed hoarsely.

She cowered, unmoving.

He panted a moment, then brought his breathing under control. "Leave us."

There was a moment's hesitation, but only for a moment. Then the guards hurried to the door.

"Every resource," he shouted, his rasp stopping them. "Every resource is to be expended. Find them."

The guards left, closing the door behind them.

Raef stared down at her. Then he limped to the door and turned the lock.

6

Janat bumped into a wall, stopped. She leaned against it for support. Every part of her body crawled. She scratched until she bled, but it did no good. Her stomach was raw, her throat burned. The giddiness of Heartspeed kept her on her feet, kept her moving, but she wanted to collapse, writhe in brambles.

"Stop it!" Meg hissed.

A grayness had slipped into the corridor. Windows, somewhere further down. It was almost dawn.

Come on, Rennika. Janat didn't want to be here when the servants arrived to stoke the morning fires and bring hot wash water. She scratched.

Meg peered out the end of the passageway into some wider corridor. The sounds of boots running in their direction echoed beyond.

"Gods, Meg, they're after us," she pleaded. There was a narrow stairway behind them. She tugged at Meg's sleeve, her back, arms, legs, neck prickling with irritation. The kitchen below must be bustling by now with cooks and maids.

Meg jerked her arm away. "We have to help Rennika."

"We can't save her by getting ourselves *caught*." She needed Boneblood. She needed to stop itching.

"Shh." Meg peered into the corridor again. She bumped back.

Come on, Rennika! Janat tugged again on Meg's cloak.

Orders were shouted, from nearby.

Gods! Janat stumbled toward the stairs. Meg was an idiot. They couldn't help Rennika. Not now.

Then Meg was with her, hustling silently down the servants' stair.

The prince consort came close to Rennika's chair, bumped his knees against its edge, and dropped his cane. He looked down at her. "I get the worthless one," he said softly. "No tribute. No magiel to make curses."

The muscles along the back of her neck clamped.

"Your sister promised me magic. 'Spells to defeat my enemies,' she said before she ran off. I could have given her a house. Protection. Food. Clothing." He leaned down and whispered in Rennika's ear, pulling the strings holding her cloak closed. "Men in my position have done as much for a mistress."

Meg offered to be his mistress? This, Rennika could not grasp. Not Meg. Never Meg. It wasn't in her. Raef must have misunderstood.

"But they bolted, saved their own skins. Left you." He pushed her cloak back over her shoulders. "Why would they do that? Abandon you? What did you do to them?" He took her arms in his muscular hands and squeezed, no sign now that he was ill. "But you are useless." He straightened. "I've been cheated."

No. No, Meg would not do that. Or Janat. And yet . . .

They had.

It made no sense for three of them to be caught, captured. They would come for her, just as she and Meg had come for Janat.

But the three of them together—magiels—could have defeated Raef.

The Regent seized her wrist. One hand scrabbling on his cane, he pulled her from the chair.

She wrenched back, panic overwhelming the ill effects of her recent struggle. But his fingers held. For all he was crippled, his arms and shoulders were powerful.

He shoved her past the chair and into the bed post. Her head cracked against the wood, surprising her, shooting pain through her headache.

"I will not be denied twice." He pushed her again, and she tripped over her dress, sprawling on her back, this time onto thick carpet. His cane struck her in the ribs. Pain.

She scuttled out of the way, scrambled to her feet, hands out for balance, searching for anything—

The back of his hand struck her face with lightning shock, snapping her head around and pitching her into a table. She shook herself—

—a candlelit chamber paneled with gold and amber—bed covered with brilliant cushions—glass panes in inky windows—

She'd been here before.

The dress. It was the one she'd worn in her vision—

Raef . . . held a knife.

She stilled, panting, hair tumbling over her face. She had to do something. Something . . .

—there was a jump in time, a blank space, not more than a moment—a snippet lived in another part of her life—

And he was before her, dagger sliding across her collarbone, slicing her cloak open, nicking her skin.

Rennika gasped and recoiled, but he tossed the knife aside and with both hands, ripped the top of her dress apart.

She shrieked, jerking her elbows over the hands violating her breasts—something fluttered to the floor—

He slapped her face a stinging blow, gripped her upper arms, and threw her onto the bed.

Panic battered her ribs—

He flung her back, climbing onto her—

Gods, no!

—what Meg had done. Your sister—not a candlemark ago—stopped my heart.

His larynx. She caught it in her mind. The front of it, the cartilage.

He pinned her beneath his thighs, fumbling at the buttons on his breeches. She wrenched herself up to claw his face.

She needed to find a time—a time when the larynx was a quarter inch farther back—

He punched her nose, and blood spewed down her face, mixing with the sweat and tears and mucus already streaming there. Searing pain, humiliation, fear screamed out inside her. Why could she not fix on his larynx?

There!

She held it. Unmoveable.

Now. Every struggle he made either crushed or clove it. His brows raised, his face hovering over hers in the candlelight. *You are no magiel!* his eyes cried out in wordless shock.

But she was.

She flicked. The hard cartilage at the front of his throat found a time in his struggles when it was farther back—and his larynx split.

His hands flew to his neck. He coughed, tried to gasp. Toppled to his side.

She gripped his throat, held her magic.

His eyeballs bulged, his face darkened. His lips opened and closed as if he would gulp air.

She backed across the feather mattress, sweat and blood hot on her chest and soaked clothing.

Gurgling, choking sounds; red froth spewed from his lips.

She held on.

How could she do this . . . hold that small piece of tissue open as blood poured down his trachea, filled his lungs, stained the bed. Pin him down as he groped blindly . . .

Yet, she did. As Meg had done.

But Meg had released him. Let him live.

The thought trickled only slowly into Rennika's awareness. Meg had stopped Raef's heart only long enough to let her and Janat escape.

Meg had left him alive. To abuse Rennika.

She slumped back against the bed's post.

Raef lay motionless now. His choking rattles had ceased.

The wind hushed beyond the window. A pale, gray light seeped between the drapes.

She backed to the edge of the bed, her own breath labored, her hold on his throat still tight.

Blood stained the pillow by his mouth.

Her foot found the floor. Slippery. Vomit.

Poised to run, she released the pressure from his throat. He lay still. The purpling of his face lessened. His eyes stared, unseeing.

She . . . had killed.

With an effort of will, she dragged herself away from the bed. Her stiff fingers tugged her garments into place, bruises and swelling and fluids making their presence known. Mechanically, she wiped her face on her sleeve, pain crackling. Then she crumpled over, leaning against the wall for support, silent moans pressing on her throat and chest.

Still, his eyes stared.

She screamed at him, ripped a shoe from her foot and hurled it. It bounced from his forehead and fell with a thunk to the floor behind him.

He lay, unblinking. The band at his neck was untouched, his death token unused.

Trembling, she pulled her torn bodice closed the best she could over burning breasts, wary for his sudden reanimation. She gathered up her cloak, her eyes never leaving his face.

He did not move.

Rennika opened the door and shuffled into the silent sitting room. No one was there. She closed the door behind her.

A low growl emerged from her throat and she sank to the floor, shaking, huddling into herself, pouring out inarticulate grief, eyes and nose and throat streaming, bruises asserting torment over her body.

Gods. She'd killed a man. The queen's consort. They would come for her.

She stumbled wildly to her feet. She had to cover herself. She fumbled about the room. Her cloak was in her hands. She flung it on and fled.

CHAPTER 38

Huwen ordered his troops roused well before dawn for the final push up the valley's headwall to Highglen. He simmered to get this unpleasantness over with and return home to Ychelle and Shalire. He'd have been here a week earlier, had rebels not harassed his every step along the way, sniping and vanishing into the woods.

He was under no illusions. An army the size of the one he commanded would not come as a surprise to his sister. Her border guards had undoubtedly sent a runner. But there was no need to lollygag into the city mid-morning. A brisk daybreak arrival was a demonstration of the gravity with which he took the situation.

Which was what, exactly?

Raef had served Huwen well in the past few years. But he was a Gramaret, a native of the country, who'd capitulated as a boy under force of threat at the outbreak of the war. And, until very recently, Raef's father had waged war on Huwen's armies, albeit pitifully, his armies slaughtered, his weapons seized, his fortresses conquered. Dwyn Gramaret remained free, for now, and the ideologies he espoused still circulated in some minds. Huwen could not dismiss the possibility that Raef was in sympathy with his father.

But equally, he could not dismiss Hada as innocent. The girl, only come of age half a year ago, might be a Delarcan, but that meant nothing. Their brother Eamon had stolen the Ruby and holed himself up in his castle in Midell. Huwen might smash his armies against that magic as much as he chose, the traitor was still safe within his borders. Even Jace, ruling Pagoras, paid only lip service to Huwen's decrees outlawing magiels, letting his captains turn a blind eye to the droves of them seeking haven there. Huwen would deal with Jace once he settled Hada's situation in Gramarye.

Which, again, was what? That she enforced Huwen's own laws more vigorously than he intended? She'd created borders, she said, so that she might evict magiels to purify her domain. Or did she build walls, as rumor held, to defend Gramarye against imperial forces once she declared independence?

But most seriously, Hada harbored Gweddien. As much as Huwen despised the Marigold scheme, the quality of the available magiel stock was poor, and Gweddien's heritage was pure. Huwen would retrieve the Ruby from Eamon; he didn't know how, but the Prayer Stone was his by right. And when he did so, he would need a strong magiel.

Additionally, according to his spies, Gweddien practiced magic for the purposes of giving Hada power—power she intended to use to defy Huwen.

How was Huwen to unify his country under the One God and bring peace to his people, when uprisers, and perhaps his own sister, carved out chunks of it from which to wage war?

You had no choice, Meg. Janat's words drummed repeatedly through Meg's head. *No hope of helping Rennika.* Not until they could fall back and plan. *Soldiers are coming.*

Meg was numb as they crept past the sleepy kitchen scullion and into the waking bailey. At least she'd killed Raef . . . maybe. Had she held his heart still long enough before they'd fled? She wasn't sure.

Janat staggered mechanically, whimpering and dazed under Meg's urgent shove, as they joined spent and bedraggled merrymakers stumbling home in the predawn gray. Shouts and the tramp of running boots echoed behind them in the bailey as they slipped through the castle gate. Soldiers, no doubt, scrambling to organize a hunt for Raef's attackers.

Across the common from the main gate, Gurd, the upriser Miach had assigned to help Meg if the mission failed, emerged from the shadows. His gaze flicked up and down street, and he silently turned to lead them at a jog toward the upper gate in the growing predawn light. The thunder of the castle's descending portcullis rang out behind them, culminating in a resounding clang.

Meg grasped Gurd's sleeve and tugged him into the mouth of an alley. Janat swayed. Her eyes were blank, mouth slack. A smudge formed at the edge of Meg's vision. "Janat's too ill to travel," Meg said in a low voice. "We have to hide."

"Where?"

"We have a place."

"The men can stand down?" Relief and disappointment and worry creased Gurd's face.

She gave a quick shake of her head. "Rennika's still inside. If she's able to get out, she'll need you. Tell Miach I'll meet him later today."

Behind them, the distant shouts of soldiers rang out from the castle wall. It would be only moments before a company of soldiers would be dispatched to comb the city.

Gurd pressed his lips closed in firm negation. "Miach can't meet you today. Maybe not ever."

She tilted her head.

"High King Huwen's troops have been spotted. He's marching on the city."

⁂

Gweddien drowsed, happy. They hadn't made love, but Hada had lain in Gweddien's arms the whole night, weeping, confessing, child and vulnerable woman, as he comforted her. Their ties were altered forever. As they would be, again, once they'd traveled to Heaven together with the Amber. Hada might have some nasty business on her hands, putting her prince consort in line, but *today*, she would meet with Yaquob. They would have the Amber.

But now, the brightening sky warned that day would soon be upon them. Gweddien caught Hada's hand and kissed it as she slipped from his bed. He rose, too, going to his outer chamber to find her a cloak and an escort back to her rooms.

A timid knock tapped on his door.

Wordlessly, Hada stepped into his breakfast room.

He scraped his tongue inside his mouth, thirsty. "Come."

It was Hada's maid. "Sieur, I wasn't sure who to speak to," she squeaked, curtseying, eyes round with fright.

Ah. The missing queen, not in her own chamber. He needed to whisk Hada back forthwith.

"The queen is missing."

"Where have you looked?" There was a pitcher of water on the side table.

"That's it, Sieur. I went to her husband's suite, and he's—" She choked on the words, face pale. "He's dead."

Gweddien turned. Dead?

He drew the girl in and closed the door. "Tell me everything. Who knows?"

The girl blinked, and for a moment Gweddien was afraid she'd burst into tears, useless. Then she spoke. "I went with hot wash water, as usual, to my mistress's rooms and saw her door was ajar. When I went to close it, I found her chamber empty. So I went to her new husband's rooms. There was no guard. There was . . . blood. On the floor." She stopped.

He waited, silently willing her to continue, no longer thirsty.

"I knocked on his bedchamber door. He didn't call. I—" She swallowed. "Sieur, I entered, and . . ."

"And you came here," he finished for her. "As you should have."

She dipped a weak curtsey. "Sieur."

What to do? Hada had to be found in her rooms, *then* discover this crime. "You did well to tell no one of the queen's empty room. I will—"

His breakfast room door opened, and Hada stepped out. "Gweddien," she commanded. "Attend me. Tuien, show us what you found."

※

In the murk of Yaquob's shop, Meg sat on the edge of Janat's pallet and dampened a rag in a bucket of water. She'd built a fire in the brazier, and the blanket on the rod in the doorway masked them as much as possible from the morning grayness seeping through the shop's outer window.

She wiped Janat's lips.

Blurs congregated in the corners of the room. Ghosts gathering.

The shaking and vomiting had come in waves, though now with poppy, Janat had drifted into a deathlike sleep.

Rennika had not come.

Meg took the bowl of puke from Janat's side and emptied it into the street. Returning, she poked through the tumult of broken glass and books and herbs tossed to the floor, for whatever was salvageable.

Meg knew nothing of Bloodbone, its form of magic, or how to counteract it. She could perform magiel magic on her sister, draw the poison from her blood as she and Janat had done for Kirst. Hane had warned them it would do no good, and as soon as they'd finished, Kirst had cursed herself again. Meg was loath to do magic that could muddy her time stream, with Rennika missing and events—she had no idea what—set in motion in the castle. With Huwen's troops coming at any time.

Worse, though. Meg could tell when she reached into Janat for a time when her flesh was healthy, that the Bloodbone had entwined itself into her muscle. Bone. Blood. Meg could not separate Janat from the charm. Not, and have her live. Her body was starving for the want of the spell.

But Meg could not sit, do nothing, and watch Janat slip deeper and deeper into coma.

She'd read Yaquob's books and scrolls, but the texts were low-level compilations of village witchery, love potions, fertility spells, and small curses. Nothing about Bloodbone.

She wracked her brain for a general principle of poisons and curses and their antidotes.

Abruptly Janat woke, springing with a cry from her pallet. She stared at the room without comprehension and spoke unintelligibly, as if still dreaming. She shivered but threw off the blankets Meg gave her, tried to vomit, then doubled over, silent.

Then she jerked back onto the pallet and spasmed in convulsion. Her breath stopped.

Kyaju!

Meg had to do something—something!

Ghosts clustered closer.

Breathe! Breathe!

Janat remained rigid, contorted, eyes bulging in a mindless mockery of terror. Tiny, choking gurgles escaped her throat.

Consequences be damned. Meg sprang onto the pallet, placed her hands over her sister's heart and stomach. She reached back in time . . .

She pulled enough clean flesh forward to calm her, buy a few minutes. Time.

※

Meg raced up the stairs and entered The Three Corners' common room. It was empty and silent, the fire in the brazier cold. No—the boy, Raoul, slept on a bench, shivering under his cloak.

"Xadria!" she called. For a moment there was no sound in the brothel, though Raoul sat up sleepily. Meg found a tankard and banged it on the bar. "Xadria!"

"What!" Xadria's croak roared irritably from a back room, and in a moment she shuffled, disheveled and puffy, from the back corridor. "You!"

Meg emptied her pockets on the bar. A half-dozen vials rolled out and a small purse with several gultra. "Boneblood."

Xadria eyed her from dark pouches. "So?"

"Come on, Xadria. You have it."

"Have you come to pay your sister's debt?" She ambled to the bar and fingered the spill of bottles and coins.

Someone appeared in the opening to the back rooms. Vellefair, his hair sticking out at every angle and a day's growth of beard giving him a querulous look.

"I'll get you the money." Meg had no idea how.

The woman shrugged. "Maybe you will." She gathered up Meg's offerings.

Raoul was suddenly by her side. Gods, the boy was silent. "I'll help you."

Meg narrowed her eyes at him.

He smiled winsomely.

"That's right," Xadria said, picking up the last of the coins. "Do business elsewhere until your bill is paid here."

Raoul tilted his head in invitation.

Vellefair scratched his head and turned back to the corridor.

"Get going," Xadria said.

Raoul snatched up his cloak and led the way from the tavern. Doubtfully, Meg followed.

Once outside in the snow and down the stairs, Raoul said, "It's in your pocket."

Piss, the boy was good. She reached into her pocket and pulled out a small purse. "Whose is it?"

"Vellefair." They walked amiably through the gray streets, waking late with the day's spent carousers. "He owes you. You paid him to take care of me, but he didn't do anything much."

In the purse were two small glass jars filled with the yellow paste. A dozen chetra. "I thought you fell asleep at your father's shop."

"I did. But I woke up and I was alone." Raoul held out his hand. "I'm hungry."

She gave him the money. "I'll be at the shop today if you want to come." Not that she would be able to entertain him.

"No." He grinned and turned, dancing backward down the alley. "I have a rendezvous."

Rennika bumped along the wall of an alley. The narrow space was lightening with morning. High overhead, the pale sky promised a clear day. At some point—when?—the chimes from the shrine to the One God had rung out. Six. She counted them. But they were silent, now.

She had to find a place to hide. A place where she could ride out her time ripples without being seen.

Her feet were shoeless, punished by a hundred cuts and the cold of the snow. Bruises on her body ached with every step. Before her eyes, Raef's face stared at her, on its side on the stained pillow, blankly accusatory. It grimaced, a silhouetted mask above her as he forced himself on her. She could not move her thoughts forward. Think ahead.

Minutes or candlemarks. They would be after her. Soldiers.

The corridor had been empty when she left Raef's room, guards dispersed to organize a manhunt. Still, she'd had to use magic, and more than enough, to slip through the roiling wasp nest of the bailey and through the tradesman's gate before it was locked and barred. But when the Regent's body was discovered, there would be demons to pay. Soldiers would come to Verlin's house. She had to warn him.

No. She didn't.

She had to run. Where? She struggled to make herself think, to yank her mind away from—

Leave Highglen. Leave Gramarye. She'd known this. She'd pre—
The letter.

She stopped, her back to a stone wall in the narrow space, and pulled her cloak open, her dress, the blood on her chest, her chemise torn.

Her letter. She'd kept it safe in her chemise. Raef had cut her clothes open. A flutter—

Gods. It was on the floor of his bedroom, beside his corpse. Further incrimination.

What was the point in running? She couldn't lead them back to Meg. And Janat.

Her life shifted.

Talanda sat on a stone by the edge of a sparkling brook in spring-scented woods with a basket in her lap, separating bright petals from marigold heads. Rennika was young, maybe nine or ten, sitting at her feet.

Her mother lifted her smile, and soft laughter stopped abruptly. "Rennikala."

Did Rennika look as stricken as all that? Even in the body of a child?

Her mother set her basket aside and took her hands. "When are you?"

Rennika's throat seized with unbidden tears, and she could not speak.

Alarm took her mother, then, and she gripped her hands harder, falling to her knees before Rennika. "Survive," she said fiercely.

Rennika nodded, mute.

Talanda gave her hands a tiny shake. "Whatever happens. Whatever it takes. You must."

And she was gone.

A laugh.

Rennika turned. The sound was carefree and joyous—

A cool, dark room smelled of earth. A peasant house made of sod and logs, a sleeping loft tucked under straw thatch. Rennika bent by a stone oven, hot from heaped coals glowing on the hearth beneath. She drew out the long paddle and breathed in the blissful aroma of bread as she laid the dark loaf on the table.

The shriek of a child's laughter drew her to the door. A curly-haired boy chased a girl just a little older than himself, dodging goats in a dirt yard. Rennika melted against the jamb with joy and relief and contentment.

A future. Her child? Or was she a servant? A guest? A refugee?

A boy, blond and pink-cheeked, raised an ax over a log on the chopping block. Toddlers—twins?—sat in the dirt gnawing on carrots—

They all turned as Rennika brought out the bread.

The cold and snow and pain returned.

She sat on a stone bench in a derelict shrine to Kyaju with no roof. A spray of summer stars shimmered in the blackness overhead. She'd been here before. She'd come to think of it as her shrine, for more than once she'd seen the accoutrements of magic laid out on a bench by a well. Some time in her future. She must visit this place often. Do magic here, often.

Janat laughed. "He gave me back the purse and said, 'And that's when the old man fainted.'" She took Rennika's hand and looked up to the stars with a smile. A future, and Janat was in it.

Happiness. Yes. She must survive. Do what must be done. For this.

CHAPTER 39

Meg woke, slumped against a wall. Fatigue was an ocean engulfing her. The fire on Yaquob's brazier had dimmed to embers and the room was chilled. But the ghosts had receded.

Janat lay on the pallet, her shift, hair, skin, pale with sweat.

Meg crawled to her, touched her shoulder.

Did she breathe?

Yes. A faint whisper.

Meg let her eyes fall closed. She slumped by Janat's side, her arm flung over her sister's shoulder.

Janat lived. For the moment.

Meg pulled a blanket over her sister and stroked her hair for a long time.

༄

Cold prickled her. Kyaju, Meg didn't have the energy to move. But shivers had taken over her muscles. She'd done something she thought she would never do. She'd smeared the yellow paste on one of Janat's sores. Then went in with her magic, balancing the entanglement of poisoned flesh with healthy flesh from Janat's past.

And again. And again.

Meg crawled to the brazier. A coal glowed. She found a handful of kindling, stoked it and blew on the flame. She huddled over its small warmth.

Meg's work would come to nothing if her sister's courage slipped. Tomorrow, or the next day, or the next. How many times had Meg dragged her sister back from the edges of cliffs, the edges of self-destruction, the edges of ecstasy? There had to be something, *something . . .*

You don't know. You can't know. Janat's words. Meg saw her in memory, huddled in the darkness beneath the wall in Glenfast under the mist of summer rain. *You wouldn't understand.*

Janat, in Cataract Crag, cleaning the innkeeper's guest room. *You wouldn't understand.*

What was Janat not telling her?

Meg and her sisters had grown up together in Archwood castle, three daughters of the same magiel mother, and the same magiel father. Why were Meg and Rennika able to face the traumas of fleeing the High King's genocide, of displacement as refugees, of being political pawns, when Janat couldn't? What was different?

It was true, they were each distinct. Janat only wanted to return to her childhood luxuries. She'd hidden in Summerbluff, trying to blend in, while Meg was fighting beside King Dwyn. She'd had her heart broken by Sulwyn, their protector who died in the infamous Battle of Coldridge. Could any of these conditions have sparked Janat's reliance on hiding from life through spell-eating? And if so, what could Meg do about it?

Meg snuggled into the covers and the warmth of the reviving fire, watching Janat sleep. Gods, she was tired.

She closed her eyes.

A sunny glade in the woods, early spring. The scent of poplars and the sound of a brook gurgling—yes, sun glinting off the surface of a tiny stream dancing over rocks. The reverberation of her time stream. Thank the Gods it had come while Janat slept, while the world was calm.

A giggle. "Do you think Tonore is handsome?" Rennika was only a child. When were they?

"Rennika!" Janat sat cross-legged on a bit of gravel by the stream, making a tiny split in the stem of a winter marigold to thread another marigold through it.

"Do you?" Rennika watched Janat's deft fingers. She already wore a crown of the orange flowers on her head. Sunshine poured into the glade, warming them. This time must've been after they'd fled Archwood, but before they'd come to Silvermeadow. Fleeing with the refugees, if Tonore was among them. Meg must've made someone a healing spell, or perhaps it was while Gweddien's mother was teaching her magic.

Janat shrugged with one shoulder. "He's all right." She grinned at Meg. "Maybe Meg likes him."

"It's Sulwyn you like," Rennika teased.

Janat gave her a sly grin. "Doesn't matter. Sulwyn's not here."

And the moment was gone.

"Ow! Ow! Ow! Not my fingers!" Tonore grimaced in spite of the laughter on his face.

It took the strength of both Meg and Janat to hold his arms against the tree as Rennika wrapped him in rope. A game of Steal the Stone, Meg remembered. Rennika had lured him away from his team, running slowly enough—almost—to be caught.

"They're getting away!" Tonore cried. His teammates were running through the woods, leaving him behind.

"Guard him, Rennika," Janat laughed. I'm going after—"

The scene shifted.

Meg stooped in a shadowed corner of a bailey, and a troop of horsemen spurred past her. Janat, dressed in a silk robe, crouched next to her, weeping softly. The main gates of Castle Coldridge opened and cavalry passed through.

And she was back in Yaquob's room by the brazier. Janat moaned.

The Battle of Coldridge. Meg and Janat had escaped as High King Huwen's forces left the castle to crush the uprisers who'd waged war against him.

Meg scrutinized Janat, awake now, staring at the brazier through bright eyes. What had she been doing in the castle, dressed so? Meg had asked her, once or twice in the intervening years, and Janat had never really answered her. She'd been captured, as magiels were in those days. Sent to the High King's magiel breeding scheme . . . but before she could be so abused, the battle had broken out and Meg had rescued her. End of incident.

"Janat."

Her sister's body tightened, and she huddled into herself.

"Janat, what happened to you?" she whispered. "In Coldridge Castle?"

A soft moan deepened her sister's whimpers.

"Janat—"

The sun crested the mountains to the east beneath a clear sky. Pristine snow, deep on the road, had slowed Huwen's troops more than he'd anticipated.

Now, like the soldiers at the pitifully weak Gramarye "border," the soldiers manning the gates to Highglen spotted his approach and scrambled laughably.

Clearly, these men had no standing orders. There seemed to be a muddle to send a runner to the castle for direction. The river below the road cascaded over ice-rimed boulders, its roar turning the city defenders' actions to mime.

Huwen halted his horse and watched as his captain, a veteran of the last four years of the civil war and no fool, approached the gate. The officer waited for the confused guards to open the gates, and when the directive did not arrive within a reasonable time, ordered his first ranks to take up offensive positions, muskets aimed.

The city guard appeared to understand what muskets were. There was a commotion, and the gates opened. Huwen suppressed a smile.

The column moved forward. His captain relieved the gatemen of their duties, and the troops fanned out within the walls to take control of each sector of the city. Huwen wanted the occupation carried out by presence alone, if possible, and no musket fired. His personal troops accompanied him up the broad, winding avenue to the castle. The cannons would arrive when the churned snow behind the army allowed.

***

Thirst.

Janat ran her tongue around her mouth. Sand. Vile. Her head throbbed, a splitting pain. Faint daylight filtered into a dim room. A brazier burned.

She shifted, every muscle crying out in pain. She let her eyes fall closed. No sound but the crackle of the flames.

Xadria . . . the man . . . Raef.

No, they were gone. This place did not smell the same. She opened her eyes again, but she didn't recognize the small, dark room where she lay. She let her fingers creep up to her chest. The Amber was gone.

She'd failed Meg. Lost the prayer stone.

"Janat?" A whisper, but one she knew. Relief and dread in equal parts. It was Meg.

"You're dehydrated, Janat. Drink." Meg was beside her with a mug of water.

Wonderful, sweet, cool water. She sipped. It was so good, so good. She struggled to sit up, took the cup and drank.

Xadria . . . had sent that thug after her. "Where are we?" Janat's voice scratched, but it functioned.

"Safe, for now." Meg took the empty cup and refilled it from a bucket.

Gods, how had Meg brought her here? Janat had a vague memory of creeping into Raef's room . . . a jumble of brawls . . . a guard capturing her. Gods, why hadn't she thought to close his throat? Getting captured probably ruined everything, too. "Meg . . . I . . ." She shook her head. She was always apologizing, always the one who'd messed everything, always—

"Hush." Meg put a finger to her lips, not against the sound of their voices giving them away to some danger, but in acceptance. She pushed the cup into Janat's hands. "Drink."

She took the cup, but only to set it aside. "Meg, I want . . ."

Meg waited. Didn't interrupt.

Janat took a chance. "I want to be different."

Meg did not flinch from her gaze. She gave a faint nod. "I want that, too." She bit her lip. "I want to be different."

Janat peered at her, not certain what she meant.

She shrugged. "I . . . don't know how."

Meg? Janat gave a small tilt to her head. An acknowledgment. Something Meg never did. Janat was not sure how to interpret this.

"Janat." Meg took a breath, then looked her in the eye. "You've said I don't understand. I can't understand."

It was true.

"Tell me."

You couldn't *tell* someone. They had to experience it. The flights of marigolds, turning to flakes of sunbeam and rising into the sky. And afterward, the smell of burnt, rotting petals that sickened like ash in her stomach.

Janat never wanted anyone to experience what she'd been through.

Meg turned her chin back with a finger. "I mean it. Help me to understand."

Janat blinked. Tears welled in her eyes. "I . . . can't."

Meg turned her chin again. "Something happened. At the Battle of Coldridge. When you were captured for the magiel breeding scheme."

The tears, unexpected, spilled, and her throat closed, heart racing. *That was eight years ago! Eight years!*

Meg's arms were around her. "Help me."

She shook her head, unable to speak.

"Whatever it is. Even if it is something I really can't understand, like you say—" Meg's embrace tightened. "Tell me. Let it out."

I can't! Don't you understand, I can't!

Meg pushed her back, lifted her chin at third time. Gazed into her eyes. Said nothing.

And then Janat melted into her, the tears flowing. "Oh, Meg, oh, Meg, it was . . . horrible. It was . . ."

It was Gweddien who'd given Janat away.

In the following years, though, Janat had, if not forgiven him, at least come to understand him. He'd had no choice. It was Wenid, King Huwen's magiel, who was the source of the evil.

Wenid was old, and what he wanted was a successor, a magiel to use the Ruby to travel to the Heavens with Huwen once Wenid was gone. But no living magiel would serve.

Living magiels had been persecuted, almost annihilated. Why would any magiel cooperate with his oppressor, carry *Huwen's* prayers to the Gods? Even if one agreed, he could not be trusted. For, once a magiel entered Heaven with a prayer stone and a royal to keep him safe, the magiel answered to no one. Unless that magiel was brought up in secrecy, in a garden of innocence, raised to uphold and believe any lies Huwen chose to tell him. Hence, Wenid had created a scheme to breed infant magiels.

Janat had known something was wrong with Gweddien when she saw him in Coldridge castle, in the chamber Wenid had supplied for Gweddien to get his magiel consorts with child. "I've seen what Wenid can do," he'd said without looking her in the eye, and his whisper was hoarse, helpless. "I'm ensorcelled." His demeanor turned cool, then, abdicating blame. "We'll do as Wenid wishes. Gently or forcefully."

Janat prepared to ensure the ordeal would have to be forceful.

Then, a change had come over Gweddien's expression. She realized later: this was when the value of her lineage had dawned on him. "By Ranuat," he breathed. "Janatelle. *Falkyn.*"

Gweddien had summoned Wenid and revealed her identity. It was only later, when she'd found Gweddien in Cataract Crag, that she'd come to understand he'd done so as a slave to his addiction.

Wenid came immediately. "Falkyn." The old magiel's eyes riveted on her. "You're sure?"

"I traveled with her for a season," Gweddien said. They'd both been refugees, hiding from royal forces.

Gods, Janat wanted to bolt, to scream, claw, *anything*—

But her wrists were tied, and guards dragged her, shrieking and struggling, through corridors to a secluded basement. A magical escape would've been impossible with both Wenid and Gweddien aligned against her.

Too late, Gweddien reversed himself. "I didn't mean for you to do this," he pleaded with Wenid as the old magiel hobbled through the keep. "I'll do what you want. I'll—"

Wenid ignored him. Whatever Wenid wanted of Janat, it was no longer merely her ability to birth a child. Though that might still come.

They entered a chill, dank cell. At a nod from Wenid, the guards released her and stationed themselves just within the door.

"*Don't drink it.*" Janat never forgot Gweddien's words. "*On your death token. Swear.*"

But Wenid's head snapped around, and he called Gweddien to heel. He poured a powder into two goblets and added a mouthful of wine to each. As soon as the older magiel gave him a mug, Gweddien swallowed his greedily. Avoiding her eyes, he curled up on the bed away from her.

Wenid held out the second goblet. "You have no choice."

She could not run, escape guards and a castle full of enemies. She could not fight him.

She tried to pull the ingredients of the potion back in time, hoping to weaken their potency, but Wenid put a hand on the back of her neck and pushed the cup to her lips. "No more delay." The wine splashed against her throat and she swallowed reflexively, stumbling to her knees.

And she was lost.

Forever lost.

To glim.

Meg sat in the silence of the dying embers, trying to envision the all-consuming bliss her sister had tried to describe, and the depths of its loss.

Enslavement.

Wenid was gone, dead eight years, but the devastation he'd wreaked on Janat endured, as bright and sharp as that first day. Meg could not comprehend the misery he'd caused, the depth of his evil.

"Later I learned what Wenid added to the wine." The tears had dried on her sister's face, and she was pale and sad. Wrung out. "The spell for finding glim has been forgotten. Magiels burned the books recording how to locate it. Glim is the only spell that can compel a magiel, utterly and completely."

"But Wenid found its secret," Meg deduced.

"Yes. Somewhere."

Janat had left her body in the instant her flesh had absorbed the potion.

She'd risen, floating and formless, lightened, buoyed, blossoming with joy, her senses bursting with vibrancy and peace and wonder, thrumming with pleasure. The *intensity* of it. Glim took her to the outer reaches of Ranuat's Heaven, to balance on a pin of ecstasy, within sight of the Gods.

Within sight of the *Gods*.

And Meg killed Wenid in the Coldridge battle. Janat never tasted glim again.

But the wanting of it, the *need* of it, haunted her every waking moment.

"I tried to kill myself when I visited my past, so I would never meet Wenid."

Meg sharpened.

"I couldn't. The flashes to my past were too brief."

Meg shook her head slowly, taking Janat's hand. "Thank you. For telling me."

❦

Gweddien leaned over the body on the bed. In a chair just behind him, Hada sat, pale and ill at the sight. Blood, darkening now but still pungent like old meat, soaked the pillow and sheets. In the brilliant light of morning, he could see the consort clearly. Last night, in the dark and panic, he hadn't been sure, but now images from his childhood came back to him. Well, well.

He touched the side of the corpse's throat and noticed that his own hand trembled. His head pounded. He needed wine. Or something stronger.

The internal structures of the consort's throat were out of place, the larynx crushed. Yet there was no bruising on the outside of the neck, as he would have expected if Raef had been struck or strangled.

The work of a magiel. A very powerful magiel, such as no longer existed in Shangril. He would report this to Hada, as well.

Two soldiers had been on duty outside the consort's door when he and Hada had arrived—on duty, it turned out, except for a critical period when Raef sent them for reinforcements. A period during which he'd been alone with a woman. Gweddien summoned them. "Was she a magiel?" he asked.

"No, Sieur," the senior guard said.

But there was no doubt this was a magiel killing. "What have you done to track her down?" An assassination, within the very walls of the castle, was an intolerable breach. The *prince consort*. Hada's guard would have to be doubled.

"Oh, we know who she is," the younger one responded. "She is a journeyman dyer and apprentice to the master draper, Sieur Verlin. A contingent has been sent to arrest her."

Indeed? Gweddien had a vague memory of a woman adjusting Hada's gown. "Have her brought—"

Boots pounded down the corridor and the door to Raef's outer chamber burst open. A handful of Hada's household guards rushed in, barely taking the time to nod their salute. "King Huwen has entered the city gate," their captain reported breathlessly. "He marches to the castle. His army is in the city."

CHAPTER 40

Meg scrounged for something to eat in Yaquob's shop. She found a half loaf of bread and a frozen block of cheese to warm by the brazier.

"So, the Amber you stole was a copy?" Janat asked, sipping the tea Meg had made.

Meg was achingly tired, but she was too anxious to sleep. The tea revived her a little. "I touched Lord Raef. He's a Gramaret. Nothing happened."

"It was never very likely."

Meg had known this. Of course. "Yaquob probably has a dozen Ambers."

"I wish Rennika would come." Janat fingered a bit of toasted bread, but she didn't eat. "She knows to come here, does she?"

"Yes." But it had been the better part of a day. Meg rose and pulled back the curtain separating the small room from Yaquob's shop. The sky outside the high window was still bright. She had to formulate a plan to find out what happened to Rennika. Get her out of the castle, if she was trapped. Meg glanced back at Janat. If rescuing one sister didn't rob her of the other.

Throngs of people seemed to be in the streets, as if there were some commotion in the square. Tonore's words, *Huwen's only a day away*. Perhaps the imperial army had arrived.

Rennika had to have been arrested. Raef's men or Huwen's. Meg had to talk to Miach. Make a plan.

Meg pushed the last of her singed bread, cool now, into her mouth and returned to the back room for her cloak and satchel. "Something's going on outside. I'm going to check."

Janat looked so frail, shivering in her blanket. "I'll come with you," she said.

No. It would be too much for her. "I'll only be a minute." Meg put on gloves and raised her hood to mask her shimmer. "You should—" She stopped herself. "I did it again. Made your decision for you."

Janat smiled.

"At least I noticed," Meg ventured.

"You did," Janat said. "And you're right. I'm still so very tired. You go."

Should she stay with Janat? But—Rennika.

"I'll tell you what I find."

Meg climbed the stair to the street and peered cautiously from the doorway. A stream of people hurried from an alley on the far side of the square, while farmers and artisans packed up their stalls. She slipped into a market aisle and touched the sleeve of a potter pulling down a snow-dusted canopy from his stall. "What's happening?" She was careful to keep her face averted.

"Soldiers," he said briefly, and she sensed he hadn't bothered to look at her. "Huwen's army. Sending everyone indoors. Curfew."

"And Lord Raef's dead," someone added, a hurried voice, passing.

Dead? Then Meg's magic must have worked. Thank the Gods. At least Rennika would not have had him to contend with when she'd woken.

"An assassin," The same voice went on. "A woman, they say, if you can believe it."

"Magiel," the potter said. He spat on the ground. "They'll find her. Lord Raef was our last hope."

Meg backed away, pulling her hood higher over her face.

✦

Gweddien ran his tongue around his mouth, his head fuzzy, as Hada, somewhat recovered now that she was no longer in the dead man's private chamber, gave instructions to the guards to call her generals to meet her within the candlemark. She also called for her serving ladies to pour a bath and lay out an appropriate—Aadian—dress in her own appartments. "Leave me, now." She nodded to the guards, who departed, closing the door to the corridor.

She turned to Gweddien, still clearly uncomfortable in Raef's outer room. "Close his bedchamber door," she said. "I don't want to see or smell that man again."

Gweddien acquiesced. If Huwen arrived finding his regent dead and his sister crowned queen, things would get difficult. To say the least.

"This is awkward." Hada nodded to the door behind him. "I have no idea how many letters Raef wrote to Huwen, but my spies obtained two before they could be sent. They're not complimentary."

Gweddien was unaware of this.

"Your advice, Secretary?" she asked.

"I thought you wanted me to buffer you from your listeners."

"*Advice!* He's on my doorstep. I spent the night in your chamber, and I am still in my nightclothes."

Gweddien gathered his thoughts. Oh, for a Heartspeed. Even a whiskey. "Your city guard did not oppose him. I think this is good."

"Good? His army's inside the *city*."

"He has cannons and five thousand men. You can't defeat him with your regional forces and if you try, you'll confirm his worst fears. Treason. And fighting will destroy your own city."

"He is going to take my country away. He thinks a woman can't rule. He'll give it to some—"

"Send an envoy to your brother, inviting him to rest and take food and housing for his men. Accomplish what you need by diplomacy. If not . . ." He rubbed his forehead, pushing at the obstinate headache. "Food poisoning among the men would be unfortunate."

She took a breath. She was listening. At least the hysterical edge of her panic seemed to be subsiding.

"Next, be aware of your brother's objective." Gweddien tried to smile, to be light, but he knew he must look as sick as he felt. "He is presumably looking for me. I think we both know why."

"His brutal scheme?" For the first time, Hada hesitated. "I . . . I would not give you to him."

This sentiment, even if futile, warmed him.

She bit her lip, and her gaze darted to the bedroom door, her face suddenly focused as though an idea had raced through links of causality. "Or . . . maybe . . . Raef may be able to be of service to his country, yet."

Gweddien tilted his head, not following.

She straightened. "Diplomacy. Nests within nests." She moved to the door, then stopped with her fingers on the handle. She turned. "And if my plan doesn't work, with what else can I bargain?"

He still did not comprehend. But he had an answer to her question. "The Amber. The merchant, Yaquob, awaits your pleasure, Majesty."

When Hada saw the merchant's face, she caught her breath. She dismissed Gweddien.

Her magiel spluttered and protested insistently, but she could not take her eyes from the free trader's face. She waited until the magiel was gone, the doors closed, and her private audience chamber secure.

Then she shook her head in shocked wonderment. "Uther?" she asked tentatively.

Her older, bastard brother quirked a tentative grin at her. "I kept insisting I had to see you personally. I didn't think you'd remember me."

She reached out for her chair, disoriented and weak at hearing his voice. Gweddien had called him . . . Yaquob.

Uther touched her elbow, guiding her to the soft padded chair. He pulled up a foot stool and queried with a look.

"Yes, of course," she whispered. Uther was dead.

He poured a goblet of water and brought it to her, then he sat at her knee-level, perched forward on the stool. "I'm sorry for surprising you."

She sipped the water. "Not often one sees a ghost in the flesh."

He lifted a shoulder deprecatingly.

She blinked, trying to get the world to sit properly under her. "Does Huwen know?"

"No one knows. Well, your consort husband figured it out, but I'm given to understand that's irrelevant now."

She nodded slowly. She was not about to get drawn into that discussion. Uther had changed. He was plumper. He wore a beard, now, which he'd never done before. He was well dressed, if disheveled from a night as her guest with no wash or change of clothes.

"I was surprised Gweddien didn't recognize me." He grinned that mischievous grin she knew so well. "But then, I was gone most of the summer he spent in Holderford."

"They found your body."

"Mutilated, I believe."

Yes . . . yes, that was true. "Why?" she asked. Her older brother. Bastard older brother by her father's maid, never to rule, but respected in their household, nonetheless. Well, respected as an adviser, as a good man. Their father's most trusted messenger, and after Father's death and Huwen's ascension to the throne, capable of becoming whatever he wished in her brother's court. Chancellor, financier, bureaucrat. She peered at him more closely. "You had wealth. You had position. Why . . ." She shook her head. "You gave it all up to become . . . a free trader?"

He dismissed her question with an offhand smile. "A long story."

"The brief version, then." She must be conscious of time, of Huwen's army. But *this*!

"There is no brief version." He held up a hand when she would have protested. "I will be here, tomorrow, as will you. I'll tell you the whole thing, then."

"I'm not so sure. You've heard Huwen marched into Highglen with an army."

His brows shot up. "Really?" He ducked a small smile. "Then . . . not tomorrow. With your leave, I will be long gone."

"I'm told you're here to sell me a prayer stone."

Something changed in Uther's expression. Something . . . *false* fell away to a solemnity she hadn't seen in him very often. "Yes. I am. Indeed."

And she knew. "It's a fake. Isn't it?"

His gravity resolved into affection. "Yes. Of course."

Then— "Why? Why bother coming here? To see me?"

"I . . . honestly didn't think you'd recognize me."

She knit her brows at him, trying to comprehend.

"I . . ." He studied her for a moment. "When we were growing up, I never knew you well."

"You're eight years older." And they were separated for long periods during the war. Separated by social class. Separated by his death.

"I never liked Huwen. Or Eamon. They were always bickering. Even Jace was spoiled."

Eamon never got along with anyone. Huwen thought the world revolved around him. She never liked her brothers much, either. Except Jace.

"The war was unfair. It took lands and rights from those who shouldn't have lost them. I filled my role for Father, but I never liked it."

"You thought I was like the other Delarcans. My brothers."

"Are you?"

She had to think about this. "I'm a woman. I'm the youngest. I'll never inherit . . . anything. I've had to fight for my place. So, yes, perhaps I am. Grasping and greedy, is that what you'd call me, then?"

"Though, I suspect, perhaps a bit more self-aware than the others." He spread his hands. "I had this Amber. I needed money. I thought I could cause a bit of trouble between you and Huwen, and maybe the uprisers would benefit." He pulled the ostentatious gem from beneath his vest, a large amber stone set in a burst of snaking golden rays.

She held out her hand, and he removed its chain from around his neck and gave it to her. She'd never seen the Amber, but she'd seen the Ruby, of course, and this was a perfect copy.

"A jeweler from Archwood made it. He'd seen the original."

"And you thought you could convince me it was real?"

He sat back with a grin of mock umbrage. "I'm very good at what I do."

"Are you a merchant or a swindler?"

"Depends on the occasion."

She laughed.

"I grew up pretending. To be royal. To be a servant. To be everyone's friend. I hardly have a personality of my own." He lifted a brow. "With your permission, Majesty, I wish you well but would like to slip out of the city, if I can, before I'm revealed. Or fighting starts. I've had my fill of fighting."

She let her fingers curl around the stone. "Might I keep this?"

He hesitated.

"I'll pay you for it. I wouldn't mind wearing it when I meet with Huwen. Leverage."

Uther pursed his lips. "Is that wise, Hada?"

Treason. Huwen still had cannons and didn't need a reason to think she was taking one of the precious countries of his empire. "No, I suppose not." She fingered the bauble. "Tell me, Uther. If you had the Amber—the real one—and a magiel to use it with, what would you do?"

"Solve the world's problems?" Then he grinned, his old charming self. "But I'm not that kind and giving. Luckily, the question's irrelevant."

"Uther. If anyone is giving, you are."

"Sorry to disappoint you, but I hate politics, Hada. Solving the world's problems is for other people to do." He held out his palm, and she let the jewel and its chain dribble back onto his fingers. "But thank you for the compliment."

She scrutinized him. "You're too moral a man to let politics stop you from doing what you think is right."

"You have too good an opinion of me."

"No, Uther." She tried to read him. "I think you're protecting someone."

His glance shot up.

"A woman?"

He smiled and stood without taking her bait. "You'll keep my secret, then?"

She stood as well. "Yes. Of course. Sell that Amber again, as many times as you can."

"Well, then." He gave her a short bow, then took her shoulders and kissed her on the cheek. "I have a small package to pick up, and then, I shall be on my way."

"Package?"

"Another long story."

༒

Gweddien hovered in the corridor near Hada's chambers, headache almost forgotten, the damn chain swinging as he paced. The Amber. He could almost touch it. Minutes.

The door opened, and Hada's guards stiffened slightly. The merchant, Yaquob, stepped into the hall and turned as Hada followed him. He took her hands in his and kissed them, and she laughed. A trifle familiar, but a positive note. She nodded to one of the guards to escort him from the castle.

Then. She must have the Amber. Gweddien's pulse throbbed, headache flooding back.

Hada nodded to him, and he trailed her to her meeting with the generals. "Is the jewel secured?" He breathed, as near to her as he could. It was perhaps unwise to discuss such things in the corridor, but soon it would make no difference.

"Hush, Gweddien. As I said before, it doesn't exist."

It was as though a quarry hammer had hit him in the chest. He stopped in the corridor, and the queen's guard had to step around him to escort her.

Doesn't exist.

What did she mean? Exactly? That the merchant had brought nothing with him?

Or had she simply dismissed Yaquob's offering?

She hadn't asked Gweddien to test the stone. Hadn't tested to see if it failed in its magic.

His heart thundered in his chest and rage rose up through him.

Hada and her guard rounded a corner. He sprinted to catch up, the damn collar constricting his neck.

He reached her just as she came to the door to the conference room. The generals would be assembled by now. No opportunity to talk.

"My queen."

She turned in annoyance. "Huwen will be here momentarily, Gweddien. I will let you know what happened in due course."

"Majesty," he bowed his head curtly, his words straining in the cage of his restraint. "A moment. I believe it is critical."

She let out a breath of exasperation. She nodded to the guards to remove themselves to a discreet distance.

"Did you see the stone?" he demanded in a sharp whisper.

"I did," she snapped back. "It's not genuine."

"How do you know? Did you try to use it?"

"No, of course—"

He threw up his hands in fists.

"Gweddien!" she reprimanded. "Leave me. *Now.* I will speak with you later."

How could she—

She gave him one last glare, then turned on her heel and entered the meeting room.

There was no air. His head was about to explode. An infuriating irritation flooded across his skin. And that *chain*!

Gweddien stared at the door, and the guards, stoic, moved to their places before it. Gweddien spun on his heel, strode down the corridor, screening his face from the puppets. A maid with a tray gave him a frightened look and twisted hastily into a servants' passage.

He drew harsh breaths through his nostrils, still marching. Ran up a flight of stairs. Back to his assigned quarters. He flung the door closed and paced, tugging the golden collar from his throat. Beneath was his death token. He held it, touched its comfort as he paced.

Gods.

There was one way. He'd known this. Since Wenid had first given him glim. There was one way to transport himself to the Heavens. Never to worry about returning to the condemnation that was this earth.

Too much Heartspeed. Or poppy. Or half a dozen other spells. A blade to the throat. A plunge beneath the suffocating waters of a well.

He roamed the confines of the room, slammed his shoulder against a wall, roamed again.

He had no knife. But he could get one.

He pulled all the spells he had on his shelf and lined them on the table before his wash basin. Some would counteract others, make him sick but not leave him forever in Heaven. Others, though. Some could be deadly.

He slumped to his bed and stared at them for a very long time, cradling his death token. Heaven was one step away.

And he knew.

He couldn't do it.

CHAPTER 41

The vendor—one of the last to still be packing up in the square—drew in a sharp breath. Rennika knew she appeared bedraggled. But that was of no concern to her now.

Cambile. He had two leaves, fresh, and was willing to shove them in her hand for a chetrum before his stall was loaded onto his cart. Rennika took both, then slunk into an alley, away from curious eyes.

Rennika had taken a chance in the crowds of refugees and gone to Highmarket Common. It was foolish, she knew, but Tyg—and Ide—they were too important to her. She'd gone to warn them.

Too late. Soldiers stood guard. Watchful soldiers, waiting for her to return.

Maybe the family hadn't been arrested. Maybe they were only detained inside and would be freed. She couldn't get near enough to know. But a patrol had come uncomfortably close, and she'd had to worm her way down to the lower town.

Here, to purchase cambile. Cambile for lust.

She couldn't return to Meg and Janat. She couldn't.

She'd tried—Gods, she'd tried—to rationalize what'd happened in Raef's rooms. Best to save two Falkyns, if one must be sacrificed. Rennika's magic was strong and she could extract herself. Raef was a highborn Gramaret, married, and too gentlemanly to harm a woman in his rooms.

No. The one fact. The one thing Rennika knew without speculation. Meg and Janat had abandoned her.

They might have had reasons. Obscure, justifiable. Noble, even.

But they had left her to the mercy of a rage-filled, impotent man bent on whatever revenge he could take.

Meg and Janat might've had confidence she would survive. But that did not discount the fact they had deserted her when she was vulnerable. The thought felt like a knife slicing her in two. As much as she might wish she was a bigger person; as much as she might wish she could understand, see a larger purpose... Rennika... had been betrayed.

She shoved a hand across her dripping nose and thrust herself down the alley amongst the rabble of panicking townsfolk.

She didn't need much. She'd never desired court life or luxuries. She only wanted to marry and live quietly.

Survive, Rennika, Mama had told her. *Whatever happens. Whatever it takes.*

Well, she would survive. She would do anything. She would escape Highglen, and all its memories.

She could make spells—Disguises, Confusions—use her worldling appearance, get out of Highglen. She might find a corner to hide in, work in a tavern or laundry, even apprentice as a dyer. Perhaps, eventually, marry, as she'd wanted for so long.

But she was tired. Oh, Gods, *so tired.*

No. She'd tasted the comforts of a home. She knew quiet community, away from the grand affairs of state. She was *done* with politics. She was done with the life of a refugee.

The temperature had dropped, a wind had sprung up, and Rennika had Cambile in her purse. She pulled her cloak closer and, avoiding the swarms of military men, stole to the river to hunt for water maca.

Survive. Whatever it takes. She owed her sisters nothing.

Without her letter from Verlin, she had no profession. Begging was for children or cripples. Magic was forbidden. She *might* plead for an apprenticeship as a dyer. Somewhere. Find a master who would not dismiss a woman out of hand. Hah.

But Raef had recognized her. He was dead now, but if he had identified her, who else might? Gramarye was a country on the edge of the wilds, and Highglen, a backwater. Down valley, in Arcan or Pagoras or Midell, there were people with long memories. Wherever she went, her one protection, her anonymity, might be compromised.

She *must* find someplace small. Out of the way. And she must not call attention to herself with magical dyes. Not be too competent. Doubly why no dye master would take her on.

She found maca root as the day was fading, then sought an apothecary, to buy nip buds. For positive outlook and clouded judgment.

Why couldn't she be simply obscure and content? All she'd wanted, for . . . how long? Years. Was to marry Yon. She could sew. She could spin and weave. She could raise worldling children, worshippers of the One God. She'd make a good wife. Make a man—some man—some *worldling*—happy.

Rennika moved on to another common. Soldiers patrolled, and townsfolk were becoming scarce. Huwen had ordered a curfew. She had to find a place.

There, in a crooked lane, was an apothecary's shop, its windows dark. No one was visible in the gloom. She sprang the lock and rummaged the shelves. Yes. Dried caddisflies. A vial of spider web dew. Muskwort milk and nip buds. She found a robe among the owner's possessions and discarded her own bloodied one. She washed her face and combed her hair.

Tonight, Sashcarnala would rise in the east. A potent time for casting spells.

Hada, dressed in what she knew to be a gown of understated but elegant Aadian fashion, swept into the salon with a handful of her most influential advisers. "Huwen!" she said as her brother, also surrounded by his closest military counsel, stood. "I am so glad you came." She curtseyed deeply before him and took his two outheld hands to kiss. "How is Ychelle? And I hear congratulations are in order on the birth of your daughter."

"Hada. They are well, or so my messengers assure me." Her brother was a young man but had aged over the years of war. King too young and inheriting a conflict begun by their father, he'd worked—hard—to unite the seven kingdoms despite continual uprisings. But he was *not* their father. He did not have their father's wisdom or decisiveness. He'd botched opportunities and made enemies, and weakened his own position. She was not afraid of him.

"I wish I'd known you were coming, so I could've prepared a suitable welcome. But my chef is preparing an Arcanian dinner."

"No need." He seated himself again. He was thinner than she would have liked to see him, but muscular, brown and lined—a lesson in hard outdoor living. "Plain food suits me."

She followed his example and took a chair next to him. "Well, I have my chefs scouring the city for something acceptable."

"My purpose is business." Though his words were hard and spare—like father's, she reflected—his eyes were weary and hesitant.

She turned to her aides. "Leave us. I haven't seen my brother in . . ." She turned to him. "A year? At least?"

Her courtiers—absent Gweddien—seemed surprised but bowed and withdrew. She looked curiously at her brother. Huwen nodded to his generals and Holder. They departed as well.

The door closed and she turned to him, waiting. He would get no confession from her. If he wanted to accuse her, the words would have to come from his lips.

"You married." Oblique. Yes, this was the Huwen she knew.

"I did."

"And crowned yourself Queen of Gramarye." The eyes were not so much cold, as testing.

"Finally." She breathed. "Father gave the country to me when I was, what? Nine years old? The regent he appointed did an adequate job, I think. At least the country's not a total ruin. But he's not a Delarcan."

Huwen eyed her as though calculating his response.

She plunged on, taking advantage of his hesitation. "I was sorry you were at the battle in Coldridge and could not be here for the wedding. Of course, I had no idea the war was actually over, and you would be here so soon, or I would certainly have waited the ceremony for you."

He tilted his head. "I think not."

He'd caught her. She hadn't expected him to be so blunt. Something he'd learned from years of war? Before her blush could betray her, she softened into a pout. "Huwen. How can you say that?"

"The border post on the road. Is that a defensive position from which you intend to wage war?"

She straightened. "No!" She gave him a look of concern. "Did my soldiers give you hostility? Either there or at the city gates?"

"No."

"Those outposts are there to mark the place where magiels may no longer be welcome. In compliance with your laws, *my king.*"

"There's no need to be churlish."

"Yet you can come here and accuse your faithful sister of . . . what?" she cried. "Of what do you accuse me?"

"Withholding my magiel."

"*Your* magiel?"

"Don't be coy. Gweddien Barcley escaped my prison in Coldridge. I've been hunting for him for two years. My men caught up to him on your border several weeks ago, and your soldiers refused to relinquish him."

"And you need him for what purpose? I've grown fond of him. Perhaps we can reach some compromise."

"You know why. I need him to father trainable magiels."

"And that is your only purpose with him?"

Huwen's eyes narrowed.

"Because his misadventures have left him unsuited to that function."

Huwen drew back.

She lifted a simple wooden box from the table before them. "I suspected you had come to ask this of me." She gave him the box.

Huwen's face had hardened before he opened the container to view its contents.

"You can blame me if you wish, but he came to me already mutilated, and with this box in his possession. You will admire the naturalism of the mummification. Magic. Apparently, some men feel a . . . a need to keep such organs near them, macabre as it might seem."

He placed the box distastefully back on the table.

"So . . . he won't be capable of siring children. You will let the rest of the magiel stay here?" she asked sweetly. "I am partial to him."

Huwen sat back in his chair and regarded her. "Where is Lord Raef?"

"Dead." There was no way to soften this, and doing so would make her look weak.

Huwen's brows raised.

"An assassin, early this morning. My captain of the household guards is still investigating, or would be if he had any authority left in my city. There would appear to have been magic involved."

"Lord Raef was Regent."

"Yes."

Huwen's finger tapped on the arm of his chair. "Father placed *him* here to govern."

"Until *I* came of age," she flashed.

"It is my understanding you undermined his decisions," he retorted, just as quickly. "The border posts, for instance. You did not seek his approval."

Again, she drew herself up. "I am a Delarcan."

"Lord Raef's authority came from me," Huwen said sharply. "He was a Gramaret, a valuable connection with the people of this country."

"And since when do Delarcans ask the people they govern for their goodwill?" she snapped. "Father never did."

Her brother glared at her.

"I never broke any of your laws, Brother. I upheld every one." She breathed hard. "I took only what was mine. This throne. I am a *Delarcan*, and I rule under your regime."

"And Lord Raef?" he asked quietly. "I think his death is convenient."

"Think what you like. But he wasn't the man you thought he was."

"No?" Huwen said scornfully.

"No." Uther had told her before he left. "His name was actually Quinlan." She let this information rest for a moment for her brother to digest.

"What do you mean?"

"No last name. Perhaps you don't remember. Why would you? *This* man was a servant in the Gramaret household before the war."

Huwen stared at her.

"He helped the true Prince Raef escape in menial's clothing by taking his place when Father took this city. The real Raef died as an onlooker, in crossfire." Uther, their bastard brother, who'd attended as servant to their father many times at state dinners recognized the impostor only weeks ago, when he came to Gramarye to sell her the Amber.

"Where do you get this information?" Huwen said skeptically.

Uther did not want her to reveal his existence. Let the dead stay dead.

"Most of the Gramaret household died in that battle. When was the last time you saw Raef?" She knew the answer to this question. Raef had been assigned his regency by letter, delivered by Huwen's Chancellor, Igua.

Huwen studied her. "Not since we were children."

Of course not. War and governance had kept Huwen far too busy to visit backwater countries that brought him no grief. As for Hada, she might've met the real Gramarye prince when she was four or five years old. She hadn't recognized him but hadn't expected to, either.

And since the outbreak of war? Raef—Quin—would've been happy to keep Huwen away. Anything he said to the contrary was mere bluff. Hada had no idea what *Quin* intended to do during Huwen's current visit. Hide? Claim the years had changed him? "His body lies in state. I invite you to view him. You can tell me if he is the same man."

Huwen looked at her through skeptical eyes. "You swear this to be true?"

"I do." She smiled to herself. For a man who'd admitted he was a professional liar, she knew Uther had told her the truth of this.

Her brother let out a long breath. "And you swear to rule Gramarye—*strictly*—under my direction and authority?"

Hada rose, then, and curtseyed to the floor before him. "My king. I swear fealty to you and declare my oath of loyalty so long as I shall live and reign."

She waited for what felt like a long moment.

Then he placed his palm on her lowered head. "Rise," he said at last. "I accept your pledge."

She lifted her face and grinned. Oh, yes. She was a survivor.

He quirked a half-grin back at her. "And I expect you to repeat that little speech in public at a suitable state event."

Flakes of snow drifted from the sky as Rennika descended the steps to the smoky room beneath the tenement. The stink of close bodies, drying wool, ale, and overcooked yak stew rose up around her. A bard in the corner played a lute, his songs drowned by the whirl of conversation. Smoke from a peat fire thickened the air, and she smelled a hint of ganja. Rennika stood by the door, scanning faces animated with talk and drink. She'd massaged a small Glamour on her face to hide the bruising and swelling of her nose. Maybe, to heighten her allure, just a trace.

With curfew enforced by soldiers on every street, no one would be leaving the tavern tonight. The upstairs rooms would be full.

The women—serving girls, drabs, and farm wives—were irrelevant to Rennika. She scrutinized the faces of men.

A big man, round-faced, black-bearded, and black-haired, quaffing back a tankard of beer.

A hollow-cheeked gaffer with graying bristles and thinning hair, frowning at his companion's argument.

A group of laughing free traders.

Jack. Verlin's collier. Sitting alone in a corner with a bowl of thick soup, unsmiling. Fair, with pink cheeks, his clothes dusted with charcoal but in good repair. Had she ever really looked at him? Muscles on his shoulders and arms from a life of hard work. His movements, sharp and angular, uncompromising.

Rennika's gaze returned to the black-bearded man, arguing a point with his finger directed at his neighbor.

She returned to Jack. A pious innocence clung to him. And he was alone. Had she ever seen him in the company of another? And the memory popped into her head. He lived in Kandenton. She smiled.

She purchased two mugs of ale, poured her potion into one, and approached his table to sit beside him.

He lifted a surprised face. He was older than she, but not old. "Rennika."

Yes, an affinity was there. He was a good man.

She set the charmed mug before him and held her own. "I didn't know you were in the city." By the Many, let him not have heard any gossip of her involvement with events at the palace. And if she had any beauty, if she had any grace, let it be convincing, just this once. "Did Sieur Verlin ever pay you for your last delivery? I did remind him. Several times."

"He did." He looked at the tankard. "Thank you." He raised it in a toast. "This delivery is my last in Highglen before winter. Any more snow and the horses can't pull the cart."

She hunched close to him, trying to catch his eye. "Last I looked, Sieur Verlin's stock of charcoal was full."

He nodded to the throng of people cramming the ale house. "I'm glad the High King's come to put things right. Still, soldiers aren't good for business."

Look at me. At no one else. She watched him. "I'm sure things will settle down soon."

"Peace. That's what's good for business." He considered the ale in his hand. Sipped.

Ranuat was with her. She waited, daring not to breathe.

He frowned and drank again. And looked at her.

Yes. She touched his cheek with her knuckle, and smiled.

He smiled back.

The soldiers on the street had looked the other way as Rennika brought Jack through the narrow alley to the tavern's stable, fragrant with the presence of the dozing horses. She closed the stable door against the cold and falling flakes, as Jack marveled at her hair and touched her neck.

He wrapped his arms about her in the soft darkness, and she folded herself inside his embrace. The cocoon of his arms comforted her, and she pushed down the flutter of apprehension of what she knew was to follow. But this was not Raef. And not Yon, either.

No. This was different. *She* chose. She had selected a good man, a man who would keep her away from politics and war. Who would ask nothing of her but a share in his life and work, and to raise his children.

She lifted her chin and offered her lips, and he kissed her heatedly. He pushed a hand beneath her hair. Then, Rennika took his fingers and led him toward the loft. She needed to seal the spell before ripples in time whisked her away.

A horse snuffled, and another flicked an ear as they passed. She climbed the ladder, Jack almost treading on her skirts.

Well, she had made the love potion strong.

She'd barely crawled onto the soft hay when Jack rolled her onto her back. "You are so beautiful," he said, a voice from a dark blot close above her, his hands running over her arms, her hips, her thighs. "I can't believe you want me." He untied the lacing on the front of her robe.

"I do," she said, and she pushed back her panic as his fingers touched her skin, sliding softly to her breast. "I do. More than anything in this world."

CHAPTER 42

Meg jerked awake, shivering. Ranuat, how could she have fallen asleep?

She peered out from behind the cast-off blanket with which she'd covered herself, a scrap found in a wreck of broken shanties. Soldiers had undoubtedly been enforcing curfew and driving the beggars away.

The street was silent. Crusted snow glittered in the faint light of Ranuat's seven murderers, overhead. She must have slept . . . two, maybe three candlemarks. It was a wonder she was alive and still at liberty. She hadn't slept all of last night. Her body must've given out.

She scanned the alley. She saw no sign of Xadria's ruffians.

She breathed.

All yesterday afternoon and evening—well into the night—she'd searched for Rennika but learned nothing of her whereabouts. She'd only managed to be hunted by soldiers, magiel haters, and Xadria's bruisers. Been forced to hide here.

Stiffly, she extracted herself from her shelter, fingers and toes numb, muscles wracked with involuntary shivers. Maybe, finally, she'd be able to return to Yaquob's shop. Janat would be worried—Meg had promised to come back soon. Ha.

She didn't have far to go. Though she spotted two of Huwen's patrols—carrying muskets—she was able to avoid them and slip into the merchant's shop. She crunched through the chaos of debris in the outer room and shifted into the warm glow of the backroom's brazier.

Janat crouched, trembling, on the pallet against the far wall. Tears glistened on her cheeks, and she stared at something on the floor before her.

A vial and a knife.

"Janat." Fear surged in Meg's pulse.

Janat's eyes darted to hers. She snuffled, her breath hitched.

Meg slid to her side, took her shoulders. "Janat, what . . ."

She licked her lips. "Take it," she hiccupped. "Get rid of it."

The vial.

Meg scooped it up, along with the knife. She hurried up the stairs, crushed the glass on the side of the building, and ground its contents into the frozen mud.

She hastened back. "It's gone," she said, softly taking her sister in her arms.

Janat's head dropped onto Meg's chest, and she breathed long shuddering breaths.

"Are you all right?"

Her sister's head nodded in her embrace. Then shook slowly from side to side. Janat swallowed. "This time," she whispered. "I found it on Yaquob's shelf. The only one."

Meg held her.

After a long moment, Janat straightened a little. "Where's Rennika?"

"I didn't find her."

She felt Janat dip her head again. Meg's return, alone, had already told her this. "You think she was arrested?"

What else could Meg think? "I couldn't get into the castle. Disguise or Confusion, nothing could have got me in. The gates were closed and locked, and manned by too many men."

Janat bit her lip, accepting this.

The brazier flickered.

"We have to leave."

Janat's head jerked up.

Meg lifted a shoulder, helpless. "We're magiels, Janat. Huwen's troops are on every street corner." She'd already—probably—left their departure too late. "I didn't tell you this before, but Raef accused us of being Falkyns. In front of his guards. That rumor is not going to stay secret."

Janat blinked but said nothing.

Meg bit her lip. She'd made Janat a promise. "Am I being too controlling? Should we consider some other . . . plan?"

Janat drew in a long breath.

"I wish . . . I could think of something else. Something . . ."

"No." Janat shook her head. "No, you're right. We can't do Rennika any good from a dungeon."

Meg tightened her hug, grief overwhelming her. "She's a powerful magiel, Janat. Probably the most powerful magiel alive."

Janat took in a long breath and pressed her lips together in acknowledgment.

"And she looks like a worldling."

The faintest hint of lessening dark came finally to the hay loft. The love potion had been strong. But just as Rennika had taken no chances brewing it—pulling each ingredient out of its time, past or future, when its potency was strongest—she would take no chances sealing it. She would repeat this act of union each night until her ties with Jack could not be undone. Already, she'd pulled his seed into herself. The first child of their love would be a boy, fair and strong like his father, and she would ensure he bore no trace of his magical heritage.

Afterward, when Jack rolled on his side and slept, she fell into another place in her life.

Rennika lifted her head. Sunshine spilled heat on her shoulder and the smell of clover and grass, and the trills of birds and the rush of running water surrounded her. Mama rolled on her back on a blanket in a meadow and lifted her up in the air.

Rennika was so small! An infant? A tot, flying on her mother's arms.

"Who do I love forever and ever?" Mama was delighted, her shifting face lit with a smile. The sleeves of her loose shift, magiel-white, fell back to her shoulders.

But no smile could come to Rennika's face. She looked deeply at Mama's cheeks and mouth and hair and eyes, trying to memorize them.

Mama's laugh cut short. She sat up, and Rennika felt herself upright, resting against Mama's knees, short legs beneath her skirt opened to either side of Mama's stomach. Mama looked penetratingly into her eyes, probing.

Then Mama gave a ghost of a nod. "You have it," she murmured wonderingly. "So young."

"Have what?"

She and Mama both turned.

Nanna, red-faced with summer heat, climbed the last few steps up the hill to their picnic. She wiped her face with her apron. Nanna . . . was so young. Not a gray hair. "Dinner," she puffed.

Mama looked into Rennika's eyes again, hugged her, and handed her into Nanna's capable arms.

Then the moment was gone, and other snippets of Rennika's life overwhelmed her—reading a book of spells as a girl with Janat in Silvermeadow, rain in the dark of night in a shanty somewhere, sliding down a snow slope balanced over her feet on a warm winter day—

And then the ripples in her time stream subsided and Rennika lay once again in the near dark, with Jack, the two of them sharing his cloak as a blanket.

By the Gods. The sketchiness with which Mama—any magiel—understood the future. How had Mama ever had confidence enough to tell Nanna to take her and her sisters out of Archwood? To know that the High King would attack?

Yet, Rennika felt a taste of the fierce desire to protect her own children. Mama must have arranged their escape because of that same passion.

Below, a hoof clopped and a horse ground oats with strong teeth. Rennika tucked herself closer to Jack's back. She would never have to use magic again.

Jack rolled over. His face was shadowed but visible in the dim light, so close to hers. His nose was straight and his curls damp. He lovingly pushed a strand from her face. "I've been thinking. We can be married in Kandenton. That's the village near my home. Or we could find a Holder of Histories here, if you'd rather, but I want my mother and sisters to see us wed. They will love you the instant they set eyes on you. How can they not?"

Marriage. Rennika closed her eyes. "And your father?"

"Killed by highwaymen." The frown that momentarily creased his brow disappeared. "I'm the master of the house now."

"Kandenton." She'd been there, years ago, with Meg and Janat. They'd midwifed a mare and her foal there. A happy time, then. It would feel like home. It would *be* a home.

"South of Kandenton," he clarified. "I sell most of my charcoal to the smithy at Silvermeadow."

Silvermeadow. Where Janat and Sulwyn Cordal fell in love.

"The house isn't much—sod and log, not like Verlin's big house, here—but it's a roof, and it'll keep us warm in winter."

Rennika snuggled into him. She had been in that house, lived it in her future. She almost wept. By Kyaju, she would make a new life. Starting now. And, she vowed, she would repay this kind and gentle man with her whole being. She would be a good wife. She would raise his children, every one, worldlings. Worshipers of the One God.

And survive.

※

Meg fingered the Amber on its chain under her robe. There was no reason to keep it, she supposed. Except that it was such an exact copy. It reminded her of Mama. Gave her comfort.

Meg and Janat had raided Yaquob's shelves one final time for ingredients and potions they might need to ease their own departure.

Now, a blanket of feathery softness covered roofs and crannies and rocks, and carpeted the frozen mud of the square. Meg had climbed the stair to gaze out onto the predawn silence and see how strictly Huwen's soldiers were carrying out the curfew. Yesterday they seemed not to be bothering common peasants unnecessarily. After an initial closure, they'd opened the gates to yak herders and tradesmen an hour before sunset, creating long inspection lines.

Tonore had horses below the city gates. She wondered if they were still there, and if he was still waiting for them.

Janat was repacking food, and Meg was trying not to tell her how to do it.

Across the square, a man hitched a horse to his cart in the falling snow as a woman closed the stable door. Refugees leaving the conflict, no doubt, trying to catch the main gates at sunup, in case the guards were opening them.

The man ran his hands lightly over his pony's flank and, taking the woman in his arms, kissed her. He lifted her to the seat at the front of the cart.

Something . . . familiar . . .

Rennika?

Gods—no. Yes!

Meg's heart skipped a beat, then slammed her chest with joy. It *was*. It was *Rennika*.

Meg's throat caught in a knot. *Rennika was safe! Safe, and well, and whole.* How? *Oh, Gods, it didn't matter how.* Rennika had freed herself.

She was safe. *Gods, she was safe.* Tears of quiet jubilation seeped into Meg's eyes.

The man climbed onto the seat beside her.

Where . . . was Rennika going? And with whom? Not Yon.

Leaving.

Rennika was leaving Highglen without coming to the shattered shop, without coming to tell Meg she was all right . . .

Rennika looked up, just then, as though Meg's gaze had called to her.

The man flicked the reins, and the horses started forward.

"Rennika," Meg cried, taking a step into the common.

"Hush! Meg's what's wrong with you?" Janat grabbed her arm, holding her back, but Rennika had seen them.

"She's alive. She's free," Meg whispered, clasping Janat's hand on her arm. "Look."

"Meg," Janat breathed, staring.

Rennika watched over her shoulder as the cart turned down the road, but she did not climb down, did not run to them. Turned, and rode away with the man from the square.

Meg stood in the swirling snow, Janat clutched beside her, watching, tears of joy cold on her cheeks.

EPILOGUE

"Uther."

Uther opened the collar of his yak hide coat. The snow was hard and crusted over enough for him to walk with Raoul on the trail without too much difficulty, but though the air was brisk, the walking had made him warm. "Yes?"

"We don't need to use the name Yaquob anymore, do we?" Raoul marched behind him. The boy's short legs would not let him move fast, but as long as Uther kept feeding him, he kept walking. Which was about all one could expect.

"No. Enough people in Highglen will say we died when the shop was attacked. The tale will fool a few people I guess, and the rest won't care."

"Good."

"Why?"

The boy was quiet for a moment. "I don't know. I like your real name better."

"Don't get used to it."

Their boots crunched in the snow, glaring white under the clear sun. They should have snow glasses like the yak herders wore, bone or wood shades with narrow slits, to keep from going snow blind. Well.

Neither of them had dark enough skin to pass for one of the leathery, tanned mountain men, though the yak coats and the bundles of market goods they carried had been enough, in the confusion of farmers leaving the markets, to allow them to pass through the city's upper gates. Uther hadn't even needed the pass Hada had given him.

"I didn't like Xadria." The boy was chatty today. Well, he'd seen a lot that was new.

"Xadria let us stay in her back room after the shop was ruined."

"But you paid her."

The high rates charged for fugitives. True, Xadria made a good profit. "She sold us these coats."

"You paid for those, too. I didn't think she was nice. She reminded me of my ma."

"Well, you're right. Not everyone is nice." They walked on for a moment. "You did a good job. Next time I need a son, I'll pick you again."

The boy was quiet. Then, he said, "Why?"

"Well, you managed those beatings pretty well."

"Those weren't much beatings. You never broke a single bone." He could hear the derisive smile in the boy's voice.

"And you're observant. You spotted the soldiers coming to smash the shop. That saved our necks."

Again, they walked on until Uther thought the subject had run its course.

"Uther."

He smiled. "Yes?"

"You had two amber necklaces, and now you have none. Why did you smash that last one?"

"Amber necklaces draw too much attention. The plan was always to get rid of the second one. If I wasn't going to sell it, I had to get rid of it."

"And the first one? Why did you want me to tell Meg you beat me and all? And steal that amber necklace from you and give it to her?"

"Didn't you like her?"

"Yes. And I think she liked you. She didn't like it when I said I was going to kill you."

"Well, I'm glad of that."

"But why?"

Hmm. How to answer? "I guess . . . because the Amber belongs to them."

ACKNOWLEDGMENTS

Of course and consistantly: the Imaginative Fiction Writers' Association and all those who helped me along the way with discussion and critiques, but particularly to my Shadow Ascension Workshop partners. Especial thanks go to Jeff Campbell, Sandra Fitzpatrick, and Adria Laycraft who read the manuscript and gave me perceptive insights and suggestions. As I did for the other books in this series, I learned a great deal about the subject matter from close friends, lovers, and family members, as well as through books (*The Anatomy of Addiction*, Mohammad Akikur, 2016), films (*Risky Drinking*, HBO) and podcasts (*On Drugs*, CBC, Geoff Turner). All the amazing people at Laksa Media have done beautiful work on this book, but my express thanks go to Lucas K. Law for his faith in me and his amazing support of this series. Finally and always, Don.

ABOUT THE AUTHOR

SUSAN FOREST is an award-winning author and editor of science fiction, fantasy, and horror. She has published over 25 short stories in Canadian and international publications. *Flights of Marigold*, the second in her seven-book series Addicted to Heaven, is not only a tense tale of political and military struggle, it is also an examination of the role of a caregiver's complex relationship with a person suffering from addictions. Caregivers are often unsung—and sometimes vilified—heroes, groping their way through a morass of conflicting courses of action with little guidance. This motif is one Susan is humbled to explore with the aspiration of provoking dialogue, and the recognition of—and respect for—those whose battles are ongoing. Visit her online at www.speculative-fiction.ca. Follow the Addicted to Heaven series online at www.addictedtoheaven.com.

READER'S GROUP GUIDE

Questions and Topics for Discussion

1. In *Flights of Marigold*, Meg is torn between caring for Janat and fulfilling her own quest. In what ways is Meg a good sister and a sympathetic character, and in what ways does she mess up? What decisions does she take that make things worse? What should she have done instead? Why?

2. Janat is a conflicted character, swinging from wild defiance to abject shame. On multiple occasions she vows to reform but fails. What forces are acting on Janat to create this inconsistency? Is her erratic behavior believable? Why or why not?

3. Huwen is seen by many as the all-powerful oppressor, and yet Hada describes him as incompetent. He has been unable to eradicate opposition to his rule despite eight years of war and the Uprisers' ineffectiveness. Why? What factors in Huwen's personality, and of Shangril's geography, economics, and social structures disempower the High King?

4. Gweddien is reviled as a monstrous villain in *Flights of Marigold*. In what ways can he be seen as a victim? Is his characterization of himself as a victim accurate, or is he merely manipulating others? Give evidence.

5. As much as Rennika loves her sisters and is happy to be reunited with them, their arrival upsets her world. Are Rennika's hopes and aspirations in her life as a dyer realistic, considering she must hide who she really is? Or is the disruption brought about by her sisters' arrival a wake-up call? Provide arguments.

6. In many ways Raoul is very adult for a young boy. What factors in his early life caused him to grow up quickly? Is his relationship with Yaquob abusive? In what ways is Raoul child-like?

7. The Verlin family represents a middle class that has been politically disempowered by the High King's occupation of Gramarye. Nevertheless, they have survived despite the far-reaching changes brought about by the war. What factors—personal, societal, political—allowed them to maintain their standing and even thrive?

8. What does Raef fear, and why? How does fear drive his actions?

9. One trope of fantasy (and other genre) literature is the "speech in praise of the villain," which shows the true immensity of the evil faced by the protagonists. How does the depiction of Kirst's use of Boneblood fit this trope? In what ways do drugs and addictions fit the role of "villain" in *Flights of Marigold*? Make a case for addictions, rather than Raef, Hada, or Huwen, as the true villain of this novel. What character most represents the evil of addictions? Why?

10. Is sugar a drug? What evidence supports this idea? What evidence shows it is harmless?

11. By importing steam technology from Aadi, Raef is a powerful force of economic and social change in Gramarye. What are the effects of industrialization on the people of Highglen? Can a case be made for industrialization as a villain? Why or why not?

12. The Uprisers in *Flights of Marigold* are fractured by competing agendas and pettiness. Why are they unable to unite against their oppressors, eight years after the initial rebellion? What has changed, to rob them of their common purpose?

13. *Flights of Marigold* is the second book in the *Addicted to Heaven* series. What techniques are used to make the story comprehensible to someone who has not read *Bursts of Fire*, without creating repetition for a reader who is familiar with the first book? How are the three sisters' travels to other parts of their personal time streams used to perform this function?

14. Of the three types of magic in the Addicted to Heaven series, two are most commonly used in *Flights of Marigold*: worldling magic, akin to herbal remedies or over-the-counter drugs, and magiel magic, akin to stronger medicines or illegal drugs. How does the metaphor of magic as drugs allow the reader to view real-world drug use through a different lens? Does this metaphor help or hinder new understandings about addictions? Why?

15. Appearance is an important motif in *Flights of Marigold*. Regardless of her supposed power, Hada must dress to impress, and Rennika is only able to maintain her lifestyle because of her worldling appearance. What other examples of characters manipulating their appearance can you find in the book? How true to life is the willingness of others to judge a person by their appearance? What examples can you find in the real world?

16. At the end of the novel, Rennika makes some unusual choices. From her perspective, why are they justified? Should she have taken different risks? Why or why not?

WHY MENTAL HEALTH AND ANTI-DISCRIMINATION RESOURCES?

There is nothing better than cracking open an epic fantasy. Swords. Sorcery. Adventure! That was my inspiration when I sat down to write this series: to create a joyous, terrifying escape from everyday life. But . . . deeper ideas crept in. Why? Well first, in the best adventure stories, characters must care deeply about things: political situations, societal conditions, personal troubles. If a character is going to fight *and possibly die* for something, that "something" must be worthwhile. But there was another process operating. As I learned when working with youth at risk, counselling does not need to prod people, precisely because whatever is on a person's mind will rise to the surface. So, too, with writing: ideas, not always fully conscious, were making their way into my fiction.

So it was, when I was discussing the Addicted to Heaven series with Laksa Media's publisher, Lucas K. Law, he asked me a very important question: what is your book about? *Really* about? Not three girls running for their lives, but underneath? What were the political, societal, and personal issues at the core of the story? And it took one blink for me to respond. Addictions.

Addictions are one type of mental illness, which is present in every family. Mine is no exception.

Alcohol is complex. Although it has taken the lives, life savings, and personal relations of family members and lovers, it has also been at the center of celebrations, good times, and significant rites of passage in my life. Our society and history (political and cultural) are steeped in this substance, for both good and ill. Scientists and the medical system still have no definitive answers about how to manage alcoholism and other substance use problems, though recent research has made steps toward better understanding.

And addictions cannot be viewed in isolation from the spectrum of mental and emotional functioning. My world, too, has been affected by multiple forms of discrimination, including bullying, discrimination based on sexual orientation, discrimination based on disabilities, and the stigma of suicide. Society attempts to function in a mechanistic manner, with expectations around time, reliability, and social norms, that are taboo to break. Square pegs struggle mightily to fit into round holes, and as a society we often view those square pegs as morally deficient. That hurts. Not only emotionally, but it hurts the individual's ability to live a fulfilling life.

Hence the importance of opening conversation. Recognition that we are not alone, that all individuals, families, and societies face these issues, provides relief and support in itself; but further, it allows dialogue to begin. Talking about issues can lead to the political will to support governments that fund research and programs. It can provide creative solutions to people struggling with their own health concerns and recognize the daily courage of those facing the uphill battle of addictions. Or, in the case of Laksa Media books, it can provide specific resources, such as the following Appendix to Mental Health and Anti-Discrimination Resources. But responsibility does not end with one half of the conversation. Look through the Appendix following. If you have any doubts about a situation in your life, if you are wondering *Is this normal or is it a problem?*, don't wait for it to progress. Prevention is easier than recovery. Check out the resources, either here, or through your community, your doctor, or your pastor. A dialogue is not a dialogue without a response.

And—what better way to begin this dialogue than through epic fantasy?

—Susan Forest, Calgary, Canada, 2020

LEARN HOW TO MANAGE YOUR STRESS . . .
LEARN DAILY MINDFULNESS.

APPENDIX:
MENTAL HEALTH RESOURCES AND ANTI-DISCRIMINATION RESOURCES

Because of the dynamic nature of the internet, any telephone numbers, web addresses or links provided in this section may have changed since the publication of this book and may no longer be valid.

A listing in the Appendix doesn't mean it is an endorsement from Laksa Media Groups Inc., publisher, editors, authors and/or those involved in this series project. Its listing here is a means to disseminate information to the readers to get additional materials for further investigation or knowledge.

RESPITE IS KEY TO YOUR WELLBEING.
GIVE YOURSELF A BREAK . . .

How is your Mental Health? Do you think you have experienced one or more of the following recently?

- More Stress than Before
- Grief
- Separation and Divorce
- Feelings of Violence
- Suicidal Thoughts
- Self Injury
- Excessive or Unexplained Anxiety
- Obsession or Compulsion
- Paranoia, Phobias or Panics
- Post-Traumatic Stress
- Depression
- Bi-polar
- Postpartum Depression
- Eating Disorders
- Schizophrenia
- Addictions
- Mood Disorders
- Personality Disorders
- Learning Disabilities

MENTAL HEALTH SCREENING TOOLS

More information:
https://screening.mentalhealthamerica.net/screening-tools

- The Depression Screen is most appropriate for individuals who are feeling overwhelming sadness.
- The Anxiety Screen will help if you feel that worry and fear affect your day to day life.
- The Bipolar Screen is intended to support individuals who have mood swings - or unusual shifts in mood and energy.
- The PTSD (Post Traumatic Stress Disorder) Screen is best taken by those who are bothered by a traumatic life event.

- The Alcohol or Substance Use Screen will help determine if your use of alcohol or drugs is an area to address.
- The Youth Screen is for young people (age 11-17) who are concerned that their emotions, attention, or behaviours might be signs of a problem.
- The Parent Screen is for parents of young people to determine if their child's emotions, attention, or behaviours might be signs of a problem.
- The Psychosis Screen is for young people (age 12-35) who feel like their brain is playing tricks on them (seeing, hearing or believing things that don't seem real or quite right).
- Eating Disorder Test is to explore eating-related concerns which may impact your physical health and overall well-being.
- Work Health Survey is for exploring how healthy or unhealthy your work environment is.
- Worried about Your Child--Symptom Checker: **https://childmind.org/symptomchecker/**

10 Ways to Look after Your Mental Health

(source: www.mentalhealthamerica.net/live-your-life-well)

- Connect with Others
- Stay Positive
- Get Physically Active
- Help Others
- Get Enough Sleep
- Create Joy and Satisfaction
- Eat Well
- Take Care of Your Spirit
- Deal Better with Hard Times
- Get Professional Help if You Need It

MENTAL HEALTH RESOURCES & INFORMATION

If you or someone you know is struggling with mental illness, please consult a doctor or a healthcare professional in your community.

Below is not a comprehensive information listing, but it is a good start to get more information on mental health/illness.

Emergency Phone Number

If you or someone is in crisis or may be at risk of harming himself/herself or someone else, please call your national Emergency Phone Number immediately.

Canada	911
United States	911
United Kingdom	999 or 112
Ireland	999 or 112
Europe	112
Australia	000
New Zealand	111

Canada
- To locate your local Canadian Mental Health Association: **www.cmha.ca**
- Specifically for children and young people (aged 5-20), call Kids Help Phone's 24-hour confidential phone line at **1-800-668-6868** English or French. More information online: **kidshelpphone.ca**
- There are a number of resource materials and list of organizations that you can reach out to on the Bell Let's Talk website: **http://letstalk.bell.ca/en/get-help/**
- Mental Health & Addiction Information A-Z (Centre for Addiction and Mental Health): **https://www.camh.ca/en/ health-info/mental-illness-and-addiction-index**
- Canadian Coalition for Seniors' Mental Health: **http://ccsmh.ca**
- List of local crisis centres (Canadian Centre for Suicide Prevention): **http://suicideprevention.ca/need-help**

- The Alex—Changing Health, Changing Lives: **www.thealex.ca**

United States
- National Suicide Prevention Hotline: **1-800-273-TALK** or **1-800-273-8255** (More resources at: **https://suicidepreventionlifeline.org/**)
- For more mental health information: **www.mentalhealthamerica.net/mental-health-information**

United Kingdom
- The Samaritans (**www.samaritans.org**) offers emotional support 24 hours a day--get in touch with them: **116-123**.
- A to Z of Mental Health: **http://www.mentalhealth.org.uk/a-to-z**
- Free Mental Health Podcasts: **https://www.mentalhealth.org.uk/podcasts-and-videos**

Ireland
- The Samaritans (**www.samaritans.org**) offers emotional support 24 hours a day—get in touch with them: **116-123**.
- Childline Helpline (**https://www.childline.ie**): Confidential for young people (under 18). Phone: **1-800-66-66-66**
- For more mental health information: **www.mentalhealthireland.ie**

Australia
- Helplines, websites and government mental health services for Australia: **mhaustralia.org/need-help**
- Kids Helpline: Confidential and anonymous, telephone and online counselling service specifically for young people aged between 5 and 25. Phone: **1800-55-1800** or visit **www.kidshelpline.com.au**
- Lifeline: 24-hour telephone counselling service. Phone: **13-11-14** or visit **www.lifeline.org.au**

New Zealand
- Helplines, websites and government mental health services for New Zealand: www.mentalhealth.org.nz/get-help/in-crisis/helplines/
- Youthline (for young people under 25): **0800-376-633**. More information online: **http://www.youthline.co.nz**
- Lifeline: **0800-543-354**
- Suicide Crisis Helpline: **0508-828-865** (0508-TAUTOKO)

International
- Mental Health & Psychosocial Support: International Medical Corps (**https://internationalmedicalcorps.org/program mental-health-psychosocial-support/**)
- International Association for Youth Mental Health (**https://www.iaymh.org/need-help/**)
- Crisis Helpline for Various Countries: **https://yourlifecounts.org/find-help/**
- Emergency Number for Various Countries: **http://suicidestop.com/worldwide_emergency_numbers.html**
- Suicide Crisis Helpline for Various Countries: **https://en.wikipedia.org/wiki/List_of_suicide_crisis_lines http://www.suicidestop.com/call_a_hotline.html**

ANTI-DISCRIMINATION RESOURCES

Discrimination is an action or a decision that treats a person or a group negatively for reasons such as:
- national or ethnic origin
- colour
- religion
- age
- sex
- sexual orientation
- marital status
- family status
- disability

What is Discrimination? For more information (Canadian Human Rights Commission):
https://www.chrc-ccdp.gc.ca/eng/content/what-discrimination

Canada
- Promoting Relationship & Eliminating Violence Network (Prevnet): Information on bullying, resources on bullying and prevention at **http://www.prevnet.ca**
- List of Crisis Centres in Canada: **http://suicideprevention.ca/need-help**
- Free LifeLine App (Apple & Android): **http://thelifelinecanada.ca/lifeline-canada-foundation/lifeline-app**

United States
- Cyberbullying Research Center: Facts, Information, Blogs, and Resources at **http://cyberbullying.org/resources**
- The **Crisis Text Line** is a not-for-profit organization providing free crisis intervention via SMS message. The organization's services are available 24 hours a day every day, throughout the US by texting **741741**.

United Kingdom
- Bullying UK Helpline: confidential and free helpline service (Phone: **0808-800-2222**). Information, advices and resources at **http://www.bullying.co.uk**
- Anti-Bullying Alliances: Resources and advices at **https://www.anti-bullyingalliance.org.uk/tools-information**

Australia
- Bullying. No Way! **https://bullyingnoway.gov.au**

Books:

The Bullying Workbook for Teens: Activities to Help You Deal with Social Aggression and Cyberbullying (by Raychelle Cassada Lohmann and Julia V. Taylor) - Instant Help; Workbook edition – ISBN: 978-1608824502

Violence against Queer People: Race, Class, Gender, and the

Persistence of Anti-LGBT Discrimination (by Doug Meyer) - Rutgers University Press – ISBN: 978-0813573151

The Mindfulness Workbook for Addiction: A Guide to Coping with the Grief, Stress and Anger that Trigger Addictive Behaviors (by Rebecca E. Williams and Julie S. Kraft) - New Harbinger Publications; Csm Wkb edition – ISBN: 978-1608823406

Laksa Anthology Series:
Speculative Fiction

The anthologies in this award-winning series have been recommended by *Publishers Weekly, Booklist, Kirkus Reviews, Library Journal, School Library Journal, Locus, Foreword Reviews,* and *Quill & Quire.*

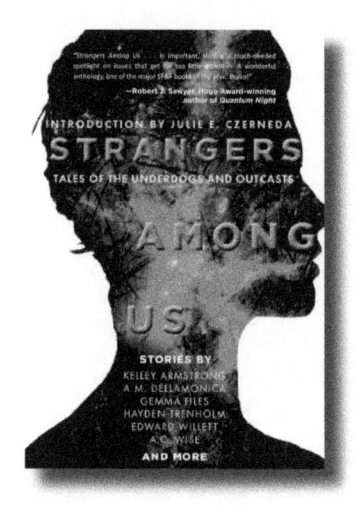

STRANGERS AMONG US
Tales of the Underdogs and Outcasts
Edited by Susan Forest and Lucas K. Law

2017 (Canadian SF&F) Aurora Award winner,
2017 Alberta Book Publishing Award winner

There's a delicate balance between mental health and mental illness.

Original Stories by Kelley Armstrong, Suzanne Church, A.M. Dellamonica, Gemma Files, James Alan Gardner, Bev Geddes, Erika Holt, Tyler Keevil, Rich Larson, Derwin Mak, Mahtab Narsimhan, Sherry Peters, Ursula Pflug, Robert Runté, Lorina Stephens, Amanda Sun, Hayden Trenholm, Edward Willett, A.C. Wise, and Julie E. Czerneda (Introduction)

Benefit: Canadian Mental Health Association

THE SUM OF US
Tales of the Bonded and Bound
Edited by Susan Forest and Lucas K. Law

2018 (Canadian SF&F) Aurora Award winner,
2018 Alberta Book Publishing Award finalist

The greatest gift to us is caring. What would the world be like without someone to care for or to care with?

Original stories by Colleen Anderson, Charlotte Ashley, Brenda Cooper, Ian Creasey, A.M. Dellamonica, Bev Geddes, Claire Humphrey, Sandra Kasturi, Tyler Keevil, Juliet Marillier, Matt Moore, Heather Osborne, Nisi Shawl, Alex Shvartsman, Kate Story, Karina Sumner-Smith, Amanda Sun, Hayden Trenholm, James Van Pelt, Liz Westbrook-Trenholm, Edward Willett, Christie Yant, Caroline M. Yoachim, and Dominik Parisien (Introduction)

Benefit: Canadian Mental Health Association

Laksa Anthology Series: Speculative Fiction

The anthologies in this series have been recommended by *Publishers Weekly*, *Booklist*, *Kirkus Reviews*, *Library Journal*, *School Library Journal*, *Locus*, *Foreword Reviews*, and *Quill & Quire*.

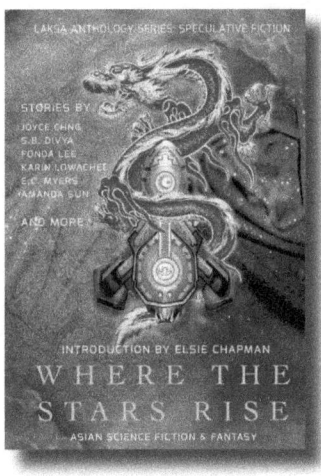

WHERE THE STARS RISE
Asian Science Fiction & Fantasy
Edited by Lucas K. Law and Derwin Mak

2018 (Canadian SF&F) Aurora Award finalist,
2018 Alberta Book Publishing Award winner

Take a journey through Asia and beyond to explore identities, belonging, and choices.

Original stories by Anne Carly Abad, Deepak Bharathan, Joyce Chng, Miki Dare, S.B. Divya, Pamela Q. Fernandes, Calvin D. Jim, Minsoo Kang, Fonda Lee, Gabriela Lee, Karin Lowachee, Rati Mehrotra, E.C. Myers, Tony Pi, Angela Yuriko Smith, Priya Sridhar, Amanda Sun, Naru Dames Sundar, Jeremy Szal, Regina Kanyu Wang (translated by Shaoyan Hu), Diana Xin, Melissa Yuan-Innes, Ruhan Zhao, and Elsie Chapman (Introduction)

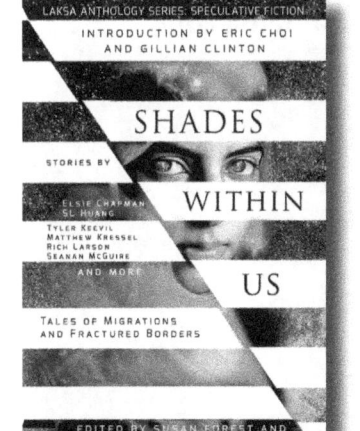

Benefit: Kids Help Phone

SHADES WITHIN US
Tales of Migrations and Fractured Borders
Edited by Susan Forest and Lucas K. Law

2019 (Canadian SF&F) Aurora Award finalist,
2019 Alberta Book Publishing Award winner

Come and examine the dreams, struggles, and triumphs of those who choose or are forced to leave home and familiar places.

Original stories by Vanessa Cardui, Elsie Chapman, Kate Heartfield, S.L. Huang, Tyler Keevil, Matthew Kressel, Rich Larson, Tonya Liburd, Karin Lowachee, Seanan McGuire, Brent Nichols, Julie Nováková, Heather Osborne, Sarah Raughley, Alex Shvartsman, Amanda Sun, Jeremy Szal, Hayden Trenholm, Liz Westbrook-Trenholm, Christie Yant & Alvaro Zinos-Amaro, and Eric Choi & Gillian Clinton (Introduction)

Benefit: Mood Disorders Association & Alex Community Food Centre

If you like *Flights of Marigold*, or *Bursts of Fire*, or any of Laksa's anthologies, please write a review or recommend the book to your public and school/academic libraries.

Thank you for supporting our projects, Canadian Mental Health Association, Kids Help Phone, Mood Disorders Association, and The Alex: Changing Health, Changing Lives.

HELP US TO CHANGE THE WORLD, ONE BOOK AT A TIME

IT'S A DELICATE BALANCE BETWEEN MENTAL HEALTH AND MENTAL ILLNESS . . .

BE ALERT!

Want to know more about *Flights of Marigold, Bursts of Fire* and Addicted to Heaven?
www.addictedtoheaven.com

Want to know more about our projects?
Sign up for our newsletters at **laksamedia.com**

LMG
LAKSA MEDIA GROUPS
LAKSA MEDIA GROUPS INC.